Praise for Sharon Bolton

"Achingly suspenseful."   —*The Washington Post* on *Little Black Lies*

"[Bolton's] crafty plotting produces an intricately detailed mystery . . . And her deft characterizations respect the psychological complexities of the three islanders who serve as narrators."

> —*The New York Times Book Review* on *Little Black Lies*

"A suspenseful and psychologically rich thriller."

> —*Booklist* (starred review) on *Little Black Lies*

"The pleasures of first-rate mystery usually lie in the plot, and Bolton has constructed a solid nail-biter. But it's the characters that infuse *A Dark and Twisted Tide* with such heart—not just the gritty, damaged Flint but her friends and colleagues, too."   —*Entertainment Weekly*

"Bolton rules the world of psychological thrillers."

> —*The Huffington Post* on *Lost*

"Realistic fear, heart-stopping suspense, and jolting plot twists keep one almost frantically turning pages as Bolton grabs us from the beginning and leaves us shaken at the end."

> —*Library Journal* (starred review) on *Lost*

"The story's atmosphere is dark and spooky, the main characters are strong yet vulnerable, and the plot is refreshingly unpredictable . . . Stunning."

> —*RT Book Reviews* (four-and-a-half stars,
> Top Pick) on *Dead Scared*

"Outstanding . . . Bolton never eases up the tension; her tightly coiled plot and heroine on the edge work perfectly in tandem."

> —*Publishers Weekly* (star
> Pick of the Week) on *l*

"Sharon Bolton is changing the face of crime fiction—if yo one crime novel this year, make it this."

> —Tess Gerritsen on *Nov*

"*Now You See Me* is really special: multilayered and sophi tough, too."

Also by Sharon Bolton
(previously published as S. J. Bolton)

Sacrifice
Awakening
Blood Harvest
Now You See Me
Dead Scared
Lost
A Dark and Twisted Tide

LITTLE BLACK LIES

Sharon Bolton

Minotaur Books
New York

LITTLE BLACK LIES. Copyright © 2015 by Sharon Bolton. All rights reserved. Printed in the United States of America. For information, address St. Martin's Press, 175 Fifth Avenue, New York, N.Y. 10010.

www.minotaurbooks.com

The Library of Congress has cataloged the hardcover edition as follows:

Bolton, S. J.
    Little black lies / Sharon Bolton. — First U.S. edition.
        p. cm.
    ISBN 978-1-250-02859-4 (hardcover)
    ISBN 978-1-250-02860-0 (e-book)
    1. Children—Crimes against—Fiction.   2. Serial murder investigation—Fiction.
3. City and town life—Falkland Islands—Fiction.   I. Title.
    PR6102.O49L58 2015
    823'.92—dc23

2015002536

ISBN 978-1-250-08067-7 (trade paperback)

Our books may be purchased in bulk for promotional, educational, or business use. Please contact your local bookseller or the Macmillan Corporate and Premium Sales Department at 1-800-221-7945, extension 5442, or by e-mail at MacmillanSpecialMarkets@macmillan.com.

First published in Great Britain by Bantam Press, an imprint of Transworld Publishers, a Penguin Random House UK company

First Minotaur Books Paperback Edition: April 2016

10   9   8   7   6   5   4   3   2   1

For Anne Marie, who was the first to tell
me I could do it; and for Sarah, who
makes me do it better

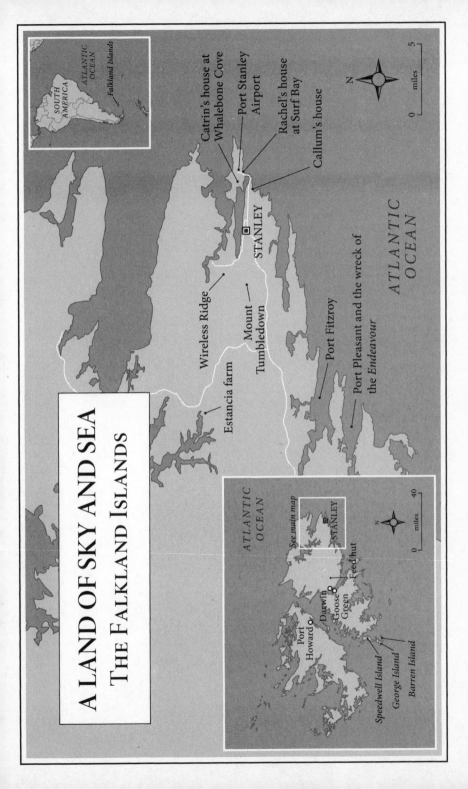

A LAND OF SKY AND SEA
THE FALKLAND ISLANDS

SOUTH AMERICA

ATLANTIC OCEAN

Falkland Islands

Catrin's house at Whalebone Cove

Port Stanley Airport

Rachel's house at Surf Bay

Callum's house

STANLEY

Wireless Ridge

Mount Tumbledown

Port Fitzroy

Port Pleasant and the wreck of the *Endeavour*

Estancia farm

ATLANTIC OCEAN

ATLANTIC OCEAN

See main map

STANLEY

Feed hut

Darwin

Goose Green

Port Howard

Speedwell Island

George Island

Barren Island

N

miles
0   5

N

miles
0   40

Ah! well a-day! what evil looks
Had I from old and young!
Instead of the cross, the Albatross
About my neck was hung.

Samuel Taylor Coleridge, *The Rime of the Ancient Mariner*

PART ONE

Catrin

I've been wondering if I have what it takes to kill. Whether I can look a living creature in the eye and take the one irreversible action that ends a life. Asked and answered, I suppose. I have no difficulty in killing. I'm actually rather good at it.

DAY TWO
Tuesday, 1 November 1994

1

I BELIEVE JUST ABOUT ANYONE CAN KILL IN THE RIGHT circumstances, given enough motivation. The question is, am I there yet? I think I must be. Because lately, it seems, I've been thinking of little else.

It is a minute after midnight. In two days' time it will be the third of November. Two more days. Am I there yet?

Something is moving. Not the water surrounding me, that seems frozen in time, but the reflection of a bird. I don't need to glance up to see that it's a giant petrel. Massive, prehistoric-looking beasts with their six-foot wing span and their huge curving beaks, they often follow the boat, especially when I'm out at night, keeping pace with me however far I go or how fast I drive.

I'm not driving now. I'm sitting in the cockpit, staring at a photograph of my two sons. I must have been doing so for some time because my eyes are stinging. I squeeze them shut, then force myself to look away.

In the distance, the mountains are dark against a paler night sky and the water around me has the appearance and texture of an old glass mirror. Still, flawed in places, not quite translucent. It does this at times, this ocean, assumes a character so unlike itself as to take you momentarily unawares, make you forget that it's one of the harshest, least forgiving seas in the world.

I'm anchored off the coast of the Falkland Islands, a tiny

15

archipelago in the South Atlantic Ocean, so distant from everywhere that matters, so unimportant on the world stage, that for centuries it escaped just about everybody's attention. And then it became the discarded bone over which two ego-driven dogs of politics picked a fight. For a few brief weeks the whole world knew about us. That was over a decade ago and the world soon forgot.

We don't forget though, and neither does Argentina. Every so often, even twelve years after it had its ass kicked, the Argentine government casts a leery eye in our direction. The Argentinians say the Islas Malvinas belong to them. We say 'up yours'.

Not that we're so very happy to be what we've become: an expensive indulgence, one of the last remaining scraps of the British Empire. We long for independence, for the income to fund our own defence. The hope is a faint one. And we never feel safe.

The photograph of my sons has faded. It's not so obvious now but in the daylight the red of Kit's jacket will be a dull pink, Ned's yellow boots a sickly cream colour.

On the water, the reflected moon is so still and perfect that it might have fallen, whole and undamaged, from the sky. It lies a little way off the stern, as slender and unsubstantial as a sliver of wood shaving. Stars are scattered around it like litter, as though someone has sprinkled them randomly over the surface of the ocean. There is no light pollution in this far corner of the South Atlantic, and every star in the sky tonight is reflected directly below me. I seem surrounded by stars. When I lived briefly in the cities of the northern hemisphere, where the stars are pinpricks of light, sometimes invisible entirely, it was easy to forget their sheer number. Back home, every time I come out upon the ocean at night, I'm reminded of the vastness of the sky.

I rouse myself, not sure how long I've been sitting here, but knowing I have another twenty minutes or so of work to do before I'm done for the night. I change the tank, check the oxygen levels, put my mask and mouthpiece in place and step off the back of the boat.

Instantly the water wraps its cold blanket around me, chilling me in spite of the protective wetsuit I'm wearing, but I never mind this. I think of it as part of the acclimatization process, the

16

transformation I have to undergo from land crawler to sea creature.

The water isn't deep, twenty metres at most. Of course I shouldn't dive by myself. I'm breaking the first rule of safety among divers even by being on the boat alone, but there is no one alive any more with either the authority or the influence to stop me, and I have little interest in safeguarding myself.

I look down, see the dive-line descending, disappearing into the darkness, then I let air out of my jacket and sink. A few feet down, I flip and start swimming towards the kelp forest that is coming into view below me.

Kelp, what most people call seaweed, grows in abundance here. Anchored to the seabed with a root-like structure, it stretches towards the light, its fronds and tendrils kept upright by gas-filled floats.

A boat was wrecked here, long ago, and since then the entire structure has broken apart to form the majestic, sub-marine architecture of the ocean floor. Huge pieces of wood, colonized by sea life, soar up from the seabed like underwater cities. Above it all, like an ancient forest, only one in constant, graceful motion, towers the kelp.

I reach its tip and continue down. In daylight, in clear conditions, the sheer brilliance of the colours around me would be astonishing. At night, seen only with the aid of my torch, they are softer, more muted. The custard of the kelp, the deep, smoky blue of the water, the occasional flashes of ruby red as crabs scuttle across the sand.

I am collecting samples of sea urchin. The kelp forests are important fish spawning areas but recently they've been in decline and one possible culprit is the sea urchin that eats away at their roots. The people I work with need to know if some new, invasive species is at large, or whether the normal population has just become a bit greedier. Potentially, selling fishing licences could be enormously lucrative for the islands' economy. The fish matter, so the kelp forests matter, so my urchins matter. Overnight, they'll be stored in refrigerated containers on the boat; in the morning I'll take them to my lab in Stanley.

A couple of metres from the ocean floor, I make my way along a path I've already committed to memory. Many divers don't like the kelp. They're repulsed by the wet plant life brushing past them; they dread the occasions when it wraps itself, tendril-like, around limbs. I like the feeling of security it gives me. I enjoy being concealed, taking other creatures by surprise, sometimes being taken by surprise myself. My scavenging missions are always more successful when I am among kelp.

Suddenly, I realize I'm not alone down here. The kelp in front of me is moving at odds with the gentle sway of the waves. Something is coming towards me. A second later a young fur seal and I are practically nose to nose. It looks into my eyes then darts away again, following a fish that is moving too fast for me to note its species. I watch them zigzag across the ocean floor, but the feeling of unease doesn't leave me.

It happens in an instant. A great shadow looms overhead, the water is pushed back against me with huge force, and a massive creature dives past after the seal. They make contact. There's a frenzied squirming and tossing of flesh. The water erupts in an explosion of bubbles, then the two creatures break apart again.

The newcomer is an elephant seal, a large male, over two metres long. It is much slower than the fur seal but exceptionally strong. They begin a frantic chase through the kelp and I am in danger.

An elephant seal wouldn't normally attack a human, it wouldn't even bother a big seal, but this one is locked into the hunt, driven by the need to kill. The water around me is already stained with the young seal's blood. If it escapes and the elephant spots me, it may just act without thinking. I freeze, crouched low in the kelp, hoping the chase will move away.

It doesn't. The fur seal heads straight for me; it's about to dive for cover in the dense vegetation when the elephant appears from above. The hunter locks its powerful jaws around the neck of its prey and shakes violently. Within seconds, the fur seal's head is loose and limp. The elephant swims back to the surface with its kill.

And that's how it's done. Quickly, brutally, with no pause for doubt or reflection. That's how we kill. I've been thinking a lot about death tonight, as I've sat on the ocean surface, as I've dived beneath it, about death and people's ability to inflict it. About my own ability to kill.

After all, I come from a long line of murderers. My grandfather, the aptly named Bartholomew Coffin, was one of the most successful and ruthless killers this part of the world has ever known. Day after day, he and his gang went out, hunting without pause or pity, watching the ocean run red with blood. Of course, Grandpa killed whales, not people, but how different can it be, really?

When I've collected and bagged my last sample I'm ready to head up. Racing the bubbles around me, I see stars while I'm still several feet under. I break surface and for a moment can't find the boat. In the time I've been below, the spell that held the ocean captive has broken and the water has started moving again. Waves rise up around me and I feel a stab of sharp excitement. I'm alone, far out to sea. If I can't get back to the boat I will die out here. For some time now, I've had a sense of my life getting very close to its end. Is this it then? Am I to die today?

Then, there it is, not twenty metres away.

Queenie has woken up. She scampers along the side deck and yips at me until I catch hold of the ladder and pull myself up. I bend to pet her, covering her in water. She runs and fetches me the old towel from her bed. It's covered in mud and dog hairs but I appreciate the thought.

Queenie is a Staffordshire terrier, tiny for the breed, a solid little bundle of muscle and silky-soft fur. Her nose, legs and the tip of her tail are white, but the rest of her is as black as the contents of my head. She is four years old and I swear there are times when she remembers the boys. When she grieves for them too.

I pull up the anchor, start the engine and head south towards Stanley, thinking about my grandfather again. Tonight, it seems, my thoughts are determined to stray along the shadowy path, where furtive plans creep like snaring roots across the forest floor, where the darker reaches of our minds run free.

Grandpa Coffin, my father's father, was one of the great whalers in the South Atlantic. He was the last scion of a dynasty of marine hunters, who left Nantucket in 1804 and arrived on New Island in the Falklands several months later. For the next two hundred years, they plundered the islands and their surrounding ocean. Marine and island wildlife around here is still trying to recover from the impact of Grandpa Coffin and his forebears.

He died when I was a child. A pity.

I turn into the more sheltered waters of Port William and adjust my course so that I'll steer well clear of the visiting cruise ship, the *Princess Royal*. From now to the end of the summer, we'll see a steady stream of such ships, stopping by for a few days on their way to South Georgia and the Antarctic. They're a mixed blessing, the hundreds of tourists who land on our shores on a daily basis when a ship is in harbour, and like most mixed blessings we love and curse them in equal measure. Tonight, it seems unusually awake and noisy, given the hour, but these ships can party hard, the sounds of the revelry reaching many miles inland.

Unnoticed by anyone on deck, I slip past and head for the inner harbour. It's almost one in the morning. Soon I'll be counting down in hours, not days. There are things I have to do still, promises I've made to others, but keeping busy has to be a good thing. I glance around the boat. I've been making sure the fuel and the water tanks are topped up. In a locked cabinet is the CO_2 tranquillizer dart gun for the rare occasions when I might need to sedate a large mammal, and also an old handgun of my grandfather's for when euthanasia is the only option. Both are in full working order. I'm ready.

Ready to find out just how much of the blood of the old family runs in my veins. I steer through The Narrows into the inner harbour and see immediately that my carefully laid plans may come to nothing.

The police are waiting for me.

2

IN THE SHORT TIME I'VE BEEN AT SEA, SOMETHING HAS happened here. Most people on the Falkland Islands live in Stanley, but it's still a small community. Only around two thousand people in some seven hundred houses. Three hours ago, when I motored out, the tiny lights of a hundred or more jack-o'-lanterns littered the hillside like stars, but they'll all have burned down by now. At this time of the morning Stanley should be in almost complete darkness. It isn't. I watch a police car drive along the coast road and there are more blue lights on the harbour front.

It's three years, almost to the day, since I last drove into harbour to find police waiting for me.

'There's been a car accident.' Three years later, I can still hear Ben's voice, crackling and shaky on the boat's radio. 'Ned and Kit are both on their way to hospital, but I don't know any more. Get here as soon as you can.'

He signed off quickly, leaving me to imagine the worst. Except I didn't. I couldn't let myself. I imagined them in pain. I imagined their small, perfect bodies bruised and broken, cut apart by razor-sharp metal. All the way back to Stanley, I heard their voices in my head, crying for Mummy, unable to understand why, when they needed me the most, I wasn't there. I imagined limbs torn from torsos, scars cut across their pretty faces. I never imagined them as lifeless corpses, lying side by side, in the mortuary.

In the grip of bad memories, I'm pushing the throttle too hard. I shouldn't be heading into harbour at this speed. There are rocks, more than one wreck, hidden obstacles that can tear a boat apart. I force myself to slow the boat and wait for my breathing, my heartbeat, to do the same. Both prove less easy to control than the throttle. And yet I have to keep up the appearance of being normal, of coping. For a little while longer the human shell around me has to hold.

Someone is waiting for me at my usual mooring, one of the retired fishermen. He lives in a cottage by the harbour with two women whom most people agree are his mother and sister, but nobody is placing any bets. His name is Ralph Larken, Roadkill Ralph behind his back. As I throw him the stern line I see that he's wearing faded striped pyjamas beneath his oilskin. They're tucked into enormous black fisherman's wellingtons and in this strange half-light they give him the look of a pirate. I jump down myself with the bowline. 'What's going on?'

'Kid missing.'

I stare at him, wondering which of us will say it out loud. He does.

'Another one.' He nods towards a group on the harbour wall. I can make out police uniforms, someone in military fatigues. 'Expecting you,' he says. 'Saw your boat lights.'

Another child missing. I was still floundering in my own grief when the first vanished, a little over two years ago, but I remember people telling each other it was a terrible accident, albeit of an undisclosed nature. When the second disappeared, those same people said we'd been terribly unlucky. And now a third?

Someone has left the group by the wall and is coming towards me. It's the young policewoman, the one whom nobody can take seriously because she is so very young, and so very tall, and because she can't seem to move without knocking something over. Constable Skye McNair is one of those people whom others claim they like because they feel sorry for her and want to be considered compassionate. I've nothing to prove so, I'll admit, I find her clumsiness annoying.

Watching her now, I think for the first time that she looks so very alive. Her hair, long, wiry, the exact shade of freshly made marmalade, is flying out around her head, and her face, pale as paper in the moonlight, tells me that she's anxious and more than a little excited. For an inch or two around her, the night doesn't seem so dark.

'Catrin, sorry.' She is way taller than I am. She stoops towards me and then sways backwards as though afraid of crowding me. 'I need to know if you saw anyone else out there tonight? Any vessels you didn't recognize?'

I tell her no. Several big, commercial fishing boats left harbour around the same time I did, but I knew all of them. A lot of the islanders night-fish, but typically in smaller boats, hugging the shore.

'Sorry, this must be so difficult.' Skye never seems to know what to do with her hands. She's flapping them right now. 'I know it's almost exactly the—'

Skye wasn't here three years ago. She was away in England at police college. And yet she knows that in two days it will be the anniversary of the day I lost my life.

'What's happened, Skye?' I glance at Ralph, who is petting Queenie. 'Something about a missing child?' I don't say *another one*. It's hardly necessary.

'One of the visiting families.' She looks back to the crowd behind us. 'Not from the cruise ship. They arrived independently, have been staying at one of the guest houses in town. They were picnicking out near Estancia at lunchtime. The kids were playing in the grass. They lost sight of the youngest.'

Estancia is a farm settlement, about twenty miles away, on the south-easterly tip of a great sea inlet.

'He's only three.' Skye looks on the verge of tears.

Three years old. The two kids who went missing previously were older, but not by much. Both were boys. A child of three, separated from his family for hours, alone at night. He'll be cold, hungry, terrified. Isn't abandonment the worst fear of the young? On these islands, at night, he will feel abandoned by the world.

'Has there been a search?'

Skye's face gives a little quiver as she pulls herself together. 'We've had people there all day. And some men have gone back again. Callum Murray for one. He went with a few men from the barracks. We're waiting to hear.'

'Is that his family?' I find the mother without really trying, a plump, dark-haired woman in her late thirties. Her whole body is clenched inwards, as though she's afraid that if she lets go she might fall apart. I know that, when I get closer, whatever flesh she once had on her face will appear to have gone, leaving it skin over bones. Her eyes will look dead. She will look like me.

Except that where it matters she's a world apart from me. She still has hope.

'That's the family.' Skye seems to be standing on one leg now. 'The Wests. It's all getting really difficult. There are people off the cruise ship too and, well, I don't want to be unkind, but they're not exactly helping. They seem to think we should be forcibly searching properties. They want a block on all boats leaving harbour from now on. Can you imagine what the fishing vessels are going to say if we tell them they can't go out in the morning?'

'I doubt many will listen.' Authority is tolerated here, but only to a point.

'And the family are anxious enough already. The last thing they need is people putting all sorts of wild ideas in their heads.'

I'm tempted to say that, given our recent history with missing children, the wild ideas will be there already.

'It's all very unsettling.' As Skye continues talking and I pretend to listen, we walk towards my car. 'We've been called out to five incidents since nine o'clock. Chief Superintendent Stopford is trying to get all the visitors back to the cruise ship, but they don't want to go until the little boy is found. It's going to be a bad night.'

Muttering what I know to be expected, that she should let me know if there's anything I can do, I slip away. Queenie leaps into the car and I head towards my house on the western side of Cape Pembroke peninsula, a tiny spit of land between the inner and outer harbours of Stanley and the ocean itself.

I'm not thinking about the missing child. Or rather, I am, but only insofar as how it will affect me. If boats are to be stopped leaving their moorings, if they are to be searched before they leave harbour, my plans fall apart. Two and a half days from now. Around sixty hours. The kid has to be found by then.

I don't take the shortest route home. Some nights, usually when the black fog in my head is getting the upper hand, something seems to take me out towards the Grimwood house. Always at night, when the chances of seeing the family are next to non-existent, something pulls me to it. Tonight, I drive around the easternmost tip of Stanley's natural harbour towards the big house with the peacock-blue roof that looks east over Surf Bay. I slow down as I round the last bend and can see the whitewashed walls, the black windows, the low gorse hedge, now bursting with yellow flowers. To either side of the low wooden gate is a pumpkin lantern, and in their intricate, accurate carving I see the handiwork of the children's grandfather. He carved pumpkins for my family, too, once.

Someone is up. I can see light in an upper window. Peter's room. I have never seen Peter, the youngest Grimwood child. He has lived the last two and a half years in my head. I see him as a fair-haired boy, skinny and oval-faced like his two brothers were at that age. He will also, like them, have his mother's bright blue eyes.

I haven't been in this house for years, not since before Peter was born, but I know Rachel's house as well as I know my own. Peter is awake in the night and Rachel will be with him, wrapping her body around his, rocking him to sleep. She'll be breathing in the scent of his hair, feeling him trembling against her and loving her power to soothe away his fears. I hate her so much at this moment it is all I can do to press down on the accelerator and carry on driving.

Yes, I think. Killing Rachel will be easy.

3

I PUSH OPEN THE DOOR TO MY HOUSE AND SENSE, immediately, the departure from the norm. There is something – a scent, the echo of a giggle, the fractional change in the atmosphere. Tiny signs, but unmistakable. They are here again.

I close the door softly behind me and look around. No bright eyes in the darkness. No scuffling movements as tiny forms press deeper into the shadows. I make a slow circuit of the large, old-fashioned room and step out into the hallway. I'm both wary and eager. It's an odd sort of hunger, this need to see the dead.

In the three years since the boys' deaths they have haunted me. Do I mean that literally? I'm not sure. I am a scientist, more likely to believe in aliens than ghosts, but within days of the accident their presence in the house became more real, more compelling than that of my husband or any of the gaggle of well-wishers who appeared periodically.

The real people left but the boys remained, drifting in and out of my life with the reliability, if not the regularity, of the tide. Always when I least expect it, I see their shadows behind curtains, the curve of their bodies under quilts on beds I still can't bear to strip. Their voices, sometimes giggling and plotting secrets, quite often squabbling, will mingle with the sounds from the television or the radio. I'll catch a whiff of their scent. The particular musky apple smell of Kit's hair a day or so after washing. The acrid smell of Ned's trainers when the shoe cupboard had been left open.

They're not sitting at the bottom of the stairs, or curled up on the sofa staring at the blank television screen. Good, I hate it when they do that. I make my way upstairs. The stair-gate that we never got round to removing is closed. Did I do that? Why would I? And yet it's rare for me to suspect the boys of having an impact on the physical environment. The odd toy, perhaps, may have been moved. A dent on one of the beds. My dog, of course, could be responsible for either.

Queenie, as usual when the boys are here, is downstairs by the kitchen door, whining. I have no idea whether she, too, senses their presence, or whether she just hates seeing me in this mood, but their visits freak her out. It's a shame, because she loved them too, but pets aren't mothers I suppose.

I'm sure I'll find them in Ned's room, curled up together like a couple of puppies, but the shape I see as I press open the door is only a large bear lying prone on Ned's bed. Not in Kit's room either. I'm moving faster now, telling myself to slow down, but feeling the normal panic of a mother who can't find her children. Even her dead ones. My bedroom is empty too. Or appears to be.

They are hiding.

I wish they wouldn't, but hide-and-seek was one of their favourite games when they were alive and sometimes they play it with me still. I start to search the house again, this time looking properly, and all the time, the storm cloud in my head is getting thicker. I'm pulling open wardrobe doors, tugging back shower curtains, peering under the spare-room bed. If I'm honest, this game has always unnerved me, even when I knew I'd find two warm, strong bodies at the end of the search.

I'm downstairs again. They can only be outside. I open the back door and the wind races in as though it's been waiting to pounce.

They're not out here. I can feel them slipping away. Two sounds cut through the rushing of the wind, both moans of abject misery. One from Queenie, the other from me.

'Ned! Kit!'

They're gone. Just as I was certain of their presence earlier, I'm sure of their absence now.

There is very little light left in my head. I'm upstairs again, in the small extension to my bedroom that I use as a study. I'm kneeling by my desk, fumbling at the pull-out drawer I always keep locked. I find what I'm looking for. I keep it sharp.

Downstairs, Queenie starts to howl.

Some time later, the fog lifts. I drag myself up off the carpet and into the desk chair. My left hand is bleeding. I put the harpoon head back in its drawer. The photograph of Rachel at my feet has been cut and stabbed to a torn, ribbony mess.

Bending, I drop the pieces in the bin. I have other copies of the same photograph. For next time.

I'm so tired I can hardly think. I need to shower and sleep, but something keeps me here, nursing my injured hand, staring at the walls around me. I keep the rest of my house much as it was when the boys were alive and Ben lived here, but over the last three years this small study space has become my indulgence room.

There are photographs of Ned and Kit all over the walls, some of them framed, most simply stuck on to the paintwork with Blu Tack. Their artwork from school is here too, little certificates they won in class, even some baby clothes I kept, all hanging from the wall in a grim, memorial montage.

'Christ, Catrin,' Ben said, when he called back to collect something from the loft. 'This isn't a study, it's a shrine.'

On the wall behind me, though, is something different. Here are photographs of two other little boys; two dark-haired, dark-eyed boys who vanished – suddenly, mysteriously. The first, Fred Harper, went missing during the sports day on West Falkland, a little over two years ago, when my grief was still raw, weeping like a fresh sore. He was five years old.

I'd heard the news of his disappearance, of course. The radio had been full of it for days and Ben, who'd been on the island as part of the emergency medical team, had taken part in the search. When I saw the story in the *Penguin News*, accompanied by a large portrait photograph, my heart leapt. Fred looked so much like Kit. I'd cut it out instinctively, hiding it away, eventually pinning it to the wall along with everything else about him that appeared in the paper over the coming weeks.

Maybe I kept the coverage as a sort of test of my humanity. If Fred was found, and I was glad, it would be a sign that there was still hope for me. And then, about a year and a half ago, the islands lost a second little boy. Seven-year-old Jimmy Brown was last seen at Surf Bay where Rachel lives. I knew the Brown family reasonably well. I was friends with the mother, Gemma, whose daughter, Jimmy's little sister, was in Kit's class at school. Ben knew the father, who worked up at the hospital as a technician.

When Jimmy disappeared, when the whole town spent days and nights searching, as his family sunk deeper into a sort of frantic despair, more than one person told me that at least I had closure. I knew what had happened to my sons, I'd been able to bury them, grieve properly, a privilege denied to the families of the missing.

'Yes, thank you,' I said to one woman. 'I do appreciate how lucky I am.'

She hasn't spoken to me since.

Below the pictures of Fred and Jimmy is another cutting, not directly related to the boys but one that touched me, at the time. A couple of months after Jimmy vanished, when the searches were still taking place, albeit more contained and without any real hope, the *Penguin News'* editor-in-chief wrote about the impact of missing children upon a community, especially a small one. He talked about a collective sense of shame, about the belief that children are a shared responsibility and that harm coming to any one of them reflects upon us all.

The piece hadn't been written with my sons in mind, but I'd found some comfort in it all the same. It had made me realize that Ben and I, and our immediate circle, weren't alone in feeling the impact of the boys' deaths. That, in some small way, our pain was shared.

The writer, Rachel's father of all people, had gone on to talk about how cultures deal with children who vanish. He wrote about how the vanishings quickly slip into local folklore, appearing first of all as ghostly sightings and then later in the oral tradition of story-telling. Missing children, he argued, are behind all the tales of children stolen by fairies, or eaten by trolls and witches. We deal with our shame by externalizing it. By blaming supernatural forces.

He'd unearthed old legends about children coming to grief here on the islands, and linked them to real-life cases of unexplained deaths and disappearances. In fifty years' time, he claimed, Jimmy and Fred would have found their way into Falkland mythology.

Ned, Kit, Fred and Jimmy. My own little collection of dead boys. Was there to be a fifth now, was our collective shame to grow ever greater?

I lean across my desk and switch on the radio. The locally run radio station is broadcasting later than it would normally. The missing child is called Archie West, I learn. He is three years and two months old. A little older than Rachel's youngest.

No, don't think about Rachel, not now.

'Just a reminder then,' says the anchorman, aka Bill from the fishmonger's, 'Archie has blond curls, brown eyes and is of a stocky build. He was last seen wearing an Arsenal football strip, red shirt with white sleeves, white shorts and red socks. If you think you've seen anything of him, get in touch with the police immediately. OK, this is Falkland Islands Broadcasting Service, Bill Krill with you for the next couple of hours, the time is one forty-three in the morning and, don't forget, tomorrow morning – or should I say later on *this* morning – we have Ray Green from the Astronomy Society coming in to tell us all about Thursday's solar eclipse: where best to see it, how to avoid eye damage and just how dark we can expect the islands to become.'

I turn out the lights, go to the window and look west. The solar eclipse on Thursday will occur at almost the exact time my plan goes into effect. This far south we'll only see a partial eclipse, but nevertheless, some time between three and four o'clock in the afternoon, our tiny corner of the world will go dark.

In more ways than one.

'With me here in the studio is Sally Hoskins,' says Bill, 'a friend of the family, who's been telling us that Archie is a lively, inquisitive child. Is that right, Sally?'

I haven't a hope of seeing the search party, of course. They are nearly twenty miles distant and there are mountains in the way.

'Yes, Bill, that's right. Archie's a lovely boy. Full of fun, full of mischief. He loves playing hide-and-seek.'

There are fewer lights down at the harbour. Skye must have persuaded the passengers to return to the cruise ship after all.

'And that's why the family didn't worry at first?'

'That's right. We assumed he was hiding. He can keep it up for hours.'

I can barely make out Mount Tumbledown. The search will be taking place beyond it.

'We all searched for over two hours before calling the police.' Sally's voice over the airwaves keeps breaking. 'Archie's parents want me to thank everyone for their support tonight. People have been so brilliant. Joining the search, checking their properties. I just want to say please keep looking. And if you know where he is, please do the right thing. Please let him come back to his family.'

'Sally, why don't you tell us a bit more about Archie?' Bill jumps in quickly. 'We know he likes hide-and-seek. What else does he enjoy?'

'Oh, you know, Bill, he's a mad keen Arsenal fan. Like all his family really. He's going through a phase where he won't wear anything but the Arsenal strip and his poor mum has to wash it overnight so he can wear it again the next day. He knows all the club songs, some of them not really appropriate for a three-year-old, but what can you do?'

I'm only half listening as Sally goes on to tell us about Archie's love of pop music. Apparently, he can't sit still when the radio plays 'Here Comes the Hotstepper'. And about how he won't miss an episode of *Power Rangers*.

'And if anyone has Archie, please don't hurt him or frighten him in any way,' she's saying now. 'If anyone has taken Archie, all we want is to get him back. Please, tell us where to find him. Please don't hurt him.'

'Yes, right. Well, thank you, Sally. But I think it's worth mentioning, just as a reminder, that the police are working on the assumption that young Archie simply wandered off from his family and got lost. That's what we have to concentrate on now, folks. A little boy has wandered away by himself, and we have to find him.

31

Right, this is Bill Krill, and you're listening to Falkland Islands Broadcasting Service.'

'Jesus, what is wrong with you people?' Sally interrupts the opening chords of the next song. 'How many children have to go missing before you actually do—'

Sally's voice cuts out. They've switched off her microphone. The music increases in volume: the reggae song that we've just heard is Archie's favourite. I picture Sally being gently, but firmly, removed from the backroom at the local newspaper office from where the radio service is broadcast. Different culture, I tell myself. In England, when a child vanishes, the default setting is to panic about paedophiles. Here, we hope he didn't wander into a sea-lion colony.

Three lost children in as many years. It's a lot to blame on sea lions.

I hear a gentle sigh that tells me Queenie has thought it safe to come back. She jumps on to my bed, snuggling into the groove between the pillows. I switch off the radio and turn on the computer. When it's fired up, I write up notes of my evening and then close the file and click on the only document I ever password-protect.

I never kept a diary before the boys died. I never felt the need, and with a husband, two young children and a job, when would I have found the time? My life before was too full for there to be any question of the need to document it. Now, with an empty heart and a meaningless life, it is as though I need this regular record of my comings and goings, my thought processes and emotional seasons, to remind myself that I still exist.

I start writing. I always detail the events of the day, not because I have any real interest in remembering what I do at work, but because what I do helps to punctuate what I feel. It's the nearest I can get to therapy, these daily outpourings of misery and rage. Mainly rage, if I'm honest, invariably directed at the woman whose photograph lies shredded at my feet. The woman who used to be my best friend.

I was eight years old when I met Rachel, she a few months younger. I was making my way along a track that was only wide enough for a child to squeeze through, so densely packed were the tussock clumps, when I came across a small, butterfly-emblazoned bottom pointing to the sky. She must have heard me, although I walk very quietly, because without turning, she held up a grubby, nail-bitten hand. It was such an imperious gesture it immediately put my eight-year-old back up.

'What are you doing?'

She wriggled backwards until I could see a small, round face with big blue eyes, creamy, freckle-free skin and very long hair that was a fraction too dark to be blonde. She had eyebrows that seemed to arch in the centre, as though she was permanently surprised and her ears stuck out from her head like those of an elf.

'Dragons' eggs,' she hissed at me. 'Don't say another word.'

Bemused, I dropped to the sand and crawled up alongside her. She was staring at two creamy-yellow shapes, each a perfect oval, about four inches long. The nest of a gentoo penguin.

'They belong to Ozmajian.' She seemed determined to communicate in a low-pitched hiss, even though we were the only two people within half a mile. 'A very powerful dragon. She was born when the thousandth heart was broken, which makes her very old, but dragon memories aren't like ours.'

At eight years old I knew that gentoo penguins often nested in the tussock, that the mother wouldn't normally leave her nest for so long and that the two of us were probably keeping her away. I knew I should suggest moving, but I admit I was curious about the dragon.

'Aren't they?' I matched her low-pitched, secretive tone.

She pressed closer, snuggling into my body in the completely unselfconscious way of very young children. 'No. Dragons can remember everything that came before, is happening in the now and what will ever be hereafter.'

Well, that needed some thinking about. 'We should probably go,' I said. 'She could be back any time.'

'Oh, she won't come back. The eggs will stay here until three moons have waxed and waned. Then the black eagles with sapphire eyes will carry them off and guard them until it's time for them to hatch. That could be tomorrow. It could be in the next millennium.'

At that age, I could identify nearly forty species of Falkland nesting birds, but the black eagle with sapphire eyes was a new one on me. In the meantime, the wind was getting up, bringing with it the tang of salt on the air and I was getting very worried about the mother penguin. If they get too stressed, they can wander off and leave a nest.

'The next new moon is five nights away.' I've always been aware of exactly what the moon is doing, even as a child. 'They won't go till then. I can come back, if you like, to check.'

She sat on her haunches, looking at me with a new-found respect. I was suddenly and painfully jealous of those shiny blue eyes. It didn't seem fair, that one person (me) should have eyes as dull as storm clouds and that the other's (Rachel's) should be the dreamy, azure blue of the ocean on a sunlit morning.

'We'll come together,' she announced. 'Now that we're best friends.'

I wasn't sure how that was going to happen, I didn't even know what she was doing there – my aunt and uncle owned the island we were on – but I was fine with the idea of having a best friend. 'OK,' I said.

'Is that your house?' She'd jumped to her feet and was pointing towards the green tin roof of Aunt Janey's farmhouse. I nodded, because to all intents and purposes it was. I was staying there for the summer while my parents worked.

'Do you have ice cream?'

I nodded again. Aunt Janey always made sure she was well stocked up before I arrived.

'Come on then.' She grabbed my hand and we raced – she was incredibly fast on her feet – through the grass, across the paddock and into the farmyard.

And that was it. From that day on Rachel and I were best friends, needing each other with a passionate intensity I don't think I've ever found in a relationship since. We couldn't have been more different. She saw world within world, linked by rainbows of endless possibilities. I saw penguin eggs. And yet we were closer than sisters, because this bond of ours was one we had chosen; closer than lovers, because lovers come and go and what we had was for ever. She was the other half of me. The sunshine on the rocks to my shady nook under a tree. The positive keys to my minor chords. She was everything I was not and all the things I longed to be, except those qualities were so much better in her and I knew it. She and I were inseparable, regardless of the distance between us. We were the past, the now and the ever more.

Until the day she killed my sons.

It's nearly four o'clock in the morning. I've been writing, and thinking, and doing neither, for a long time. I switch off the computer and am crossing the room to join Queenie when I hear the noise outside.

This one, I can't ignore, can't pretend is the weather.

I couldn't pin down when it started. It could have been going on for years, maybe only during the last couple of months, but more than once, if the wind's been in the right direction, I've heard something in the late evening that has made me wonder if someone is outside my house. I've heard movement that seems at odds with nature, shufflings that might have been footsteps. Several times, Queenie has been agitated, keen to get outdoors, and yet hanging around nervously in the doorway when I open it. Earlier in the year, when the evenings were darker and before I'd drawn the curtains, I had a sense of eyes outside in the darkness, looking in at me.

Nobody on the islands locks their doors, but I've started to and I'm glad of it now, because what I heard left little room for doubt. Someone is out there. I leave the bedroom. Queenie snores on. She plays numerous roles in my life, but guard dog isn't one of them.

Downstairs, without switching on lights, I step to the window.

The land around my house is unusual even by Falkland standards. It is a monument, an outdoor museum if you like, to whaling. Pride of place is given to the skull of a blue whale. It stands on the front lawn, reaching nearly nine feet high, jaws gaping as though frozen in the act of gobbling up food. A near perfect skeleton of an orca lies nearby. Over by the fence is the spine of a sperm whale, caught by Grandpa off the coast of South Georgia. Between that and the house is a shoal of dolphin skeletons. Most of the collection was acquired by my grandfather. The weapons, too, were Grandpa's: the harpoons and lines, the massive cannon-like gun. The prevailing message of the museum, though, is entirely down to my father. He brought it all together, not to glorify whaling, but to condemn it. *Between 1886 and 1902, over 20,000 whales were killed with this gun*, reads the sign below the cannon. Dad was deeply ashamed of the havoc wreaked by his ancestors on the seas. He spent his life trying to redress the balance.

The sound I heard, seconds ago, was a clattering, as several pieces of metal fell together. Something has dislodged the collection of whaling spears that stands over by the gorse hedge.

A shadow crosses the outline of the orca skeleton and I edge closer to the door until I can see the big, dark shape. As I recognize the outline, my heartbeat starts to settle. And then pick up again, for a different reason entirely. I watch the man in my garden straighten first one spear and then another, before I unlock and open the door.

'Bit late for trick-or-treat.' It comes out before I have time to question its wisdom.

Callum Murray puts the last spear in place and turns round. 'I saw your light on. And I thought I saw you in the garden. I wanted to make sure you're OK.'

I don't respond to that. What is the point? I'll never be OK. Then we hear the sound of a horse whinnying. Which we shouldn't, really, given that there are no horses kept anywhere nearby.

'Sounds like someone's stealing your horse.' I'm joking, I suppose. I've never seen Callum on horseback. I doubt the islands have a horse big enough to carry him.

'I walked over.' He strides to the edge of the garden and looks down the road. The horse must be out of sight because he quickly loses interest and comes back. 'Are you OK?' he persists.

Callum Murray is not a kelper. He is a Scotsman who fought in the conflict, a former Second Lieutenant with the Parachute Regiment. When he left the regiment, not long after the British victory, he bought a cottage a couple of miles outside Stanley. If people ask him whether he's here for good, he says he's keeping his options open.

'Did you find the child?' I ask, more because I feel the need to say something than because I can't guess.

36

His eyes catch the light from the upstairs window. In the day-time, they are unusual, the result of a genetic condition known as heterochromia iridum, making his right eye blue, his left green. In the moonlight, though, those odd, quirky eyes are nothing more than a gleam of light. 'We're starting again in four hours,' he tells me.

There is a sound in the distance, coming towards us on the wind. A helicopter is approaching.

'Chances are he's fine.' I try to sound as though I care. 'He'll have wandered around till he was exhausted, then curled up somewhere and slept. You'll find him in the morning.'

'I bloody well hope so. It was all getting ugly earlier. That's mainly why we went out again, to calm things down.'

Why is he doing this? Why is he here, in the small hours, pretending I have any interest in what's going on around me? I should go inside, close the door. Lock it. 'Skye said something about the people from the cruise ship being difficult.'

Callum's eyes flick up to the sky, back down to me. 'They were the least of it. Fred Harper's family flew over this afternoon. They've been playing merry hell with Stopford for giving up too easily two years ago.'

'It happens, though,' I say. 'Farmers lose sheep all the time. They get stuck in the peat and sink. Or they go over a cliff and the tide takes them. Ponies and calves fall into the rivers. If they're small enough, they get washed away. Every now and again we lose people too. It's terribly sad, but it happens. This isn't a national park.' I don't mean to sound patronizing but Callum isn't making this easy.

The helicopter, a Sea King, is overhead, hanging in the sky the way dragonflies hover above ponds. The dry, peaty smell of the hills, so different to the scents of the sea, seems to be clinging to Callum's jacket. I am reminded, as I always am when he is close, of how very tall he is.

'Is this thing directly above us part of the search?' I say. 'Because if something falls out of it, this isn't a good place to be standing.'

This close to Callum cannot be a good place to be standing.

'They were waiting for us to finish,' he says. 'So we wouldn't confuse the equipment.'

The Sea King moves on, having ascertained that neither of us is a three-year-old boy. Callum and I are alone again.

'I'm going to get some sleep.' I turn and walk inside, locking the door. Only when I know I'm out of sight do I let myself relax, lean heavily against the nearest wall. He walked over? Why would he do that? Callum's house is at least four miles from mine.

Upstairs, Queenie snores on, as I switch out the lights and creep to the window. Callum is turning away, as though he'd been waiting for my light to go out. I watch him walk across the garden and stride over the low picket fence.

Four miles from my house to his, if he's taking the conventional route. Given the way he's heading, I'm guessing that he isn't.

About a year ago, I was awake late, and happened to see him walk past the house. On an impulse I couldn't begin to explain, I followed. I watched as he left the road, approached the high barbed-wire fence, loosened three of the strands, and then slipped through into the minefield.

The minefield?

There are several around the islands, mainly along the coast, planted by the Argentinian army during the invasion. Conservative estimates suggest there could be around thirteen thousand potential explosions lurking in the peat and sand. One day, we're told, they'll be made safe. In the meantime, given that they only account for around 16 per cent of our unused land mass, they are simply fenced off.

I let him vanish into the darkness before approaching the fence myself. The three strands of wire that he'd moved had been clipped through, and he'd attached small hooks to put them back in place. He'd made his own secret entrance into a field that, over a decade after the conflict, was still riddled with deadly traps. Every step he took through that field could be his last.

Tonight, as I stare out at the now empty road outside, I wonder if he's heading there again, if he's going to walk the minefield, to find out if this night, right now, is when it's all destined to come to an end.

And I thought I had problems.

I climb into a bed that feels unusually large and empty, even with my snoring, wind-expelling dog hogging the best place. This is normally the hardest time of the day, when there is nothing left to do but dwell on what I've lost. Sleep never comes quickly.

Sometimes, at night, in that half-dreaming, half-awake state we occasionally find ourselves in, I feel the boys creep into bed beside me. When it happens, I lie still, swimming in their presence, revelling in the smooth silk of their skin against mine; smelling their hair, feeling their tiny limbs wrap around me. On mornings after I dream this way, I wake in a cloud of pure happiness, both unexpected and bewildering, and so distinct from the misery that follows as to be close to unbearable.

Don't come tonight, boys. I'm not sure I can take much more. Just this once, leave me be.

4

'ANYONE HEAR THE GOVERNOR ON THE RADIO FIRST thing?' Brian is saying, as I arrive at what I always think of as the family business.

Grandpa Coffin had several daughters, each in their way as determined and blood-thirsty as he, and one son, who proved a massive disappointment. My father established Falkland Conservation, the charitable trust that protects wildlife in the islands for future generations. I honestly don't think he meant it as a personal affront to Grandpa, but Mr Coffin senior always took it that way.

Brian is an ornithologist in his late fifties whom my father employed twenty years ago. He still clambers up and down cliffs, checking on nesting sites and tagging chicks, despite being around ten years too old and three stone too fat. He'll be found one day, cold and battered, at the foot of a cliff. If anyone were destined to die on the job, it's Brian.

As usual, his ample buttocks are spreading over my desk. For years I've been telling myself that, one day, I'll come in early and cover it with superglue.

'Can't imagine he had anything valuable to add.' Susan is in the kitchen area clattering around with coffee mugs.

'Corporate propaganda,' says Pete, our gap-year student. 'Can't have anyone thinking the kid did anything other than wander off by himself.'

'Well, he couldn't.' Brian wriggles on the desk. 'It's obviously what happened.'

The boss clears his throat. John Wilcock is a small wiry man with dark hair and sallow skin, who has sported the same sleek, dark moustache for the last two decades. We believe that we are cousins of sorts, possibly through marriage a couple of generations ago, but neither of us can be bothered to work out the exact relationship.

'Cat, there's been a change of plan.' John rarely bothers to wish me good morning, which suits me fine. I have no interest in small talk. 'Your group wants to join the search. I said you'd drive them out there. Act as team leader.'

The original plan was that I take a party of visitors round to George and Barren, two small, wildlife-rich islands off the south coast of East Falkland. The two human inhabitants, my Aunt Janey and her husband Mitchell, are something of a tourist attraction too. Janey is the only person I know to have successfully hand-reared a penguin chick. She found 'Ashley' trying to keep warm in campfire ashes and has spent the last fifteen years teaching her to sit up and beg, belly-slide along the roof of the shearing hut and prise snippets of fish from pockets.

'People need to do something.' Susan can tell from my face I'm not too keen on the idea. 'Nobody feels good about enjoying themselves when there's a kiddy out there on his own.'

'We hope he's on his own,' Pete pipes up.

'Yeah, not helpful, Pete.' At barely eight thirty a.m., John is already stressed. 'Don't rise, Brian, we really don't have the time.'

'If these people are willing to give up their outing, we should be willing to guide them,' says Susan.

I pick up the phone and let Aunt Janey know she doesn't need to bother baking this morning. I count four expletives in her response, which is mild by her standards. 'I got my frigging witch costume out of the loft as well.'

'Like anyone would notice the difference. And Halloween was yesterday.' I put the phone down on her grumbling.

'You need to meet at the police station.' Susan loves telling me what to do. 'All the search leaders are getting their orders from the police commissioner at nine.'

41

Finally, the buttocks shift and Brian stands in front of my desk, scratching parts of his body that I'd really prefer not to dwell on.

'Do I offer the guests a refund?' I say this purely to wind up John.

'No, you bloody don't. This was their idea, not mine.'

Our collection of flags is banging in the wind, as are the remnants of our Halloween decorations; the calm of last night is over. As I drive towards the police station, I pass people heading the same way. I see faces I've known all my life and complete strangers. I spot home-made posters fastened to fencing and slow down enough to see that they are blown-up photographs of the two boys who went missing before. *Still Missing*, they say. Archie isn't going to be allowed all the attention.

A plastic skeleton, freed from its restraints by the wind, hurtles across the road in front of my car and it doesn't feel like a good omen.

There is only just space for my car outside the police station.

'Catrin!'

I turn and see the tall figure hurrying towards me, oilskin coat flapping, red scarf flying. A red-gloved hand is waving hard, determined that I should wait, and I feel my insides sinking. One of the few people I haven't managed to freeze out over the last three years. One of the very few who won't give up.

'I'm coming with you, OK, darling?' Mel is out of breath. 'These wellingtons cost a bloody fortune and I am not losing them in a peat bog. I don't care how many kiddies are running round lost, I'm sticking with someone who knows what they're doing.'

Mel is easily one of the better-dressed people on the island, spending a fortune importing clothes from the capital cities of Europe and South America. I look down at the spotless new wellingtons. 'They're pink.'

I'm tapped playfully on the shoulder. 'I know. You can actually buy pink Hunters now. What is a girl supposed to do?'

I've often thought that if ever I laughed again, it would be at something Mel said. At six two, thirteen stone and blessed, I'm informed, with an unusually large penis, Mel isn't a girl of any description. He isn't even a transvestite: his clothes, while beautifully cut and very colourful, are nevertheless clothes made for men.

He's the chef in the Globe Tavern here in Stanley. Two nights a week he leaves off cooking and leads a sing-song around the piano. After seven in the evening, it's literally impossible to get any more people through the door.

'Darling, I'll loiter by your vehicle while you're inside.' He relishes the word *loiter*, rolling it around his mouth like an extra-strong mint. 'Don't hang about though. Perishing wind will blow a whore's drawers off.' He leans against the car door, like a tart on the look-out for punters.

Around us, the crowd in the car park has grown bigger and PC Skye seems to be in charge. She is even paler than usual. Her hair is a mess and I think she might have slept in her uniform. I remember her as a child, always grubby, with bloody knees and torn clothes, the kid with ice cream in her hair, or chocolate stains on her shirt. As I walk towards the door I can hear her trying to persuade the ever-growing crowd to organize themselves into groups of a dozen people, to make sure they have transport and to each elect a group leader.

A clatter of high-pitched voices catches my attention and I spin round to see the community school kids walking down the road. My stomach flips because right there, at the front, is Christopher Grimwood, Ned's best friend.

He's grown. Absolutely shot up in the year or so since I last saw him. His head will be on a level with my shoulder. His face has changed too, losing much of its baby roundness. His jaw has lengthened, his nose developed a pronounced bridge. The pain comes like a freak wave.

In my head – in my heart – Ned is still eight, the age he was when I lost him. He still has chubby knees and fat hands and when he looks down, the puppy fat around his neck gives him a double chin. And yet, now, in Christopher, this awkward, gangly boy on the verge of leaving his childhood behind for ever, I see what Ned would have been today. His perfect skin might be showing the first signs of acne, he'd have an attitude like a walrus with a sore head. He'd be me, all loaded up with testosterone, an absolute fiend, making my life close to unbearable – and my longing for him almost brings me to my knees.

I hold it together, of course. I've had three years to perfect the art of appearing OK. Inside the police station, I find my name is on a list behind the desk and I'm directed towards the meeting room.

I join a group of ten including three in military uniform and two police officers, one of whom is the most senior on the islands.

He's a tall man, neat and measured in his movements. I always think of him as *Stopford, Bob, Chief Superintendent*, because that's how he introduces himself to strangers. He is a man who has read a few books and watched a few documentaries, managing to convince himself, and quite a few others besides, that he is considerably brighter than evidence would suggest.

Pouring coffee from the jug on the table is the head teacher of the school, a man called Simon Savidge who became something of a hero in what, only half jokingly, is referred to as the Falkland Islands' Resistance. In the early stages of the Argentinian occupation, while the islanders were waiting for the British Task Force to arrive, Simon made contact with the troops via a forbidden radio, keeping them informed about Argentine movements on the ground. He was head teacher back when I was in high school and seems to have been in post for ever. His son, Josh, is the most senior detective on the islands.

There are no vacant seats, but then a chair scrapes back along the floor and I see my ex-husband getting to his feet. There is more grey in his hair than when I saw him last and he looks thinner. 'Have this one, Catrin.' He holds the back of the chair, ready to slide it beneath the table as I sit. Ben is always kind to me, in public and in private. I don't particularly like it, if I'm honest, I find it patronizing, but to object would imply that I resent him and the break-up of our marriage. I don't. It wasn't Ben's fault that our marriage failed. It was Rachel's.

And mine, I suppose, in fairness.

So I sit, and pretend not to notice that his hands remain on the back of my chair. Opposite us, the chief fireman is talking to Robert

Duncan, owner of the local radio station and weekly newspaper, the *Penguin News*.

In his early seventies, but with the energy of a man a couple of decades younger, Robert is over six feet tall and stick thin. His hair is thick and white, surrounding his head like the mane of an old lion. He has a white moustache and a white goatee beard.

Another key figure in the resistance, he was broadcasting live when the Argentine soldiers arrived, defiantly playing his own take on patriotic tunes. 'London Calling' by The Clash blared out across the airwaves as the Argentinian commander marched his platoon up to the studio building. The main door splintered beneath Argentinian boots to the sound of the Sex Pistols singing 'God Save the Queen'. Rob kept the airwaves open all the time he was arguing with the South American soldiers who'd come to close him down. Time has not mellowed him. Today, I doubt there is a single figure on the islands more complained about or better loved than Rob Duncan. He is also Rachel's father.

It occurs to me, then, that Rachel is likely to put in an appearance and that that will be a step too far. I cannot be in the same room as Rachel. I'm on the verge of getting to my feet when I see mismatched eyes watching me from the corner of the room. Callum hasn't slept. His sandy hair needs washing and his beard has that particular mix of brown, blond and ginger that tells me it's around thirty-six hours since he shaved. I have a feeling that, if I leave, he will follow. And then Ben might too.

The door closes and *Stopford, Bob, Chief Superintendent* has the floor. Major Wooton, the military's Civilian Liaison Officer, stands to his left, and I know we are about to see the usual jostling for position, with Stopford claiming authority and Wooton, expertise.

'We estimate the absolute maximum distance a child that age could have travelled in eighteen hours is ten miles.' Stopford steps to one side and I can see the large map of East Falkland on the wall behind him. Someone has drawn a red circle around the point at Estancia where the child was last seen. A good wedge of the circle consists of ocean.

'Major Wooton is going to take a platoon and start here.' Stopford points to the centre of the circle. 'He and his men will make their way out to the perimeter. At the same time the rest of us will start from the outside, allowing for the beaches of course, and work our way in.'

'Are we ruling out the possibility that he didn't wander away by himself?' Callum doesn't move from the corner of the room. 'From what Skye tells me, there were other vehicles around the area yesterday.'

'All local cars.' Stopford barely acknowledges Callum. 'We've spoken to everyone concerned. No one saw anything of the lad.'

Stopford goes on to explain that it will take between four and five hours to complete the search.

'What are the school kids doing?' Callum again. 'We don't want a bunch of over-excited children running round. We'll end up with more than one lost.'

'God forbid. The kids will search the beaches. Just the older ones. Eleven years and upwards.' Stopford nods towards me. 'Catrin's colleague Brian is taking the lead on that. They'll stay in sight of an adult at all times. A lot of the mums are coming along to supervise.'

That's where Rachel will be. On the beach, keeping an eye on Christopher. I'm double glad that the younger children are not involved. Seeing Christopher has been bad enough. Seeing Michael, who will be eight now, the age Ned was, the age Kit would have been, would be too much.

'Ben?' Stopford is looking directly behind me to my ex. 'Anything you want to add?'

'We have an ambulance on standby and Mrs West, Archie's mum, is going to stay with it so we know where she is at all times.' Ben clears his throat before continuing. 'When we find him, he'll be cold and hungry. Get him warm, give him small sips of water, but don't feed him. If he's injured, don't try and move him. Just stay with him until I, or one of my colleagues, can get to you. That's it.'

'Right.' Stopford claps his hands together. 'Let's make it happen soon.'

As the group files out, the sheen of optimism that Stopford has painted looks brittle enough to blow away with a strong breath. They did this before. Twice. They set out with Land Rovers, horses and quad bikes to scour the terrain and told themselves they'd find the child quickly. That nothing bad happens here.

'Can I hitch a ride with you, Catrin?' Ben catches up with me on the way out. I can't think of a good reason why not, but I know Ben does nothing without a purpose.

We head out in convoy. In my group, all but Mel, Ben and me are visitors, but the rest look fit and are dressed for the job in walking boots and waterproofs. The bloke driving the hire car behind is my biggest worry at the moment because the road is only going to take us so far.

Driving across camp is hard. Even people who've lived here all their lives get stuck trying to cross rivers, scramble over stones, manage steeply sloping terrain. If I have to keep stopping to tow him out of trouble, we might as well not have bothered giving up our trip to watch penguins. I've already told him to follow my tracks exactly without getting too close, to accelerate and brake hard as I do, take steep ditches diagonally, keep his foot off the clutch as much as possible and use the diff lock when he needs to. He also needs to look out for obvious colour changes in the vegetation that usually indicate soft ground. Agreeing to all of it, he looked a little nervous, rather than impatient, and I took that as a good sign.

On the edge of Stanley, we pass the waiting ambulance and I catch a glimpse of Archie's mother, about to climb into one of the passenger seats. She turns her head to watch us drive past.

'Someone told me you were in charge of the medical team.' A woman speaks to Ben. 'Shouldn't you be with the ambulance?'

'There'll be nothing to do in the ambulance until the child's found.' Ben is giving her his professional smile. He was always good at handling patients and he still has the swarthy, Latin looks that charm most people. 'Until then I can be more use out searching.'

Visitors here are shocked by how quickly we leave any semblance of civilization behind. Those few hundred who don't live in Stanley are spread out over an area roughly the size of Wales, much of it consisting of smaller islands. When you leave Stanley, you pass into a landscape that is bare, almost primal, with no linear roads, very little in the way of trees or greenery, and in which human habitation is almost absent. Outside Stanley the few settlements you see will be isolated farmhouses, surrounded by outbuildings and abandoned, rusting vehicles.

A few miles more down the road and the convoy separates. Some vehicles continue the twenty-five-mile journey towards Estancia. As instructed, we leave the road and head west. Immediately, the vehicle begins to pitch and sway.

'Oh my life, it's like trying to get your leg over in a force eight.' Mel, beside me, is clinging to the passenger seat.

Stony silence from the back. I catch Ben's eye in the rear-view mirror. He gives me a half smile. We've both heard it all before.

'Why do you have so many soldiers here?' one of the women asks, in a distinctive Welsh accent.

'Two thousand military personnel stationed on the Falkland Islands at any one time,' the man next to her says. 'That's roughly one soldier for every Falkland citizen. On the off-chance the Argentinians come back.'

Nobody answers immediately. I was in my final year at university during the conflict. Ben was doing hospital rotations in the UK. Mel saw it all from the relative security of the MV *Norland*, the civilian vessel he was working on that brought the Parachute Regiment south. None of us feels entirely qualified to comment on what the seventy-four days of occupation were like for the resident population. Besides, in the best tradition of *Fawlty Towers*, islanders don't like to talk about the war. Maybe we feel all the conversations we'll ever want on the subject have already taken place. Whatever the reason, we just don't.

'Lot of British taxes go into making you people feel safe,' says one of the men.

'You ever woken up to the sight of an invading army marching down your high street, darling?' Mel may not be a native kelper but he isn't going to let that one go. 'Ever been under house arrest? Had to obey a curfew? Been locked in a community centre with nearly fifty other people and only one working toilet?'

'What's your point?'

'My point, sweet-cheeks, is that the good people of Argentina, who believe these islands belong to them, are three hundred miles away. Britain, on the other hand, is eight thousand miles away and the current prime minister does not have the mighty cojones with which Mrs Thatcher was blessed.' Mel holds his stare.

'So, if you have a soldier for every civilian member of the population, how come this is the third kid to go missing?'

'Hold on tight.' I swing the car into a ditch. There are grunts from the back, some muffled cursing from Mel, but we make it up the other side and drive on. Callum, driving the vehicle ahead of us, disappears into a steep dip, sending up a pair of alarmed geese in his wake.

'Kelp geese,' I say, because the group with me might as well get some of their money's worth. 'The male is pure white, which makes him easy to spot. The female has very distinctive black-and-white striped breast feathers. You normally find them on the coastline but there's a freshwater pond in this dip. Almost there – hold on, everyone.'

Once up the other side of the dip, I slow to a halt. When I jump down, the spot we're standing on is bare rock but the ground will get boggy as we head west. Callum and his team have continued on.

I've walked over camp many times, through tussock grass, following the stone runs, through the bogs. Every time I do it, I'm hunting for something, usually creatures much smaller, better camouflaged and a lot more accomplished at evading predators than a human child. If he's here, he should be easy prey. I watch for incongruous colours, for movement that isn't caused by wind, for the furtive scuffling sound that tells me something is panicking.

I lead my group further across my wild, windswept homeland, and as I do so, I'm thinking about the mother we passed on the road. When Ned was fifteen months old, I lost sight of him for a few minutes. We were on the beach. I'd gone to the water to check on a possible oil slick and left him higher up among the dunes. When I looked back, he'd vanished.

Impossible to describe the horror of that moment, until then the worst thing that had ever happened to me. The ability to think, to reason, left me completely. I got to the spot where I'd left him, called his name, ran on into the grass and there he was. He'd crawled after a cormorant chick, was watching it hop around the grass.

'Catrin, are you OK?' Ben has drawn close, is looking at me with undisguised concern. I'm sweating in spite of the wind, breathing far too quickly. I nod, but I'm still more than half lost in bad memories. Because that time on the dunes wasn't the worst thing to happen to me, not by a long chalk. The worst time came later, when I was far out to sea, and my husband called me on the boat radio.

There's been an accident. Rachel's car went over the cliff outside the house. She left Ned and Kit alone in it. God knows why. The handbrake must have been dodgy. Maybe one of the boys pulled it off. Nobody knows. They're both on their way to hospital. Get here as soon as you can.

When I recovered enough to think it through, I realized Ben had known when he called me that they were both dead. How could he not? He was there, at the house, when it happened. He saw them being pulled from the water. They were both killed instantly and he is a doctor, for heaven's sake, he understands the condition of being dead. He simply hadn't dared tell me. He hadn't dared risk what I might do, two hours out at sea, with such dreadful knowledge in my head. He thought I might do something terrible in my grief, that I'd destroy my own life too, and he couldn't risk that. Not with my being six weeks pregnant.

'What are you doing on Thursday? Do you have someone with you?'

'I'll be fine.' I keep my eyes fixed ahead. I cannot let Ben suspect that I have anything in particular planned for Thursday. Especially not that I am planning to kill my former best friend. 'It's been three years. People move on.'

'I moved on.' I can't see Ben's face, but I know he's close. His voice has dropped so that only I can hear it. 'I found a way to deal with it. You didn't, love.'

I keep walking, but I hear the long, sad sigh.

'I still care about you, Catrin.'

'I've heard elephant seals can be aggressive.' Mel has caught us up, thank God. 'If the lad came across one of those, he wouldn't stand much of a chance, would he? Sea lions too.'

'Possibly not.' I look back to make sure none of the others are in earshot. 'But not something we have to worry about if he came this way. It would be very unusual to see either this far inland.'

'What about birds? Would they attack a three-year-old?'

This, I admit, is a possibility. Skuas are known for attacking humans. During nesting season, locals and visitors alike venture near their sites armed with large sticks. 'It would depend on how hungry they were, to be honest, and at this time of year there's a lot of food around.' I try to give Mel a reassuring smile. He's a sweet man and there's no point in him being upset. 'We probably don't have to worry about him being pecked to death by birds.'

'Everything OK, Catrin?' Callum's voice comes over the radio. I can see him in the distance, on slightly higher ground, and I realize my group has almost stopped moving. I raise my hand to tell him we're fine. He turns away without responding and his group press on. I do the same.

'Tell me something, darling, do you think I'm wasting my time?' Mel has slung a rope, rancher-style, over one shoulder.

'Trying to keep your boots clean? Almost certainly.'

'With Lieutenant Murray.' Mel gives an exaggerated sigh directly into my ear. 'That great, big, gorgeous hunk of ginger. I only came back to this God-forsaken lump of rock for him.'

Unlikely as it sounds, Mel and Callum met during the conflict, on board the MV *Norland*, when Mel was head steward. According to Callum, the typically homophobic soldiers were pretty hostile to Mel at first, but such was his good nature, efficiency and sheer brilliance at the piano, he won them all round. By the time they got here, he'd practically become the regimental mascot.

'I really don't think you're his type, mate.' Ben's voice has an edge that makes even Mel stop and think before he says anything else.

'We've reached the bog,' I tell my group. 'It's about thirty metres wide, so we go in single file from here.'

One of the women looks nervously at the thick covering of fern and pale wild grasses, the dark earth beneath. 'What if he fell in here?' she asks. 'He could be at the bottom right now. We could walk right past him.'

'We're still some way from where the child went missing,' I say. 'It's very unlikely he made it this far.'

'But the third child to vanish. You must be asking yourselves why?'

51

I don't try to hide the sigh but Ben beats me to it. 'Imagine a child goes missing on Barry Island, with nothing to suggest anything more sinister than he fell in the sea.'

She listens, flattered by his attention.

'Over a year later, a child vanishes in Rhyl,' Ben continues. 'You don't necessarily connect the two. We're talking similar distances, similar timescales. Then another year goes by and a third child, a bit younger than the others, is lost, but you still have every hope of finding him. You wouldn't be screaming about serial killers and paedophiles – and neither are we.'

She seems satisfied with this. At any rate, it shuts her up for a bit. Of course, what Ben's just related is the best-case scenario, a child found soon with nothing more to show for his adventure than a ravenous appetite and a few bruises. It doesn't explain why all the attempts to find him yesterday failed.

The radio bursts into life again. I call for quiet and the others gather round. Some way in the distance I see Callum's group doing the same thing. My heart beats a little more insistently. In my group someone starts to speak, someone else shushes her immediately. Callum is looking my way again. I stare back, thinking how much easier it is to do this when he's at a distance, when there's no danger of eye contact. Then I see Ben watching me.

On the radio I hear a reference to flies, to maggot activity.

'Oh my God,' says the Welsh lady in my group. 'They've found him.'

5

AS THE WELSH LADY JUMPS VERY QUICKLY TO THE OBVIOUS but wrong conclusion I'm shaking my head, sending my own private message to the man on the hillside.

'It can't be Archie.' I raise my voice and give the radio to Mel while I address the group. 'Maggots can hatch in twenty-four hours but to do so they need much warmer conditions than they'll find on a Falkland night, even one in late spring. Archie would have to have died almost before he was missed. Even then . . .'

Mel taps me on the shoulder and gives me the thumbs up. 'Dead sheep,' he says. 'I've asked them to deliver it to the Globe for tonight's dinner.'

We don't find him. By two o'clock in the afternoon, we've walked the area twice. He isn't here.

Back at the police station, food has appeared and the search parties fall on it. Mel practically falls on Callum. I hang behind, wanting to leave. After a few minutes, the search leaders are called into a separate room.

'There's talk of a vigil tonight,' Stopford announces. 'The radio's been full of it all morning. Calling for people to camp out. Build fires. Give the lad something to aim for, apparently. Bloody daft, of course. They're more likely to set half of camp on fire and I can't see how that's going to help him much.'

'The ground's probably too wet to catch fire, Bob,' says Ben. 'And it's understandable. No one wants to think about the kid being out at night by himself. If half the island is camping out too, then he isn't by himself, is he?'

'I think we have to consider the possibility that he may have left the island.'

Everyone turns to the speaker, Major Wooton. A hush settles over the room.

'Going where?' I say, which is sort of pointing out the obvious. Tierra del Fuego on Argentina is three hundred miles away. South Georgia is nearly a thousand miles in the other direction. Other than that? Well, Antarctica, if you have weeks to spare.'

'One of the other islands, obviously,' Wooton says to me.

'Well, that narrows it down.'

Wooton glares.

'I don't mean to be difficult, but there are over seven hundred of them.'

Callum clears his throat. 'I think what Major Wooton is driving at is that it's starting to look as though he didn't leave the area by himself. And, let's be honest now, these islands have form when it comes to missing kids.'

Silence. A stubborn one at that, and it's clear what everyone is thinking. We're a small community. We all know each other. Go back a hundred years and half of us are related. There is no crime here other than parking tickets, the odd bit of teenage pilfering from the shops and fairly regular but largely harmless merry-making at the weekend. Our prison houses drunks. The idea that someone could have abducted Archie West is monstrous.

'We need to close the ports,' says Wooton, as though there are dozens of them. 'No one leaves the islands.'

He's panicking. No one can leave the islands, even without his macho posturing. There isn't a flight out till tomorrow, even if it were possible to smuggle a three-year-old child on an RAF plane.

'What about the cruise ship?' Ben says. 'That's due to leave on Thursday.'

I mutter excuses and wander outside, helping myself to a couple of small sausages as I go. In the car park, I let Queenie out of the car and feed them to her. She licks my hand until it can contain no trace of anything but dog slaver.

There is a noise behind and I know who has followed me out. 'Someone has to think the unthinkable,' Callum says.

'No one on the islands would hurt a child. It must have been one of the visitors.'

He shakes his head. 'Visitors might have the will but not the means. Someone who doesn't know the islands would have nowhere to take him. Wouldn't know where to hide him.'

I say nothing.

'The same group of visitors weren't here seventeen months ago when Jimmy Brown disappeared from Surf Bay. They weren't here twenty-seven months ago when Fred Harper vanished from Port Howard.'

Trust Callum to be quoting facts at me. 'No one's taken him.' I turn to face camp. 'He's out there somewhere. He fell in the river and got washed out to sea, or into a bog and for some reason he hasn't floated yet. The best way to find him is to systematically clear the area of livestock and then have the army do another heat search. We're looking for a body now and that's terribly sad, but we might as well face facts.'

We glare at each other.

'The cruise ship will be searched this afternoon,' he says, after several seconds. 'Stopford was reluctant to agree but we talked him into it. Wooton is going to release all personnel not needed for basic guard duty. They'll do the fishing boats as well. With our own private army, we'll be able to rule out the visitors by the end of the day.'

If the boats are being searched today, we should all be in the clear by tomorrow. Able to move around freely again. In the meantime, this conversation is going nowhere. I should simply climb in my car and drive away.

'Isn't it always the parents?' I say. 'Maybe Stopford needs to have a long, hard chat with the West family.'

He half smiles, and there's a pitying look in his eyes as he turns away and walks back towards the station. He thinks I, and the rest of the natives, are simply refusing to accept that someone we know could be bad. That there could be a monster among us.

55

Mid afternoon, I decide I need something from the store, so take Queenie for a quick walk around town. I'm conscious of it being almost time for school to finish and the knowledge makes me walk faster than usual, keeping my eyes down. I find it too hard to see the kids racing out of the gates, and I don't want mothers trying to be kind to me. It's impossible to miss Callum's Land Cruiser, though. It's probably the only car on the islands that particular shade of forget-me-not blue.

Just as I realize he's most likely in Bob-Cat's Diner, even as I'm thinking that I might actually – no, I'm not going to do that – I see him. Sitting at the counter, directly in front of the window. He hasn't gone home yet, he's in the same clothes he was wearing this morning. He isn't alone.

There's a small child, a child I don't know, but one about two years old, leaning towards him, his little feet balanced precariously on the lap of the woman sitting beside Callum at the counter. A woman wearing pale-coloured jeans tucked into riding boots and a sweater that's exactly the blue of her eyes. Callum is with Rachel.

Someone walks past me on the pavement. I have a feeling it's Roadkill Ralph, but I can't take my eyes off the diner window.

I haven't been this close to Rachel in three years. In such a small community it would be impossible to avoid her completely, but on the few occasions I've seen her, I've always made myself scarce. If she turns now, she'll see me. They both will.

I can't move. Something is rooting me to the spot.

She looks great. Her hair is longer than I remember. She's a bit plumper, maybe, but it suits her. And she's laughing. She's looking up at Callum and both of them are laughing, while the child hangs between them. They look like a family.

I'm going to be sick. As saliva floods my mouth, I turn and drag Queenie back down the street.

Later that evening, I can barely summon the energy to eat and clear away afterwards. I never sleep well, and it doesn't take much exertion above normal to send me into a state of complete exhaustion. The search for Archie resumed in the afternoon, but in a less focused way. The police and military all left to search the various boats around the islands, leaving the population and the visitors to their own devices. I went to work, where the radio and a constant stream of visitors kept us up to speed with the day's lack of any sort of progress.

Fewer than two days to go. Around forty hours. Tomorrow I'll write the letter that will ensure Queenie is taken care of.

'I moved on.' All afternoon, I've had Ben's voice in my head. 'I found a way to deal with it.' Ben dealt with the loss of our sons, who were as important to him as they were to me, by finding another woman to love, by replacing the family he'd lost with a new one. Could I have done that too? Should I have tried?

Too late now.

As the daylight fades, the wind picks up and the skeletons in the garden start to creak and groan. For a short while, Queenie rushes from the front to the back door, barking at phantoms in the dark. She's quickly unsettled by my moods. It isn't really cold enough to merit a fire, but I feel the need for its comfort, and Queenie loves nothing more than curling up on a scorching hearthrug. I pour a glass of red wine and tuck myself into the big armchair. Most evenings, if I'm not working, I either read or watch movies. We don't have live television on the islands. Our programmes are courtesy of the British Forces Broadcasting Service, chosen for their likely popularity with serving soldiers. We have a thriving movie video library, though, and most of us make good use of it.

Not tonight. Were I to choose a romantic comedy, the faces of the leading actors would morph into those of Callum and Rachel. A murder mystery? Guess whom I'd be picturing as the corpse? The ticking of the clock seems unnaturally loud. The child has been missing for nearly thirty hours now and it feels as though the islands are waiting for something.

Queenie jumps to her feet as the banging resounds through the house. This is not the polite tap of a close neighbour. This is someone demanding entrance. My heart starts to thud in my chest. Queenie's frantic barking doesn't help.

There he is, Callum Murray, right there on my doorstep, claiming my attention in person just as he does, so much of the time, in my head. He has the grace to look embarrassed.

'Sorry, I know it's late, but I think someone should search the wrecks. We should start with the *Endeavour*, that's the most likely, then the *Sanningham*.'

Remembering this afternoon, seeing him in the café, I want to hit him, but that would require too much in the way of an explanation. 'What are you talking about?' I say, instead.

'I've been thinking about places he could have been taken.' Callum steps back, as though not to crowd me. 'Everyone's checked their outhouses and their barns and their peat sheds. He isn't anywhere obvious. He's where no one would think to look.'

'He's at the bottom of a bog. He'll float in a few days when his body fills up with gases.' I know I sound heartless, but the last time I saw this man, he was grinning at the woman who killed my children.

'The *Endeavour*,' he repeats. 'Catrin, are you listening to me?'

The *Endeavour* was an Antarctic supply ship that sits now on the seabed off the coast of Fitzroy. It will be the small hours before we're back.

'He can't be on a wreck.'

'Ask yourself where you'd hide a three-year-old,' Callum says. 'Somewhere he'll be safe until you need him again, but with no possible way of escape and where no one else would think to look.'

There's a time lag in our conversation. He speaks, but it takes me a second or two to process the content.

He doesn't wait for me to answer. 'The *Endeavour* isn't much more than an hour's drive from where he went missing. It's largely out of the water, but too far out for wading or even swimming to shore to be a possibility.'

'You're saying someone grabbed him, drove him to the coast, put him in a dinghy, motored or rowed out to the *Endeavour* and stowed him in the wheelhouse?'

'Or the *Sanningham*, but the *Endeavour* is more likely because you wouldn't have to drive close to Stanley to get him there. Are you saying it's impossible?'

I want to. Except . . . 'Have you shared this with Stopford?'

'He's still tied up at the harbour with the cruise ship.'

I know about the police activity at the harbour. My own boat was searched earlier. The constable who stopped by the office to collect the keys told me that no boat, skippered by resident or visitor, will be allowed to leave harbour without police permission while Archie West is still missing. It is very much in my interests that the child is found quickly.

I give in to the inevitable and find my jacket and keys.

'You can drive,' I tell Callum as Queenie follows us to his Toyota. 'I'm wrecked.'

He jumps in and starts the engine. 'Yeah, I imagine Archie West's feeling pretty jaded right now. Not to mention his mum and dad.'

There's no real answer to that, so we head for the harbour in silence.

The town is busier than it should be, people on the streets, beer bottles in hand. We have a mild problem with alcohol abuse on the islands. Noise, skirmishes, minor vandalism. In all fairness, there isn't a lot else for the younger people to do in the evenings, but it's usually, if not reasonably good-natured, then basically harmless. Not tonight, though. I don't like the purpose I can see in these groups. I don't like the way people stop talking and watch us drive past.

We explain ourselves to the constable on duty who agrees to let Chief Superintendent Stopford know our plans. The boat is searched, quickly, once again and then we're on our way out towards The Narrows.

Normally, there's something rather magical about harbours at night-time. Even I'm not immune to the beauty of coloured light dancing on water, the playful sounds of water round hulls. Tonight, though, the tension hovers around the masts like gulls hanging on the air currents. The suspicion that arose when the child wasn't found is spreading like an infectious disease.

We turn south around Cape Pembroke and the Antarctic wind hits us full on. Queenie shoots me a look of disdain and does her usual half run, half fall into the bow cabin, as I become conscious that this is the first time Callum and I have been alone, properly alone, in years. I wait for him to say something, make some comment about the search, or the plans of either police or military.

He remains silent, and when I turn I see him sitting on the side couch, arms on his knees, head down.

The sea gets bigger. Both the wind and the tide are against us and it's going to take longer than the usual hour to reach the wreck. The waves are five, six feet high. They hit the bow and droplets of water scatter like pebbles over the hull, running down the glass panes of the wheelhouse windows. Callum hasn't moved.

'If you're not feeling too good, you're probably better on deck.'

'I'm good. I don't get seasick.'

Seasick or not, something is bothering him. He's the colour of the water that is splashing over the bow, a sort of sickly grey-green. Sensing me watching him, he lifts his head.

'I know you don't want to hear this, but there's a killer on the islands.'

I'm conscious of my heartbeat picking up, of a chill that has nothing to do with wind or weather creeping up on me. 'This isn't Glasgow, or Dundee or London.' I'm trying hard to keep my voice light, as though I'm half joking. 'We only have a couple of thousand people. What are the chances of one of them being a psychopath?'

His stare hardens. 'Well, I'm no actuary, but I'd say greater than the chances of three boys between the ages of seven and three disappearing in three years.'

It seems a good moment to concentrate on steering.

'I was at Port Howard when Fred vanished. So was Stopford. I begged him to search all the visiting boats but he refused. He said the owners would check themselves, that if the little boy was hiding on any of them, he'd be found without a disruptive and distressing search.'

I don't answer. No point. I can tell he's far from finished.

'Think about it, Cat. Two of our biggest events, Sports Day and the Midwinter Swim. Loads of people milling around. Kids wandering away from their parents. If you were a paedophile, isn't that when you'd choose?'

I shake my head. He just doesn't get it. He doesn't get that that sort of thing simply doesn't happen here.

His raised voice is as shocking as a sudden cold wave. 'Jeez, Catrin, what happened to you?'

I look at him then. I forget the boat completely. That he, of all people—

'Sorry.' He's on his feet. 'That was a stupid thing to say.' He runs his hand over his face. 'I haven't slept in God knows how long.'

I turn back to the wheel. 'Archie didn't vanish during an event. He was just picnicking with his family.'

'So maybe he's becoming an opportunist. He could have been stalking Archie and his family for days.'

'He?' Callum is directly behind me. I can see him in the glass of the wheelhouse, not quite as tall as I would expect him to be. His feet are planted wide apart to give him balance in the rolling sea.

'Paedophiles and child killers are usually male.'

If the boat pitches suddenly, he'll fall into me.

'When Fred vanished, some teenagers said they'd seen a young kid wandering off towards the beach. They followed but when they got down there, no sign of him. Which suggests to me, he didn't make it to the beach. When Jimmy went, more than one person thought they'd seen him near the parked cars.'

'None of them were sure, though, from what I can remember.'

'Why do you think they all vanished near water?'

He's not going to let this go.

'If a child is going to come to harm here, the chances are it will be in the water.'

'I think he's got a boat. I think he lures the kids on to his boat, somehow, and then' – Callum lifts his hands, spreads them wide – 'there is no end to the places he can take them.'

'Why are you telling me this?'

'Because the woman I knew would care.'

I can't even look at his reflection any more. The woman he knew had two sons to protect. Of course I'd have cared had there been a killer on the loose when Ned and Kit were alive. As it is, I care so little I can't even take what Callum is saying seriously. He's right. What has happened to me?

We travel on, Callum resumes his seat, I stare at the sea. Some time later, when we're still a little way from the *Endeavour*, I jump when he taps me on the shoulder. He's looking out of the wheelhouse window towards land. On the beach and stretching back miles into camp, small fires have been lit. They dot the countryside like fireflies. I slow the boat almost to a halt.

We stand side by side for several minutes, letting the boat find its own course, watching the orange beacons sprinkled across the hillside like fairy dust. Then Callum unzips his jacket. 'I'll take the wheel.' He steps to the helm. 'You need to look at something.'

As we move again, faster than I would go given the size of the sea, I take the folded papers he's holding out to me and then his seat on the side bench. It's still warm from his body. He's handed me three sheets of A4. It's a spreadsheet, a list of names.

'What's this?' I know most of these people. I see Rob and Jan Duncan, Rachel's parents. Simon Savidge. My colleague, Brian. The Governor.

Callum pushes the throttle further and the boat starts to ride the waves. 'These are the people who were at the Sports Day on West Falkland when Fred vanished and at Surf Bay when Jimmy did.'

I flick through to the second page, and the third. 'Seventy-five in total.'

'There were more. I took out those aged under sixteen and the elderly ladies.'

I make a point of raising my eyebrows as a wave crashes over the bow but he doesn't take the hint. 'And the ones in bold?'

'Men, between the ages of sixteen and seventy-five. Able-bodied. Forty-one prime suspects.'

'Mel's on this list. You think because he's gay he has to be a child molester?'

'I'm on it too. So is the frigging Governor. Those names marked with an asterisk have a boat, although to be fair, most people here have access to one.'

'How did you pull this together?'

'I started with those I could remember, then looked at the sports teams I knew had taken part. It's easy to get hold of team sheets. I asked other people who they could remember. Skye McNair helped a bit. Unofficially.'

'Has Bob Stopford seen it?'

He makes an exasperated movement and the speed increases

again. 'Course he bloody has. Trouble is, he's not listening. I'm an incomer. I don't understand island ways. I'm judging what happens here by the standards of Glasgow's sink estates. He used those exact words.'

We're going recklessly fast. A big wave now could swamp the wheelhouse. 'What do you want Stopford to do?'

'Go through this list and find out where each person was when Archie disappeared. If they can't account for themselves, he should search their properties. He won't do that, though, because then he has to admit that I'm right.'

'Why should that be such a big deal?' I stand and gesture that I'm ready to take the wheel back. 'I'm not saying you are right, but if you are, why would it be such a problem for Stopford?'

We swap places again. Callum tucks the spreadsheet away but doesn't sit down. He stands behind me, holding on to the roof beam for balance.

'Wouldn't he want the challenge of working on a big case?' I ease back on the throttle, but gently. He notices, though. He misses nothing.

'It won't be just about him, though, will it? The Governor, the Legislative Assembly, the Foreign Office, hell, probably the entire British Government, all have an interest in keeping this place under the radar screen. If you start making a nuisance of yourselves, if you put your heads above the parapet again, for the wrong reasons, then the groundswell of opinion that you're not worth the effort or the expense any more might just become uncontainable.'

'You're saying we can't afford a serial killer?'

He shakes his head, as though despairing of my naivety. 'Of the whole frigging world, Catrin, the Falklands can least afford a serial killer.'

I ramp the speed up again and we travel on.

On the south coast of East Falkland there is a long, narrow harbour called Port Pleasant and, at the harbour entrance, the low-lying Pleasant Island. It is just about becoming visible as a darker smudge on the horizon. The *Endeavour* lies in the narrow strip of water between the smaller and larger islands. Large boats rarely come in here, which is just as well because the *Endeavour* is dark metal, low lying in the water and in the dark, other boats could easily ram it. On a rough night, you'd mistake it for a wave until you were practically upon it.

I keep an eye on the depth as we get closer. My boat has a shallow hull but the tide is low and there are rocks scattered around this stretch of the coast. I can see the wreck now. It sits on the ocean floor and its bilges and lower cabins will be flooded, but it's a tall boat and the wheelhouse at least is out of the water.

About twenty metres away I stop and release the anchor. As the grinding sound of the mechanism wakes my dog, Callum takes a deep breath and runs his hands over his face. For the last twenty minutes he's said nothing.

'We'll have to do the last bit by dinghy. I hope you're prepared to get wet.' As I check the anchor is holding, pull on oilskins and speak a few words of reassurance to Queenie, Callum hauls the dinghy from the cabin roof. I hand him a life jacket, grab my kitbag and we climb down. The dinghy has an engine, of course, but at a shake of Callum's head I don't turn it on. He picks up the oars and we move silently through the water.

The wreck looks enormous from the water. It rises up before us, black and dead. Maybe sixty or seventy years ago it was left behind by those it served well. Not for the first time, I wonder if ships feel pain when their days on the sea come to an end.

It's swaying in the rough sea. As we get closer, it rocks and pitches in a sad echo of how it used to move on water.

I dive wrecks from time to time, but I never really enjoy doing so. They attract a particular sort of ocean life into their secret places. Boats belong on top of the waves, not beneath them. Wrecks speak of lost hopes, of wasted lives, of dreams that didn't survive the storm.

This is a horrific place to keep someone imprisoned. I can think of few crueller things to do to a child. On the other hand, if he's here, imprisoned, then he's still alive.

'How do we get on board?' We are approaching the bow and I can't help feeling that the old ship is watching us, that there is something sentient on board, and that our presence is unwelcome.

Maybe Callum is more right about this than he knew. I have a moment to feel glad he's with me, this six and a half feet of muscle, then remember that I wouldn't be anywhere near this place if he hadn't bullied me into it. The deck must be twelve feet above us. There is no way up that I can see.

'There's a ladder at the stern. Starboard side.'

Starboard side is facing away from the shore. Callum pulls hard, and we move into the deeper shadow between the great hull and the moon.

'Wait here.' He stows the oars in the dinghy and stands up.

'You're going up on your own?'

As he reaches out, I see his hand shaking. 'We really don't know what's up there.' He tugs at the ladder, testing its strength. 'If anything happens, if I'm more than ten minutes, get yourself back to the boat and call for assistance.'

He really does expect to find something on this boat, I realize. His silences on the trip over. His sickly green colour. Shaking hands. He's scared.

Climbing quickly and silently for so big a man he disappears over the side and I'm alone on the ocean.

6

I LISTEN, FOR THE SOUND OF FOOTSTEPS, FOR THE VOICE OF A small child, and hear nothing but waves slapping the hull and wind screeching around the nearby hills. I want to stand up, to follow Callum up on deck, or cast off and get back to my own boat. I don't want to be here, tethered to this dead ship.

How long has it been?

I keep listening, but the wind is strong and the water pulls and sucks at the iron hull of the ship, as though trying to lift it from its grave on the ocean bed. Callum might have vanished into the night.

How long can it take to search a wreck? The wheelhouse is above the water line but much of it has been damaged by the elements. There will be a cabin to its front that is the most likely prison for a child. All the other cabins and storage space below will be flooded. There really isn't that much to search and I would have heard something by now.

Some way off, my boat is rocking on its anchor. I think I can see the gleam of Queenie's eyes on the side deck.

He's been gone too long. I reach into my kitbag and find what I'm looking for, then tuck my grandfather's handgun in my pocket before reaching for the ladder. Meaning just to climb and look, I take one rung and the next until I can see over the side.

Constant movement on deck. Water is splashing over it every few seconds and then racing back to the sea. Clouds overhead cast drifting shadows. I search, for the glimmer of movement that isn't water, for darkness that isn't empty. There is no sign of Callum. A big wave hurls the *Endeavour* to one side, almost throwing me off the ladder. Suddenly, climbing aboard seems the safer option.

I'm on deck now, but rooted to the spot. The iron beneath my feet is covered in wet silt, rough with clinging shellfish. Weed is everywhere, some left strewn by wind, some growing of its own accord. The wreck is in the middle of a kelp field and the vegetation is trying to claim it. The wind grabs hold of my hair, pulling it up around my head. I reach into my pocket and pull out my grandfather's pistol, hoping my hand doesn't shake too much. I am not, particularly, experienced with firearms. My footsteps squelch as I move closer to the wheelhouse and the dank darkness of the ship seems to wrap itself around me.

It smells vile. It smells as though the carcasses of long-dead animals are rotting here, as though unspeakable things have crawled out of the water to feed on them.

The door of the wheelhouse is missing and I can see only blackness inside. I draw closer still and a tall figure takes form. I'm startled, have half turned to run, even as I realize it can only be Callum. He is standing upright, completely still. I see his shoulders rise and fall. His head is fixed, looking at something in front of him. Something I can't see. It cannot be a scared but still living little boy, because if it were, he'd have bent to pick him up by now, would be carrying him back towards the dinghy, grinning in triumph, the way he always looked when—

I've reached out, laid my hand on his left shoulder. He spins on the spot, knocks my hand away so forcefully I drop the gun and stagger back. The stagger is what saves me, or possibly the weed on the floor that gets beneath his feet and brings him to his knees. Without my stagger, his stumble, those reaching hands would surely have found my throat. He's on his feet again in an instant, but I didn't fall and have a split-second advantage.

I'm out of the wheelhouse, racing for the side of the boat, have almost made the ladder when he catches me. I hit the deck flat out. He's on top of me. Impossible to move with that weight pressing down on my chest. His hands are around my throat. I reach out and my hand closes around something hard. A backward twist of the elbow and I make contact with his skull. His weight lifts as he rolls away, grunting. I spring forward, twist round and his eyes meet mine.

There is blood dripping from the wound I made on his temple.

'What are you doing?' Instead of getting away while I can, I whimper like a child. 'Callum? It's me. What the hell are you doing?'

One hand goes to his bleeding head. The other stays on the deck to keep him steady. 'Christ, what did I do?'

For a few seconds we crouch, a yard or so apart, holding eye contact. Then I stand quickly and back away. I see the gun on the deck by the wheelhouse and race towards it.

'No, don't go in th— Christ, is that thing loaded?'

I spin round. 'It is. It put down a one-and-a-half-ton beached killer whale last year with a single shot to the head. I'm guessing your brain's smaller.'

'I'm not arguing on that one.'

'Now talk to me. Do you know who I am?'

He gets up, but slowly, not wanting to alarm me. Or give me an excuse to fire. 'Catrin Quinn, née Coffin. You're thirty-four years old and you live on a cliff above Stanley, in a house with the creepiest frigging garden I've ever seen.'

He waits, and sees in my face that this probably isn't enough.

'I'm Callum Murray, former Second Lieutenant with the Parachute Regiment, originally from Dundee in Scotland. Sir Bradley Rose is Governor of the Falkland Islands and back home in the UK, John Major is Prime Minister. Want me to go on?'

'No. Are you OK?'

'I'm OK.'

I flick my head backwards, indicating the wheelhouse. 'What's in there? What did this to you and what is it you don't want me to see?'

His face tightens. 'We need to call Stopford. Let's get back to the boat and get him on the radio.'

'What's in there?'

He shakes his head. 'Stopford.'

Going into the wheelhouse means turning my back on him, but I don't think it's Callum I need to be afraid of any more. So I spin round and step inside. Apart from the thin beam of light gleaming from the torch he dropped, the wheelhouse is in darkness. The stench is stronger in here, as is the sense that I am surrounded by the sort of creeping, half-rotten life forms that inhabit nightmares. I find myself thinking of the poem Rachel loved so much, the one she was always quoting at me. The one she thought I'd like, because I always loved the sea. I didn't, I hated it, but I'm remembering too much of it now.

> *The very deep did rot: O Christ!*
> *That ever this should be!*
> *Yea, slimy things did crawl with legs*
> *Upon the slimy sea.*

I bend to pick up the torch, slipping the gun into my pocket, and hear Callum step inside with me. 'Bow locker. Port-hand side. If you're sure.'

I'm far from sure. But I aim the torch and see the child's foot. It seems to tremble in the thin beam, like old movie footage. The world tilts and I'm not sure whether it's the *Endeavour* knocked by another big wave, or just me.

I step closer: three, four steps and shine the torch along the full length of the child's body, from head to sneaker-clad foot.

'Jimmy,' I say.

This isn't the corpse of Archie West. The ankle-bone sticking out of the canvas, lace-up shoe is almost skeletonized. This could not have happened to Archie in a day. Also, these remains are too big to be those of a three-year-old, even a five-year-old. Not Archie, nor Fred. We've found Jimmy.

'I'd say so.' Callum is in the doorway of the wheelhouse. 'Looks about seven years old.'

The little boy in front of me, just a tiny bit younger and smaller than Ned was, is still wearing scraps of clothes, including both shoes. There are tufts of hair on his head still. Most of his skin is gone. The flesh that gave him firm, plump cheeks, a stubby chin, strong little arms and matchstick-thin legs is gone too. All that is left of Jimmy is the calcium framework that should have been allowed to grow, to get stronger, to turn him into a large, healthy man.

> *I looked upon the rotting deck,*
> *And there the dead men lay.*

Coleridge. I remember now. Samuel Taylor Coleridge's *The Rime of the Ancient Mariner*. A ghastly piece of work. Ned will look something like this. My angel is a corpse in the ground now, slowly rotting away as this child is. Ned has been dead for longer, his body will be showing a more advanced state of decay. I have never thought of this before. In my head, Ned is still the pale, but otherwise entirely familiar little boy who slips in and out of shadows at home, chasing his ghostly brother from one hidey-hole to the next.

It's as though I'm looking at Ned, as though someone has forced me to dig up his grave and confront the reality of what he's become.

The boat sways, the torch beam falls and I feel the weight of two large hands on my shoulders. The temptation to lean back into them, to close my eyes, is almost irresistible.

'His skull looks weird.' Callum has taken the torch from me and is aiming it at Jimmy's head.

Somehow I manage to answer him. 'He hadn't lost his milk teeth.' Without facial flesh and skin, two rows of dentition can be seen around Jimmy's jaw, one above the other, waiting to push through. Perfectly normal for a child that age, but so very, very odd to see.

Ned lost a milk tooth days before he died. The lower-right central incisor. I still have it, in a tiny heart-shaped box by my bed. If this were Ned, I'd be able to see the gap. I can't bear this. I can't.

Callum lowers the torch. 'I see his dad in the Globe sometimes,' he says. 'He works up at the hospital.'

He had a sister in Kit's class. I try to say this out loud, to prove I'm OK, but I can't. Emily, I think she was called. A pretty little thing.

Callum takes hold of me again, but I shrug him off, because

something has occurred to me. 'The others could be here too. Archie, even Fred. We have to look. 'Archie!' I call out. 'Archie, can you hear us?'

I feel his breath in my ear. 'Cat, there's nowhere else they can be. This and the cabin are the only spaces above water. I'd checked the cabin before I saw him.'

It's not that I don't believe him, I just need to see it for myself. I push at the narrow, arched wooden door that takes me into the triangular-shaped cabin at the front of the boat. Someone, Callum I imagine, has opened the three lockers. They are all empty, apart from a few inches of water. The cabin floor, too, is under an inch or so of water. There is nothing in here.

The steps leading below deck are on the starboard side of the wheelhouse. As I head for them, Callum catches hold of me. 'No way. You are not going below deck in the middle of the night.'

'What if Archie's down there?'

'If Archie's down there, he's dead too. There are only two steps above the water line. It isn't happening, Catrin.'

He takes advantage of my hesitation to push me out of the wheelhouse. He's right, of course. There is nowhere else in here a body can be hidden and any below deck aren't going anywhere in a hurry. The adrenalin that brought me on board, that made me fight and win against a man twice my size, that gave me the courage to search for a dead child, is gone. I'm exhausted and more miserable than at any time in the last three years. I honestly wouldn't have believed that possible.

'You were right,' I whisper as we head across the deck. 'Well almost. Congratulations.'

'Aye, it's a blast being brilliant.'

No need for stealth on the return trip. We use the outboard and are at my boat in seconds. Queenie gives a little 'hurry it up, will you' yip as I cut the engine and Callum ties the dinghy up.

'Radio reception isn't great here.' I climb up after him and he turns to pull me up the last foot or so. 'We should motor round the headland. It's more sheltered there too.'

The next harbour along is Port Fitzroy, another anchorage I

know well. While I'm securing the boat, Callum makes the radio call to Stopford. Knowing any number of others could hear it too, even at this hour, he keeps details to a minimum. I take off my oilskins and turn up the heater. He joins me, taking the seat opposite in the cabin that always feels ridiculously small when he's in it. He too pulls off his coat. Queenie cuddles up close to me and stares at him.

'I'm assuming that was a flashback,' I say. 'On the *Endeavour* just now. When you lost it.'

He pulls a face that indicates agreement. And one that reveals his shame.

'You told me they'd stopped. You said you didn't have them any more.' It doesn't escape me that I sound like a wife with a grievance.

The cabin light behind me is shining directly at him, because his odd-coloured eyes are apparent. I find my own eyes flicking from the green, to the blue. I could never decide which I preferred.

Shortly after Callum and I first met, he told me about the post-traumatic stress disorder that he, like so many soldiers from the Falklands conflict, suffers from. His particular mental illness – because that's what it is, make no mistake about it – usually takes the form of flashbacks to the conflict itself. For hours at a time he goes to another place entirely. A darker, more violent place. I looked up PTSD once. Flashbacks are a common symptom.

'When I told you that it was true. They pretty much stopped within a year of my moving back here. I can't really explain why being here helps, but it does. Or rather, it did.' He drops his head into his hands, pushes his fingers through his hair. 'A couple of years ago, they started again. Normally, if I feel one coming on, I make sure I'm alone.'

He's talking to the cockpit floor now. 'They're triggered by stress. Anxiety. It was stupid of me to come out here. I'm not good around water. Not since – sorry, you don't want to hear this.'

'What do you mean, you're not good in water? I've seen you swimming. What's water got to do with anything?'

He looks up, stares at me for long, long seconds. 'Cat, do you really not know?' he says, eventually.

'Not know what?' Suddenly, my heart is hammering. I have a

feeling that I really don't know. And that it might be better if I carry on not knowing.

'The day Ned and Kit died, I was there.'

It is as though he has hit me again. I know practically nothing about the accident that killed Ned and Kit. I know that the car in which they'd been left alone started to roll, that one of them had probably been playing with the handbrake, that it went over the clifftop outside my house. That it fell twenty feet into a high tide.

'I saw the car go into the water. I was the one who got them out.'

Callum was there. He saw it happen. And he didn't save them?

He's off the seat now, kneeling in front of me. 'I had to climb down after them. It's not steep there, as you know, not particularly high, but it took time. The car had sunk before I got to the water. I pulled Kit out first, then Ned. I pulled them on to the rocks and I was praying they were just concussed but I had to go back and make sure there was no one else in the car. I knew it was Rachel's and I thought she might be in it too. Or her kids.'

I think I knew that someone had been at the scene. I hadn't known it was him. No one had talked to me about the details and I hadn't asked. I hadn't gone to the inquest.

'The impact killed Ned and Kit, Catrin. They didn't drown. They were dead when I got them out.'

I knew this, I think, yes I did. That much seeped through the drug-fogged haze that was my life in the weeks following the accident. Ned and Kit didn't drown. They were killed instantly. I have always taken some comfort in that. But the terror! Those last few seconds, as the car fell—

Callum is holding my hands. 'There's something else,' he says.

I'm not sure I can deal with anything else.

He reaches into the pocket of his jacket. It takes me a moment to register the object that he pulls out and, when I do, I think I'm going to be sick. I gulp down something vile then stretch out for it. He hesitates for a second before handing it over.

'That's exactly what I thought, when I saw it,' he says. 'It was on the deck, caught behind some chains. I recognized it straight away, but I don't think it can be. What are the chances?'

I'm holding a stuffed rabbit, with long ears, glass eyes and a blue jacket. The colours have faded, it's been shrunken by the seawater, but I'd know it anywhere. Benny Bunny. Kit's favourite cuddly toy. When Kit and Michael were tiny, Rachel and I both bought identical toy rabbits for our youngest. Kit loved his so much. I had to prise it from his sleeping fists to wash it. It was with him in the car the day he died. I haven't seen it since.

'They were pretty common on the islands a few years ago, weren't they?' Callum is saying as I can't take my eyes off the toy. 'It probably isn't Kit's. The beach here is quite popular for beach-combing. All sorts of things get washed in by the tide. I really don't think it can be Kit's.'

I nod again.

'I'd seen Jimmy's body, I was on my way back to you when I saw it.' I think Callum is talking non-stop because he's afraid of what I might do. 'I think it was the toy, rather than the body, that brought on the flashback. The next thing I remember is you whacking me over the head with that piece of iron.'

'Did it hurt?' I take my eyes away from the rabbit to look at the wound on his temple. It doesn't seem too bad, but I bet he has a hell of a headache.

'God yes.'

'Good.'

'Did I hurt you?'

My throat is still sore but there's no serious damage done. What he would have done if I hadn't stopped him is another matter. 'I'm OK. But you should probably see someone.'

'I already do.'

His hands are shaking. In spite of the warmth of the cabin, of the thickness growing in the air as the kerosene fumes fill it, we are both still cold.

'I'll get you some aspirin.' I stand up.

'Shhh. Did you hear that?'

He gets to his feet, squeezes around me and goes out into the cockpit. Puzzled, not sure whether to be alarmed or not, I follow and find him on the stern deck.

The sound of the wind and the ocean. The sound of loneliness. The sound of distance from everything. Then something else.

Something musical, beautiful, heartbreakingly sad. Whale song.

'They must be close.' The wave of sound dies away and I reach back inside the wheelhouse for binoculars.

Callum is spinning slowly on deck, trying to locate the source. 'I've never heard anything like it before. I thought whale song could only be heard underwater.'

The sounds have gone for the moment, all we can hear is the rumble of the waves and the wind coming off the hills. 'It's unusual but it happens. There are stories of whales having conversations with people. Even with dogs.'

'What are they?'

I put my fingers behind my ear to indicate that I'm listening and wait for it to start again. A moment of nothing but water sounds and then a long, low growl followed by a purr like that of an enormous cat. Then the tone changes completely to one tuneful, high-pitched, almost a keening sound.

'I don't think it's one of the dolphin species.' I lift the binoculars and look in what I think is the right direction. 'They make more of a chirruping, clicking noise.' I can't see anything. It's too dark, the animals are too far away. 'Could be humpbacks, they have the most complex song, but they're not that common here.'

'They sound sad.'

The sounds have settled into the rhythmic repetitions that bear some similarities to human song. Then there comes the whoosh of a blow. I give the binoculars to Callum but he can't find them either. They're not in this bay, but somewhere close. We listen for five, maybe ten minutes until the song fades into wind and wave. Then we go back inside. We don't sit down. Something has changed. Suddenly, it's not the dead child, or the missing one that's uppermost in my mind.

'How long before Stopford gets here?'

He shakes his head. 'I'd like to say just over an hour, but he can't mobilize as fast as we did. You should get some rest.'

We both look to the closed door of the bow cabin. I know exactly what he's thinking. I'm thinking it too.

'Callum, about— I'm sorry— I just—' I have no idea what it is I want to say.

He gives me the first smile I've seen on his face in a very long time. Although I don't think I've ever seen a smile quite this sad before. 'I know,' he says. Which is good. Because I don't.

Queenie joins me on the bunk, her fur damp from the spray, and doesn't complain when I cling to her. We lie together, awake and shivering. We listen to Callum moving around in the main cabin, we hear the pumping of the heads, then silence as he settles down to rest.

The wind gets up. Storms come from nowhere in this part of the world. The boat starts to rock and pull against its anchor and an eerie whistling comes from the headland. Just as I'm dozing off, I hear the whales again. Two distinct species this time, the steady mournful song of the large toothed whales, and the lighter, chirrupy notes of a dolphin species. Callum was wrong, I think, as I try not to wake properly. They don't sound sad. They sound afraid.

When I was fifteen, my father and I rescued a young pilot whale from drowning. We were out in his large, flat-bottomed boat, fishing. Fishing, with my father, meant lowering massive nets at previously selected spots. Periodically, we'd scoop them up, counting, photographing, making notes before releasing the captured fish. We'd been at it around an hour when we noticed the large shape in the water. Grey-black, smooth, motionless.

'What is it?'

'Young pilot, I think.' Dad moved us closer. 'Can you see the round head? And that pectoral fin looks quite large.'

'Is it dead?' The whale proved emphatically that it wasn't by exhaling loudly.

Something was wrong though, even I could see that. The whale was hardly moving and its tail end seemed to be weighted down in the water.

'I'm going to have a look.' Dad was already reaching for his snorkel and mask.

He approached the whale slowly, he wasn't stupid, and swam the length of the animal's body towards its tail. After a couple of minutes he came up and swam to the boat.

'It – she – is caught up in a fishing net.'

I helped him on board.

'It's wrapped around her tail and both pectorals, stretching up as far as the dorsal fin. She can't swim and her rear end is being weighted down.'

I looked at the sleek dark shape in the water. She seemed to be edging closer to us, had turned her head so that she could see us. 'What will happen to her?'

Dad was out of breath. 'Eventually she'll get exhausted trying to stay near to the surface. She'll sink and drown.'

'Dad, we have to do something.' At fifteen, you still think your father can achieve anything he puts his mind to.

I watched him think about it. Approaching a frightened, injured whale was an incredibly dangerous thing to do. One unpredictable flip, and we'd be in the water. On the other hand, if we did nothing, she'd die for sure.

We helped her, of course, it was never really in any doubt. I'd have cried all the way home if we'd left her and I imagine Dad would have too. We paddled right up to her and then, with me on board and Dad in the water, we began the painstaking process of pulling the net away.

Fishing nets are massive and very strong. We had two knives but mostly we had to pull. After thirty minutes or so we'd got the dorsal and one pectoral fin free. Discovering she could move again, the whale swam forward in a surprising burst of speed, taking us with her for a hundred metres or more, before she tired again and we resumed work.

After another hour the second fin was free and it was all looking a lot more hopeful. Another ride around the bay and the whale calmed enough for us to get the rest of the net off her tail. We lay back in the bottom of the boat until Dad found the strength to get up and start the engine.

The whale hadn't gone. She was hovering about fifty metres off to port. As we started to motor she came with us, surfacing first on port, then on starboard. She breached high into the air before diving deep, only to emerge somewhere we least expected. We watched breach after breach, tail lobs and fin slaps in a spectacular display of aquatic acrobatics. She stayed with us until we reached Stanley harbour when Dad cut the engine again. As the propeller stopped spinning, and silence fell over the sea, the creature came right up alongside until we could see her liquid black eyes peering at us. We leaned out and stroked her smooth, round head. She left us then, flicking her tail in a last, joyful salute.

'What did you call her?' Rachel asked me later.

I shrugged. Dad and I had been working too hard trying to save her, we hadn't thought to give her a name.

'One day, when you're lost on the ocean and about to drown, she will appear and save you,' Rachel announced, in the emphatic way of hers that told you there was no point arguing. 'When she does, give her a name.'

Dreaming of Rachel has woken me, as it always does, and with that grinding, impossible-to-settle rage that her mere presence in my head always brings. I get up, trying not to disturb Queenie. In the main cabin all seems still.

Midnight has come and gone. It is Wednesday. One more day to the anniversary of the boys' deaths. One more day until everything changes.

The door opens quietly. Callum shouldn't be asleep at all, given that the bench he's lying on is two feet shorter than he is. His feet are propped up against the cabin wall, his shoulders hunched uncomfortably against the side of the fridge. He is sleeping, though. His breathing is heavy, his face completely relaxed.

I take deep breaths, forcing myself to calm down, to stop shaking.

Callum sleeps so deeply, an army legacy of having to snatch rest whenever he could. We used to joke that a lit firework under his bum wouldn't wake him ten minutes after he'd dropped off.

I will never get this chance again.

I walk over, my bare feet making no sound. I'm calmer already. I'm not shaking any more, or if I am, it's for a different reason. I kneel beside him and lean closer, until I can feel his breath against my face. Closer still. I can smell coffee, the oils in his skin, whatever he last washed his hair with. I touch my face against his, feel his skin, the stubble of his beard next to my cheek, then let my lips meet his.

I stay like that for long seconds, breathing in time with him, willing him to wake up, praying that he won't. Then I see him, once again, grinning down at Rachel, and I can't bear to be near him.

I'm disturbed once more before morning. A boat has come alongside. I hear lines landing on deck, feel the gentle thump of another vessel's fenders. I think I hear my name and wait to be roused. The call doesn't come, and so I drift away.

DAY THREE
Wednesday, 2 November

7

I'M AWAKE AGAIN BEFORE DAWN, BUT LIGHT IS GROWING AS I step out on deck. Queenie and I are alone. The sounds I heard in the early hours were those of Callum being picked up by the police boat.

A fret, or sea fog, has arrived in the night and the harbour entrance is filled with white mist. It looks solid enough to run across, a wall of white. It looks like a giant wave, stretching between the two cliffs, and for a moment I have a sense of it moving towards me. It looks like a barrier, something that will stop me leaving this safe harbour, and maybe I should listen to what nature is telling me. Maybe that wall of mist is here to keep me safe.

But the light grows, the clouds take on the soft, ivory warmth of the sun's first beams and the wall begins to break. After a while, I can see the point where the ocean meets the sky on the other side of it. Whatever is waiting for me there, the mist is letting me through.

There's traffic on the shipping channel, and I hear that the search of the boats last night proved fruitless. Archie West, the little lost Arsenal supporter, has been missing for two nights now. I also hear some of what's going on around the headland.

When I turn into Port Pleasant I see immediately that I'll get nowhere near the *Endeavour*. There are two police vessels, a military boat and a dive boat anchored close to it. Callum is standing on the bow. Sound travels a long way here and he obviously heard me coming. He turns to talk to someone on board and then Stopford appears. I watch the two of them climb down into one of the police launches and head my way.

'Catrin, what do you know about the tides round here?' Stopford doesn't waste time once he and Callum are on board. 'People tell me a lot of stuff gets washed in here.'

'That's true.' I talk to Stopford but I'm looking at Callum. His beard, that odd mixture of blond, red and brown hairs, is clearly visible around his chin and lower cheeks. There are grey hairs in it too now. His face is thinner than when I first met him. Or maybe he's just tired, having had little or no sleep the last two nights. As if confirming my thoughts, he sinks down on to the wooden slatted seat that runs around the side deck and Queenie leaps into his lap. He reaches out to stroke her muzzle and his hand is shaking.

'What we're trying to figure out is whether the little lad was left on the boat, or whether he could have been carried around by the tide and got stuck in the wheelhouse.' Stopford raises his voice to get my attention.

I think about it for a second. Port Pleasant, like a lot of the inlets around Falkland, is long, thin and undulating. And it has the island directly in the middle of the channel. It's a collecting ground for all sorts of floating debris. Even, I imagine, that of the human variety.

'It's possible,' I say. 'A big wave could have brought him on to the boat and after that, it's not difficult to see how he could have become stuck. Is it Jimmy?'

Stopford's face tightens. 'Too early to say. We'll get him back. Hopefully the dentist can help us out.'

I think back to the small skull we saw in the torchlight, to the double dentition that freaked Callum. 'Did you find anything else on board?' I don't mean anything else, of course, I mean *anyone* else. I just don't want to say it.

'Not yet. But the divers will be here most of the day. If necessary we'll tow the wreck itself back to Stanley. I'd appreciate you and Callum keeping quiet about what you found here. Until we've had chance to confirm identity and talk to the lad's family.'

Half the islands' population will know about the body we found by now, but I nod my agreement and so does Callum. Telling us to stay in touch, Stopford climbs back on to his launch and returns to the *Endeavour*.

'Anything I missed?' I ask.

Callum shrugs. 'Jury's out on whether we found a murder victim, or the trapped remains of a tragic accident. No prizes for guessing which camp Stopford's in.'

I think for a second. 'So where does that leave Archie? I mean, the search for Archie?'

'There was talk about searching all the other wrecks. Or at least the ones that have some sort of sheltered accommodation out of the water. That's something. It'll take time though.'

'We need to get back. You're frozen. You should go inside. Try and get warm.'

Somewhat to my surprise, he doesn't argue. When he goes into the cabin, Queenie follows him as if she's his dog, not mine.

I start the engine, lift the anchor and head out. After we've cleared the bay and I'm confident I can put the auto helm on, I steal quietly over to the seat in the wheelhouse where Callum left his jacket.

The toy rabbit is in one of the inside pockets. There's hand stitching around one ear where the original seam came loose and someone – me, I think – sewed it back up. I feel sure that this is Kit's toy. I can't begin to calculate the odds of it ending up on the *Endeavour*, the odds of both this and the body of poor Jimmy Brown doing so, but this is the last comforting thing my baby ever saw. I tuck it inside my shirt. It's filthy, cold and wet against my chest but I wouldn't have it anywhere else.

As I drive into Stanley the fishing fleet are setting out for the day. I reverse into my mooring and tie the boat up. I haven't heard from man or dog the whole trip back. So I'm not entirely surprised to see both of them curled up on the main bunk, snuggled under rugs and dead to the world. Queenie opens her eyes. I wait for her to scramble off and join me but she stays in the crook of Callum's arm.

Just before I leave the boat, I tuck Benny Bunny into a drawer in the wheelhouse. I want him close, next time I head out from harbour. I want him with me at the end.

I'm weary. Body and soul. Weary of being forced to think about children who mean nothing to me, of putting what little energy I have into looking for boys who are not mine. I never used to be so cold. I'm not naturally a monster. There was a time when I'd have been as distressed as anyone by the losing of Archie, by the finding of Jimmy. There are days when I think the old me is almost gone.

Now, for the short time I have remaining, I want to be left alone, with the only two people I care anything for. Even if they are ghosts. But at this stage I cannot do anything that will draw attention to myself. I have to go through the motions, just for one more day.

So I head for the office, to see if normal business has resumed or if we're spending another day searching for Archie. Susan is in something of a flap.

'Your Aunt Janey's been on the phone. Needs you to call her right away. Problem over at Speedwell.' She is holding the phone out to me and I have no choice but to take it and dial my aunt's number.

Speedwell is an island off the south coast of East Falkland very close to George and Barren. Aunt Janey and her husband own it and live on it some of the time. She answers so quickly I know she has been sitting by the phone. 'Catrin? We've got a big problem. Whales on the beach. Hundreds of them.'

Susan is watching me. I pull a face to let her know it's bad. 'Are they alive?' I ask Janey, and to be honest, I'm hoping they're not.

'Most of them. But the birds are starting to have a go at them. Catrin, it's really horrible.'

It takes a lot to upset my Aunt Janey. I tell her I'll be with her as soon as possible, just as John arrives.

'Mass stranding on the south coast of Speedwell,' I tell him. 'Well over a hundred, according to Janey. Pilot whales, most likely, from her description.'

Neither of my colleagues replies immediately. It's the sort of disaster we dread, can never really prepare for.

'We'll have no help.' Susan has gone pale with distress. 'Everyone will be looking for the little boy.'

Ordinarily, with a major marine incident, we could rely upon both the police and the military for assistance. But with a child still missing the chances of them sparing personnel are slim.

'I've got that fisheries meeting this morning,' says John.

The meeting has been planned for months. We're discussing selling fishing rights in certain stretches of water. It's important. The islands need the revenue. John has to go to the meeting. Which means I'm in charge. Susan will have to stay in the office as a central point of contact.

'But it's your field, right?' Susan looks to John for confirmation.

'Cetaceans are Catrin's speciality.'

I nod. 'I know what to do.'

'I can get on the phone.' John is the first to pull himself together. 'Explain the situation to Stopford and Wooton. See what they can spare us.'

'The radio too,' I tell him. 'People should be able to decide for themselves.' I want to tell him that Archie is almost certainly at the bottom of a bog or been swept out to sea, but there may still be a chance to save the whales. I don't. Maybe it's the memory of that tiny skeleton, lying alone on the *Endeavour* all this time, but I don't.

'What do you need?' he asks me.

'Couple of helicopters with load-bearing capacity would be good. Failing that, as many people as possible. Small boats with big engines, jet skis will do, ropes, stretchers, buckets and lots of large sheets or groundsheets. And spades. Lots of spades. Did I mention buckets?'

Susan makes a list, as John goes to find his phone book. 'I can be there by mid afternoon,' he tells me.

I spend the next half-hour getting everything I need. Pete arrives and makes himself useful. When John has finished his calls, we talk through the various scenarios. None of them inspires us with anything other than a sense of dread. We all hope Janey has been exaggerating the scale of the problem. I don't say that Janey never exaggerates.

As I'm about to leave PC Skye arrives. 'The Chief Superintendent asked me to pop in,' she says. 'We'll do our best to get some people over to Speedwell, but we have to concentrate on the search for little Archie.'

'Clear the area of livestock and do another infrared search,' I tell her. 'You'll find him.'

Her eyes fill up. I forget how young she is. I forget that it's possible to be so fresh and vulnerable that the death of a complete stranger can have a serious impact upon you.

'Mr Stopford would prefer you to stay here,' she goes on. 'You and Callum. In case he needs to talk to you again.'

'I'll be contactable by radio all day.'

I haven't given her the answer she wants but she chooses not to pursue it. 'I'm sorry I can't come to Speedwell,' she says. 'The boss has put me in charge of liaising with Archie's family.'

I want to tell her I can't imagine anyone better, but I've rather got out of the habit of kind words, so I nod. She hovers for a few seconds, then walks into the door on the way out and disappears rubbing her hipbone.

Pete helps me load the equipment and we set off. Back at the harbour, my boat is empty. I feel a moment's qualm about leaving Queenie with a man who is clearly emotionally unstable. I was prepared to be lenient when it was my own safety at stake but if he hurts my dog, I will kill him.

There is nothing to be done. I don't have time to track them down now and in any event, Queenie has been coping with emotional instability for three years. I doubt she'll notice the difference.

We don't take my boat. It isn't fast enough. The RIB will get us there in an hour so even if people have already set off overland, we'll still beat most of them to it.

'Pilot whales?' Pete has to shout his question at me above the roar of the engine as we leave Stanley harbour.

'Probably.' I take the RIB up to its top speed. Janey is a true daughter of Grandpa Coffin, she knows her whales. Besides, pilot whales are among the most common to be involved in mass beachings.

'It won't be pretty,' I shout back, which is something of an understatement. Of all possible marine disasters – oil slicks, pollution incidents – the grounding of a pod of large mammals is one of the trickiest and most distressing to deal with.

As we near Speedwell we pass other boats heading the same way. One of them appears to be from the cruise ship, which isn't great news. Island people will be pragmatic, ready to pitch in if there's anything sensible they can do, stoical if not. Visitors from overseas, with no real understanding of the natural world, will be a different matter.

'Why?' Pete is mouthing at me. 'Why does it happen?'

I couldn't answer that one in a few words and sign language. No one really knows why it happens. My father, who made something of a life's work studying whale beachings, argued that they were akin to road traffic accidents. Any number of things could go wrong, but the result was the same. Animals can hit ships, be attacked by predators; in the northern US, pneumonia is a common reason for beachings. The animal could have a virus, a brain lesion, parasites. Quite often animals are washed ashore posthumously.

With a mass beaching though, there's something else going on. Strong social cohesion within a pod of whales means that if one gets sick or is injured and swims into shallower waters, it's quite likely to be followed by the rest of the group. The whole pod then gets in trouble.

Some scientists believe the echolocation systems that whales use to navigate are less adept at picking up the gently sloping coastlines around the Falklands. The whales simply don't see the beach until it's too late.

The environmental lobby are quick to blame man's habit of pillaging the planet, that military sonar can cause whales to lose their bearings, stray into shallow water and end up on the beach. On the other hand, there are reports of cetacean strandings dating back to Aristotle. My own belief is that Dad probably had it right. Lots of different causes, the same horrible result.

We see our first whale when we're still a quarter of a mile from the beach. Dead, belly up. Janey was right. This is a long-finned pilot whale, sleek and black, with a bulbous nose. An adult, female at a guess, about four metres long.

As we approach land, we see more whales. Some of them are floating in the shallows, gently bumping up against the shore with each new wave. Most are on the beach, in a grim, straggly formation.

'Jesus,' says Pete.

There are several other boats in the bay, all creeping in. I count around twenty people on the shore, most of whom will be from the nearby settlements, although I can see a few of the red anoraks worn by visitors from off the cruise ships. I spot the bright blue baseball cap that Janey invariably wears to contain her mass of dark curls when she's out of the house.

She wasn't exaggerating. There are well over a hundred. Possibly closer to two hundred. The surf around the water's edge is red with blood. Some of the animals are being dashed against the rocks. And the petrels haven't waited for the whales to die.

When I glance at Pete he looks close to tears. I take the RIB up to the edge of the bay and head in. 'I need you to be OK.' I sound harsh, I know, but this is going to be hard enough without human sentimentality.

He sniffs. 'I'm OK.'

A man jogs along the shore to meet us. It's Mitchell, Janey's husband. Pete throws him the RIB's painter and he pulls us in.

'One hundred and seventy-six, I counted twice,' Mitchell tells me. I nod my thanks. Counting them would have been my first job and Mitchell has saved me the trouble. More people are arriving all the time. They're wandering about among the whales. Some of them are going to get hurt.

I pick up my bag, gesture to Pete to bring the stretchers and stride up the beach. When I'm close to the biggest group of people I give two short blasts on my whistle.

'I need your attention, ladies and gentlemen. Can you all gather round and listen up.'

Not everyone is listening. I give one more blast, shout at a man who is ignoring me. 'Mate, I need you over here now. We're running out of time.'

I go on quickly, while I have their attention.

'My name's Catrin Quinn. I work for Falkland Conservation and my speciality is cetaceans. I'm in charge of the operation.' I don't say rescue operation. I don't want to give them false hope. 'Thank you for coming. Now, when you approach the whales, move slowly and quietly. They are very distressed and we don't want them any more frightened than they are already. Be very careful. Keep away from their tails and their mouths. Watch for them rolling on you. They can still hurt you a lot more than you them. No children or animals are to go anywhere near.'

Everyone is listening to me now.

'The first priority is to keep them cool and wet. Protect them from the sun. Put sheets and covers over as many as you can and keep them soaking with seawater. Those of you with spades, start digging channels to get water to the whales. I'm going to go along the beach now, marking them with flags. Red means they're small enough to be stretchered back to the water. My colleague Pete is in charge of that, and he'll tell you when we're ready to start lifting. Blue is for the bigger ones that we can try to harness and pull back in using the boats. Black means cover them up and keep them cool.'

'How do we get the black ones back?'

I look at him. Big, middle-aged, self-important. In the red anorak that will make it easier for the ship's steward to spot him when it's time to herd all the passengers on board. He thinks he's being clever, catching me out.

'I'm hoping the RAF will spare us a helicopter,' I say. I don't tell him that airlifting a whale back into the water is a time-consuming and tricky task. Even if we do get a helicopter and some men to help on the ground, the chances of our saving more than one or two are slim.

'The best thing you can do for them now is make them more comfortable. And try to keep those birds off. OK, let's go.'

'Come on, you heard the woman.' Janey's voice follows me down the beach. 'Get some chains formed.'

Starting at one end of the beach, I begin examining the whales. Pilot whales are the second largest of the oceanic dolphins, orcas being the biggest. The males can grow up to six and a half metres long. Not massive, by the standard of whales, but big enough. They're playful creatures, fond of following boats, riding bow waves, and they have this habit of spy-holing, when they hang vertically in the water and peep their heads out to give you a good looking at. They are one of my favourites of all the cetacean species.

After forty minutes, we're ready to start lifting the smaller whales. Out on the water, a flotilla of boats is on standby to nudge and coax them into deeper water.

'We need to roll them on to the stretchers.' I have to shout to make sure everyone can hear me. 'Take care because, although they're big, they're quite delicate and they're in pain because the weight of their bodies will be pressing down on their internal organs. Sand in their blowholes will be very distressing. On the other hand, once we start we should work as quickly as possible.'

No one knows how to begin, so I kneel down beside the closest whale and gesture for others to join me. I slide my hands under her body just as a large pair of hands that I recognize appears at my side. Others copy us.

'And lift,' I say.

We can only raise the creature an inch or so, and only then for a second, but Janey is at the head, and her friend Katie at its tail and they've done this before. The man next to me gives us the muscle we need.

'And slide,' Janey says, and the two women slide the groundsheet beneath the whale.

'Nicely done.' I turn to Callum. 'Where's Queenie?'

'In my car on the mainland. Asleep probably. Stopford's not very pleased with you.'

I raise my eyebrows. 'But he's happy for you to be here?'

'I'm bigger than he is.'

Six of us stand on either side of the whale, bend and take hold of the groundsheet. Callum, being the tallest, moves to the head.

'And lift.' The whale gives a huge sigh. We can't hold it for long. 'And walking.'

This whale is only feet from the sea. Callum strides off and we do our best to follow. The water laps up around my legs and I don't look down. I don't want to see that I'm wading in diluted blood. The whale is panting, emitting small distressed sounds, but Callum is deep enough now to lower it and let the water take some of the weight.

'As soon as the groundsheet's removed we need to get clear,' I say. 'Ready, and let her go.'

We loosen the improvised stretcher. The whale hovers in the water for a second. I can see her getting ready to roll.

'Callum, get out of the way.'

He moves to the side as the whale rolls on to her back. Her tail flicks and catches me on the thigh. I stagger but stay upright. 'Get to shore, everyone.'

Other groups are following our example, wrapping and lifting the smaller animals. Slowly, but steadily, the whales around us are being returned to the sea.

'Any news?' I ask. 'About . . . you know?'

Callum looks round to make sure no one is in earshot. 'Nothing I was told directly. Rumour is that the military will start searching the wrecks today. Less encouraging is that both Fred Harper and Jimmy Brown's families have apparently made contact with Archie West's. There's talk about them getting in touch with British newspapers.'

'Well, I'm sure that will help enormously.'

'It won't help Stopford's efforts to play the whole thing down. He's under pressure from the Governor, too. The powers that be really don't want this place getting a reputation for being a dodgy place to bring a kid.'

I look at the chaos surrounding us. Right now, this doesn't feel like a great place for anyone to come for a couple of weeks' R and R.

'How many can we save?' Callum asks.

I've been wondering the same thing. Fewer than a third of the beached animals are small enough to lift. If everyone on the beach stays for the rest of the day, without food and rest, if we get additional help from the military, we have a chance of getting around seventy back into the sea.

'Reinforcements.' I look towards the dunes and breathe a sigh of relief. Just one squad, around a dozen soldiers, but a whole lot better than nothing. I thank the red-haired, freckle-faced sergeant in charge and ask him to get his men helping the lifting teams, while I harness one of the bigger whales. If we can get a larger one back, I'm going to contact the RAF and beg the use of a Chinook.

With military help, we can save even the biggest whales and suddenly it feels like the right thing to do. More than that, it feels as though, for the first time in years, I have a purpose. An interest in the living.

Blimey, how did that happen?

With a sudden burst of energy, I jog back to the shoreline. Callum is waiting, but he's not looking at me. 'Cat, they're coming back.'

8

THE WORDS I'VE BEEN DREADING. EVEN SO, I TRY NOT TO
hear them.

'The whales.' Callum is looking about fifty metres off
shore. 'The ones we rescued. They're coming back in.'

I walk to the water's edge. I have to make sure Callum's right,
although I have no doubt he is. I can see three, no four, of the
smaller whales we carried out nosing their way back to shore.
Beaching themselves again. Around me, other people are noticing.
Word spreads and the rescue effort stops.

'Why are they doing that?'

'What's going on?'

I tell myself it's not the end of the world. These waters have a
healthy population of pilot whales. We can afford to lose a couple
of hundred. These things happen. Everyone is looking at me.

'Are they the same ones?'

'They're not going to beach themselves again, are they?'

It's exactly what they are going to do. No one knows why they do
that either, but it's all too common. Either the beaching was
deliberate in the first place and they're not going to let human
sentimentality get in the way of the plan, or they simply can't bear
to leave the group behind.

'Keep going,' I tell Callum. 'Try and get some more back.'

'Come on, everyone, we're not giving up now.' I leave Callum behind and step into the water. Aunt Janey and her friend, Katie, follow, and one or two others from the islands. We stride out, meeting the returning whales head on. Janey slaps her hands on the surface. Someone else shouts at them. Janey resorts to language that would scare me away. It works, for a while. The whales hang back, some even turn away, but their hearts aren't in the retreat. They're hanging around, or looking for another route, staring at us with their big, reproachful eyes. One way or another, they're coming back in.

I allow six more whales to be carried out to sea before I admit defeat. We can't spend any amount of time in the water, it's too cold. Now, we just have to see what happens.

What happens is that they all come back. They nose their way towards shore, pushing through the corpses of those already dead, squeezing past the dying. They roll and flap and push themselves out of the water, back on to the sand.

The dismay around me is pitiful. Some of the women and youngsters have started to cry. The men look pale, are blinking hard, rubbing their faces. It isn't fair. These people have tried so hard and they deserve something back. Unfortunately, nature doesn't work that way.

'What now?' Callum is keeping his voice low. I suspect he knows what comes next. I shake my head at him and he follows me as I walk towards the sergeant. The three of us move away from the crowd.

'I have to euthanize them,' I tell the sergeant. 'It doesn't matter how many times we carry them out, they'll keep coming back in.'

The soldier, who isn't much more than a boy himself, looks shocked. He turns back to the carnage on shore, at the sheer numbers involved.

'What if we get them deeper?' says Callum. 'Tow them out with the RIB?'

I knew this would happen. Arguments and counter-suggestions that do nothing other than prolong the inevitable and increase the distress to the animals.

I shake my head. 'When whales re-beach themselves, there is nothing anyone can do.'

A pause, while they try to come up with another answer and fail. 'How are you going to do it?' asks the sergeant, who is looking younger and less sure of himself by the minute.

'Gunshot to the head. If you and your men can assist, that will be a big help. If you can't, then I need to ask you to clear the beach. No one is going to want to see this.'

Callum runs a hand through his hair. 'Catrin, is there really no alternative?'

I feel anger welling up. This is going to be difficult enough and I need these two on side. 'No. If we do nothing, they'll die slowly and painfully. It could take some of them a couple of days. Continually dragging them back is just going to increase their distress and exhaust these people.'

'I'll talk to my CO.' The sergeant walks up the beach. At the water's edge, people are still carrying the smaller whales back, trying to shoo the returning creatures out of the shallows.

'Do you not . . . I don't know, need some authority to do this?' asks Callum.

'Who do you suggest I ask? God?'

'Where's John?'

The implication that my judgement isn't sufficiently sound, that I need to check with my boss infuriates me. Does he honestly think John and I didn't discuss exactly this possibility before I came out here? That we didn't carefully count and sign out the number of bullets I was going to need?

The sergeant returns, radio still in hand. 'My CO can't approve a cull without proper authority. He's phoning the Governor's House.'

'Your CO has no authority over this beach or over me,' I tell him. 'I'm getting started.'

I stride away. I think I see the sergeant gesture to one of his men to stop me but Callum gets to me first. 'Give it a minute.' He's speaking very quietly, his voice just above my ear. 'The Governor's staff will phone John who'll back you up. You might not need this guy's authority to go ahead, but you do need his help.'

'What I need is for him to stay out of my way.'

He grabs my shoulder, physically stops me moving. 'Catrin, there must be fifty people on this beach. Fewer than half are local. They won't understand what you're doing and why it's necessary.'

The sergeant is talking on the radio. It will take time, precious time, for his boss to call the Governor, for the Governor to call John, for the persuasive, soothing words to be said. Time when the whales are suffering and I'm hanging round thinking about one of the worst jobs I can imagine.

'They don't have to understand,' I tell him.

'What will you do if they decide to protect the whales? Form a physical barrier between you and them? Half of them have cameras. You can't do this without the army's help.'

He's right. I hate him for it, but he's right.

Aunt Janey, meantime, knows something's up. She and her friend walk up the beach towards me. Pete and Mitchell have brought the RIB back in and they're coming over too. I'm not completely on my own. It just feels like it.

'I'm going to invite everyone to our house,' Janey says. 'We can show them round the farm and that side of the island. I've got cakes in the freezer. And Ashley's got a new trick. She actually sits up and begs now.'

I manage a weak smile. Her plan, if it works, will get the visitors off the beach. They won't see me shoot a hundred and seventy-six whales in the head. A crunching on the sand tells us the sergeant is on his way back. He's squinting in the sun and his freckles stand out sharply against his pale face.

'My CO can't authorize me or my men to take part in the actual cull,' he says. I'm disappointed but not surprised. No senior army officer is going to want to see pictures of his men shooting helpless animals. 'We'll give you space to work, offer what assistance we can,' he finishes.

I nod my thanks. It's better than nothing.

'Are we sure we've given it enough time?' Callum is looking out across the beach, at the ranks of panting, miserable animals.

'We've had a clearer view out on the water,' says Pete. 'Every single whale we returned to the sea is making its way back in. Some have done it twice.'

Mitchell nods his agreement. 'We're not going to get a different result if we put it off another hour.'

Enough. I turn to the sergeant. 'Can you ask people to leave the beach? They've all worked incredibly hard but they need to leave it to us now.'

'I'll come with you.' Janey takes the young soldier's arm and gently pushes him over towards the waiting crowd.

'Let's hope it's that easy.' Callum takes up the rear and follows them.

Telling me he'll get the gun, Pete heads back to the RIB and I'm alone.

A petrel swoops so low I can feel the rush of air above my head. The unexpected bounty has made them even more aggressive than usual. Knowing I can't put it off, I head over to the crowd who have already heard the worst from the platoon sergeant.

People start shouting at me as I approach. Some are genuinely trying to be helpful, they have suggestions for helping the whales that they honestly think I haven't thought of. Others just want their voices to be heard above the crowd. The headache I hadn't realized I had starts pounding at my temples.

I hold my hand up.

'I'm sorry it's come to this, but it was always a strong possibility,' I say when they're quiet enough to hear me. 'In roughly fifty per cent of cases, whales re-beach themselves. Nobody knows why they do it, but to continue with the rescue operation now will only add to their distress. Euthanasia is the kindest solution.'

I wait. Let my eyes drift from one shocked face to another.

'You should probably leave the beach now. Thank you once again.'

A flurry of questions and protests follow me as I turn away. One young woman runs past me, heading for one of the bigger whales. A soldier sprints after her and grabs her by the arm. I walk on. Crowd control is the military's job now.

I take a less direct route back to Pete, stepping among the dead and dying animals. We know so little about these creatures. Apart from the relatively small number, mainly of the dolphin species, which we keep in captivity, we have so few opportunities to study them. Much is talked about the intelligence of whales and dolphins. Their brain size, in absolute terms and in relation to body mass, suggests that they deserve a place among the most intelligent species on the planet. They exhibit problem-solving abilities and creative thinking. They show evidence of strong social cohesion, form long-lasting and intense relationships, have been known to display cross-species cooperation. It is even believed that they are self-aware, can recognize themselves in mirrors and on video footage. But the truth is we have so much more to learn.

Do they know what I'm planning, I think, as I walk among them, shooing away petrels, stopping to scoop up water and pour it over noses. It seems to me that they do. That there is a tremor of awareness running through this pod as I make my way back to my gun.

'Have you ever killed anything before?' Callum has fallen in step beside me.

I have to think for a moment before shaking my head. I've never shot game for sport. I've been present when animals have been euthanized but I've never been the one pulling the trigger.

'Want me to do it?' he offers.

I shake my head. My responsibility.

'What do you want me to do?'

'Be my last line of defence. If the sergeant and his merry men can't hold the crowd back, I need you to.'

We've reached Pete by this stage. He has a case with the spare ammunition. He hands me the gun.

There is nothing neat, quick or painless about euthanizing a large mammal. The bullet tears into flesh, sending pieces of it flying in all directions. Blood spatters, just as it does at any crime scene, and it isn't long before I'm covered in it. I could stand back, out of reach, but that would increase the chances of missing with the first shot. Even with a good, clean shot – and I am a good shot, I learn that day – the brain takes time to shut down. The animal emits a lonely, mournful cry as it feels itself dying, and that is echoed by those around it. Soon the beach is filled with the sound of whales singing their last. Pete is crying long before we've finished. I feel damp

100

trickling down my cheeks and wonder if I am too, but when I put up my hand to brush the tears away, it comes back red. It's blood, not tears, that is running down my face. The slaughter isn't saddening me, I realize, before I'm halfway done. It's adding to my rage.

Callum remains untouched by it all, moving from one dying creature to the next, always shielding me from view, never stopping the accusations ringing in my ear.

I come across a large female. As I step in close I can't help but remember the pilot whale that Dad and I rescued all those years ago. The one who'd be fully mature now, of breeding age. The one I was supposed to name if I ever came across her again. 'Hello again, Rachel,' I whisper, a second before I shoot her in the head.

9

RACHEL WAS CHARGED WITH CHILD NEGLECT. APPARENTLY, leaving two lively young children alone in a car on a clifftop for nearly fifteen minutes didn't qualify as manslaughter. When the trial came around (a judge had to be flown in from the UK especially for it) she was six months pregnant. She pleaded guilty and was given a twelve-month sentence, suspended because of the advanced state of her pregnancy and her two young sons. Her driving licence was taken away for two years. If you were a kindly sort, you'd probably say that the guilt she had to live with was punishment enough.

A week after she was sentenced, Ben took a good hard look at me, realized that what was going on in my head and body was more than grief and admitted me to hospital. I'd caught an infection, probably the result of four months of complete neglect and stress, and although I recovered, my son didn't. He was stillborn, three weeks prematurely. When I held him for the first and only time, his body still warm from my own, I swear I heard a high-pitched twanging, like the sound of a guitar string breaking, and knew the only remaining cord tethering me to life had gone. I saw myself, a wrecked vessel, the last safety line frayed, drifting into the peril of the open sea.

What followed after was entirely predictable. After eighteen months Ben had largely come to terms with his loss. He was still young, just thirty-seven and so much stronger than I, but he couldn't deal with a wife who had ceased to function as a human being. Oh, I dragged myself to work each day, did my job competently enough. I managed to keep the house on the acceptable side of squalor. I bought food and did my share of cooking it. I walked and fed Queenie, and wrapped myself around her when I needed reminding that bodies are supposed to be warm and hearts to beat. I even let Ben have sex when I sensed he needed the comfort of physical intimacy and tried not to shudder as his hands roamed over me. But the woman Ben had married wasn't there any more and neither he nor I knew where to find her. When he told me he was moving out, that he was going to live with a young radiographer from the hospital, I wasn't remotely surprised. It was a relief, frankly, not having to try to be normal around him. I barely noticed he was no longer in the house. I cleaned less, ate less, spoke to no one not connected with work. The day I heard his son had been born I wept so long and so loudly that Queenie fled the house. After that the woman I'd become resumed the pretence of being OK.

Nobody leaves the beach. Even with the temptations of cake, new-born lambs and a penguin that does circus tricks, no one will follow Aunt Janey to the other side of the island and she won't leave me in the face of so much hostility. They stay and watch, call 'shame' and take photographs as I walk from one animal to the next. 'Murderer!' they yell, as I take aim and send a bullet into the brain of a creature that is much more noble and beautiful and deserving of a place on this earth than its killer. I don't look back or ahead, I just carry on going, walk to the next, aim and shoot. Over and over again I kill, and long before the daylight starts to fade there is little doubt remaining that I've become what they're all calling me. A murderer.

Only once do I stop. Mid afternoon, when around thirty whales are still alive and suffering. I stop because a group of newcomers bypasses the soldiers and gets right up to me. So engrossed am I in my grim task that I know nothing of their presence until they say my name.

I turn and take a few seconds to clear the dark fog that's been growing in my head since I started killing. Callum isn't by my side. Occasionally, he's been stopping to double-check the whales I've shot are properly dead. So he's a couple of metres away, crouching by a young female.

Seven people. All locals, although I can't immediately think of names. Then I recognize Gemma Brown. Whose son's body I may have seen on the *Endeavour* a few hours ago.

'We need to know what you saw on the wreck last night.' It is a man who speaks to me, most likely her husband, Jimmy's father.

'You're going to have to talk to Bob Stopford, guys.' Callum strides closer. They all ignore him.

'We just want to know what you saw. Which one it was. That's not asking too much.' A different man, similar to the first, maybe his brother, the boy's uncle. It doesn't seem too much to ask, but how can I tell these families that the corpse I saw was unrecognizable? That the little boy they once loved no longer exists.

'What was he wearing?' Gemma, the mother, is the most practical. I think of the canvas trainer I saw, dark blue, with laces that might once have been cream. A few words from me would confirm her worst fear. Or prolong the agony. I can't tell her, it would be shockingly irresponsible.

'I'm sorry, I can't help you. You need to talk to the police. I'm sure they'll have answers for you as soon as possible.' I try to turn away, someone catches hold of my shoulder.

'What the hell were you doing there anyway? Who goes out to a wreck in the middle of the night?' The man is in my face, tall and threatening.

'Catrin, the gun.' Callum, speaking softly, steps to my side. I relax my hold on the gun and let him take it, just as the group confronting me notice it too. A different emotion entirely creeps over their faces. A couple of them take a step away.

'Going to the wreck was my idea.' Callum tucks the gun into his waistband. 'We were looking for the missing tourist kid. Catrin gave me a lift. Now, we are very busy here and you need to talk to the police.'

Two of the soldiers have joined us. 'Sergeant, these people need to leave the beach.' Callum is standing for no nonsense but I'm the one who gets Jimmy's dad's parting shot. He looks around, taking in the dead animals, the crimson beach, the spatters on my clothes and skin.

'Jesus, what is wrong with you?'

He turns, and the others follow him from the beach.

By late afternoon, all the whales are dead. John, Brian and a police officer arrive and we start the collection of data. No one has the heart to say that every cloud has a silver lining but the information we'll gather today will be shared with cetacean scientists all over the world.

Slowly, at last, the beach empties, until it's just Conservation people, the army and those few who are here for me. Aunt Janey brings sandwiches that no one can eat and hot coffee that we can't drink fast enough. She also brings a change of clothes, for which I'll be grateful before the day is over. She presses me to stay, promises me my old room is always ready, but I have less than twenty-four hours now. I have to be back in Stanley tonight.

When what little that remains to be done can be handled by John, Brian and Pete, I walk to the next beach, which is all but empty of living creatures. Every bird within a five-mile radius will be feasting on the dead whales by now. I strip down to my under-wear and walk into the water. It feels cold enough to stop my heart. I walk further, submerge myself completely, rinse the gore away from my body, face and hair, and all the time I know that no matter how long I live, it will never leave the inside of my head.

For a moment, I'm tempted to keep walking, start swimming, until the cold gets too much for me, because maybe I can appease the anger of the people who saw me kill today, if I give myself in payment for the whales.

10

AROUND A YEAR AGO, WITH NO REASON TO GO ON LIVING, I started to give serious thought to no longer living. My parents and my children had died, my husband had moved on, my best friend had become someone I couldn't bear to have in my head, never mind in my life. There was Queenie, of course, and I felt bad about abandoning her, but I figured Ben would take her and she'd be fine with that. I started leaving extra food out for her, in case there came a day when I seized the moment and didn't make it home, but she's a greedy little beast and I had to stop when she got too fat.

One Sunday morning, I kissed my little dog goodbye, straightened the house, and drove the boat all the way round the coast to New Island on the westernmost edge of the Falklands.

Over the years, my family have owned a lot of land on the islands but New Island has always felt like home to us, because it was to New Island that my ancestors first came and established their whaling operation. A little way off the coast there is a wreck of a ship called the *Isabella*, that got into trouble carrying a cargo of mother-of-pearl. Decades later, fragments are still found on the shore, some cut into the little tesserae used in mosaics, some still attached to the shells. Rachel was enchanted by the place, renaming it Treasure Island. On my wedding day, I gave her a necklace and earrings made from *Isabella's* mother-of-pearl and she cried for so long I had to redo her make-up.

When our older boys were six, our younger two just four, we took them to Treasure Island. We lit fires, sang songs, watched penguins mooch about and the black-browed albatrosses sitting on their doughnut-ring nests and in an hour and a half on the beach, we collected twenty pieces of mother-of-pearl. I think it was one of the happiest times of my life.

If anywhere could bring home to me what I'd lost, make the leaving behind of this empty life at all easier, it would be New Island.

So the Sunday morning I decided to end it all, I didn't bother with a wetsuit, figuring the cold would ease my passing. I attached a tank with only ten minutes of air and went down. I went in a diagonal line to take me away from the boat. By the time I hit the ocean floor I had roughly five minutes of air left. The water was nearly thirty metres deep and visibility poor. I thought about my sons and let the pain wash over me. I thought about the possibility of seeing them again, although I've never really believed in the afterlife. I heard the sucking, rasping sound of the air running out.

I sat, glued to the sand. When my lungs began to fight, I pulled off the tank and ripped the mouthpiece from my face. My stomach was starting to pulse, my ribcage felt on the point of bursting inwards. I knew it was only a matter of seconds before the urge to draw breath became impossible to resist and when that happened water would flood in and the venture would no longer be within my control. And, at the moment when I think my vision was starting to blur, a beam of sunlight made its way down to the ocean floor. There, directly in front of me, was a small, iridescent fragment that wasn't rock, or shell, although it was once created inside one. A piece of mother-of-pearl.

Rachel. She was right there with me at the bottom of the sea. I saw her twelve-year-old self, face aglow with the shining, gleaming things washed up on the beach. I saw her, tearful and beautiful, on my wedding day. I saw her in the knife, fork and spoon set she gave Ned at his christening.

Seconds later I was on the surface, clutching the shell fragment.

I tried again, of course, I am not so easily dissuaded from a purpose. I stockpiled paracetamol, and succeeded only in making myself very ill. I took a sharpened kitchen knife into the bathroom and after several half-hearted attempts to make a dent in my own flesh, hurled it at the mirror. I read everything I could get my hands on about the psychology of suicide, trying to find out what it was that I was lacking. In the end, I got the message. I was too angry to take my own life. Unless, of course, I could take Rachel's first.

Standing here in the sea, letting the cold water wash over me, as if anything could ever make me feel clean again, I realize that any lingering doubts have finally slipped away.

I've been wondering if I have what it takes to kill. Whether I can look a living creature in the eye and take the one irreversible action that ends a life. Asked and answered, I suppose. Nearly two hundred dead mammals on the next beach are testament to that. I have no difficulty in killing. I'm actually rather good at it.

It's dark when Aunt Janey's boat drops Callum and me back on the mainland. When I say goodbye, I hold her so tightly and for so long that I feel sure she must suspect something. I'm in luck though. She puts it down to the stresses of the day.

Queenie greets Callum and me rapturously, leaping high into the air with excitement, but that could be because she hasn't eaten for hours.

'I can still smell blood,' I say, as we set off across camp.

Callum shifts in the seat. 'Janey didn't have anything to fit me.' He smiles. 'And I'm far too much of a wimp to wash in the sea.'

Taken unawares, I smile back. We have a daft tradition here on the islands called the Midwinter Swim. On the day of the Winter Solstice, which occurs here in June, a couple of hundred foolhardy types gather at Surf Bay and – well, not swim exactly, more run into the water, dunk their heads and run out screaming. In the old days, Callum took part every year. The first time I saw him in swimming shorts, I thought a man from Norse mythology, one of the heroes of old that Rachel talked about, had stepped out of the sea. His hair was quite long then, and it shone strawberry blond in the winter sun. His skin was pale, freckled, and covered in fine, gold hairs. He was massive, magnificent, so very, very male. It was four years ago, a few weeks before I met him properly for the first time. I was a very different woman back then.

I lost more than my sons, when Rachel's car plunged over the cliff.

11

I WAKE SUDDENLY, WITH NO IDEA OF THE TIME OR WHERE I AM. Then I realize I'm lying across the front seats of Callum's Land Cruiser. His coat is below my head, a tartan-plaid rug over me. The car smells of the slaughter we left behind on the beach at Speedwell: blood, the shore, flesh already beginning to rot.

Queenie is with me, not curled up between my stomach and thigh, as is her habit when we both sleep, but upright on her haunches, her tiny ears pricking. She's alert, on the watch for something, staring out of the windows. Maybe she can see something out there. I can't. Her breath, and mine, have misted the windows over.

'Callum?' I don't expect a response. I don't get one.

I've been dreaming. Bad dreams of gunfire and flesh ripping apart. Of blood and bones exploding into the air. I was somewhere very dark. All around me was noise and I was very, very afraid.

I sit up, wipe the windscreen, then the passenger window. Queenie jumps on to the driver's seat to get out of my way, but she's watching my every move.

'Where'd he go?'

She sticks her nose against the window then looks back at me. Her ears flatten. She doesn't know either.

There are no keys in the ignition.

The night air, thick with the smells of gorse, peat and the sea, streams into the car as I climb down. The stars look like droplets of ocean when the sunlight catches them but there is no moon. It's too dark to see much beyond the Diddle Dee, the dense, woody shrub that grows along the roadside like the frayed edge of a ribbon.

I find the small torch I always carry with me, and make my way round the car. There is a wide, deep ditch beyond the Diddle Dee to either side of the road which means I'm somewhere between Darwin and Stanley. I shine the torch as far as it will reach. No sign of Callum.

A sudden explosion of sound and light in the distance has my raw nerves tingling. Fireworks. As the coloured sparks fade I'm remembering more of my dream. Mud and slaughter. Darkness and deafening noise. The battle for Goose Green.

When I first got to know him, Callum told me many stories about the conflict, but only light-hearted stuff. He told me about stealing a sheep to make mutton stew, about the wine store in Stanley that took a hit and caused the streets to run with wine and beer. He didn't tell me anything about the death, the mutilations. He shared nothing of the real horror of the Falklands war.

So I found it out for myself. I read every account I could get my hands on. It wasn't from Callum that I learned of his regiment's five miserable days on Sussex Mountain after their landing, surrounded by bleak hills and lifeless slopes, trying to keep warm in the face of a ceaseless mid-winter wind. He told me nothing about that, but I knew all the same about their failure to dig trenches in solid rock or waterlogged ground, about their grasping at shelter of any kind, even a gorse bush.

I know what he went through on this hillside.

While I'm still undecided about what to do, Queenie takes off along the road.

'Piglet, stay!' Without thinking I use Callum's old name for my dog. She pulls her nose out of the Diddle Dee and looks back at me. Then sets off again.

'Did he go that way?' Queenie is no sniffer dog but she could usually track down the boys when they were hiding.

She yips at the ditch. I stand on tiptoe but there's nothing I can see, beyond dark heathland and endless black emptiness. Then she runs a few metres further down the road. I follow, as another flurry of bangs erupts.

In all the time I knew him, Callum told me nothing about his regiment's overnight march towards Goose Green, about crossing eleven miles of countryside in the winter darkness. I learned from written reports that the Paras marched silently through flat, barren land, knowing the enemy outnumbered them and had had time to plan their defences, to become thoroughly entrenched.

I fail to see a dip in the road and stumble.

The moor the Paras crossed that night in 1982 became a mantrap. Men fell into bogs, twisted ankles on hidden rocks, learning to hate the land they'd sailed so far to protect. They drew closer to where they knew enemy soldiers were waiting, wondering whether the first sound of gunfire might be the last thing they heard. Ever.

Callum did tell me that on that first march they were made to turn around and retrace their footsteps twice, so that by the time they finally engaged in battle they were soaking wet and exhausted. He told me that due to some gigantic cock-up, the BBC announced to the world that the British army was poised to liberate Goose Green, effectively giving away its plans to the enemy.

Callum, already stressed by our adventure on the *Endeavour* last night, has spent the day surrounded by death. He watched me shoot one animal after another, heard nearly two hundred gunshots. For hours today, Callum has been subjected to the heartbreaking sound of animals dying. He's listened to people crying, to shouts of recrimination. Now he's somewhere in the darkness, on the same hillside where he once fought a terrible battle.

Callum, when I first knew him, had firearms. He kept them in the locked box in the back of his Land Cruiser. I should have checked that box.

Queenie's white face appears on the other side of the ditch. With a growing sense of unease, I jump down.

Callum told me nothing about the trenches, the ditches both sides dug to offer protection from hostile fire. It was from others that I learned about the Paras stumbling into enemy trenches to find them festooned with childish reminders of home: toy cars, comic books, letters, photos. He didn't tell me about finding rifles with religious pictures on the butt and severed hands clinging to the triggers. He didn't tell me about headless corpses, about faces with huge gaping holes, about men, still living, whose limbs had been blown clean off. About flesh melting away beneath horrific phosphorus burns. He didn't tell me that napalm had been dropped.

I found all that out by myself.

I can see torchlight. Directly north of my current position. About a hundred metres away. I keep moving, as the Paras did, twelve years ago. Queenie stays a little way ahead.

I should never have let Callum stay on the beach today. Driving back across camp at night, hearing fireworks that can sound so much like gunfire, might just have been enough to tip him over the edge. To spark another flashback.

So now I'm miles from anywhere in the middle of the night and somewhere close to me is an emotionally unstable, trained killer who might think he's back in 1982 and about to go into battle. And who might be armed.

Somehow, I manage to keep moving.

As the Paras neared the site of the battle, they started taking fire from all directions. Mortars, bullets, grenades and anti-tank weapons came at them as they leapfrogged their way forward, one tiny patch of cover at a time.

That's what I'm doing now. Leapfrogging forward, getting closer and closer without being seen.

As they neared the enemy position, the Paras heard the almost crippling news that their commanding officer, Colonel H. Jones, call sign Sunray, had been killed in a suicidal charge against a machine-gun post.

Sunray is down. Repeat, Sunray is down.

I really need to find Callum.

I reach the top of a ridge and get a better view of my surroundings. I can see the car and the lights of Mount Pleasant air base, three or four miles away at most. Queenie has vanished.

I pick up my pace as much as I dare. Another ridge and I can see a small building. I know where I am now. The building is an animal-feed storage hut. This is my land, but I rent it out. It's years since I've been here.

I've lost sight of the torch completely and I can't help feeling that it, and the man carrying it, have gone inside the hut.

113

Towards the end of that first battle, when the Argentinians knew they were beaten, a white flag appeared on a heavily fortified schoolhouse. Three men from Callum's own company went to take the surrender. Callum must have been watching as the men drew near, confusion arose and fire opened up. The men were killed, as were all the Argentinians in the schoolhouse.

I draw closer to the hut and no one shoots me. I see no sign of anyone inside but I'm sure I'm being watched. I get close enough to pull open the door.

The food-storage hut of my memory is not as I remember it. The floor is wood, as it always was, to keep the damp away from the sheep fodder, but someone has made a rudimentary attempt to introduce some human comfort. A single mattress has been pushed against one wall. It has a pillow and an old, stained patchwork quilt. The hut smells of human waste and I can see a pile of small brown faeces in one corner.

'Callum.'

'I'm here.' I turn and see his shape, dark and massive, blocking the doorway.

'What's going on? What is this place?' I'm scared. I don't like being here, trapped in this rank-smelling hut. And I don't like what I can see of Callum, nothing more than a large, dark silhouette.

'I saw Archie. Or I think I did. Standing by the side of the road, watching us drive past. Sorry, I didn't think you'd wake up.'

'You saw him?' I turn round, taking it all in one more time. 'Is this where he's been?'

'I guess so. Looks like someone was feeding him.' Callum is looking at crisp packets on the floor. From behind, Queenie squeezes in and makes straight for a chocolate wrapper.

'And giving him beer.' He nods towards the beer can near the pillow. 'It's nearly full. Looks like the kid didn't like the taste. Thank God for that, a can of lager could do some serious damage to a kid that size. Leave that, Piglet.'

Callum seems rational. His voice is even, his breathing regular. Not a flashback then. Thank God. 'So where is he?'

'Christ knows. He can't have gone far, but we need help. We can't search this area in the dark by ourselves.'

One last look around the hut and I follow him out. Queenie comes reluctantly.

'I've been shouting but I think he might be scared of a bloke. Maybe you should try.'

I do. I shout Archie's name, I tell him he's safe, that we'll take him back to his mummy and daddy, but he either doesn't hear us or doesn't believe us. We shine torches to both sides of the path, but if Archie is behind the rocks and bushes, he keeps to his hiding place.

'How did you manage to lose him?' I ask, when I need to give myself a break from yelling.

'I couldn't stop too quickly or you and Piglet would have gone through the windscreen. By the time I'd jumped down, he'd squeezed through some bushes and vanished again. I yelled, went in the direction I thought he'd gone, but I couldn't find him. I was about to give up when I saw that hut.'

We're back at the road now, the car about thirty metres away.

'At least he's alive.'

'Yep. He needs to be found tonight though. I only saw him for a second but he didn't look good. He looked like a ghost. Hang on. Cat, did you leave the driver door open?'

Callum jogs ahead to the car. I'd do the same thing but I can barely put one foot in front of the other. I watch him reach the vehicle, peer inside and stop dead. I can't see the expression on his face.

I pick up my pace as he leans into the car. My heart is starting to thud. I'm running as he stands up again. This time two pairs of eyes look back at me. Callum is holding Archie West.

Not a ghost. Not dead at the bottom of a peat bog. Not under dirty blankets in some paedophile's house with fingermarks around his throat. Not rotting slowly in a long-abandoned, sea-swept wreck. While Callum and I have been searching the moors, this clever little boy has climbed into our car.

'Sitting on my seat, bold as brass.' Callum frees one arm and pulls out the blanket. 'He's bloody cold though.' Archie is passed from Callum to me and, for the first time in three years, I have a living, breathing child in my arms.

12

'NO WAY DID HE WANDER THIS FAR BY HIMSELF.' CALLUM switches off the radio and changes up a gear. 'It wasn't an impulsive kidnapping, either. Someone planned it. Someone prepared that hut.'

'He doesn't seem hurt, though.' I look down at the silent, shivering boy in my lap. Archie's face is pressed against my shoulder. His eyes are closed but I don't think he's asleep.

Callum says nothing.

'Abuse leaves signs. Apart from a few cuts and bruises, he looks OK. And he's still dressed.'

Callum drops his voice so that I practically have to lip read. 'That hut stank of sex.'

I'm shocked. I smelled a small boy's wee and poo, the earthy aroma of peat and, I think, the beer from the opened can. I didn't smell . . .

'Can Stopford and his colleagues process a crime scene?' I ask. 'Do they even have the equipment?'

Callum swerves to avoid a hole in the road. 'They're going to need help for a case like this. They certainly can't afford a cock-up. It's only a matter of time before it's all over the British press.'

'What about the army? They have military police.'

He shakes his head. 'They work to a completely different set of rules. I guess someone will be flown in from the UK.'

'He'll have his work cut out, trying to keep that cruise ship here.' Some way in the distance, I think I can see lights. People are coming towards us. 'Not to mention all the visitors who came independently. They'll all have schedules.'

Callum doesn't reply.

'What?'

Still nothing. He drives me nuts when he does this.

'You think I'm kidding myself that it could have been one of the visitors?'

'It's not completely impossible, I suppose.'

We both fall silent. The lights ahead of us have become a string. Vehicles getting closer all the time.

'I'm thinking of going home.' Callum is staring at the convoy coming our way. For a second I'm confused. Does he mean now? After we've handed Archie over?

'Scotland, I mean,' he adds. 'For good.'

We drive on. He doesn't take his hands off the steering wheel, or his eyes off the road.

'It's not that different to here. On the coast anyway. Crap weather. Lots of big noisy birds. Everyone knowing everybody else's business.'

The truck stops, suddenly. I look for the pothole, the stray sheep, the dead dog. Nothing, the road is clear. Callum has turned my way. I stare ahead, at my reflection in the windscreen as the car rocks gently with the beating of my heart.

'Come with me,' he says.

It feels like hours before Queenie and I get home and I'm struggling to put one foot in front of the other. I throw off my clothes and then the two of us huddle beneath the quilt. Exhausted though I am, it takes sleep a long time to come.

One of the things I had cause to reflect on, as I grew older, was that as we cast our net of love ever wider we make ourselves stronger and weaker at the same time. When I was very young, three people comprised the universe: Mum, Dad and me. At age eight, Rachel leapt into the mix and my little trio gained an extra voice, loud and rich, to sing its harmonies. When I lost both my parents, at far too young an age but these things happen, Rachel and Ben held one hand each and stopped me from falling. For a few years we were three again, and then we cast out silvery strings around us and reeled in the boys. First Ned, then Christopher, Kit and Michael, four tousled-haired, strong, noisy, smelly, cheeky little boys, marvellous, joyful individuals that together were as close as a pack of wolves. They'd have licked each other's wounds if they'd had to. Then I became pregnant for the third time and Rachel told me she was trying again too. The four were to become six and we knew, we just knew, they'd be two more boys. Some women are born to bring warriors into the world and that was our role. For a few brief years, it seemed the world wasn't big enough to hold all the love in my heart.

And there was Callum.

I sleep for an hour and dream about slaughter. Then I sit in the garden, wrapped in a quilt, with Queenie on my lap, amid my own personal collection of dead whales. As the sun comes up I feel as though I am being slowly swallowed by death and it seems entirely appropriate.

'Come with me,' Callum said last night, minutes before we gave little Archie to his weeping parents. *Come and live in Scotland, so very like Falkland, where the weather is dreadful, the people nosy and the wildlife big and noisy.*

As if on cue, a bird swoops low directly in front of me. It is an albatross, huge and powerful, a bird that, even here, is rarely seen flying above land, and suddenly I'm thinking about Rachel's favourite poem again.

The 'Ancient Mariner' is on a long voyage south when, in a senseless act of violence, he shoots dead an albatross. Throughout the rest of the story the dead bird, worn around the Mariner's neck, symbolizes the guilt and grief the old man feels.

I sometimes think we all have an albatross around our necks.

The living, breathing one above me finds an air current and sweeps high, then turns and heads out to sea. I watch it until the fleck it has become is indistinguishable among the clouds.

I'm sorry, my love, it's too late. I'm leaving today and I'm never coming back. But it's not you who's coming with me. It's Rachel.

DAY FOUR
Thursday, 3 November, 15.45 hours

13

IT'S TIME. THE *DAILY MIRROR*'S FRONT-PAGE STORY – sensationalist, ignorant nonsense with its ridiculous photograph of me on the Speedwell beach – gives me the excuse I need. No one tries to stop me when I say I'm going home. They assume I'm upset, that I need some time to myself.

I don't think I've ever felt calmer in my life.

The furore in the office, though, has given me one big problem. I didn't have time for the phone call. I'm winging it. I step outside into a sort of creepy twilight, as though the world has fallen into the shadow of something sinister. For a moment, I'm frightened. Then I remember the eclipse. Were I to look up right now, as people around me are doing, I'd see the moon eating away at the sun's light.

I am not a superstitious person, but this seems entirely appropriate.

I switch on my headlights as I set off. The houses, shops, offices of Stanley fly past. The road curves upwards. I'm heading out of town.

Someone tries to stop me. I see a shape, eyes that I know, but it's too late. Too late to stop the car, engage in conversation, be a normal person. I am not a normal person. I'm a killer. A monster. Thanks to my picture on the front page of a national British newspaper, the whole world knows what I am.

They don't know the frigging half of it.

I drive faster than I should given the poor light but this road is always quiet. I turn the corner and see the whitewashed house with the blue roof. Rachel's house.

There is someone in the road. A child. For a second I think it is Archie West, materialized out of the bushes at the side of the road again, and that his appearance marks the final stage of my descent into madness. Then my head clears enough for me to see that this isn't Archie. Nor is it either of my own boys. This child is thinner than Archie, maybe a little smaller, with fairer hair and bright blue eyes, but altogether more substantial than the ethereal figments of a disturbed mind that have been haunting me for three years.

This child looks like Rachel. This is Peter. Peter Grimwood, her youngest son. And this is an opportunity that even my darkest prayers couldn't have asked for.

Run now, Peter. Turn and run.

He's in the middle of the road, staring at me as I hurtle towards him. He is frozen in place. Unafraid. Staring.

How much easier it will be, to take the child, instead of the adult. How much more devastating for Rachel, to lose her baby rather than her own life. Perfect revenge.

I jump down hard on the brakes and the car slides to a stop. Peter is feet away from me. He cannot be alone.

He is. I can see Rachel's car in the driveway but there is no sign of her, or the two older boys who should be home from school by now. I wind down my window and listen.

Nothing other than the cries of the skuas and the grumble of the ocean. And the uncontrollable hammering of two hearts.

Run, Peter. Forget everything you've been told. Monsters are real and this one's coming to get you.

Leaving the engine running, I get out of the car, fully expecting him to turn and flee, to disappear back within the safe confines of the family garden. He doesn't. He continues to stare. I wonder, for a second, whether it is the sight of the vanishing sun that has scared him, the sudden darkening of his bright world, but no. It is me that he's looking at. He has never seen me before in his life but there is recognition in those harebell-blue eyes. Or maybe I have acquired the ability to hypnotize. The way a snake can.

Last chance, Peter. Break the spell. I'm a step away. An arm's reach away. A single blow away.

The spell holds. Peter doesn't move. So I do.

122

PART TWO

Callum

'Shoot him! Fucking shoot him.'
   'You shoot him!'
   Hope fading in the lad's eyes. None of the men with the stomach to kill a frightened kid. A single bullet. A sharp upward stab of the bayonet. The kid falls to the mud. My bullet. My bayonet. Sometimes, the buck just stops.

DAY FOUR
Thursday, 3 November, 10.30 hours

14

I ARRIVE IN STANLEY MID MORNING AND GRAB A LATE breakfast at Bob-Cat's Diner. It's a long, thin, single-storey building with a bright orange tin roof and matching tabletops. Pictures on the walls are faded, cheap-framed photographs of the harbour. Which is pointless, really, seeing as how the diner has one of the best views of the harbour in Stanley.

Back home environmental health would slam a demolition order on the place. There are grease stains on the walls and dead flies in the lampshades. And you're a braver man than me if you venture into the lavatory out back. But, as Bob-Cat points out regularly, nobody ever died within twenty-four hours of eating here.

I open the door and step into the familiar smell of burned fat. There are a couple of visitors at a table by the window and some blokes from the fishing boats at one end of the serving counter. A bunch of local workmen are stretching 'smoko' out for as long as they can. The traditional morning break, 'smoko' means tea, a fag and cake. It's the bane of most employers' lives.

'What you smiling at?' Roberta Catton, also known as Bob-Cat, scrapes bacon from the grill and slaps it on a bun. She adds an egg, over easy, and swirls brown sauce to form the letter C for Callum. As she says, it's the little touches that make the difference. She's been serving me breakfast for a long time now. She doesn't need to ask what I want any more. She also knows I won't always answer her daft questions.

'Coffee's a bit stale.' She leans against the counter. 'I'll make some fresh.'

In over ten years of coming in here, I've never known Bob-Cat offer fresh coffee. You drink what's in the pot till she has to shake out the grains, and if you've the balls to complain you're reminded that you probably have a kettle and a jar of instant at home.

I say nothing. I'm not about to push my luck. Bob-Cat's coffee isn't bad when it's fresh.

'You'll have a lot to talk about this morning,' she grunts.

The plate she's given me isn't chipped, and she's wiped it free of grease. And she's added a napkin, a small, ripped square of kitchen roll, but it's more effort than she'd normally make. She wants something. Not too difficult to guess what.

'What happened to doctor/patient confidentiality?' I say this to make a point rather than because I've a snowball in hell's chance of keeping anything quiet in this place. Once a fortnight for the past three years I've had hour-long appointments with a counsellor and, within a week of the first, everyone on the islands knew I was seeing the local shrink. (Except Catrin, as I learned Tuesday night.) They've all been pretty good about it. While ex-patriots here are known as the three Ms – Mercenaries, Missionaries and Misfits – former servicemen are cut a lot of slack.

I've never asked which of the three Ms I am. I've never needed to.

'Nothing confidential about those lads being found. One alive, one dead, God help us.' Bob-Cat looks offended. For such a tough-talking old broad, her feelings are more easily ruffled than her hair. It's vertical right now. Three inches of wiry, black and grey hair, standing up on top of her head and doing some pretty weird things to either side. She's one of those local women with neither the time nor the patience for the niceties of being female. Running the diner is a second job for Bob-Cat. I called it her hobby once and she nearly bit my ear off.

I watch her turn away to do something to the coffee machine. It starts to hiss and I half expect her to slap it.

Her other job is farming. She and her husband run a

smallholding outside Stanley with a few sheep, a couple of pigs, and a small army of poultry. Her hands are stained pale brown by the peat she digs for fuel and she invariably has grime under her fingernails. Her skin is tanned and wrinkled, but the flesh beneath it is holding up well. She could be any age between forty and sixty. She's not short of a bit of meat on her, but no one – no bloke anyway – would call her fat. I've seen her hold her own in arm-wrestling contests with some pretty hefty guys. She's in the Globe most nights of the week.

'It was all over the radio last night.' She's still talking about the boys, Archie and Jimmy, shouting back over her shoulder as she wrestles with the coffee machine. Around us, conversation has stopped. Of course, they all know everything already, but they want to hear it again, first hand.

I got used to it years ago, the relentless nosiness.

When you're hundreds of miles away from the rest of the world, when news from outside is always too little, too late, then the world you inhabit, however small and sparsely populated, assumes a terrific importance. In the Falkland Islands, everybody knows everybody else's business.

Bob-Cat pours the coffee and puts it in front of me. 'Watch the mug,' she says. 'We've had a lot of breakages this week.'

Two days ago I dropped one of her mugs and paid well over the odds for it. I'm not about to apologize again. On the other hand, the coffee she's put down smells like the answer to all my problems right now and I have five minutes to take a thirty-second walk. I can afford to be generous.

'Bloody radio can be a pain in the arse.' I bite deep, thinking once again that there is a God and he enjoys a good fried breakfast. Folk would go to war for Bob-Cat's bacon. It's thick as a flash-fry steak, moist like young chicken and exactly the right blend of sweet and salty. Bob-Cat imports honey from South America and cures the meat herself. The salt comes from the ocean. The result, every time I eat it, feels like the best thing I ever put in my mouth. Maybe the Argies got a whiff of it twelve years ago.

She's waiting for me to go on. Everyone is.

'Profits at the Globe must have taken a dive,' I say, after

swallowing faster than I would have liked. 'I think everyone came out to meet us. Complete gridlock for about a mile.'

I'm only going to talk about Archie, I decide. That story had a happy ending. Jimmy's family don't deserve to be gossiped about.

'I told 'em.' Bob-Cat is shaking her head in a nobody-listens-to-me kind of way. 'I said they should stay where they were, leave the road clear for the police and the ambulance, but would they listen?'

I'm pretty certain I drove past Bob-Cat's old Land Rover in the line last night, but I'm not about to argue. I have less than three minutes to go and there is no way I'm leaving any of this food.

Once we were back in the truck last night, with Archie wrapped in my blanket on Catrin's lap (pissing off Piglet no end), we discussed whether to radio it in. Well, I discussed it – out loud – with myself. Catrin listened, wide-eyed and tight-lipped. When I decided that putting his parents out of their misery at the earliest opportunity outweighed the likelihood of getting half the population of Stanley out to meet us, she nodded her agreement. So I called Bob Stopford on what is supposed to be a secure channel but, of course, is anything but. We heard the news being broadcast less than fifteen minutes later.

'I think perhaps I made the wrong decision,' I said, when the headlights of our reception committee appeared on the horizon. Meeting one car on the Darwin Road and getting round it is no big deal. Getting round a couple of dozen or more was another matter entirely, given the depth of the roadside ditches. And yet somehow, this shaking, silent little lad had to be handed over to his parents and secured in an ambulance, which would then have to manoeuvre itself past all the other cars to get to hospital.

'You didn't.' Finally, a word out of her. 'His parents know he's safe. They've known for an hour. You have no idea what that means to them.'

'Even if the sun's coming up before they get their hands on him?'

She was staring at the line of lights, curling its way towards us like a giant serpent from science fiction. 'They won't let a traffic jam get in their way.' Her hands were white with tension and I realized this was probably the first time Catrin had touched a child since her own had died.

'Well, at least it's over now,' says Bob-Cat. 'And no harm come to the lad.'

Her news brings me back to the present. I'd been planning to drive up to the hospital later in the day to check on young Archie. 'Do we know how he is?'

She nods over at one of the workmen. 'Ron's sister-in-law's niece works at the hospital. Lad's stable.' She waits for Ron to confirm. He nods his head slowly and pinches his fag out between his thumb and index finger.

'Very dehydrated.' Bob-Cat runs on before Ron has a chance to open his mouth. 'Possible pneumonia, but they've had antibiotics in him overnight and they're hopeful. No major injuries. A few cuts and bruises.'

She leans across the counter. I can smell smoke, coffee and stale alcohol on her breath. 'No sign the lad's been interfered with, but you can't always tell, can you?'

'Actually, I think you can. Especially if the interference was penetrative.'

Her eyes narrow. Bob-Cat can go from friendly to mean as hell in the blink of an eye.

'Who's treating him?'

A nasty smile. 'Ben Quinn. Catrin's husband.'

I know she wants me to correct her, say ex-husband, so I don't. I make a mental note, though, not to bother going to the hospital after all. If what she's told me is right, it's about as good an outcome as anyone could have hoped for.

I thank her for breakfast, finish the coffee, remember to pay her – like she'd let me leave otherwise – and walk out into the wind.

I have a few streets to navigate, but I always quite like walking around Stanley. Most of the houses here are built of what the locals call 'wriggly tin'. It looks like horizontal wooden boarding and when the wind gets up it creaks and whistles like a bunch of wheezy old ladies in a bingo hall. Most of the houses are painted bright colours, which I always think is about defiance more than décor, as though a good strong storm couldn't send half of them hurtling across the ocean.

As I near the junior school PC Skye is coming out of the gate. She gives a little start when she sees me and her eyes drop to the footpath.

'Morning.' I stop in front of her. Calling by the police station is something else I agreed to do this morning.

'Callum. Hello.' She takes her hat off and starts tapping it against her thigh like a tambourine. 'How are you this morning? I mean, recovered from your adventure?'

'Aye. As is Archie, from what I understand. No ill effects at all, is what folks are saying.'

Her face stays troubled, telling me all I need to know.

'The rumour going round is that he wasn't hurt, Skye. If that isn't true, you're doing nobody any favours with a cover-up.'

She looks over her shoulder. And past mine to further down the hill. 'Nobody's covering anything up. As far as we can tell, Archie wasn't hurt. Apart from being very cold and hungry, he seems fine.'

'So what's the problem?'

Another glance around. 'He says he was taken by a man. Which doesn't really make any sense. Who'd take him and not do anything?' She shrugs. 'Chief Superintendent Stopford thinks he's probably confused.'

I bite back the obscenity. 'He may be confused, but he didn't walk thirty miles on his own.'

She steps to one side. 'I really need to get back. You can ask Mr Stopford directly later.'

Even I'm not daft enough to forcibly restrain a police officer. I let her go and carry on up.

A few paces past the school I see a toddler in a buggy on the opposite side of the road. He's red in the face, straining against the reins, trying to be free and crying at the same time. I'm about to cross the road to check him out when I recognize both child and buggy. This is Rachel Grimwood's youngest, the kid who got me in trouble for breaking Bob-Cat's crockery earlier in the week.

Then I see a woman's bottom sticking out of the back seat of a Land Rover a couple of metres away and I know it's Rachel's because of the jodhpurs and riding boots. And I have a knack of being able to recognize women by their arses. The car isn't hers,

132

though, it's Bob-Cat's. I'd know that skanky old pile of tin anywhere.

For some reason, Rachel is rooting around in the back of Bob-Cat's car.

I shrug. It isn't any of my business. And the kid seems fine. Pissed off, but fine. I carry on up the hill.

Dr Sapphire Pirrus is not a medical doctor of any description, certainly not a psychiatrist, but she's been on all the right courses, has the right certificates on her walls and, above all, knows how to listen.

Her house is sufficiently elevated for me to have a good view of the harbour. 'Paperwork,' Catrin told me, when I'd asked what she had on today. 'The whale beaching will keep us busy for days.' Paperwork will keep her in the office all day. It's her boat I'm looking for, though, among the fishing vessels, yachts and ferries darting about the harbour. I think I see it moored up but it's difficult to tell from here. Some distance away, anchored in the outer harbour, lies the cruise ship, the *Princess Royal*. It should already be heading for South Georgia, from there to Antarctica. Passengers will have paid a small fortune for their trip. They won't want delays of any kind.

And yet everyone on the islands hopes the abductor of Archie West is on board that ship. Stopford can't let it go.

Sapphire opens the door and steers me into her consulting room at the front of the house. As usual, there is the faintest whiff of patchouli oil about the place. Sapphire was the child of hippy parents, long before hippies became fashionable. Her family came to live on the islands forty years ago when she and her brother and sister were small. They came dreaming of a simple life, of self-sufficiency.

'You well?' I ask, as I take my usual seat in the wooden-framed armchair facing the window. I can still see the harbour, still watch the boats. 'Cold clear up?'

Her lips twitch as she takes the seat opposite mine. It throws her when I ask her about herself. She's a woman who likes to compartmentalize. The hour I pay for is my time, to be used talking about me and my problems. I don't always go along with that, because I

133

won't be the needy, self-absorbed loser I imagine too much counselling could turn me into.

'Quite a couple of days you've had.' She picks up her notebook and makes sure the pencil is close to hand. She never holds the pencil, just lifts it from time to time to make notes. I suspect this is deliberate, because the one time she forgot she played with it endlessly, twisting and turning, stabbing and rolling. When Sapphire holds a pencil, she gives away how nervous this whole business makes her. Or maybe it's just me.

'Are you supposed to listen to gossip?'

'Small island.'

I don't tell her that actually, the islands are massive, pretty much the land mass of Wales, and that it is the population that is small. I'm conscious that if I piss her off too much, she might refuse to carry on seeing me.

'You look nice,' I say instead, which is probably worse. She does though. She's tall and wiry, thin rather than slender, but she wears her clothes well and she favours bright colours. Today she's wearing the sapphire of her name, a cardigan that reaches her knees. Her legs are long, slim. With a name like Sapphire you'd expect her to have blue eyes, but her eyes are a pale grey, very similar to the hair that curls to her shoulders. Her skin is pale too.

I asked her once how a little girl who didn't have blue eyes ended up being called Sapphire. She pursed her lips for a few seconds, clearly wondering how she could get away with not telling me.

'My older brother is called Mistral,' she said in the end. 'My younger sister is Blaze. I'd say I was the lucky one.'

As I say, hippy parents.

'What would you like to talk about first?' The tone of her voice tells me that all kidding around is done for the day. There's only ever really one thing I want to talk about, but I feel like a girl if I start with that.

'I had another flashback,' I tell her instead, and describe the incident on the *Endeavour*, or what I can remember of it. She listens without interrupting, making occasional notes, a slight furrow appearing between her pale eyebrows. Her reaction when I tell her about finding Jimmy Brown's body is muted, letting me know it isn't exactly news to her, but when I get to the really interesting part (as far as she's concerned, anyway) she starts tapping the pencil on the arm of her chair.

'You hurt Catrin?' she says when I'm done. 'Physically harmed her?'

'Not as much as she hurt me,' I say, remembering how she coshed me with a crowbar. Certainly not as much as she could have hurt me, I think, remembering the gun she'd produced.

On the wreck I'd seen enough of the semi-automatic pistol to make me stop and think. Later, on the boat, after Catrin had gone into the cabin, I found it for a closer look. Several decades old, it was a Ballester-Molina, basically an Argentine copy of the famous American Colt M1911. The Colt was reproduced all over the world, sometimes becoming the weapon of choice over the original. The British Army in the Second World War used the Molina on several clandestine operations. Quite how that particular one got into Catrin's hands I have no idea, but some of her forebears weren't exactly peace-loving.

All in all, the Molina is a pretty respectable weapon. I hadn't taken seriously Catrin's ability to use it. The woman I'd thought I knew couldn't point a gun at a living creature and pull the trigger. Just shows what I know.

'I'm not trying to make light of it,' I say. 'God knows, Catrin's the last person I'd knowingly hurt.'

'Tell me everything you can remember. From climbing on to the boat to when you came back to yourself again.'

I try, but flashbacks are like dreams. If I don't capture them in the seconds after I come out of them, they quickly fade. 'Something to do with the bombing of the *Galahad*, I think.'

'Your regiment watched that happen, didn't it? You were camping out at Fitzroy at the time?' Sapphire, like all islanders over a certain age, is well versed in the history of the conflict. On 2 June 1982, the Chinook put us down on the stark, snow-swept hillside above Port Pleasant. We were due to rest up as the powers that be prepared for the final onslaught into Stanley. Battle weary from taking Goose Green, we dug ourselves in and watched two ships, the *Sir Galahad* and the *Sir Tristram*, slip into the harbour below us, bringing troops

135

and ammunition. To our amazement, the troops remained on board, effectively making both ships sitting ducks in the event of an Argentine bombing.

A few days in, it happened. We heard the approaching Skyhawks, the answering roar of machine guns, and watched men leap from a burning ship into a burning sea. The gunfire, the Hawk engines, the exploding ammunition should have been deafening. Maybe it was. Maybe the screaming of tortured and dying men was only in our heads. All I know is that it sounded very real at the time, and it still sounds real when I get the flashbacks.

We ran down to the beach and discovered we couldn't touch the survivors because their blackened skin came away in ribbons. The stench of gunpowder and phosphorus filled the air, threatening to burn the inside of our lungs and even that was preferable to the smell of burning flesh. To this day, even the whiff of a barbecue makes me want to throw up.

'And Catrin's two boys, Ned and Kit. They were part of it. But there's nothing logical about these flashbacks when they happen. Imagine a drugged-up, drunken nightmare. The scariest images you can think of racing into your head one after another.'

'It makes a lot of sense.' Sapphire is leaning towards me. I can smell the heavy, musky perfume she's wearing. 'In a state of some stress, compounded by being with Catrin, you went to the place where you had one of the worst experiences of your life. And then, not only did you find the body of a young child, albeit not the one you went looking for, you also found a toy that belonged to yet another dead child. One that meant a great deal to you.'

'It may not have been Kit's rabbit.'

She gives a brief, dismissive shake of the head. 'Doesn't matter. In that moment, you thought it was. I'm not surprised all that triggered an episode. What does surprise me is why you put yourself in that situation in the first place.'

I shrug. 'We all wanted to find the bairn.'

'There are two thousand servicemen on the islands who could have gone. Are you sure you didn't want an excuse to be alone with Catrin?'

Sapphire takes no prisoners. Five minutes into our session and she has me bang to rights.

'Have you thought any more about what we talked about last time?'

I stand up and walk to the window. A fishing vessel coming into harbour is leaving a trail of white water on the sea and a flock of scavenging birds hangs in the air.

'Callum, within a year of coming to live here, most of your PTSD symptoms had gone. You were well on your way to becoming healthy.'

I know what's coming. I've heard it before.

'Then, almost immediately after the Grimwood car accident, the violent flashbacks began again.' I can hear from Sapphire's raised tone that she's spun round in her seat to face me. 'It doesn't take a genius to work out that they're directly related to what happened that day, to the fresh trauma you were personally involved in.'

'How's your da?' I ask her. 'Ready for his big night?' Sapphire's father is in charge of the firework display on November the fifth.

She ignores that. I don't blame her. As distractions go, it was pretty lame.

'Three years on, there's no sign of them improving. In fact, judging by what you've just told me, they're getting worse. Unless you've been hiding something, you've never exhibited physical violence before.'

'I hide nothing from you,' I tell her. I'm lying, of course.

'It seems to me that Catrin and her grief are having a direct and damaging impact upon your mental health. She's refusing to get over her loss and, while she's in your life, you're not getting over what happened either.'

I turn quickly. 'She lost two children. Three children.' I hear my voice break and know I've made a mistake that Sapphire will spot. 'How soon was she supposed to get over it? Six months? A year?'

'You need to talk to her. You know you do.'

'She's not strong enough.'

One pale, perfect eyebrow lifts. 'She slaughtered nearly two hundred whales yesterday. I'd say she's tougher than she looks.'

Stalemate. I'm annoyed. From the look in her eyes, Sapphire's pretty narked too. But she's the professional. She gets it together first.

'You think you can't talk to Catrin about something so painful because you're worried what it will do to her?'

'Maybe I'm worried what it will do to me.'

I get a very firm headshake in response. 'I don't agree. This has always been about what's best for her. My point remains that it shouldn't be. There are two of you involved in this.'

'She lost everything.'

'Well, arguably, so did you.'

I take a deep breath.

'There are other women in the world,' she tells me, not for the first time, but her voice is gentler than usual. 'There are other women on the islands.'

I smile, which isn't difficult. For all that she gives me a hard time, I like Sapphire. 'There's you,' I say. 'Although you might think it unethical.' As I wait for her to respond I realize I'm only half joking. Sapphire is definitely shaggable, even if she is a decade older than me. Even if she is married. Suddenly, shagging Sapphire feels like the best idea I've had in ages. Right here, right now. On the thin beige carpet, or across the desk, watching the boats heading out to sea. Her eyes have fallen to her notepad. I wait for her to look up. The answer will be in her eyes and I'm going to act on it.

'It would be completely unethical,' she says, in a flat voice, keeping her eyes on her notepad. I feel like a dick.

The atmosphere in the room has turned awkward. I wonder if I should leave, even though there are twenty minutes of the appointment to run.

'How was Catrin last night? When the two of you were bringing home the child. That must have been very difficult for her.'

Sapphire is usually reluctant to spend too much of our time talking about Catrin. That she should bring her up again probably means I'm forgiven. Or that she's picked the best way she knows of getting my attention off her. I cross the room again and sit, resolving to behave for the rest of the session.

'Quiet. As though she couldn't really take it in. But then I was much the same, after Speedwell. I think we were both on autopilot.'

She nods, her signal that she wants me to go on talking.

'She was unusually silent. Even by her standards. There was none of the "How did he get there? What were the chances of us driving past at that moment?" – none of the reaction you'd expect. She almost, I don't know, took it in her stride. As I said, on autopilot.'

'Do you think it might offset public opinion? The fact that she was instrumental in finding the boy?'

'What public opinion needs offsetting, exactly?'

'She killed two hundred whales.'

'She euthanized two hundred dying animals.'

'Not everyone will see it that way.' Sapphire's voice has a definite edge to it now. She knows what she's doing, goading me about Catrin.

'Islanders will be fine with it.'

'Some of them. Maybe most of them. But there'll always be a few who will question it. Did she act too quickly? Had she really tried everything? And there's been a lot of talk among the visitors, I understand.'

'They'll be gone in a couple of days. I wouldn't be surprised if that cruise ship leaves today.'

She nods again, although I know she doesn't agree with me. And she's touched on something that, I admit, does worry me. Catrin should be able to rely on the support of the people around her. After yesterday, I'm not sure she'll get it.

'Do you still love her?'

The question takes me by surprise. She has never asked me outright before.

'You're very protective,' she says. 'Not just with me. That race over to Speedwell yesterday was all about watching her back, wasn't it?'

I nod, because trying to pretend otherwise would be a waste of my time and hers. 'She's not the woman I knew. I keep hoping she'll come back, even a glimpse, but she's a shell. A – what do you call it – a cardboard cut-out.'

'I agree with you, but that's not what I asked.'

I lean back and close my eyes. Do I still love Catrin? I practically proposed to her a few hours ago, shocking myself as much as her.

'Come with me,' I said, meaning come with me to my home on the other side of the planet. Leave this place and its crippling memories and build a new life. Dare to believe you could be happy again. She didn't answer. Didn't say a word for the rest of the drive back. I'd like to tell myself she's thinking about it, but even I'm not that thick.

'All I know is she's become a part of who I am. I don't particularly like it, any more than I like suffering from PTSD, or some of my mates from the regiment like their missing limbs or scarred faces. I've just learned to deal with her being there.'

'Interesting that you compare your feelings for Catrin to war wounds.'

'Which do you think I'm trivializing?'

'I think your feelings for Catrin are like a shell strike that keeps burning. Three years after the affair finished, she's still hurting you.'

She's right. I've always known that she's right and, at this moment, I don't have the energy to keep arguing.

'So what do I do about it?'

'Well, I think you start by talking to her.'

'I do talk to her. I spent most of yesterday with her.'

'I'm not talking about chit-chat. I'm talking about what happened between you. Why it happened. Why it ended.'

I look at my watch and decide time is up, whether it really is or not. 'It happened because it couldn't not. It ended because she couldn't deal with anyone or anything after her sons died. There really isn't anything to say.' I stand up and put cash on the desk. Usually I make some quip about her giving satisfaction. Not today.

'Oh, I think there is.' She follows me from the room and along the corridor. She's never before continued a conversation once the session is over. 'The child she was carrying when the boys were killed. The one she lost.'

I know what's coming. I open the door and don't look back. I don't need to. Her parting shot is perfectly audible.

'Callum, you need to know if that baby was yours.'

15

I DON'T GO HOME. GOD KNOWS I'VE ENOUGH WORK TO BE doing but this isn't going to be one of those productive days. Instead, I drive to a beach a couple of miles outside Stanley. I get out of the car and set out across the dunes.

There's a storm coming in. The wind has picked up, is tossing huge waves against the shore. The birds – Catrin could name them in an instant; they're just big, noisy birds for me – are having a ball above my head, diving and rolling and screaming their feathery heads off.

This is one of the less popular beaches, even with islanders. The rocks are mostly too low to offer any shelter but pretty much prevent ball games. They also make it next to impossible to keep your eye on young kids. On the other hand, they make ideal habitats for all sorts of nesting critters so it's long been one of Catrin's favourite spots.

It's also a great place to run if you think continually dodging and weaving around rocks is good for your reflexes and flexibility. Which is how she and I met.

I was running, fast and hard, feeling pretty good. Life was good. Since moving to the Falklands permanently, the bad dreams and waking flashbacks had more or less disappeared. Whether it was being around the people and the way of life we'd been through it all

141

to protect, being close enough to the demons to see the whites of their eyes, or simply having enough peace and quiet to think, my head was in a better space than it had been for years. I was healthy, too. Fit, strong, running regularly, lifting weights, playing football. Work was going well. I was making a living, putting something aside, with real hopes of a big breakthrough one day. And I was having a dalliance with a woman who worked for the Governor's office. We both knew it wasn't going anywhere. Or at least, I did, and really hoped she did too. Whatever, busy cock, healthy mind, as the lads in the regiment used to say.

All was well, my life as complete as it could be, with no idea that anything was missing. And then I turned round a taller clump of rocks and it was like someone had taken a pneumatic drill to that life and opened up a ruddy great chasm that just one woman could fill.

They were a hundred yards away across the sand when I caught sight of them. A woman and two kids, walking towards me along the beach, around the rocks and pools that littered the water's edge. They all wore shorts and pale-coloured, light sweaters. They held hands. The younger kid was furthest from the sea, his shorts still wet from the splash. The woman's hair was long and dark, like the kelp at the water's edge.

I ran wider. No one relishes the thought of a big bloke thundering towards them. They'd been intent on something in the water but they looked up as I drew closer. I had a sudden thought and stopped.

'There's a colony of seals back there.' I raised my voice so that it would carry through the wind, speaking directly to the woman, gesturing back the way I'd come with a jerk of my head. 'Getting quite aggressive. You might want to keep the youngsters away.'

'They're southern sea lion pups,' the older boy called back across the beach. 'They're about six weeks old. Their mummies haven't left them. They're forging for food in the sea.'

'Foraging,' his mother corrected him.

I stepped closer, until I could make out the coarsening of her skin and the wrinkles in the corners of her eyes that put her in her late twenties, possibly around thirty. Pretty much the same age as me.

'You're the soldier,' the boy told me.

I risked walking closer still. The younger boy backed into his mother's legs.

'I'm Callum.' I looked at the mum. 'Callum Murray,' I added. She nodded, as though she already knew.

'Have you got a gun?' The older kid was at my feet now, looking directly up.

'Not any more.' It wasn't strictly true, but I had a sense it was the answer his mum would prefer. Close up, it was hard to take my eyes off her. Her face was tiny, perfect, every feature exactly the size and shape it should be. She wasn't wearing make-up. This wasn't a face for make-up. Cosmetics of any sort on this face would give it the look of one of those spooky china dolls.

Her eyes, watering in the wind, were the colour of the rocks around us. Her hair was long and straight, constantly moving in the breeze. Close up, it was more like the kelp than ever. Her skin was the warm ivory of the sand. She looked like the beach come to life.

The kids were dark too. The older one the image of his mum, the younger with darker hair and brown eyes. Even at such a young age, there was a set around his jaw that made me think he'd take after his father.

'We're the Quinns,' she said, as her fingers tightened around the kid leaning against her. I wondered if that had been deliberate, her labelling them as a family unit. *We are complete and whole. Do not think of trying to break us.* 'This is Kit. Ned is the one with the obsessive interest in warfare.'

I waited, eyebrows high. She wasn't getting away with that.

'Catrin,' she said, after a moment. 'My husband's Ben. He works at the hospital.'

Yes, definitely a message there. *I am not available. Don't even think about it. Leave us now.*

'Also, and I can't be sure about this, but I think there could be a pod of orcas just offshore. If they've come to hunt the seals, you really shouldn't . . .' I looked down from one kid to another, feeling sure she'd get the hint. Did she really want to risk feeding the kids to a hungry killer whale?

She, too, was looking down at the kids, her face suddenly alive

143

with excitement. 'Now that sounds like something we should see.' A last, dismissive glance at me. 'Thank you.'

She set off, jogging easily, the kids keeping up. In minutes, they were approaching the rocks that separated the safer part of the beach from the seal colony. Sea lions. Whatever.

I went after them. The animals I'd seen had been stocky, aggressive and numerous. They'd given me a good barking at as I'd run around the outside of their colony and I did not like the idea of this bunch of tiny humans getting chewed. Even if the mother seals didn't come back from their forging expedition. Even without the added threat of the killer whale pod.

Woman and children disappeared behind some rocks and I picked up my pace. When I could see them again, I was relieved to find them perched on a wide, flat rock a safe distance from the animals. Catrin saw me and smiled to herself before pointing to where a black, triangular-shaped fin moved lazily some distance from the shoreline.

I stopped running and strode over to join them, choosing a rock a little way down the beach. Close enough to talk, but not so near as to be intimidating. The smaller kid, Kit, was on his mother's lap, the bigger one cuddled at her side.

'There are three, possibly four,' she said, eyes still fixed on the black sail in the water. 'Small pod, maybe juveniles out on their own for some fun. They're waiting for the sea-lion pups to try the water out. This shallow bit of beach is a very popular nursery pool.'

'Mummy, I don't want the whales to eat a pup.'

She wrapped an arm around her older son. 'I don't think they will, sweetie. Look, the penguins have spotted what those big orcas are up to.'

It was as though the surf suddenly sprang into life as a clutch of sleek, fat penguins appeared at the edge of the water. They jostled and bullied and flapped their little arms hysterically in their bid to be out of the sea. Behind them, four black sails moved in.

The sea-lion pups yelled back at the newcomers, who were invading their space, getting tangled in the kelp, filling the beach with noise. At the same time, seabirds appeared from nowhere, flocking towards the ocean where, I'm pretty certain,

144

the water was starting to turn red. The whales had got something.

Closer to shore, the beach was turning into a wildlife rave, as the penguins reached the rocks and started bouncing around like balls in a bingo drum. As they left the water behind, they carried on jumping, leaping from rock to rock, getting further from the water. The younger kid burst out laughing.

'These are rockhopper penguins. Can you see their big yellow eyebrows? Watch them now, they'll leap all the way back up the cliff to their nests.' She turned to her boys. 'Why don't we go up the easy way and see how the chicks are getting on?'

She'd seen the kill the whales had made at sea, was keeping the attention of her sons away from it. As she and the boys got to their feet, I stood up too. 'Well, it looks like you guys know what you're doing. I'll leave you in peace.'

'It was nice to meet you.' She stretched out a hand. For a small, clumsy moment, I wondered if she were reaching to me. I think I even started, looked down as if to take it, and then I realized she was reaching for the older kid. He grabbed her hand and walked backwards, staring at me as his mother dragged him away. When I knew I couldn't watch them any more without looking creepy, I ran on. Another hundred yards and something made me stop. I turned to see Catrin Quinn looking back at me across the rocks.

I knew then. She did too, although it was another four months before I made her admit it.

A gull flies low, screaming. I'm probably too close to its nest. Do gulls nest in November? I haven't a clue. Catrin used to talk to me for hours about the wildlife of the islands. I didn't take any of it in. I just loved the sound of her voice.

I turn and head back to the car. There are no answers for me here.

My therapist with a ridiculous name is right. Two and a half years ago, when the snow was thick on the ground, a woman whose heart and soul was broken gave birth to a tiny, stillborn boy. I need to know if he was mine and only Catrin can tell me that.

After the day on the beach I started seeing Catrin around town. I found out where she lived, where she worked part-time, in which department her husband worked. I learned which nursery she took her boys to on the mornings she was in the Conservation. I started being in Stanley when I was likely to see her, hanging around, watching for her boat coming and going, double-checking registrations of similar silver Land Rovers in case they were hers. Am I making myself sound like a stalker? I was. I simply couldn't help myself.

I started running on that same beach every day because that's where she might expect to find me and after two weeks had gone by, she was there, alone this time.

She didn't make it easy. She had two young kids, a busy life. The last thing she needed was someone who could bring the whole thing tumbling down like a house of cards. When I dropped hints that I wanted more than a passing acquaintance, she backed away.

I joined the Stanley social scene, attending dances and film nights and whist drives. Whist, for fuck's sake, that's how bad I had it. I was rewarded time after time by the sight of her with her husband. He was a decent enough bloke, and I felt bad about what I was doing, but I was also pretty certain he wasn't in love with her. Not the way he maybe had been once. There was a coldness about him. He never touched her in public, never put his hand, possessively, on the small of her back, never stroked her hair, or clasped his fingers around her wrist. I never saw him kiss her. Probably just as well. I might have landed him one and that would have been tricky to explain.

I never left a function before they did. I watched her drive them away – she never really drank – and then I'd go home, tormented by the memory of her dark hair swept up high so that her shoulders and neck were bare, by the curve of her instep when she wore heels. I'd think about what it must be like to touch her and I'd jerk off and tell myself if it didn't happen soon I'd lose my mind.

And then one day, after I'd known her a few months, I caught her struggling to carry some boxes up from the boat. It was raining and her hair, more like the seaweed than I'd ever seen it, was streaming down her back. I took the boxes, carried them to her car and suggested coffee.

'I'd rather have a stiff drink,' she said to my surprise.

Ten minutes later, we were in the Victory Bar with a couple of large bourbons and she was telling me about a wreck she'd been diving. Thanking God and all his sweet angels for a scuba-diving course I'd done with the regiment, I laid on my enthusiasm for the sport as thick as I dared. Maybe it was the whisky, maybe I'd worn her down, but as we finished our drinks, she dropped her eyes to the tabletop.

'I'm going out there again on Friday.' She ran a finger through a water splash on the wood, as though her mind was loose and carefree. I wasn't fooled. Her other hand was shaking like a maraca in a salsa band. 'I need to collect some samples. You could come, if you want.'

I pretended to think about it. 'I have a call I need to take Friday morning,' I said. 'I can probably rearrange it though. Thanks, that'd be good.'

For the three days that followed I barely slept. I lived on soup because my constricted throat wasn't letting solid food through. On Friday I waited at the little-used jetty in Whalebone Bay, not far from her house. When she'd suggested picking me up there, rather than be seen leaving Stanley harbour together, I'd known. Shit, I'd known from the moment I laid eyes on her. It had never been a question of if. Just a question of when.

She was ten minutes late. At five minutes I decided she wasn't coming. She'd got cold feet. It had all been a big wind-up. She was, at that moment, in one of those girly coffee mornings, giggling with her mates about the gullibility of blokes. Stupid ex-squaddie blokes, at that. I honestly wasn't sure how I was going to live through the next hour. Then her boat appeared around the headland. I couldn't see her. The sun was glinting off the windows of the wheelhouse, but I could make out that fat little dog of hers at the bow.

She threw me the rope, I caught it, jumped on board and pushed us off.

'That's not the way the health and safety people prefer us to moor up.' She put the engine into reverse to clear the jetty then swung it round and we headed out to sea.

'The wind's getting up.' I wrapped the rope around my lower arm and made it off. 'If it gets too choppy you might not want to go down with an amateur like me, and I'd hate to miss the chance to see the *Mary Jane*.'

147

I was a fucking liar. I couldn't give a toss if we didn't dive. In fact I'd prefer it. All I cared about was getting on her boat and getting far enough out to sea that nobody could get in our way. We were halfway there already.

We did dive. Catrin was determined to keep me at arm's length for as long as she could and if she wanted to keep up the pretence of coming out here to explore the wreck, I was prepared to go along with it. We pulled on wetsuits and tanks, masks, snorkels and fins and jumped over the side.

The water was cold enough – almost – to cool me down. The sun had more or less gone behind the cloud by this time so visibility was poor. I followed Catrin's hard-kicking fins and the beam from her head-torch deeper and deeper, and wondered if anyone had ever had sex at the bottom of the ocean before. I followed her into the hull of the old whaling ship, brushing the tickling kelp out of the way, sliding between iron plates, sometimes feeling my way when I lost sight of her torch beam. Periodically, she'd stop, wait for me to catch up, and direct the beam on to a brass plaque or a pile of harpoons. I pretended to be interested, when all I wanted to do was catch hold of her hair, drifting round in the water like it was alive, and pull her to me. I could see the glint of her eyes behind her mask. She was fast down there, much faster than me, a strong swimmer. Down there she wasn't afraid of me.

When we'd been everywhere accessible on the wreck, we swam out through a hole in its starboard hull and she turned to make sure I was following. I reached out, took hold of her hand.

We floated, in the swirling shadows at the bottom of the ocean, our weight suspended in the water, her face on a level with mine. I pulled her closer, spat out my mouthpiece and kissed her hand.

She panicked then, reaching for the mouthpiece, pushing it towards me. I smiled, took it from her, and slowly, to show her I wasn't worried, put it back. When I gave the thumbs up, the signal to swim to the surface, she nodded.

Back on the boat, we chilled down fast. Shivering, we pulled off our equipment. She let me peel off her wetsuit and wrap a towel around the black swimsuit she wore underneath. Her hair hung down to her waist, dripping on the cockpit floor. When I was naked but for swim shorts, I took her through the wheelhouse and into the cabin at the bow.

Being in the Parachute Regiment, I'd made dozens of jumps, but I've never forgotten the first. The near-paralysing terror as the plane soared high and I knew there was only one way back to earth and that was free-fall. The realization that the moment was upon me, that I was going out of the airplane now. The certainty that death was seconds away. And then the mind-blowing joy of being in the sky, speeding like an arrow, that sense of absolute, infinite power, the feeling that anything was possible. That's how it was for me the first time with Catrin.

To this day, I only have to close my eyes to remember the ice-cold silk of her skin against mine as she pressed closer, seeking warmth at first, and then because she couldn't pull away. Or her hair, clinging like wet string. The heady thrill of having the woman of my dreams become the woman biting at my neck, running her hands down the backs of my thighs, taking me between her hands and letting her fingers play until I could barely think straight.

She was so deliciously naïve. She'd only ever known Ben and he clearly hadn't been the adventurous type. She gasped and squeaked and told me no, but she wriggled like an eel, bucked like a new-born foal and clung to me with a strength that surprised me.

When it was over, when I was flat on my back in that tiny bed, looking up at the wooden panelled ceiling, and she was curled up against me, her head on my shoulder, arm possessively across my chest, I told her I loved her.

She didn't say it back for some time. It didn't matter. What I felt seemed to be enough for both of us. By the end of the first month I was begging her to leave Ben. I carried on doing it, right up until the moment when he left her and she looked back at me with those empty eyes. I think that was the moment I gave up.

I go home and start work. The west coast of the US, where I do most of my business, is five hours behind us and it's getting to the time when people I need to talk to will be at their desks.

Tonight I'll hit the town and get hammered, I decide. Stanley will be in a good mood, the worries over the disappearance of Archie

West put to one side. The Globe will be packed, with locals and visitors alike. The band will play and the ladies won't be averse to a bit of mild flirting. Sapphire is right. Catrin is not the only woman on the islands and maybe a warm, willing woman is exactly what I need right now.

I rattle off an email to a mate called Sam in Palo Alto. I have an ISDN line in the house that my employers arranged when I moved here and staying in touch with the outside world isn't a problem for me. Bar the military, I probably have the best IT system on the islands. Which is why I'm the first to hear about the storm breaking back in the real world, just as the one over Falkland releases its might on the land around me.

It starts innocuously enough.

You've been in the news a bit, writes Sam.

Huh? I reply. My fingers are too big to make keyboard work easy and I rarely waste words.

You're all over the papers. Here and in the UK. South America's having a field day.

Again, *Huh?* I'm still not that interested. John Major will have sent the Argies a yah-boo message and they'll have a cob on. It happens from time to time. Or the Governor might have made some entirely premature announcement about oil reserves around the islands.

I'll see if I can attach a pic. Stand by.

I stand by. Or rather, I get up, make coffee, have a piss, stare at the rain bucketing down outside and come back ten minutes later to see an email with image attachment has landed in my inbox. I click it open, see the scanned image of the front page of the *Daily Mirror*, and realize that Catrin's part in the safe return of little Archie West will make no difference to how she's viewed on the islands. Her part in the discovery of Jimmy Brown's body, and putting to rest seventeen months of agonized unknowing for his parents, won't make the slightest impression on how she appears on the world stage. Even I, ignorant ex-Para that I am, know a golden story when I see one.

The picture is one taken by one of the tourists on a pretty good-quality camera. The definition is excellent. He must have used a zoom lens because I don't remember anyone getting that close. I'm in the shot, although you'd have to look hard to spot me as I'm half turned away. Pete, the other person in the foreground, is looking down, as if sickened. It's in colour, so I get the full impact of the blood around the beach, in the water, running down the face of the woman who takes centre stage.

It is a picture of Catrin, her flying hair giving her the look of an avenging fury, standing beside a six-metre male pilot whale. The gun is in her hand. She's looking down at her kill. The faintest whiff of smoke floats around the gun muzzle. The animal's jaw opens in what isn't, but looks like, a scream. The headline says it all:

Killer Quinn

16

THE RAIN HAS SLACKENED BY THE TIME I REACH STANLEY. It's a temporary respite though. Out to sea, more cloud is banking up. I'm relieved to see Robert Duncan's car parked outside the offices of the *Penguin News*. Tracking him down would have wasted more time. The counter from which the paper is sold once a week is empty, so I lift it and in the back room find all three regular staff of the *News* in the office, all on the phone. Robert sees me, holds up a finger and carries on talking.

I do not want Catrin seeing that photograph. I don't want anyone here seeing that photograph. I'm pretty certain that, if I have to, I can shut down email correspondence in and out of the islands for a couple of days. I can't get near the military's comms, of course, their security's too good, but all civilian traffic is well within my capabilities. People will just assume there's a problem with the telephone connection. They'll get on to their suppliers, who wouldn't give the Falklands top priority, and after a day or so, I'd let it all trickle through again. A couple of days, maybe three, might be enough time to let the storm die down. People soon forget and in a couple of days the world will have something else to outrage about.

What I need to know is whether the news is already out. Whether Rob and his team have already seen the story currently in my jacket pocket.

'Well, I'm sure they'll get back to you as soon as they can.' Cathy,

Rob's chief (only) reporter, is looking frazzled. 'The Conservation only have a very small staff and I imagine their lines are quite busy at the moment.'

Looks like I'm too late.

'Callum, what can I do for you?' Rob has finished his call. He steps around his desk. I take his outstretched hand in my right and with my left pull the picture from my back pocket. 'Have you seen this?'

He only needs to glance. 'Phones have been going mental for an hour. Friggin' tourists.'

'Does Catrin know?'

He nods again, unhappily. 'She must do. I had to tip John off when we got the first call. We haven't been able to get through to them so I imagine they're taking more calls than we are.'

'And that's saying something.' Mabel, Rob's mum and the office junior, has finished her call. 'News International are chartering a plane, Rob. We can expect them early tomorrow afternoon.'

'For a bunch of fucking dead whales?' I'm incredulous. 'Sorry, Mabel, Cathy.'

Rob's phone rings again. He grimaces an apology and turns away to talk. I hear him say 'expected environmental disaster', and know he's going to be some time.

'It's not just the whales, Callum.' Cathy's phone is ringing but she's ignoring it. 'They're making a connection between her shooting the whales and the disappearance of Archie West.'

For a moment, I'm stumped. 'How the hell are they managing that? There is no connection.'

Deep frown lines appear between Cathy's brows. 'Of course there isn't. But you have to see their point. We have an abducted British child, and an island woman instrumental in a mass slaughter.' She holds up a hand to stop me. 'Yeah, we know it was for the right reasons, but try telling that to people whose experience of whales is limited to watching *Free Willy*. Added to that, the woman in question, who has a history of emotional instability, drove into town last night with the same abducted kid.'

'Catrin is not emotionally unstable and she found the fucking kid.'

153

Mabel stands up and crosses to the kitchen.

Even easy-going Cathy is starting to look put out now. 'Maybe, but that's not how the early news bulletins are telling it. According to them, she disappeared from the beach, covered in blood, and turned up in Stanley several hours later with the kid in her arms.'

'Fuckin' bullshit! I was in the car with her. She was asleep for most of the journey. It was sheer bloody fluke we saw him when we did.'

Mabel is back, standing directly in front of me, holding a bottle of washing-up liquid. I look down. At it; at her.

'Mind your mouth, young man, or I'll wash it out,' she tells me. 'This might be a newsroom but we're not on Fleet Street and we're not the ones writing this crap.'

Mabel is half my height, probably a quarter my weight and yet I have a feeling that, were I to smile right now, I'd regret it. 'But I'm allowed to say crap? Right?'

She waves the Fairy Liquid in my face. 'No, I'm allowed to say crap because I'm ninety-two and I don't give a shit. You can say yes ma'am, no ma'am, sorry to give offence ma'am, but if I were you I'd be out of here and trying to find Catrin.'

'She also found the body of Jimmy Brown, in a bay she's known to frequent.' Cathy's a bit braver with Mabel to back her up.

'What are you talking about? It was my idea to search that wreck.'

A firm shake of the head from Cathy. 'Not the story we're hearing around town.'

Rob has finished on the phone, so I turn my back on Cathy. 'Do we know for certain the kid on the *Endeavour* was Jimmy?'

He looks at me over Mabel's head. 'They did the initial examination yesterday afternoon. While you and Catrin were at Speedwell. It was definitely Jimmy. They had dental records.'

I wait for him to go on.

'His family have been told, obviously. Now we have to wait for a pathologist to arrive.'

We have no one on the islands qualified to carry out post-mortem examinations. When a death requires investigation, someone has to be flown over from the UK. It will be several days, maybe a week or more, before we know what happened to Jimmy.

Rob pulls a face. 'Not that we're expecting to find out much more than we know already. According to what they found yesterday, there's no obvious cause of death and the remains of clothes suggest he wasn't interfered with. Bob says we'll probably never know what happened to him, but there's a lot to suggest that a child going into the sea at Surf Bay could easily have washed up in Port Pleasant.'

The phone starts ringing. Unable to stop himself, Rob picks it up.

I turn to Mabel. 'So Stopford's happy again. Archie found alive and well, poor wee Jimmy's death an accident. No monsters on the Falkland Islands.'

'Oh, I wouldn't go that far,' says Cathy.

Mabel glares at her to be quiet. 'The best thing you can do right now is get Catrin out of Stanley for a while,' she tells me. 'Get on board that boat tonight, drive to New Island, or anywhere, and hole up till it blows over. This place will be crawling with journalists tomorrow and I really don't think she can cope with that.'

On my way out, I glance back at Rob, who is standing at the window, still on the phone, but looking up at the sky, down at his watch, back up at the sky again, and telling the caller to get a blinking move on or he'll miss it.

It's five minutes to the Falkland Conservation, probably faster to run, so I set off and within two minutes know I've made the wrong decision. Catrin's Land Rover comes hurtling towards me. There isn't time to leap bodily into the road, which is probably just as well because I'm not convinced she'd have stopped. She speeds past, and I have no option but to turn and run back to my car.

When I get there I'm winded, my breathing shallow, which is not a good sign. In me, an approaching flashback is similar to what other people might describe as a panic attack. My heart starts to pick up speed and lose its usual regularity. In other words, I get palpitations. My breathing gets a lot faster. I feel light-headed, get a sense of unreality, as though the world around me has detached itself. I'm getting all that now. Plus, the world around me is turning darker. I shake my head to clear it. It doesn't work. I'm losing my grip.

Normally, when I feel this way, I take myself off somewhere quiet, lie down and try to get my breathing back under control. If I catch it in time, I can sometimes prevent the onset. This is not a good time to be lying down. I need to find Catrin.

I take a few deep breaths and jump into the car. She's about eight or ten minutes ahead. I head east along a rapidly darkening Ross Road, and when I've driven past most of the town, turn inland to pick up the Airport Road. A few more minutes and I can head directly north towards her house. I tell myself to keep breathing, to stay calm.

I'm almost at the point where I turn when I see her hurtling towards me again. She screeches to a halt, reverses a couple of feet, then mounts the verge at the side of the road to get past. As I watch, mystified, she doesn't make eye contact, doesn't even glance my way. It might be an empty truck she's manoeuvring around. With a spray of mud, she's off the verge and speeding away in the opposite direction. The world darkens again and I can't go on.

The rain wakes me and I scramble to my feet. I have no idea how or why I'm outdoors but I know I'm not dressed for being out in camp. I'm wearing a light denim jacket, jeans, shoes that I'd normally wear to the pub or around the house. Not what I was wearing earlier in the day. Some time, in between chasing Catrin up the coast road and winding up here, I've been home.

It's punishingly dark. No stars, no moon, no glow from the imminent arrival of the sun. I press the illuminated button on my watch and the sudden spark of light becomes the flash of gunfire.

I cry out, look round in alarm. Then take a deep breath and tell myself it's over. That the flashback, and the events that sparked it, are over. Neither leave me that easily.

Thirteenth of June 1982. The assault on Wireless Ridge. My company had already sustained heavy losses at Goose Green, we weren't ready for another prolonged attack. We waited, in the mud. The guns fell silent. An order, one that I had to give: 'Fix bayonets, lads! No prisoners.'

The order comes and we go. A charge into a black nightmare. No way of knowing where the enemy is or what sort of land we're crossing. Into the stinking mud of enemy trenches, to find them abandoned. On again, with mine the voice that pushes the lads on. 'Keep going. Let's do it. This is what we're here for.' The key to success in battle is to keep moving forward, regardless of personal cost.

Calling up artillery support with disastrous consequences. Shells crashing down on us, losing more men in friendly fire. 'Keep going, lads. This is what we trained for.' As if anyone could be trained for this living hell. A terrified young Argie, jumping up in front of us, hands in the air.

No prisoners.

Impossible to explain to people who've never known combat, who can quote the Geneva Convention but have no idea what it's like to be in a hostile situation, that in the heat of battle, you don't take prisoners. Capturing and securing a single enemy soldier could tie up three of our guys in circumstances when everyone is needed for the forward push.

This is a kid in front of us. A teenager, begging not to be killed.

'Shoot him! Fucking shoot him.'

'You shoot him!'

Hope fading in the lad's eyes. None of the men with the stomach to kill a frightened kid. A single bullet. A sharp upward stab of the bayonet. The kid falls to the mud. My bullet. My bayonet. Sometimes, the buck just stops.

I'm sweating, in spite of the cold. Shaking in the aftermath of the flashback I always dread. For me, the worst night of the war, the night I killed a terrified, unarmed kid.

When Catrin and I were together, she used to talk about a poem that her friend Rachel was keen on and such was my infatuation at the time with all things Catrin, I looked it up. It was long, I remember that much, and also that I didn't understand most of it, but three lines stood out for me:

For the sky and the sea, and the sea and the sky
Lay like a load on my weary eye,
And the dead were at my feet.

I'd like to be able to forget those three lines. I can't. I know what it's like to be surrounded by dead men. To fall over them, to walk on top of them. There are times when it feels like the dead are always at my feet.

I check my watch again. It's after two in the morning. I reach into

157

my jacket pocket and thank God my Swiss army knife is still there because it has a small torch attached.

I'm by the stone run, the same one that crosses the road to Estancia. I can follow it down. It'll be bloody miserable going, but I won't get lost. I set off, keeping to the edge of the trail of boulders, flicking the light on to them every few seconds to make sure I don't stray. Already the pictures in my head are fading. The tightness in my chest starting to uncoil.

I try to call up the last real thing I can remember before the flashback kicked in. Catrin. Up near the Grimwood house. Following her back into town. Seeing her boat disappear out of harbour and knowing there was no way I could follow. From the way I'm dressed, I know I went home briefly, showered and changed, and I can remember the Globe, not long after four in the afternoon. A few of the guys from the fishing fleet were in there. Also a couple of folk from camp. Some off-duty squaddies from the base. I'd learned that Stopford had managed to get the cruise ship to agree to stay another night, but after that, he was going to need a court order to keep it here.

I'd started with beer, quickly moved on to Scotch. There'd been music playing and none of the bands ever start before eight. I have no idea what time I left the pub.

Ahead of me, a shape is emerging more solid than the night, paler than the hillside it sits on. My Land Cruiser.

I'm considered unconventional on the islands for a number of reasons, not the least of which is my choice of vehicle. The patriotic locals typically choose the British Land Rovers, occasionally Range Rovers or Land Rover Discoveries. My Toyota Land Cruiser, a 1974 FJ40 that I bought off a dealer in Texas, is the only one of its kind here.

I climb into the front seat, pull my jacket off, find the rug – the same one that wrapped Catrin and Archie last night – and pull it around myself. Somewhere in my immediate future there is one hell of a hangover waiting its moment to pounce.

The flashback has almost gone, the worst pictures faded. And yet something else, clinging on. Another memory, much more recent. I'm on the hills above Port Fitzroy. The sky is still light and I am looking at Catrin's boat, far below me in the bay.

Real or not? Why on earth would she head back to the place where we found a corpse a couple of nights ago? And if real, when? Before the pub or after I left? The light means nothing. It is light till nearly ten this time of year. And if I did look at Catrin's boat, anchored in the bay, is she still there?

At last I reach the road and set off towards Stanley. While I'm still half a mile out of town I know that something has happened and so self-obsessed am I right now that I'm convinced it's something to do with me. I hurt someone earlier. Blinded by drink and dark memories, I ran into them and drove on, oblivious. I see blue flickering lights and know they must be looking for me.

I head down towards the harbour, waiting for the shouts of recognition, for the police car to pull out in front of me. At nearly three in the morning, Bob-Cat's Diner is open.

There is a platoon of soldiers heading towards the police station.

I park and tug my soaked jacket back on. If I'm really lucky, I might down a hot coffee before they take me.

'Look what the cat dragged in.' Bob-Cat puts a mug down on the counter and lifts the coffee pot, which I guess beats racing to the door and yelling, 'He's here, he's in here!'

'What's going on?' I grab the coffee almost before she's finished pouring.

'For your information, when a man offers to buy me a drink, he usually stays around long enough to pay for it.' She slops milk into the mug and adds two sugars. I don't take sugar. She knows that. 'If I'd known I'd have to pay for my own drink, I'd have ordered half a lager.'

There is some hope, I think, in Bob-Cat's annoyance being primarily about being cheated out of a drink.

'Can you remember what time I left?'

'You left in between ordering my drink and paying for it. That'll be five pounds sixty please.'

Knocking off a pound fifty for the coffee, I guess I owe Bob-Cat for a large Bacardi and Coke. I pay up, thinking I might have got off lightly. And yet I can't shake this feeling, the one that tells me that, whatever I've just been through, something worse is coming.

'What's going on?' I ask her, when I assume we're cool again. She gives me a look that says, *And which banana boat dropped you off?*

'Seriously?' I gesture outside. 'This can't all be about an unpaid bar bill.'

Her eyes narrow. 'We all assumed you'd got some sort of advance warning. That that was why you scarpered.'

'Advance warning of what? Are the Argies on their way back?'

Outside, a couple of squaddies look set to join us. They're stamping their feet, shaking the rain off their jacket collars. The door opens and a blast of wet, cold air hits us. 'Got some coffees, love?'

'Coming up.' Bob-Cat turns her back on me.

I get up, swallow down the coffee and head out. Up the hill, outside the news office, Rob Duncan is holding up an umbrella. Beneath it, I can make out the form of a woman. He's bundling her into the passenger side of a vehicle. She seems to droop, to be held up only by the man at her side. Then the door is closed, Rob bangs on the roof of the car and it heads away.

This is all looking frighteningly familiar. I see it in the shocked faces of people hurrying from one inadequate shelter to the next. I see it in the hurried movements of the police officers, who slam car doors and jog from vehicles to station, holding up the flats of their hands to ward off questions.

People seem to be converging on the town hall and I head up there. Inside, I see two distinct groups have formed. Over in the red corner, the visitors. I see Archie West's dad with a gleam in his eye and an energy in his movements that were entirely missing last time I saw him. In the blue corner, by the serving counter, are the locals. There's a group I don't know particularly well and I wonder if they've come from Port Howard, whether it might be Fred Harper's family. Everyone is wet. No one has thought to put the heating on and the air in here is almost as chill as outside. I have a moment to be thankful that, soaking as I still am, I'll be mistaken for part of the search.

How do I know there is another search going on? That another child has gone missing? I just do.

I step up to a group I know. Terry from my football team. John who works with Catrin at the Falkland Conservation, Chad from the ironmongers. One or two more. All blokes.

'Any news?' I say, because it seems the safest thing.

160

A couple stare at me. One bloke looks at the floor. Then one voice from the rear of the group pipes up. 'I think we're all hoping you and my ex-wife can work another one of your miracles.'

I curse myself for not checking more carefully. I hadn't spotted Ben Quinn. He'd been behind Chad, but steps out now and faces me. I avoid Catrin's ex-husband if I can. It was a habit I got into even before I started seeing her. I avoid looking at him, speaking to him, even being in the same room as him. I can't remember the last time the two of us made eye contact, as we're doing right now. He hasn't changed much. Spanish eyes staring out of sallow skin. Dark hair, where the grey hasn't yet touched it. Little Kit is shining out of him, and I wonder how Catrin stood to be around him for as long as she did.

He's a slim guy. Fit enough, I guess, but a few stone lighter than me. Even half drunk, I could flatten him. The fact that I want to is because I'm half drunk. At least, I hope so, because what does it say about me otherwise? It's not as though I can blame the guy for being an arse with me. I did shag his wife.

What happened between Catrin and me has never been public knowledge, so far as I'm aware, but if rumours exist, there's a chance he's heard them. Whatever. In the end, he was the one who walked out.

'I take it the feed shed where Archie West was kept has been checked.' I don't address this to Ben particularly, but I don't drop my eyes. That would look as though I'm backing down and it's suddenly very important that I don't.

'It was the first place they looked.' It is Chad who answers. Ben and I are eyeballing each other like a couple of kids with more testosterone than sense.

I still don't know which child is missing. Not that it matters all that much. I don't know most of the kids in Stanley.

'If you know where Catrin is, we're a bit worried,' says John. 'No one's been able to contact her since this afternoon.'

'I haven't seen her since I dropped her off at home this morning,' I say, which is stretching the truth – it was the early hours when I drove Catrin home – but I'm enjoying winding her ex-husband up. As his eyes narrow still further I decide I'm being a dick. I nod my goodbyes and head out. As I step out into the night, I feel a hand on my shoulder. There is nothing friendly about the way it stops my progress forward. I turn and am not remotely surprised to see that Quinn has followed me out. Well, I guess this day was coming.

'She blames you, you know. For what happened to the boys.'

I'd been bracing myself for the punch, wondering how hard I'd be justified in hitting him back. I hadn't expected that.

I shake my head. 'You're wrong. She didn't even know I was involved until a couple of nights ago.' I wonder if I should tell him I'm sorry for his loss, that they were great kids. I decide if I do that, he'll land me one for sure.

'I'm not talking about your big rescue attempt. We all know what a hero you were that day. I'm talking about the fact that, as Catrin sees it, she was screwing around and the boys were killed as a punishment.'

'That's bollocks.'

He has a way of blinking heavily, of closing his eyes for a fraction too long. 'Course it is. But in my ex-wife's messed-up brain, it makes perfect sense. What she did with you cost her her kids. So if you're indulging in any sentimental daydreams about happy ever after, I'd forget it.'

I can't hit him. If I start I'll never stop. Then she'll blame me for killing her ex-husband as well.

'Which kid?' I say, because I have to move this on and it seems as good a way as any.

'What?'

'Which kid is missing? I haven't been in Stanley all evening. Which kid has been taken?'

He steps back, shaking his head, as though I'm not worth any more of his attention. He tells me though, calling over his shoulder as he heads back into the hall.

'Peter Grimwood. Her friend Rachel's youngest.'

DAY FIVE
Friday, 4 November

17

I'M RUNNING UP THE HILL. PEOPLE ARE STARING. THEY THINK I know something. I'm being stupid, drawing attention to myself like this, but I have to keep moving or I'll start thinking. The police station is out. If I could catch Skye on her own, I'd probably get the basic facts out of her, but not in front of her colleagues.

Peter Grimwood. I've seen him a couple of times this week. Him and his mother. Couple of days ago he nearly scared me to death with a toy gun. Funny kid. Bit quiet and clingy, I'd thought.

Rachel's kid, missing? This can't be good. On any level.

I bang on the door of the news office and open it a second later. I know they're all still here, I could see them through the window as I ran past. Cathy is leaning against her desk. Mabel, in a pink velour tracksuit, is hovering in the kitchen doorway and Rob stands in the middle of the room. They all three stare at me. A phone is ringing. Everyone ignores it.

'Rob, mate. What can I do?'

Rob lifts one hand to push imaginary hair out of his eyes. 'Go home. Check your shed, your peat shed, your garage, under your bushes. Anywhere a small boy could be hiding out. Then be back here at first light to join the search. It's all anyone can do.'

At that moment, he looks every one of his seventy-plus years.

'You can take Rob home,' says Cathy. 'Or better still, up to Rachel's. She shouldn't be on her own.'

'Where's Sander?' Sander is Rachel's husband. He works in the Secretariat.

'Away,' Rob tells me. 'Flying back tomorrow. And she isn't on her own. Jan's with her.'

A look between Mabel and Cathy tells me they don't think much of Jan's ability to take care of her daughter in a crisis. I barely know Rachel's mother, but I've heard she has a keen sense of drama.

'Jan can't cope with Rachel and both boys,' says Mabel. 'And it's not as though we're actually answering the phones here.'

On cue, another starts ringing. Rob's hand reaches out and his mother stops him with a yip. She crosses to a line of hooks and pulls a coat down.

'You're not a newsman right now, Robert, you are the news, and you of all people know the mess you'll get yourself into if you start talking to people who can quote you. Come on.' She shoves the coat at him. 'Callum's going to drive you home. Cathy will take me. The last one turned up safe and sound and Peter will too.'

'I drove past Rachel's house earlier,' I say as we head out of town. 'What time was Peter missed?'

'Shortly after four. When everyone was watching the eclipse.' Suddenly, Rob won't look at me. 'Cathy had just dropped the older two home from school. Rachel called the police at half past four after she and the boys had searched the house and garden.'

The email with Catrin's photograph came through shortly before three in the afternoon. I arrived in Stanley roughly an hour later. It must have been about four when I followed Catrin's car up the hill.

'What time were you there?' he is asking me. 'Did you see anything of him?'

'Earlier,' I lie. 'I didn't see anything of Peter,' I add, grateful to tell him something that's true.

I head up the same hill that I followed Catrin up just hours earlier. How far in front was she? A couple of minutes? Ten? Easily enough time to reach the driveway of the Greenwood house, as I'm doing now, turn in the soft mud surrounding it and then bomb it back down the hill. I try to remember whether I made it up this far and can't. So much of this afternoon has been lost to the flashback.

But this is the easiest place to turn round, so chances are I did.

I shunt backwards and forwards and wonder if I'm deliberately trying to hide previously made tyre tracks. And, if I am, what the hell I think I'm playing at. Rob jumps out as soon as I pull the brake on. He disappears into the house before I have time to wish him goodnight, leaving me no choice but to follow.

As I make my way inside, I'm thankful for one thing, at least. Rob has just reminded me about yesterday's eclipse. I knew about it – we all did – I'd just forgotten, given everything else going on. Still, good to know the freaky unscheduled darkness was a natural phenomenon, not a sign of approaching lunacy on my part.

In daylight, this is one of the nicer houses in Stanley, standing high above Surf Bay, in a large, sloping garden. The kitchen smells of instant coffee, oxtail soup and burned toast. Feeling awkward about being inside uninvited, but even more uncomfortable about bailing, I find Rob in the sitting room where his wife, Jan, is huddled under a blanket with Christopher, Rachel's eldest.

'Is there news?' She sees me and her eyes widen.

'Callum drove past here earlier in the day.' Rob turns back to me. 'Have you told Bob Stopford?'

'What time was it? Were you alone?'

'Some time before four,' I tell Jan. 'Alone. I didn't see anything of Peter. And I haven't told Stopford yet. Hi, Chris. How's your mum doing?'

A few months ago, I gave a talk to the older kids at Chris's school about the future of information technology and how, one day, household computers will change our lives and the world. Chris had been one of the brightest, the most interested.

His face grows paler. 'I think she'll be better when Dad gets home.'

'Shouldn't you be in bed?' his granddad asks him.

'I can't sleep. Michael's in my bed and he sticks his elbows in me.'

I look at my watch. Not far off four in the morning, making it nearly twelve hours that Peter has been missing. Jan tucks the blanket up higher around her shoulders.

'Why don't I light a fire?' I look at the peat burner. It's been swept and cleaned, there are firelighters and kindling in a basket to one side. It's ready to go and will give me something to do. 'Do you know where the matches are, Chris?'

I follow Chris into the kitchen. He's going to be tall. His dad, Sander, is. So is Rachel, for a woman. Chris was always a couple of inches taller than Ned.

'When was the last time you saw Peter?' I ask, when we're out of earshot of the grown-ups.

'He was in his cot when I got home from school. His nappy was wet. I changed him.'

'Then what?'

'Michael was calling for me. We were going to go down to the beach to watch the eclipse.'

His eyes drift from mine. He thinks he's in trouble. He ran outside, faster than his toddler brother could follow, and now he's blaming himself. I pull out a chair and sit on it, so I'm on a level with the kid.

'Where was your mum?'

'Lying down. In her bedroom. That's where she usually is when we get home.'

'He's tired, Callum. He needs to be in bed.' Rob has followed me in from the living room.

'You found the other little boy, didn't you?' Chris says to me. 'Are you going to look for Peter?'

'Of course, we all are. Did you bring Peter downstairs?'

'I carried him,' Chris tells me. 'Then I put him down. He's quite heavy.'

'He's a monster,' chips in Rob. 'I can barely lift him myself.'

'What happened then, mate?'

'I ran down to join Michael. We have a den on the beach. We were playing there. We stayed until we heard Mum shouting for us. That's when we knew Peter was missing.'

'Rachel phoned the police at four thirty,' says Rob.

Chris is looking at me. 'Will they light fires for Peter? Like they did for that other little boy?'

I stand up. 'It's a bit wet for fires tonight. But that other little boy is safe and sound now. You need to remember that.'

Chris stays where he is. 'Jimmy wasn't safe, though, was he?'

Rob and I make eye contact. Neither of us has anything to say to that.

'The police searched the wreck in the bay yesterday.' Chris is looking defiant now. He knows this isn't something we want to hear. 'They were looking for that other little boy. The one from West Falkland. That makes four now.'

'Bed,' says Rob, for want of anything else.

'Will you take me?' Chris asks me.

'I'll take you up, Chris.' His grandmother has been hovering in the doorway, watching us.

'I want Callum.' Exhausted though he is, Chris is determined to get his way.

After Rob nods his permission and Jan gives an exasperated shrug, I pull off my shoes and follow Chris upstairs, not without a few misgivings. I have no experience of young kids.

On the upper floor, I can see four open doors, one closed. Behind the closed one, I imagine, is Rachel. Chris pauses on the threshold of one door before walking past. As I follow him, I see a small form huddled in a single bed. The next room along is Peter's. I lean in and switch on the light.

Surely this should be sealed off? A crime scene? Resolving to touch nothing, I lean over the cot and catch the faint whiff of piss. Hard to tell in this light but I think I can see a stain where Peter's nappy leaked earlier. There is a changing mat on the floor, an opened pack of nappies at its head. There are three left in it. A dirty one is in the corner of the room.

I find Chris in the next room along. 'This is Michael's room,' he tells me, explaining the posters and toys that seem too young for a near teenager. 'You're going to look for Peter, aren't you?'

'Yes. Everyone is.'

'Where will you look?'

'I guess we'll start close to home. If he's wandered away by himself, he won't have gone far.'

'We checked the garden. Michael and I looked everywhere. We went down to the beach too. And the old boathouse down there. He isn't anywhere near the house.'

'Chris, if you remember anything, anything at all, you have to tell the police. Or me, if you prefer. Do you promise me?'

He nods and snuggles down. 'Will Mum be OK?' he asks,

as I leave the room. I can't remember what I tell him, only that I look back at Rachel's door and hope that her non-appearance means she's asleep, that she's having a few hours' break from all this.

As I approach the living room, I hear voices that I know are not meant for me.

'. . . of all people should be here!'

I push open the door. I still don't have shoes on and I can move quietly for a big bloke. Both Rob and Jan turn, surprise on their faces and something else too. Something I don't think is worry about their grandson. Rob has been making half-hearted attempts to light the fire. Ignoring the atmosphere, I edge him out of the way and have it going in a few seconds.

I've been in this house before, but years ago. I remember good-quality furniture and decent paintings on the walls. During the evenings, candles glowed softly, the air was scented. There were always flowers. Kids' clutter was never far away but not more than the odd toy lying around. Tonight, the room looks as though no one's bothered to tidy it up in weeks and the whole house has a stale smell to it. This is more than a few hours' neglect by a terrified mother.

'How's Rachel doing?'

Jan and Rob exchange a look.

'In shock, we think,' says Rob. 'Shaking. Can barely talk. Trying to hold it together for the older boys but—'

'Sander knows, I take it?'

'I spoke to him,' says Rob. 'Not the easiest conversation to have over a long-distance line but he had to know.'

'What time, exactly, did you drive by this afternoon?' Jan doesn't wait for me to reply. 'We know you left the newsroom shortly before four, you couldn't have been here much earlier. Were you with Catrin Quinn?'

I know nothing about Peter's disappearance, and yet suddenly I'm feeling guilty as hell. Jan has backed towards the kitchen door and I realize she's edging nearer to the phone.

'What's Catrin got to do with this?' I get to my feet.

'Rachel saw her here this afternoon.' Rob can't look at me any more. 'Seconds before Peter went missing. Just as it all went dark. She saw Catrin pick him up. By the time she ran outside, they'd both gone.'

'The police are looking for her. They'll find her. And if she's hurt my grandson . . .'

Rob puts a hand on his wife's shoulder. 'We're all upset, Callum. Maybe it's better if . . .'

I don't need telling twice. I find my shoes, pull them on and step outside.

'Obviously we all hope there's been some misunderstanding.' Rob has followed me out.

'There's no misunderstanding, Rob. Rachel saw her.' Jan comes up to me, catches hold of my arm. 'It's twenty-four hours since she apparently found the other boy. He was on her land, on her property. And all those whales she killed. Not to mention the dead child on the wreck. Nobody believes that was coincidence. She's not well, Callum. You have to help us find her, before she does something terrible.'

With one thought in my head, I drive to the harbour. Catrin's car is here and her boat still missing. So I head up to the hills above Port Fitzroy. The darkness in the sky is beginning to soften. I drive on and leave the road, heading for the cliff. In the light, I can get right to the edge. In the semi-darkness it seems risky, but I need to know if her boat is down in the bay.

I drive as far as I dare, then get out.

I'm so cold that even walking forward is painful, but the rug from the car helps a bit. I carry on and the light grows.

So close to the edge, the wind is a demon. It tugs at the rug, determined to claim it for its own. Below me, surrounded by rocks that look like teeth, among clouds that swirl and a sea that strikes hard, is Catrin's boat.

There is no life, no movement on board, and I have no way of getting in touch. If I call her on the radio, the whole world will hear. If I go down to the harbour, try to commandeer a boat and get out to her, I'll be stopped or followed.

A flicker of white against the steel grey of the water catches my eye. A large white bird is flying low, barely skimming the surface of the sea. As it nears Catrin's boat, it gains height. I can make out massive, black-tipped wings and a hooked beak. It hovers above the boat and I'd give a lot right now to be able to see what it can.

What's going on down there, Catrin? What the hell are you doing on that boat?

I think about climbing down, swimming out, and know I wouldn't make it.

I tell myself that Catrin would not hurt a child. That she drove past the Grimwood house yesterday and saw Peter, maybe playing in the garden, maybe watching at the fence. She saw him and it hit her hard, because her own son – my son – would have been almost exactly the same age. It hit her hard and she needed time alone. She went to where she always goes when she needs to get her head together, out to sea.

If she saw Peter, why didn't I see him?

The wind pushes me back, as though afraid of what might happen if I get too close to the edge. There is another vessel, steaming around the headland, approaching Catrin's boat at speed. A police boat. They've found her.

Catrin and I drove past the Grimwood house at roughly four in the afternoon. By ten minutes past four Rachel had missed her youngest son, was already searching. Fewer than a dozen cars a day drive along that road. That there should be three, in less than ten minutes?

And Rachel claims she saw Catrin pick the kid up.

Catrin has suffered more than anybody I know. I've seen suffering and I still say it unreservedly. She's been damaged beyond recognition, probably beyond repair, but she still wouldn't hurt a child.

I have to go on believing that. Or I might as well step off this cliff now.

The police vessel slows as it approaches Catrin's boat. I see Queenie run on deck to greet them. Then she appears. She's moving slowly, looks half asleep. Catrin, who is normally so quick, so agile on a boat, seems drugged. She catches a rope thrown to her and makes it off. I watch a police officer board her boat, then another. A third. With Queenie in her arms, Catrin is helped to make the crossing on to the police boat. She's taken below, her head guided down to prevent it banging on the cabin roof. There are no cuffs that I can see, but it's pretty clear what's going on. Catrin is under arrest.

18

WAY BEFORE I GET BACK INTO STANLEY THREE HOURS later I'm praying for more rain. A bloody great downpour, a thunderstorm, a frigging hurricane would do. Anything to get this lot off the streets. People are everywhere. Bob-Cat's Diner is full. The pub has opened early. There's a crowd outside the post office. People are drifting in and out of the town hall. Two days ago, when we looked for Archie West, there was a sense of purpose that you could almost touch. Everyone was determined to get out and find the lad. It's all very different now and this isn't compassion fatigue. A lot of these faces I don't recognize and feel sure they must be off the cruise ship, drawn ashore by the sense of a drama unfolding.

They'll all know about Catrin's arrest. If they think she did it, they'll be waiting for the police to force a confession, for her to tell them where Peter is. No one will be looking for him.

It's nearly eight o'clock in the morning. Resisting the temptation to speed back into town after watching Catrin being taken into custody, I'd driven home instead, taken a shower, put on dry clothes, eaten. I'd forced myself to be calm, knowing that Catrin, like any other arrested prisoner, would have to be processed. She'd be booked into the system, have fingerprints taken and be photographed. She'd be offered a solicitor and, if she accepted – I hope to God she did – there could have been a couple of hours'

173

delay before one was found and woken. The first interview could have taken an hour and by then they'd have to break.

That crap should all be over with by now and the initial excitement, at the station at least, will be starting to die down. They'll have time to talk to me.

Heads turn my way as I park. Already, I'm tainted by my association with the woman they know has fallen under police suspicion. God help me, there is a TV crew, here to cover the beached whale story, only to be met with a completely unexpected bonanza. One guy holds a camera on one shoulder, the other has one of those big furry microphones that hover out of shot. A woman in an apricot-coloured coat has hair that looks solid. A warm shade of blonde, it curves around her head. The wind blows her scarf across her face. Her hair doesn't move. Someone tips them off and as I climb out of the car, they're heading over.

'Callum Murray, your close friend, Catrin Quinn, has been arrested this morning. Do you have any comment to make?'

I step to one side, she bounces in front of me. Her make-up is caked thick on her face. It might work on camera; in real life it looks grotesque. 'Are you still telling people it was coincidence you and she found Archie West on the hillside two nights ago?'

I sidestep around her again, treading on the cameraman's toe in the process. 'Watch it, mate,' he mutters.

'What happened? Did he assault you?' Apricot lady turns her attention from me and I stride ahead. She bolts round in front of me again. 'Do you have any comment to make about the child's body you found on Tuesday night?'

Luckily I'm at the door. There is a constable on door duty. Apricot tries to follow me. Constable Bouncer holds her back.

'All right, Neil.' I nod to the sergeant on the desk. 'Is Catrin here?'

A silent nod tells me she is. Behind us, the Apricot gang are arguing that they have as much right to enter the police station as anyone else. Bouncer is holding firm.

'Can I see her?'

Neil blinks and squares up to me. 'She's being interviewed.'

'Does she have a solicitor?'

His eyes fall to the counter. He's not sure.

'Has she been charged?'

Blank stare.

'When can I see her?'

He looks over at the door. 'Come back later.'

Someone behind the Apricot gang wants to come in. Constable Bouncer is torn. His hesitation costs him ground and there is a sudden flood of newcomers into the reception area. Sergeant Neil is distracted. Bouncer is flustered. Former Second Lieutenant Murray is a canny bastard. I back away and slip quietly into the inner corridor.

I'm not going far, just to the office on the right where Skye has her desk. She looks up.

'Neil let me through,' I tell her. 'It's chaos out there.'

She nods, pulls a face. 'I'll say.'

I cross to her desk, pull over a chair and sit down. 'Skye, tell me what's happening with Catrin.'

She blushes and fiddles with a button on her shirt, as usual finding it difficult to make eye contact. People have told me that Skye has a crush on me and I've suspected the same thing myself. I've never acted on it, even if she is the only woman on the islands I could snog without getting a sore neck. To me, Skye is an overgrown kid. But if she does have a soft spot, I'm going to exploit it to the full now.

I lean forward. 'Catrin and I go back a long way, Skye. All a long time ago, but I probably know her better than anyone. I can help.'

Skye is young enough and keen enough to want to chase any lead. 'Do you want to make a statement?'

'Of course.' I'm sure I can think of something if I have to. 'Preferably to you. But first, I need to know what's going on. Has Catrin been arrested?'

She nods, unhappily. 'If you ask me, it was a bit premature. I'd have just brought her in for questioning. But coming right on the back of Archie West's abduction, and with all the press attention, I guess the Chief Superintendent didn't want to take any chances.'

'Has she been charged?'

'Not that I know of.'

'What are the facts, Skye? What have you got?'

175

She shakes her head. 'I really shouldn't.' Then she gets up, strides to the door and shuts it. 'What the hell,' she says. 'I'm sure it's all over Stanley anyway. When did anything ever stay quiet here?'

I wait. I probably look patient but I know my time is running out.

'Catrin was seen driving up the hill towards the Grimwood house yesterday shortly before four o'clock,' she tells me.

'By who?'

'Someone who works at the boatyard. Ten minutes later, he saw her again, only this time going the other way, towards the harbour.'

I wait, give Skye time.

'She stopped outside the house. Rachel Grimwood was at her bedroom window. She saw Catrin get out of the car and she saw her carrying Peter.'

'The kid could have got out into the road. Of course Catrin stopped for him.'

'She was seen – Catrin I'm talking about now – getting on board her boat with a very large bag or bundle.' Skye really isn't enjoying passing on the bad news. 'Something she was struggling to carry.'

'What does she say it was?'

Skye shakes her head. More knowledge than she has.

'Is that it? She drove past the house, picked the kid up out of the road and carried a bag on to her boat?' I lean forward, reach out as though to touch Skye's hand, then pretend to think better of it. 'Skye, this is dangerous. While your people are focusing on Catrin, they're not looking for Peter. Have you seen the circus outside? No one is looking for Peter.'

I stand up and cross to the window, turning back when I reach it. 'The weather's taken a turn for the worse. Peter will have it a lot tougher than Archie did. A small kid won't survive in the open for long in these conditions.'

Her face crumples, and I feel sorry for her, but there's more at stake than Skye's feelings. She makes a sudden movement that doesn't seem designed to go anywhere or achieve anything and knocks a pencil holder off her desk. It clatters to the floor.

'There's a storm forecast for this evening,' I tell her, which isn't true that I'm aware of.

'The army are ready to start searching.' She crouches down to retrieve the pencils. I'm pretty certain she bangs her head on the side of the desk but she bites her lip and doesn't complain. 'But the Chief Superintendent told them to hold off until we've had chance to interview the prime— to talk to Catrin.'

'He's a fool.'

'There's also a team of divers searching the bay where her boat was anchored last night.'

I cross back to her desk and find the last pencil for her. As I hand it over, I take her hand. It feels large and warm in mine, so different to Catrin's tiny, always cold hand. 'Skye, I need two things. I need to talk to Catrin and I need you to get that search going as soon as possible. There'll be another lair somewhere. An old hut, a food store, an outbuilding.' I let her go and lean back on my heels. 'Look, it's obvious that whoever took Peter also took Archie and we already know Archie was taken by a man.'

In my pocket, I still have the spreadsheet I showed Catrin on Tuesday night but there's no need to get it out now. I emailed it to Skye months ago.

'Forty-one men between the ages of sixteen and seventy-five were at both the West Falkland Sports Day and the Midwinter Swim. A handful of those will not have alibis for when Archie and Peter went missing. Good old-fashioned police work will find the man who's taking the kids, Skye. You can find him yourself; this morning, if you put your mind to it.'

She rubs her hand as she gets to her feet. 'Actually, Archie is pretty confused about what happened. He's also talking about a woman.'

'What?'

Skye takes a step closer to the door. In the corridor an alarm runs the length of both walls. She only has to touch it and my time is up.

'The latest thinking is that Archie was taken by a man and a woman working together.'

'Ridiculous,' I say. Not at the notion of Archie having two abductors, but at the entirely new idea I can see running through Skye's head. If Catrin, in her new role as child abductor, had an accomplice . . . ?

'Catrin has no alibi for the time Archie went missing,' says Skye. 'She was working at home, all afternoon, by herself.'

'Yeah, so was I,' I say, which probably isn't the wisest response in the world, given the turn this conversation seems to be taking. 'So were half the people on the islands.'

'There was a toy on her boat. Rachel recognized it as being Peter's. I'm sorry, Callum, but it doesn't look good.'

I feel massive relief at being confronted with a piece of evidence I can blow out of the water. 'What sort of a toy? A rabbit, by any chance? Looking a bit worse for wear? It isn't Peter's. Catrin and I found it the other night on the *Endeavour*. Her own son had one exactly like it.'

'Yes, Rachel told us that. We think maybe seeing Peter with a toy she recognized was the last straw for Catrin.'

'Catrin wouldn't hurt a fly.'

Skye raises her eyebrows. Fair point.

'And there were hairs on her sweater. Fine, short, blond ones. Definitely not hers. Not yours either. They'll have to be sent away, obviously, but—'

'They were probably Queenie's. She carries that dog around like a baby. Stopford's going to spend a fortune having dog hairs tested. Where is Queenie, by the way?'

'In the pound. I think she bit someone.'

'Good.' I step to the door and pull it open. 'Can I at least see the dog?'

19

IN THE TIME IT TAKES QUEENIE TO EAT WHAT I'D PLANNED FOR dinner, shit in my garden and leave dog hairs all over my bed, I've managed to hack my way into the police computer system. To be fair, it was harder than some I've encountered. Of course, it will be wasted effort if nothing relating to Catrin's arrest or subsequent interview has been transcribed yet.

I start with Stopford's private email account and find a request issued first thing this morning to the military up at Mount Pleasant to conduct a dive search of the bay where Catrin was anchored overnight. In the response, I learn that the search is to begin mid morning and hopefully conclude by mid afternoon. They also offer to get tidal experts predicting where something dumped overboard at Port Fitzroy is most likely to drift, in the event of nothing being found immediately.

I find another email to the forensic science laboratory used by the Metropolitan Police in London informing them that clothing taken from a suspect in a child abduction case will be flown over in two days' time. A third is following up the request for detective assistance from the Met. Yet another is exploring the possibility of a forensic pathologist being flown to the islands to re-examine the body of little Jimmy Brown. Stopford is covering his back. An internal memo instructs all police personnel that a search of the land around the Grimwood home will not go ahead for the time being. As evidence suggests that Peter was driven away from his home, Stopford sees little point in investing valuable man-hours on a search that is likely to prove fruitless.

Twat.

I dig a bit deeper and find the transcript of the interview carried out with Catrin this morning. It was conducted by Detective Sergeant Josh Savidge, son of the headmaster of the local school. Savidge Junior is the most senior detective presence on the islands. He's accompanied by Detective Constable Liz Wilkins. Catrin has chosen not to have a solicitor present.

I skim through the opening formalities, the reminder to Catrin that she is allowed legal representation, and her declining it again.

Savidge: What time did you leave your office yesterday afternoon, Mrs Quinn?

Catrin: I wasn't particularly conscious of the time, I'm afraid. Mid afternoon.

Savidge: Your colleagues tell us it was coming up to four o'clock, not long after the photograph of you on the front cover of the *Daily Mirror* arrived by fax. And just as the eclipse began.

Catrin: That sounds about right.

Savidge: So, just before four o'clock then?

(Short pause.)

Savidge: For the benefit of the tape, Mrs Quinn, can you answer the question verbally?

Catrin: Yes, I imagine it was around four o'clock when I left.

Savidge: Alone?

Catrin: My dog was with me. Where is she, by the way?

Savidge: Why did you leave then?

Catrin: Have you seen the photograph of me that millions of people all over the world are looking at?

Savidge: Answer the question, please, Mrs Quinn.

Catrin: I was upset. I wanted some time on my own.

Savidge: Where were you planning to go?

Catrin: Home.

Savidge: Which way did you head?

Catrin: I went up the Airport Road, the easterly arm.

Savidge: That's not the most direct route, is it?

(Short pause.)

Wilkins: Mrs Quinn?

Catrin: No, it's not. But sometimes I drive that way.

Wilkins: Why?

Catrin: There are very few roads on the Falklands. Sometimes I just get bored.

I stop reading and lean back in my chair. No sound from upstairs, not even the gentle rumble of canine snoring. Back to the transcript where, not surprisingly, Savidge hasn't accepted a desire for variety as the reason Catrin drove along that particular road yesterday. He's pushing her. She doesn't want to answer. He persists. She gives in first.

Catrin: That road takes me past Rachel Grimwood's house. I used to spend a lot of time there, when I was younger, when my sons were alive. I suppose it reminds me of when I was happy.

(Indistinct murmuring.)

Savidge: Mrs Quinn, we spoke to Christopher Grimwood yesterday, the eldest child. Nice lad. Just turned twelve.

Catrin: Christopher is my godson. I know who he is.

Savidge: Yes, exactly. When did you last spend any time with him?

Catrin: I'm sorry, you want to know when I last saw Christopher?

Savidge: Yes. When did you last, I don't know, have a meal with him? Go for a walk with him? Sit and watch a television programme together?

Catrin: I haven't spent time with any member of that family in three years.

Savidge: Three years? And yet he's your godson?

Catrin: Josh, you know perfectly well what happened three years ago. You know why I don't see Rachel or her family.

Savidge: Yes. And we were very sorry to hear of your loss back then.

(Short pause.)

Catrin: Are you waiting for me to say thank you?

Savidge: I'm waiting for you to tell me why, given that you no longer want to associate with the Grimwood family – for understandable reasons, by the way, but given that, why you drive unnecessarily past their house. Why you spend so much time parked outside it in the dark.

Catrin: Who says I do?

Savidge: Christopher. He's seen you. His bedroom window overlooks the road and he says he's seen you more than once, parked outside at night-time. He'd made a note of your car registration, so there really isn't any doubt it was you he'd seen.

Catrin: I'm sorry to hear that. I wouldn't have wanted to frighten Christopher.

Savidge: So you admit you park outside the Grimwood house in the dark, on a regular basis?

Catrin: Yes, I suppose I do.

Savidge: How often?

Catrin: I'm not sure I can answer that. I don't keep a record.

Savidge: Once a day? Once a week?

Catrin: Less often. A couple of times a month.

Savidge: Always at night?

Catrin: I drive past at other times. I only park at night. When I think no one will see me.

Savidge: Why?

Catrin: I've told you. I have memories of that house.

Savidge: Parking outside it at night strikes me as being the action of a pretty disturbed mind.

(Short pause.)

Wilkins: Mrs Quinn?

Catrin: Sorry, was that a question?

I get up to stretch my legs. To anyone who knows her well, Catrin is just being Catrin. She doesn't suffer fools gladly and Savidge isn't the sharpest knife in the box. Unfortunately, I don't have to be in the room to know she isn't winning any friends. They might not be able to prove she did it, but while their attention is on her, they're not looking for Peter.

The irony does not escape me. I have been banging on for

months that there is a killer here and nobody has been paying the slightest bit of attention to me. Now, finally, they're coming round to my way of thinking and they've decided it's Catrin.

I go back to my desk.

Savidge: Tell us about what happened yesterday. When you drove past the Grimwood house again. Only in broad daylight this time.
Catrin: I drove up the hill. I turned the last corner before the house and saw Peter in the road.

I can practically see the increased interest in the room. Savidge and Wilkins exchanging glances. Both sitting up a little taller in their seats.

Wilkins: Peter was in the road?
Catrin: Yes, right in my tracks.
Wilkins: What did you do?
Catrin: I pulled over. Switched my engine off. Got out, went over to him, picked him up, put him on the other side of the garden gate, made sure it was locked and he couldn't get out again. Then I turned my car round and drove back down the hill.
Wilkins: Why didn't you knock on the door? Hand him over to his mum, make sure he was OK?
Catrin: I knew he was OK. A small kid can't get out of that garden if the gate's closed.
Wilkins: Most people would want to talk to his mum, don't you think? Let her know what happened. Especially given how dark it was.
Catrin: I'm not most people. I'm the mother who lost her children because of that woman's recklessness. I never talk to Rachel.
Savidge: You really hate her, don't you?

Don't answer that, Catrin. Please don't answer that.

Catrin: I hate her more than I'd ever have believed it possible to hate someone.

For a while I can't read on. I get up, go upstairs and cuddle Queenie. I make coffee and stare out at the hills.

Catrin doesn't care. Even in the transcript that's obvious. She has nothing left to lose. She doesn't care if people think she killed the kid. She's already the woman capable of slaughtering nearly two hundred whales and, as she's perfectly well aware, in many people's heads, that's far worse than killing one child.

Determined to see it through, I go back and skim through the rest. I read about Savidge asking about the blond hairs on her sweater and Catrin explaining, with thinly disguised impatience, that if they are Peter's they transferred when she picked him up and carried him back to his garden. I read about him asking what large bundle she was carrying out to her boat, and her explaining that it was bedding from the main cabin that had got wet the day before.

Made wet by me, I imagine, when Queenie and I crashed the other morning. I can corroborate that. Also the rabbit I found on the *Endeavour*. I'm going to need to talk to them soon. I check my watch again. I'm not sure how long they can hold someone without charging.

Savidge moves on to talk about our trip to the *Endeavour* on Tuesday night. About why we went, what we found. Catrin answers everything put to her with brutal honesty, except that she makes no mention of my attacking her. She does, though, admit something I wasn't aware of. That she often anchors in Port Pleasant and the adjacent Port Fitzroy overnight, that she knows the bay, and the wreck of the *Endeavour* as well as anyone.

I need to talk to them. Searching the *Endeavour* was my idea, not hers. If anything she was pretty reluctant to take me out there.

Savidge, in the transcript, is asking Catrin what she dumped overboard in Port Fitzroy this morning. She's denying she dumped anything. He's insisting she was seen doing so. She's challenging him to say who it was. He can't. Or won't. She's claiming that if she did want to dispose of a body, she wouldn't pick that bay because the water isn't deep enough. She says there are any number of other spots around the islands where the chances of a weighted body being found are tiny. I'm willing her to shut up, even though I know the conversation is already over in real life, because that sends Savidge off on a whole new tangent. Where would she dump a body? Is it something she's given much thought to?

When he gets nowhere, he moves on. Did she see anyone else on the Airport Road? No, she didn't. Did she take Peter Grimwood from his home yesterday? No. Did she take him on to her boat? No, she left him safely in his garden. Where was she three days ago when Archie West was taken from his family? At home, working. No, no one can confirm that, she lives alone.

She breaks his flow to ask what will happen to her dog. Savidge doesn't know. He presses on. Does she think it coincidence that Archie West was kept in a hut belonging to her, one that relatively few other people would know existed? She has no opinion on the subject. Did she take Archie West from his family? She'd never seen Archie West before finding him on the Darwin Road the other night.

It goes on, until even I'm exhausted. The interview takes a little over an hour. I search for more but can't find it. If she's been interviewed again since, no record has been made on the system.

I pick up the phone and eventually get through to Neil at the police station. I make an appointment for later in the day. With a bit of luck, I can get the toy rabbit discounted as evidence against Catrin.

Archie was taken by a man and a woman? He isn't making a lot of sense, according to Skye. If the kid's confused, the man and woman he's talking about could easily be me and Catrin. A man and woman took him away from his family? Or a man and woman took him back? Christ, all we need is for some half-arsed attempt at an identity parade, Archie to recognize Catrin, as he almost certainly will, and the frigging wheel falls off.

I get on the phone to a firm of solicitors in Stanley who confirm what I was already pretty sure of. In a serious case such as child abduction, Catrin can be held for up to four days without being charged. If the search for Peter Grimwood doesn't start properly for four days, the kid will be dead.

I call up people I know at Mount Pleasant and learn, to my huge relief, that a search is already underway. That a platoon of soldiers are searching the ground round the feed hut where Archie was held. It's a start, but I don't hold out a lot of hope. If the same person has taken Peter – and what else is possible? – then he, she, they, will have somewhere else to take him.

With no idea what to do next, I go back to the Grimwood house. When I arrive I find two police cars parked outside and crime-scene tape around the turning area. People in white overalls are working it. Better late than never, I suppose. I draw close and clear my throat.

'Found anything?' I know they shouldn't answer me. I also know they probably will. I'm not disappointed.

'Footprint.' One of them is pouring some sort of pale-coloured liquid into a hole in the ground. 'Just the one. Rain must have washed the rest away, but one is enough. Someone stood here recently. Big bloke, from the size of his feet.'

Catrin's feet are tiny.

I leave them and push open the garden gate. Christopher and Michael are both on the swing seat not far from the house. They jump up when they see me and head my way.

'Hi, you two. Any news?'

'Dad's plane's been delayed,' Chris tells me. 'He can't come back till tomorrow.'

'That's a shame. You must all want him back pretty bad.'

When Michael's eyes start to look pink around the edges, I regret not saying something more uplifting, like how their mum is lucky to have two such sensible, grown-up boys helping her out, or some such bollocks.

'Where's your mum right now?' I ask.

'She's lying down. Gran says she needs to sleep.'

Christopher is the one who needs to sleep, if you ask me. I'm not sure I really understood what shadows beneath the eyes meant until now. It's as though someone has rubbed their thumbs in purple paint and drawn them down from the corner of Chris's eyes diagonally across his cheeks. 'Have you come to look for Peter?' he asks me.

'We can look together, if you like.' I suggest this because I know that families in these situations often feel an overwhelming need to be doing something, anything, that feels productive. 'We can go down to the beach.'

'We've been already.' Chris reaches out and takes his brother's hand. 'We went first thing this morning. Before anyone else was awake.'

'We looked yesterday too.' Michael is still wearing pyjamas. He's pulled a fleece on top to stay warm and there are trainers on his feet, but otherwise he hasn't bothered with clothes. 'As soon as Mum couldn't find him, we looked everywhere.'

'She did the house, we did the garden,' says Chris. 'He's been taken away. He isn't anywhere here.'

'People think Auntie Catrin took him.'

I crouch down so I'm on a level with Michael. 'Who's saying that, buddy?'

'We overheard Gran and Granddad talking this morning.' Chris answers for his brother.

'She's in prison,' chips in Michael. 'Gran says she's sick in the head because her own sons died and now she wants to hurt Peter.'

I take the boys gently by the shoulders and walk them over to a group of upturned barrels arranged in a circle.

'Guys, did either of you see Catrin at your house yesterday? About four o'clock? Just before Peter went missing?'

Their eyes fall; first Christopher and then his brother shake their heads.

'Did you see anyone? Any other cars?'

More headshakes. And yet these two were in the garden when both Catrin and I each drove past. I guess when kids are in their own little world, they see and hear nothing beyond it.

'Have you noticed anyone else near the house? Not necessarily yesterday, but in the last few days? Maybe even the last few weeks? Anyone you don't know that well? Maybe someone watching you?'

'The policeman yesterday asked us that,' Chris says. 'I told him no one. No one apart from Auntie Catrin.'

'Gran says she hates us.'

'Catrin doesn't hate you,' I tell them. 'She's just very sad.'

'Mum's sad too,' says Michael. 'She cries a lot. Not just about Peter. She cries about everything.'

'Sometimes it seems like everyone's sad,' says Chris. 'They always were and always will be.'

Well, ain't that the truth?

20

QUEENIE'S TAIL IS BANGING AGAINST THE PASSENGER DOOR when I get back to the car and it occurs to me that if she's going to be my house guest for the next four days, I'm going to need dog food. I have another hour and a half before I'm due at the station. Shopping is as good a way as any to kill time, I suppose.

'Callum!' Someone calls my name as I close the car door. John, Catrin's boss, is hurrying towards me. I wait, let him get close, conscious that there are still too many people on the streets of Stanley and that a lot of them seem a little too interested in me.

'How you doing, John?'

He gives me that sly, almost furtive, smile of his. I've got nothing against John but I never feel entirely comfortable around him. Big men often don't around small men. Small men have a lot to prove. Small men can take you by surprise. You'd be surprised by how many small men carry long, sharp knives.

'Have you seen Catrin at all today?' he asks me, and I resist the temptation to answer no, on account of her being under arrest on suspicion of child abduction. I shake my head.

'She needs to talk to a solicitor.' He steps from one foot to the other, looking down. 'From what I can get out of Neil at the station, she's refusing one. I tried to talk to her, but she won't see anyone.'

'They've got nothing on her,' I say with more conviction than I feel. 'They'll have to let her go in a couple of days.'

'That's just it, they think they've got a pretty solid case.' He leans closer. 'Neil told me they're confident of being able to charge her later today.'

This will be about the rabbit. Without that, and the purely circumstantial evidence of her being at the Grimwood house yesterday afternoon, what do they have?

'They have fingerprints, apparently.' John answers my unasked question.

'Whose fingerprints?'

'The little boy's. Catrin was wearing a sort of leather shoulder bag yesterday. His prints are on it.'

I tell myself it means nothing. Peter's fingerprints will be on Catrin's bag for the same reason his hairs might be on her sweater. She found him in the road, picked him up and put him back in his garden.

I don't like it, though. If Peter's hairs were on Catrin's sweater, they may be in her car and on her boat too. There is a chain of evidence building that, while bogus, is looking more and more convincing.

'And fingerprints on that gun she keeps on the boat. Fresh ones, apparently, although how they can tell that is beyond me. She's handled that gun recently.'

She handled that gun when she and I were on the *Endeavour*. Thank God she didn't fire it, and not just for my sake.

'She really needs some sensible advice,' John is telling me now.

What she needs, I'm thinking, as I say goodbye and walk up the hill, is for Peter to be found and the real abductor identified.

'Callum!'

John has followed me. 'Look, there's something else. I didn't want to say anything but I have a feeling no one's looking out for her and whatever problems she might have, she needs support.'

'She needs Peter to be found and for this crap to be over with.'

'Callum, did you know the other two boys who went missing?

190

Jimmy Brown was local, you probably saw him around. The other family, the Harpers, they came over from time to time. Did you know them?'

I shake my head. 'Sorry, pal, why's it important?'

'The library will have old copies of the *Penguin News*. Both boys had their photograph in the paper when they vanished. Take a look. I don't recommend you go to the Duncans direct on this. They'll probably have pictures at the police station too. People are starting to make the connection, my friend. You need to as well.'

He shakes his head, as if wishing there were more he could do, then he turns and walks back down the hill.

Still an hour before I'm due at the station. The library in Stanley is in the community centre so I head over there and dig out the archived copies of the *Penguin News*.

Jimmy disappeared in June 1993. I find his story on the front page of that week's issue and take a photocopy.

My attention is caught for a moment by a story about both boys, or more specifically, about the impact their disappearances will have upon the islands. According to Rob Duncan, the author, they'll pop up in our folklore in a few decades' time, as kids who were whisked away by the fairies. And within a year, he claimed, there would be ghostly sightings of them on the islands' beaches.

I remember reading it before, wondering if it hadn't been a bit insensitive, although it had been written in the context of we're all still praying for Jimmy's safe recovery. Rob was right about one thing, though. There really is nothing worse for a community than a missing child. I'm not sure this one will cope with another.

Knowing I can't afford to be distracted, I leaf back through to August 1992 and copy the story about the missing Fred Harper. I put the papers away and take my two photocopies to a table by the window.

Oh no.

I sit down and pull them towards me, hoping the fleeting first impression won't stand up to closer scrutiny.

Jimmy was seven years old and lived with his family in a house in Stanley. Fred was five, from a settlement on West Falkland. There is nothing to suggest the two families knew each other particularly

191

well. They had nothing especially in common. Except that the two boys were alike enough to be brothers.

Dark hair, dark eyes, dark skin, both showed the Spanish influence that colours much of the population here. Both looked a hell of a lot like Catrin's two kids.

No one has argued louder, or with more passion than me, that there is a killer on these islands. No one has claimed more frequently than me that three missing kids, never mind four, goes way beyond coincidence. Finally, the rest of the population is coming round to my way of thinking.

Jesus Christ, what have I done?

Several hours later, I wonder if I've achieved anything at all. To say the police weren't convinced by my story of finding the rabbit on the *Endeavour* is an understatement. They wanted to know why we didn't say anything at the time and, while the discovery of the dead child wiping the rabbit temporarily from our minds makes perfect sense to me, it doesn't seem to impress them in the same way. Neither does my insistence that it was my idea and mine alone to search the wreck in the first place.

I was even shown a copy of my own frigging list. With Catrin's name added. When I tried to argue, they told me that Catrin had been seen, by more than one person, at the Surf Bay swim. She was on the clifftop, apparently, watching the swimmers through binoculars. And while nobody can claim to have seen her at the Sports Day, according to the harbour master's records, her boat was in Port Howard harbour at the time.

By the time they let me go, it's clear they have Catrin and me labelled as a very odd couple and I'm a short spit from being under suspicion myself. Only when I get home do I remember I should have bought food for Queenie. She turns her nose up at the can of tomato soup I open for myself, and isn't impressed by an offer of cornflakes. It's too late to go back into Stanley and my only choice seems to be to get something from Catrin's house.

I can kill two birds with one stone though, collect some clothes and take them to the station in the morning. It will give me an excuse to ask to see her again.

I don't drive. Catrin's house is only four miles from mine across country and I'm ridiculously tense. Nothing calms me like walking, which is odd, if you think of it, given that my first experience of crossing Falkland countryside on foot was one of the shittier episodes in my life.

But there is a world of difference, I've discovered in the intervening years, between crossing a strange land in the dark, wearing soaking-wet kit, heading towards an imminent and violent death and, on the other hand, hiking over moors I've learned to know, under a golden moon, with the scents of the sea mingling with those of the land.

As the sun disappears, just a gleam of silver on the horizon gives me a direction to aim in, but it's enough. In about fifteen minutes I'll hit a narrow river and that will take me more than halfway. At that point, I turn my back on the sunset, if any of it's left then, and tab directly east to Catrin's place.

I make good progress, Queenie trotting along at my side, getting sidetracked now and again by scents and scufflings, but pitching up again when I whistle. The wind starts to pick up as we near the airport and from here I can see the lights of Stanley.

As the white outline of the house above Whalebone Bay comes into view, Queenie knows she's nearly home. She's running ahead as we find a thin, trodden path that takes us down to the garden edge. The night is so dark I can barely make out those bloody fish skeletons, even when we're close. God, the press will have a field day when they see Catrin's house. To anyone who bothers to look, the message is clearly anti-whaling, but a few carefully chosen camera angles and a bit of clever editing will tell a different story. They could easily give the impression she lives in a graveyard, make her out to be some sort of ghoul.

People here rarely lock their houses. I lock mine, but old habits die hard. Catrin never used to, but when I check the back door it doesn't move, so I find the stone planter under the dining-room window and sure enough, the key is in its usual place.

Inside the house, Queenie runs around as though all sorts of stuff has been happening in her absence. She sniffs the floor, the walls, cupboard doors, races upstairs and comes thundering down a minute later. While she does that, I stand in the kitchen, getting my bearings. I've never been in here without Catrin. Without Catrin, it feels like a very different house.

I find Queenie's food in the utility room, load up my rucksack then head upstairs. At the end of the corridor is a room with a white door. Closed.

I've never been in Catrin's bedroom. On the few occasions we met here – usually it was at my house or on the boat – she took me into the spare room. As gestures of loyalty go, it always struck me as too little too late. I'd been inside his wife, for God's sake, it was hardly going to matter if I went in his bed too, but if it was important to Catrin to preserve the distinction then I was happy to go along with it.

I'm strangely nervous, though, as I push open the door and step inside.

The king-size bed is neatly made, a patchwork quilt that looks genuinely old folded over its lower half. The quilt is made from all colours, all fabrics, and looking at it gives me a sense of a couple of generations of Falkland women, sitting in the lamplight, sewing their way around this giant work of art. I see Catrin's grandmother taking a tiny, dark-haired child on a tour of its memories. 'And this is the dress I was wearing when I met your grandfather. Oh look, this lined your pram when you were a baby, do you remember?'

We could have spent years, Catrin and I, huddled beneath that quilt, her telling me the history of every piece of fabric in its making.

The room is L-shaped and I can see round the corner to an office space. Desk, filing cabinet, chair. The bottom drawer of the cabinet is open. A desktop computer has been removed, recently I'd guess, judging from the cables lying around on the desk and floor. A laser printer remains, an old Hewlett Packard model; the cable that would have connected it to the desktop hangs down towards the carpet. Closer, I can see a ring of dust.

Three of the walls are covered in photographs of Ned and Kit, alone, together, with their parents. There are pictures they drew at school, even pages pulled out of medical records. The fourth wall is blank, although I can see drawing-pin holes and Blu Tack.

Queenie starts and races out. I hear her on the stairs then scampering across the hall on the ground floor. I start opening drawers, trying not to be distracted as the scent of Catrin drifts up. I find trousers, a sweater, socks. In her underwear drawer I find things I bought, out of some needy, male compulsion to see her in clothes I'd paid for. It's largely about territory, isn't it, our dealings with women?

Another door leads to a bathroom and I guess she'll need a toothbrush, toothpaste. On the back of the door she's hung her pyjamas and I can't help myself. I lift them to my face and breathe her in. In three years this feels like the closest she's been to me. I close my eyes and can almost believe she's here, right now, in the room with me.

'Hi,' she says.

I jump, let the silky fabric drop, feeling ridiculously guilty. I'm imagining nothing. She's right there, in the doorway. Queenie, at her feet, is in danger of knocking them both off balance, her tail is wagging that hard.

She's shrunk, is my first thought. Her clothes are huge, hanging off her at the shoulder, turned up at the wrist and ankle. Her hair is lank and dull, pulled back from her face. Her eyes look enormous and almost silver in the half-light.

'They told me you had Queenie. Thank you.' She bends to pet the dog, keeping her eyes on me.

'I thought you might need some clothes.' I feel the need to explain why I'm here, in her bedroom, uninvited.

'I do.' She half smiles, looks down at herself, lifts her arms. 'These are Skye's. I'm not sure we're quite the same size.'

'They let you go?'

Her head drops fractionally to one side. 'No, I waited till they were looking the other way and made a run for it.'

'How did you get here?' I haven't heard her car. Mind you, the wind is blowing up a real hooley by this time.

'Broomstick.'

She does this. She loves it when I'm the dumb squaddie and she has all the answers. Then she sees something in my face and takes pity. 'Skye dropped me off.'

'What's happening? Why?'

195

She shrugs, but doesn't move from her place in the doorway. 'The divers finished their search of Port Fitzroy and found nothing. Which means everything they have on me is circumstantial. Bob Stopford decided they don't really have the facilities to keep prisoners over extended periods and, let's be honest, it's not as though I'm going anywhere.'

The turn of events is so sudden I'm struggling to take it in. 'It's over?'

She frowns at me. 'Of course it's not over. The divers will go down again tomorrow. I have to report back to the station tomorrow. Actually, could you give me a lift to the harbour? My car's still there.'

'First thing in the morning I'll be glad to. I walked over.'

She nods and the elephant in the room throws back its head and trumpets so loud I think the roof might come off. She hears it too. 'Anything you want to ask me?'

'Nope.' Elephant or not, I'm not going to say it.

'You're a fool,' she says, but her face has softened. I see her body twitch, as though she is a half impulse from crossing the room to join me, and I know that she has to be the one to make the move.

'Have you seen Rachel?'

It's been three years since I've heard Catrin mention Rachel. I shake my head, assuming she means since the child went missing. 'I've seen her parents. The two older boys. Not Rachel herself.'

'Did they say how she's doing?'

'In shock. Struggling to take it in. Pretty much what you'd expect.'

'Are people looking for him? The way they did for Archie? I couldn't get any sense out of Stopford and his jokers. Have they got searches organized?'

Shit, this is Catrin. Real Catrin, not the ghost I've been chasing for so long that I'd almost forgotten things were ever different. She must be seeing something on my face too. The lines on hers fade. Her cheeks seem to plump out. Is she actually on the verge of smiling at me?

'I have been half out of my mind, worrying about you,' I tell her.

Not a smile, not yet anyway, just perhaps a memory that such things were once possible. 'I've been in custody less than twenty-four hours.'

'I'm talking about the last three years.'

Do it, Catrin. Half a dozen steps towards me, that's all it will take. I actually think she's going to, when the sound of shattering glass cuts through the storm. Downstairs, someone has broken a window.

Then we hear the explosion.

21

C ATRIN'S EYES ARE WIDE WITH SHOCK. 'THAT WAS A GUN. There's someone downstairs with a gun.'

'It was a firework,' I tell her, spinning her around and flicking off the light. Catrin's bedroom is at the back of the house, the sounds we heard came from the front. 'Probably kids messing around,' I add, although I'm less sure about that last bit. 'Wait here.'

I jog downstairs, thankful I didn't turn the lights on earlier, and that Catrin didn't either, because there is a chance that whoever is outside won't know we're here. There is a stone on the kitchen floor and the firework that followed it through the window. Home-made, what we used to call a banger. As kids we'd toss them into the crowd on Bonfire Night. Well, I did, until I got my arse royally tanned by my da. I cross to the back door and turn the key.

Outside, I can hear the revving of engines. Not cars. Quad bikes. They are getting increasingly popular on the islands, especially with the youngsters. You need a licence to drive a car here, but not to ride a quad bike off-road. And quad bikes can go places most cars can't. I've seen kids as young as twelve hurtling around the countryside on four-wheel-drive bikes.

I can see nothing outside, so I head back upstairs, meeting Catrin halfway and dragging her with me. In the small front bedroom that once belonged to Ned – that still looks spookily like the occupied room of an eight-year-old boy – I creep to the window. Catrin follows, resting her chin lightly against my shoulder. The wind has really picked up by this time, buffeting the walls of this old building, whistling around the roof. No wonder we didn't hear the bikes approaching.

'Lot of people out there somewhere,' Catrin whispers in my ear.

There are headlights outside and, from what little I can tell, parked cars stretch some way down the road, effectively blocking it. Not everyone arrived by bike.

'Stay back. Stay behind me,' I tell her.

The security lights below us are on, giving us a temporary advantage. We can see more than the people outside can. The wind has blown away the clouds and the white forms of Catrin's macabre garden ornaments gleam in the artificial light.

'Why couldn't you have gnomes like normal people?' I mutter under my breath.

Then I see the torchlights. I count three, four, six at the front of the house, dotted among the skeletons and weapons. I watch them move closer. Shadows take substance. Movement becomes human form. A lot of people drawing nearer, and something tells me they're not early carol singers. I've not known islanders behave like this before.

I see a light outside, a naked flame, flickering close to the ground. Then something, a rocket, comes hurtling towards the house. It sails harmlessly overhead.

'Look out the back,' I tell Catrin. 'See if they're at the back as well. Don't let them see you.'

Another rocket comes flying towards us. It misses the window, hits the wall and falls harmlessly to the ground. Another may follow it. Another may not miss. If they keep sending fireworks into the house they're going to set it alight. I shake my head to clear it. The *Sir Galahad* in flames. Screams of burning men.

She's back, in the doorway behind me. 'They're at the back of the house. I counted three of them. Who are they?'

Nine torches. At least nine people, but given the number of vehicles, quite possibly more. 'Get me the phone, Cat. Don't switch on any lights.'

There is a loud banging on the door then I see someone step back and look up. A torch is shone upwards but it hits another window first and gives me the chance to get out of sight. Something tells me these guys don't know we're here. They're expecting Catrin to be in custody and there was no vehicle to give away either her or my presence.

So if they don't want us, what do they want?

My question is answered a second later by several of the torches moving away from the house towards the whale skeletons. In a flickering beam I see a hammer being swung and striking the orca skeleton. Glued and nailed together, it's suspended on a plinth, to give the impression of a large mammal moving swiftly and gracefully through the water. The plinth tumbles under the force of the blow and the skeleton hits the ground. Another swing and the tail breaks in two. Another, and a fin is shattered.

Someone else has a spray can and goes to work on the long pointed skull of the blue whale. A third vandal picks up a harpoon and hurls it towards the house. You wouldn't put him in the javelin team but his example is soon copied and spears start to fly in our direction. We hear some of them striking the walls.

Further back, smaller pieces of bone are being thrown over the hedge, to land on the beach, a couple of dozen feet below.

'They're wrecking everything.' Phone in hand, Catrin is wide-eyed with dismay. While the whale graveyard might be deeply unpleasant to some people, certainly to me, it's part of her heritage, part of the islands' history. 'I'm going out,' she announces.

'You're fucking well not.' I grab her with one hand, the phone with the other, and dial 999 with my thumb. While I'm waiting, the entire orca skeleton goes over the cliff and the crowd outside gets to work on the dolphins. Catrin is trembling at my side and I'm not sure how long I'll be able to hold her.

As I'm explaining the situation to the desk sergeant at the police station, people outside start picking up the stray harpoons again and hurling them at the house. I hear another window break.

It will take fifteen, twenty minutes at best, to get a police car out here. With the road outside blocked by vehicles, that time could be doubled.

200

'These people all think I took Peter.' I notice she doesn't say killed Peter.

'It's not just about Peter.' I hate saying this, but she has to realize what she's dealing with here.

'What then? The whales? I know no one liked that, but people here understand it was necessary.'

I push her back closer to the door as fireworks continue to explode outside, as increasingly shrill cries of encouragement accompany the bones and whaling memorabilia going over the clifftop.

'The two boys who went missing before Archie and Peter? The two local boys?'

She stares back at me, scared, not following. 'Jimmy and Fred?'

'People have realized they looked a lot like Ned and Kit. And the first of them vanished not long after the boys died. People aren't thinking straight, Cat. Their kids are disappearing and when people are scared enough, they turn on their own.'

Downstairs, Queenie starts barking. We're out of time. They know we're here.

'Get on the phone again,' I tell her as I head for the stairs. 'Tell the police to get a frigging move on.'

More shouts from outside. Something else hits a window. It doesn't break, but it's only a matter of time.

'You can't go out there.'

'The police will be here in ten minutes. I'll keep them talking.'

She tries to hold me back but I have gravity and a five-stone weight advantage on my side. I tell her to make the call, then wait for me at the back of the house. I stride across the kitchen, my heart hammering in my chest. No one likes to go into a hostile situation blind and I have no idea who's out there or what they have planned. What I do know is that I have to act fast, take them by surprise. I open the door, step into the security light, then close and lock the door behind me. The key goes into my pocket. He'll be a brave bloke who tries to get it from me.

'What do you want, guys?' The question is polite enough. The tone of my voice says don't mess with me. Privately, I'm shitting myself, but if I let them know that, it's all over.

201

A torchlight shines directly into my face. Then another. Fuck's sake!

'We want to talk to your girlfriend. Get her out here.' A woman's voice and I'm pretty certain not an islander. That accent was estuary, not the soft, almost West Country burr that a lot of the locals speak with. I turn my head to one side. If diplomatic negotiations break down, I need to see what's coming. If the police set out straight away, they're ten minutes away at best. For now, I'm on my own.

'Who wants to talk to her? And get that friggin' torch out of my face or I'll ram it up your arse!'

There are jeers from the oncoming line, but the beam falls. I can look directly ahead again. Shapes stand out against the remaining sculptural forms of the whale graveyard. Adults, wrapped up for the weather in thick coats. Hats and scarves partially covering faces. Anonymous. I hear more vehicles approaching but it's too soon for them to be police.

'Anyone here I know or are you all off that cruise ship? Because if you are, you probably want to think twice about getting yourself in trouble with the law here. That ship won't wait while you get bailed.'

Silence. I sense an advantage. 'You'll pay a thousand quid a head for flights home. I doubt your travel insurance will cover that one.'

'Nobody's going to be in trouble with the law.' A bloke steps forward. Big, though not quite my height, and soft around the edges. Not from the cruise ship. I'm pretty certain he's Jimmy Brown's father. 'We just want to talk to her.'

'She's been talking to the police all day. They're dealing with it. Go home.'

A woman comes striding towards me, pushing past the bloke. Then another follows her. I don't know either of them. She comes right up to me. Mid forties, with the coarse skin and lines around the mouth that suggest a drinker. I can smell alcohol. This is trickier. A bloke would be wary of me. A woman less so. She'll tell herself I daren't touch her. She'll be right too, not in front of so many witnesses, especially as I'm pretty certain, at the back of the crowd, keeping a very low profile for now, I can see the gleam of a camera lens. That frigging TV crew have followed this lot out here.

The woman stands inches away, trying to intimidate me with proximity. 'There is a two-year-old kid missing.' She points into my face with a gloved forefinger. 'Four kids missing in three years. Do you even give a shit?'

'Get her out here!' The line of people presses forward again. These are not just visitors. The locals are hanging back but they're here. The Brown family certainly, probably one or two of the Harpers as well. Behind the tarnished skull of the blue whale, I can see the black and white tufts of Bob-Cat's hair.

Still too long before the police get here. These people are scared. Their children are being spirited away and they feel helpless. Fuelled by drink and bolstered by numbers, they've found an outlet for their frustration. There is no way on earth they're getting the key out of me, but more than one window has already been broken. They can get in.

'You want to talk to Catrin?' I look over the woman's head towards a man who I'm pretty certain is Archie West's dad. 'The woman who found your son, by the way. The woman who handed him back to his mother not twenty-four hours ago? Is she the one all this is for?'

He has the grace to look ashamed of himself, but others still feel they have the courage of anonymity. Some kids at the back actually start singing the Queen song, the one about the woman they call the Killer Queen. I hold up both hands.

'OK, you win. I'll get her.'

That surprises them. They stop with the stupid singing but they're drawing closer all the time.

'Give me two minutes. But she's coming out to talk, that's all. She's one woman, who hasn't done anything wrong. She's had a hell of a day and you can treat her with respect.'

Gobby Cow pushes after me as I step back to the door. 'How about I come in with you?' she says.

I lean down, talk directly into her face, so that only she can hear me. 'How about I break your ugly nose?' I straighten up. 'Two minutes.' I call out as I unlock the door and open it. 'And nobody hurts her, or you'll have me to answer to.'

I slip inside and turn the key. Catrin is waiting in the hallway. She looks past me to the back door. 'I'll talk to them. I'm not afraid.'

'Yeah, well I am.' I drag her through the house to where I remember there being a laundry room. Washing machine, wire-framed dryers stacked neatly against the wall. And a large window, directly above the sink, that overlooks a secluded part of the garden.

I had sex with Catrin in this house more than once. Her husband worked less than twenty minutes away. Years ago, I had my escape route all planned out.

'There are people at the back,' she hisses at me, as I open the window and climb on to the sink.

'They'll be round at the front now, waiting for you to come out.' Not without some difficulty – maybe I'm bigger now than I was three years ago – I squeeze myself outside and drop to the ground. I hold out my arms to help her down and she gives me Queenie.

Great.

Keeping the dog tucked under one arm, I help Catrin with the other. The wind will hide any sound she and I make. I just have to hope the dog stays quiet. Once we're all three outside I give myself a second to take stock.

We're in the small fenced area where Catrin keeps her bins. I leave the window open, so they'll know we got out and, hopefully, won't be tempted to trash the house, and then I push open the swing door and peer out. Nobody that I can see and, in any case, I can deal with the odd straggler. I give Queenie to Catrin and then drag them both along a narrow, paved path that leads to the bottom of the garden. Once over the fence we're in open country. We've lost the cloud cover, though, and the quad bikes will follow us easily.

Back at the house the chanting has begun again. I hear a loud knocking and know they're running out of patience, but we've reached the fence. I vault over it, take Queenie and put her down, then lean back to lift Catrin.

A rocket screams overhead, trailing tiny coloured sparks of fire as I pull Catrin forward. In Skye's borrowed clothes she's not exactly dressed for a hike across the moors but we have to get a move on.

Sensing a change in the mood behind us I glance back to see the torches dancing about randomly. Above the wind I can hear shouts of frustration.

'Guess they know we've gone.' At my side, Catrin sounds breathless already. Three years ago, she was fit as a flea. Now, I'm not sure she's going to cope with a four-mile hike in the dark. Still, I've carried heavier weights across Falkland countryside at night.

A torch beam falls on to the ground directly in front of me and there is an answering cry from behind. We've been spotted. I pick up speed again but whatever Catrin's got on her feet, it isn't running shoes. She's struggling to keep up and behind us I can hear the roar of quad-bike engines. This is bad. Back at the house, with the moral high ground, we might have faced them down. Now we've become prey, hunted by a mob, it's an entirely different story.

Options? Hide? Turn and face them? Beat one of them up so badly the rest back off? Making a sudden decision, I switch direction and head for the road.

'They've got cars. We can't get away on the road.'

'We're not going to. We're going to cross it.'

I wait for the protest. For Catrin to realize what's on the other side of the road and tell me I'm insane. We push through gorse and Diddle Dee. There are still some clouds above us and every now and again one gets blown across the moon, effectively cloaking us in darkness. Every time that happens, there's a chance we'll slip out of sight and so I press on as fast as I dare. It's not easy, tabbing across Falkland countryside at night when you're under pressure. There are clumps of tussock, holes and burrows, great stretches of peat bog and even streams and ponds where you least expect them. And rocks, embedded deep in the ground, low but sharp, vicious as man traps.

The bikes are getting closer. When I look back I see the headlights. They're heading straight for us.

Finally, the road. We can move faster, even without light. Mind you, so can the guys chasing us. I turn left, keeping a firm hold on Catrin. We have about forty yards to go but it's uphill and she's breathing heavily.

'You're out of condition.'

'You're out of your mind.'

We've reached the fence. I don't normally enter this particular field at this point, so I haven't prepared it. 'Do you trust me?' I ask.

Over her shoulder, coming up the hill hard on our heels, I can count three headlights.

'Seems the least I can do.'

I grin at her, then drop to the ground and roll. The barbed wire snags at my jacket but I pull free. The ground is soggy, but there isn't time to find a better spot. She follows me and then Queenie scrambles through.

We're in the minefield.

22

I KEEP CLOSE TO THE FENCE UNTIL I CAN GET MY BEARINGS.
There is a bare outcrop of rock a little way north of our current
position and when we reach that, we can head west. A sheep
trail takes us most of the way through. Behind me, Catrin is carrying the dog again.

'Piglet won't set anything off. Put her down.'

Woman clutches dog even tighter. I stop and face them. 'Cat, the
field's full of sheep. They're too light to set mines off and so is she.
Just don't let her chase them or we could all get shot.'

I'm not entirely joking. The minefield is rented by Chase
Wentfield, a local farmer, who takes a zero-tolerance approach to
dogs bothering his livestock. Meanwhile, the headlamps are still
following us and, on the road side of the fence, they can move faster
than we can. We reach the outcrop and I pull out a compass to
double-check. I wouldn't normally, and I'm not sure we can spare
the time, but I sense Catrin is still pretty nervous.

'This way,' I tell her. 'Stay directly behind me. And put that
bloody dog down.'

I set off jogging along the sheep trail. Catrin's so close behind me
she's practically tripping over my heels but that's good. We need to
disappear into the gloom before the headlamps catch up with us or
those daft bastards might be tempted to follow. When I've run
nearly a hundred yards I turn and look back. The headlamps are still

there, shining into the field, but quad bikes can't come in here. So far, no sign of anyone following us on foot. I pull Catrin low and after a few minutes we watch the bikes turn and head back down the hill.

'I love it when a plan comes together,' I tell her.

'Brilliant.' She's still clutching Piglet. 'And losing the odd limb will be a small price to pay.'

When I stand and start walking again she follows me like a baby elephant chasing after its ma. 'Maybe we should spread out a bit,' I tell her. 'Then if I get hit, there's a chance you'll miss the worst of it.'

'Oh, very funny. Are you going to tell me how you do this?'

'Got a map.'

She thinks about this for a second. 'You've got a map? Acres of the islands have been out of bounds for over a decade because nobody wants to get blown up and you've got a bloody map? Have you told anyone?'

'Nobody asked.' I look back. Nothing but darkness behind.

Catrin, too, has stopped moving. I know that look. If Queenie weren't in her arms her hands would be on her hips.

'Of course people know I've got it. Or rather, the military know. The trouble is they can't trust it. I had it off an Argie prisoner at the end of the war. His squadron laid the mines, so he knew exactly where they were. The British government want to do their own sweep and until they can spare the funding, the minefield remains.'

She's looking round. At the bumpy uneven ground, the scattered rocks, the ghostly white shapes in the distance that are probably sheep. 'How many mines are there?'

'A hundred and forty?'

'You're kidding me. And you remember where they all are?'

'God no. I just know this path's safe.'

She takes hold of my hand and looks back. 'They're gone now. They've given up. We can go back to the road.'

It's been a long time since Catrin held my hand. I realize she's shaking and I don't think it's just the fear of being blown up. I unzip my coat and pull it off. Wrapping it round her gives me the excuse to pull her closer, to do something I used to love. I tuck my hands behind her neck and pull her hair free.

She remembers. I see it in her eyes, in the tiny shudder she makes as my fingers touch the back of her neck. 'I can't believe you're coming on to me in the middle of a minefield,' she grumbles.

I want nothing more than to kiss her. Staring down, at the face that is little more than shadows, I have a sense that something is changing. For the first time in years, I feel something akin to hope.

'Come on.' We set off again. After several steps, we're still holding hands.

'All this time, I thought you were playing some twisted game of Russian roulette coming in here. I thought you were seriously disturbed. You could have told me you had a map.'

I had no idea Catrin even knew I came into the minefield. 'You been spying on me?'

'Don't flatter yourself.'

We walk on. Queenie, finally on the ground again, picks up a scent of the sheep and I have to growl a warning. She looks up at me like a wilful kid. I bare my teeth at her.

'Stop bullying her. Hang on a minute. How can you be sure the map's accurate? It only takes one your Argentinian friend forgot to mention and you're gannet food.'

'Actually there's a few he forgot about. I set one off last May. Cracked a couple of ribs when I landed.'

She stops dead. 'Really not funny.'

'Really not kidding.'

I put her out of her misery. 'The Argies weren't very good at laying mines. They dug them too deep, and they completely underestimated the impact of the peat soil.'

As we walk on, I tell her the story of the night, not long after we landed, when we were heading for the Argentine defensive positions at Goose Green. We advanced on the left flank, close to a beach, across an area we were soon to learn that the Argies had mined. One of our company, an eighteen-year-old gobshite from Glasgow, set off an explosion and flew twenty feet into the air. He landed on boggy ground, picked himself up and carried on running

209

forward. Several more mines exploded that night. Not a single one of our lads was harmed. Not by mines, anyway.

'The Argies thought we were fucking supermen.'

I'm smiling at the memory. In the midst of the hell that was the Falkland liberation, you had to find your light relief where you could.

'I've missed your soldier stories.'

I keep walking. I can't answer that. Once I do, the conversation will move on. It won't be the last thing she said to me.

'Callum, what do you think happened to him? Rachel's little boy, I mean.'

Bloody good question. And one we really need to answer. 'We know he wasn't taken by road, because we were on it, so only two possibilities that I can think of. The first is that someone approached the property from the beach and then got him away by boat.'

'Which means he could be anywhere on the islands.'

'The other is they came from camp.'

'And carried him off on foot?'

'Actually, I was thinking quad bike. Or horse.'

She accepts the suggestion immediately. Lots of people on the islands still keep horses for getting around camp. Rachel has a couple herself.

'If any of those is true, there would have been tracks. On the ground around the house if it was a bike or horse, at the top of the beach if it was a boat.'

'There could well have been. But the police didn't look for them because they were focused on you.'

'And the rain's washed them all away.'

'When I was there yesterday the crime-scene team had found a footprint. Or so they thought. A large one. A bloke's. I think they got a print of it before the rain.'

She's silent for a moment, thinking about it. 'I still can't believe it's someone on the islands,' she says. 'Everyone's lived here for years. People don't suddenly turn into paedophiles overnight.'

Over the years, people have often asked me why I came back here after the conflict was over, why I've stayed so long. The truth is, I came for Catrin, even though I didn't know her at the time, and for people like her.

One of the things I love about this woman at my side, about everyone here, is their innocence. This tiny archipelago is like a bubble, isolated from the rest of the world, in which people have the chance to be their very best. Here, the cult of the individual, so common in the Western world, is largely unknown. There is no in-bred sense of entitlement here. No one here talks about 'me time'. Here, life is about graft and sweat, about making the very best life out of a harsh environment and, big difference now, about helping others along the way. This is a community. It's a team.

Margaret Thatcher, who's practically become the patron saint of the islands after her handling of the invasion, talks about society being redundant, of the individual being king. If she truly knew and understood this place, she'd never spout such a load of old bollocks.

Other than the conflict – and even then, the invading Argentinian army behaved pretty well towards the islanders – kelpers have no experience of the worst the human race is capable of. They don't know that it can take years to make a monster.

After half an hour, we reach the end of the minefield and duck under the fence. Catrin is visibly relieved. I'm freezing. We've cut nearly a mile off our journey though and we soon pick up the stream that takes us directly to my house.

'Is this bringing back memories?' She's still struggling to keep up, but that wind is piercing and I can't slow down. At my feet, Queenie seems to be limping along too and I wonder if I'll be carrying them both before the night's out. 'Of, what did you call it, yomping?'

'Lady, wash your mouth out. The Crap Hats yomped. We tabbed.'

'Two words for exactly the same thing.'

'Bollocks,' I say, although technically she's right. Yomping is a Marine term. There was always a healthy 'cap badge' rivalry between the Marines and the Paras. We had a lot of respect for them, but it only went so far. When Stanley was retaken, the bosses wanted the Marines to raise the Union Flag over the islands once more. For symbolic reasons, whatever that meant. As far as we were concerned, the Cabbage Heads had lost it in the first place and there was no way we were giving up ground. We'd been the first battalion ashore, the first to give the Argies a good pasting, and we were bloody determined to be the first into Port Stanley. We were too.

'Tabbing involves heavier packs and an extra couple of miles an hour in speed,' I tell her, and I'm not going to be argued with. 'Boys yomp, real men tab.'

One last fence, a short distance downhill and I can see my house. At my side, Catrin gives a massive sigh. 'Would I be pushing my luck if I said I was hoping for hot water?'

I have a sudden mental picture of Catrin in the tub, her skin glowing pink in the steam, and tell myself to slow down. There's been progress tonight, but still a hell of a long way to go. 'I can probably manage a hot dinner too, although it might be microwaved.'

When she speaks again her voice is quieter, more serious. 'Cal, do you think Rachel thinks I did it?'

I honestly have no idea. I never got to know Rachel particularly well; when we do meet, we stick to social niceties. 'She's known you longer than I have. If I know you didn't do it, she must too.'

'You don't though. And neither does she. You might hope, or even believe, but you don't know.' She's slowed down, is hardly walking forward at all. All very well, but she still has my coat and the night isn't getting any warmer.

'I know you,' I tell her.

'You knew me three years ago. You knew me before. I'm very different now.'

'People don't change that much.' I'm telling her what I need to believe: that in her heart, Catrin is still the same woman. 'No matter what they've been through, deep down they stay the same.'

'I think we both know that's not true.'

Almost home. I know what I'm hoping for and it isn't, particularly, hot water and hot food. I tell myself I must not push her. And then I do the exact opposite. I push her. I stop and face her. We stand together on the narrow path.

'I spoke to Ben last night. He knows about us. Did you tell him?'

Her face clouds over when I mention Ben. I really want her to say that she told him. God knows I begged her to often enough. When you have nothing, small victories mean a lot.

She knows exactly what I want her to say, but she's the woman who never lies. 'It wasn't me. It was Rachel.'

'You told Rachel?' She'd always insisted that Rachel could not know.

She can't meet my eyes. I sense she's reluctant to say this, even now. 'No, I didn't tell her. She found out. She saw us together one time. We were, well, I don't imagine there could have been much doubt about what we were doing.'

I wait for more details. I can't think when Rachel could have seen us. We were pretty careful.

'That's why she was at the house that day, when she left the boys in the car.' Catrin is talking to the ground at our feet now. 'She was nearly an hour earlier than we'd arranged. She went to meet Ben, and she told him about us. My best friend was in my house, break- ing up my marriage, trying to destroy my family, when my sons fell to their death. An accident, a moment's carelessness, I might have forgiven. But not that.'

Shit. I don't know what to ask first. Did Ben tell her this? Why should Rachel want to hurt Catrin so much? Why did none of this come out at the inquest into the boys' deaths? What I ask is the least relevant and most selfish thing I could come up with.

'Were you ever going to tell him?'

I don't get the slap I probably deserve. For a long time I get nothing. Then, 'I was afraid,' she says. 'Ben was just so – depend- able. I loved you so much, but you were a total wild card. I had no idea whether I could rely on you, and I had two children to think about.'

Oh, I'm glad she brought that up. 'Three children. You had three children to think about.'

She backs away, tries to step around me. I reach out, but she's already moved out of reach.

'Was it mine?' I call after her as she strides ahead. I know she isn't going to tell me. Not now anyway. Still, the ball has been played. It's in her court.

We walk on, we're almost home.

213

'Cal, I need to ask you something about computers.'

'Should be within my grasp.' I'm sulking a bit.

'I need to delete some files. If I go into File Management and delete them, are they gone for good or are they still on the hard drive somewhere?'

Ask me something hard. 'Still there. I can delete them properly for you, if it's that important.'

'Can you tell me how to do it?'

As I start to wonder where this is going, we reach the last ridge and are a stone's throw from the house. 'If it's your home computer, though, you might have to wait. It wasn't in your bedroom earlier. It must have been taken in as part of the investigation.'

She stops walking. Just as I see that there are two police cars waiting outside my house. I stop too. When she turns around I don't like what I see on her face. She slips off my coat and hands it to me. 'Thank you,' she tells me. 'Not just for the coat.'

We've been seen. Stopford is getting out of one car with Josh Savidge. Skye is in the other, with two more constables. They start walking towards us.

'Better late than never, I suppose.' I feel the need to act as though this is no big deal. That, of course, given what we left behind at Catrin's house, the police are going to be waiting for us.

'I was wrong,' she says. 'About Ben being the reliable one. You're the one who's been there for me, who never gave up. I'm sorry.'

And there's the smile. It's only there for a second, but it's real. Then it's gone. 'Callum, don't do anything stupid. You can't protect me any more. Don't get yourself in trouble.'

'Cat, this is bullshit. They've probably just come to make sure you're OK.'

'Look after Queenie, please. I think Ben will take her, but until he can get something sorted out. Promise me you'll look after her.'

'There's nothing they can do. They don't have any evidence.'

'Oh, they have enough. More than enough.'

She starts walking forward. I put out a hand to hold her back and she gently brushes it away.

'I'm really sorry, Callum,' she tells me. Then she walks ahead. As the night grows colder, I stay where I am. I watch her meet the police head on. I watch her hold out her hands for the cuffs, I see her listen without arguing as they arrest her again. Then I watch them take her away.

Queenie is seriously upset. Scratching at doors, whining, racing from one side of the house to another. Not sure whether I want to yell at her or join in, I start wandering the rooms myself.

Catrin wanted me to delete something on her computer. No, she wanted me to tell her how to do it. The police have her computer. Whatever it is she didn't want me to see, they've seen. Knowing they'd seen it, she went with them without arguing.

Catrin's computer is a stand-alone model. There'd been no lead that would have connected it to a modem. No modem either. She had no way of sending emails or accessing websites. She'd have used it for admin, for storing information. That means there's no way I can access it directly. To transfer information she'd have needed to save it on to a disk and download to another computer. If that's been done already I can pick it up at the police station.

Within minutes I'm back in the police system but I find nothing. I get up, light a fire, force food down my throat, feed Queenie and try again. Nothing. I keep trying. Finally, an hour before dawn, I find it. Her files have all been downloaded and saved, but one in particular has been opened and read several times in the past few hours. I open it too and find a diary. I had no idea she kept a diary. Maybe when she and I were together she didn't. The first entry is dated a little under three years ago.

In different circumstances, I would not dream of violating Catrin's privacy. But everyone connected with the islands' police force will know the contents of the document in front of me by now. I start reading. I finish as the sun is starting to appear on the eastern horizon.

DAY SIX
Saturday, 5 November

23

THERE MUST BE SOME MECHANISM IN OUR HEADS THAT acts as a kind of filter when really bad things happen. Protecting us from the full force of the blow, it lets the bad news trickle through, drip-feeding, giving us just enough to deal with, before calling a halt and making us take a break. Certainly, in this first hour after reading Catrin's diary I'm struggling to take it all in, to make sense of any of it. For this first hour, I'm numb.

Catrin kept a diary, that much I know. It started out as a record of grief, an expression of wonder that someone could go on living with so much pain. I deal with that, as I wander from room to room, step outside to let the cold air hurt me. Catrin kept a diary, and in it recorded the clear progression from grief to burning rage, then a cold, pitiless determination to get revenge.

In reading Catrin's diary, I have discovered a woman I had no idea existed. A woman whose pain was so great, that she was prepared to become a monster rather than go on living as she was.

I thought nothing, ever again, could shock me to the core. I've seen mates blown apart by grenades on nights when I've been so cold I've been tempted to put my hands on the guts spilling out of their stomachs just to stay warm. I've seen dark-skinned boys running around battlefields looking for their missing arms. I've seen men bigger than me sobbing for their mothers, as they die lonely, freezing deaths on the opposite side of the planet. I thought it was impossible to shock me. How wrong I've been.

The knocking on the door takes me completely by surprise.

She's back. It was all a mistake. The diary was nonsense, a fake, some twisted work of fiction. I race to the door and pull it open. Not Catrin on my doorstep.

Rachel.

24

S HE SMELLS LIKE A BEER MAT IN THE GLOBE A FEW HOURS after the final whistle in the annual soccer match. Mascara smudges under her eyes suggest she hasn't washed or looked at herself in the mirror for days.

'I need to talk to you.' Her eyes don't quite focus on mine.

I step back to let her in, but I'm wary. I can't imagine why Rachel would be here. She and I barely know each other. Catrin talked about her a lot but never wanted the two of us to spend any time together.

'She'll know,' she used to tell me. 'If she sees us together, she'll know immediately.'

'Would that be such a bad thing?' Unlike Catrin, I never wanted to keep our affair secret. I wanted everyone to know. I wanted to shout to the world that she was mine. Christ, I'd have tattooed 'Property of Callum Murray' on her forehead if I could.

'It's not fair to force a confidence on her.' Catrin hadn't even pretended to think about it. 'She and Sander are friends with me and Ben. It would be putting her in a very difficult position.'

So the secret had stayed a secret and Catrin, who shared everything with her best mate, now had something in her life that she couldn't share. Mind you, it's beginning to look like Catrin had more secrets than either of us knew about.

Rachel shudders when she's out of the wind, like a dog putting its fur to rights after a soaking. She's generally considered to be one of the best-looking women on the islands, but I could never see it. Even before worry for her son stripped her face of any life, she was always too bland, too blonde, for my taste. There are dark roots peering through that blonde hair right now, and those famous blue eyes are bloodshot.

'Catrin's been arrested again.' She isn't dressed for the weather. She's wearing riding jodhpurs and a thin, long-sleeved T-shirt. Both look too tight, strained over her flesh and bumpy in the wrong places. Knee-high boots. No coat. 'The police found a diary on her computer. People are saying it's tantamount to a confession, Callum. That she's confessed to killing Peter.'

Christ, does confidentiality mean nothing to these people?

Rachel sees something on my face and takes a nervous step backwards. 'You knew, didn't you? How did you know?'

I don't want this right now. I can't deal with bereaved, hysterical mothers, I'm too close to hysterics myself.

'Catrin was here when the police came for her. A couple of hours ago. Rachel, you should be with your family. Let me drive you home.'

I turn to the door, meaning to open it, to steer her out, and catch a whiff of horse. She must have ridden over.

She steps back again, holding out one hand as if to ward me off. 'I need to read it for myself,' she tells me. 'I won't believe it otherwise. Not Catrin. She wouldn't.'

I think I'd give anything to have that certainty back. That belief in Catrin. Except, I've read the diary. And now this woman wants to as well. I can't let her do that.

'Rachel, there'll be all sorts of rumours flying round the next few days. You should listen to none of them. If there is a diary, it'll come up as part of her trial.'

'That will be months away. I need to know now.'

I'm not budging from the door. Her face blanches, her eyes fill up. 'I'm his mother, Callum. I have to know what's happened to him. I can't stand everyone at the police station knowing the details and me not.'

'Rach.' Without thinking, I use Catrin's name for her. 'I don't know what you think I can do . . .'

222

'You can find it.' She steps forward, reaching out as if to touch me, not quite daring to. 'Her computer's at the police station. Her files will have been copied and you can access them. There is nothing you can't do with computers.'

I start to shake my head.

'I know more about you than you think. I knew about the two of you. I knew from the very beginning. She could never hide anything from me.'

'Rachel, I'm not sure what you mean, but—'

'It was obvious. She physically changed when your name was mentioned. She sat upright, stopped whatever she was doing, so she wouldn't miss a word that was being said. I could practically see her ears flapping.'

'I need to take you home.' I look round for something to pick up, some signal I can make that her time here is up. The woman didn't bring a coat, a bag, anything. Short of opening the door and bundling her out, there's nothing I can do.

'She mentioned you more than she talked about her husband. Any excuse to drop your name into the conversation. I saw her eyes when she looked at you. Catrin didn't know how to keep a secret. She certainly didn't know how to lie. I knew when she'd been with you, and I knew when you hadn't called her for a couple of days.'

No, I can't deal with this, not now. I feel bad for the woman, but my universe has been rocked too. 'You're upset. You need to be with your so— with Chris and Michael. They'll be wondering where you are.'

'I didn't say anything.' She seems to be trying to placate me now. 'I would never have said anything. I was waiting for her to tell me.'

She didn't say anything to Catrin, but she told Catrin's husband? I need to close this down, get her out of here. 'Rachel, there was nothing to tell. You've got this wrong.'

'I know she never loved Ben the way she loved you. I'm not sure she ever really loved him at all, but once you appeared, it was all over for them.'

This woman is way smarter than Catrin. Or maybe just more manipulative. Catrin would never wheedle and flatter her way to what she wanted. She'd ask, straight up. If she didn't get it, she'd argue the case, but it would be clean arguments. Catrin argued like a man. She would never dream of exploiting someone's weakness the way Rachel is doing now. And Rachel is lying. Small lies, but lies all the same. If Catrin was telling me the truth – and I've never known her do otherwise – Rachel caught us in the act.

'I'm phoning your parents.' I stride round her and head for the phone at my desk. Big mistake. She follows me, of course, and Catrin's diary is still open on my PC. All Rachel needs to do is move the mouse and the file will appear. I turn abruptly and put myself in between desk and visitor.

'Rachel, you don't know what you're asking. Whatever Catrin might or might not have written in that diary, it's not going to be stuff you want to read.'

She doesn't back down. No way, I realize, is this woman going to back down. 'Of course it's not. I don't want Bob Stopford to come to my house later today, sit me down and tell me he's very sorry but they've found my son's body. But I know he's going to, because Catrin's diary will have told him where Peter is. I don't want to be avoiding the newspapers six months from now, because all the details of how she killed him will be in there. I don't want to tell Chris and Michael that their baby brother is never coming home. I don't want to meet my husband off the plane later today and tell him I let his baby get killed by a madwoman who used to be my friend, but I'm going to have to do all these things and if I can know for certain, if I can read it in her own words, then it might start to sink in and I can begin to deal with it.'

Oh crap, double crap, a whole fucking lorryload of crap.

'Come and sit down.'

She lets me take her into the sitting room. Queenie, curled up on the rug, opens her eyes and appears to start. She gets up slowly, not taking her eyes off Rachel. I push Rachel into a chair by the fire and pour us both a drink. Then I sit down at her side and look her directly in the eyes. No easy way of doing this.

'Rachel, I'm truly sorry, but I think Peter may be dead.'

She gives a cry, something in between a wail and a scream. Her hands come up towards her mouth and she seems to bite down on something directly in front of her face. I wish I'd never started this, but know I have to see it through.

'I'm sure she didn't hurt him. Or frighten him. She isn't cruel. I'm sure it was all very quick, but it does look as though he's dead. I'm so sorry.'

Rachel closes her eyes, starts rocking backwards and forwards. She'd told herself anything was better than not knowing and now she's discovering that not knowing has a lot to recommend it. Then she looks back at me and shakes her head. 'She wouldn't. I just know it. She wouldn't.'

She's slipping out of focus. I take a deep breath and rub my eyes. Then she's in my arms and I honestly can't say which of us is sobbing. Or which of us is sobbing the hardest. When, minutes later, we're calmer, we find that Queenie has crept into the gap between us.

'You've read the diary already, haven't you?' Rachel whispers.

'You shouldn't read it,' I say. 'You should trust me when I tell you no good will come of you reading it.'

She's pulling herself away from me. 'And yet I have to. Is it on your computer?'

I don't stop her this time. I pick up Queenie, trail after her and the three of us sit down at my desk.

The first two-thirds of it are hard enough to read. They are the private thoughts of a woman barely able to keep functioning, so great was the weight of her grief. Anyone would find them tough. For two people who loved her, both of whom, arguably, were directly responsible for her misery in the first place, they are close to unbearable. Rachel is clinging to my hand before she gets to the bottom of the first page. When she finishes the second, I prise myself free to get kitchen roll. I'm going to need it too.

When I come back, she seems diminished. Outwardly, pretty much the same as I left her, staring directly ahead at the computer screen with eyes that might have forgotten how to blink; inside, though, something essentially human has slipped away.

I sit down, put the kitchen roll between us, and we carry on.

As I read, for the second time, about the ghosts of the little boys

Catrin sees around her house, of the voices she hears calling for her out at sea, I think any half-decent lawyer should be able to pull off an insanity plea. I read about how her husband faded in front of her eyes, how his colours became muted, his voice muffled, as he simply drifted out of her life. I reread her decision to stay on the islands rather than make a new life for herself elsewhere. Here on the Falklands, she tells herself, no one will ever ask her if she has children. No one will ever expect her to be normal.

There is no mention of me. I have ego enough to notice that. It's as though I stopped existing for Catrin the day I didn't save her children.

The passages Rachel needs to see, the words that, when read in any court, will convict her former friend, are towards the end. On 19 October this year, Catrin wrote:

People would tell me to forgive Rachel; that what happened was an accident, nobody's fault, that she is suffering too. They'd say that only through forgiveness can I begin to heal. As though healing were even remotely possible. Or desirable. I cannot bear the thought of a life without my sons. In this half-life left to me, this existence in the shadows, they are still with me. I cannot let them go.

Rachel jumps when she sees her own name on the screen. In the words of the song, she ain't seen nothing yet.

The truth is, I don't hate Rachel, the woman I once knew, because she's no longer that woman for me. She isn't human in my eyes now, any more than I am. She's become an event. A living disaster. A void sucking every last beam of light from around me. She's the reason the world has lost all balance. While she's around, the universe is tilted and those of us on the underside are on the brink of falling straight down into hell.

I'm not looking at the woman beside me any more. I can't.

The piece that I have no doubt will eventually become known as Catrin's confession begins on Tuesday, 1 November, the day after Archie West's abduction.

226

A child has gone missing. I have no interest in who he is or how it happened. I don't care whether he's found tonight or in six months' time when his bones have been picked clean by birds. I have no interest in any living child, but I can't get the sight of his mother out of my head. She was disappearing before my eyes. Folding inwards. Her shock and helplessness were simply beyond her capacity to cope.

I thought she looked like me. All the way home, I was seeing my own face in place of hers. And then, just as I was parking up, I saw her as Rachel.

'Enough?' I ask, more than happy to leave it there.
Rachel shakes her head.

Which would be worse, I wonder – knowing your child is dead, that he died quickly and painlessly, or not knowing where he is, who has him, or how much he might be suffering? How many hours of not knowing, of imagining the very worst possible, can any woman deal with before she loses her grip on reality?

Before she suffers like I am suffering?

Rachel drops her head into her hands and starts to sob again. I give her time. I know better than to suggest again that we stop. 'Three years with this inside her,' she says, eventually. 'Does it get any worse?'
'I'm afraid it does.'
'OK, carry on.'
'Rach—'
'Carry on.'

It was as though someone had switched the lights on, as though everything that had been in shadow was suddenly plain as day. Why couldn't it have been Rachel standing there on the dock, falling apart? Rachel suffering as that poor bitch is doing. Why not Rachel dying inside, right now, instead of curling up on her son's bed, rocking his warm body back to sleep? Why isn't she staring at that bed, cold and empty, wondering where on God's earth he is?

*

As we get closer to the end, there is a picture I can't get out of my head. Catrin, standing pale as stone beside the body of a large pilot whale, his blood spattered across her face, the smoke still rising from the gun in her hand. I see her standing in the exact same way, over the body of a dead child, and know that, thanks to the article in the *Daily Mirror*, the whole world will soon be doing the same.

The last entry is Thursday, 3 November, the day after the whale beaching. Catrin must have written it within hours of handing over little Archie West to his parents. The reunion had had everyone witnessing it in tears. It had left Catrin unmoved.

I've been wondering if I have what it takes to kill. Whether I can look a living creature in the eye and take the one irreversible action that ends a life. Asked and answered, I suppose. I have no difficulty in killing. I'm actually rather good at it.

Today is the anniversary of the boys' deaths. It is three years to the day since Rachel's recklessness ended their lives and mine. Three years since I began plotting how I might redress the balance. For most of that time, I've been thinking about how and when I might kill Rachel. Now, I'm wondering whether that might not be enough. Whether I might actually go one step further.

There is nothing of me left. I have just taken one hundred and seventy-six lives. What's one more?

25

WITHOUT ANY REAL IDEA OF WHERE I'M GOING, OR what I'm going to do when I get there, I head back into town after Rachel rides away. Catrin needs a lawyer. I can call into the firm in Stanley and speak to one of the partners about representing her, in the early stages at least. Later, someone specializing in criminal cases will have to be found and flown from Britain. It will be cripplingly expensive. Fortunately, neither Catrin nor I are particularly short of money.

Apricot-coat lady, now wearing bright scarlet, is doing what I think is called a piece to camera outside the front of the police station, so I carry on past and turn into the private car park behind. I go in through the rear door and find myself in one of the back offices.

Neil, the desk sergeant currently away from his desk, spots me and stands in my way. 'Out. Use the front door like everyone else.'

'The film crew are blocking the way in,' I lie. 'You want to get them shifted or you'll have complaints.'

Muttering, he leaves the room.

'I want to see Catrin,' I tell Skye, the only other person in the room. She shakes her head. 'She's being interviewed.'

'Does she have a lawyer present?'

'She refused one.' Skye leans across the desk and closes the computer file that she and Neil had been looking at. Not before I catch a glimpse of it.

'Does she have an appropriate adult?'

Skye blinks at me.

'Catrin is emotionally very fragile. Probably mentally unbalanced. UK law dictates that she should not be interviewed without the presence of a properly trained appropriate adult.'

It's about 80 per cent bullshit, 10 per cent guesswork. I'm just willing to bet that Skye and her colleagues aren't exactly up to date on the law surrounding the interviewing of vulnerable witnesses. Even so, she isn't easily intimidated. 'I'm sure that's been considered,' she tells me.

'So who is with her? Who is her appropriate adult and what training does he or she have? Skye, the whole bloody world will be watching this case. You can't afford to get anything wrong, not least because I am going to hire the best lawyer in England to defend her.'

'Well, good for you.' Skye looks like a pissed-off teenager.

'You're missing the point. How is it going to look for you and the rest of the woodentops here if she gets off on a technicality because you haven't followed procedure? You'll all need a posting to South bloody Georgia to get away from people here.'

Not easily intimidated, but I get her in the end. Telling me to wait where I am, she leaves the room and her footsteps disappear down the corridor. I step to the computer. She's closed the file, but I pull up the history and the file she was looking at is at the top. It's the footprint found outside the Grimwood house.

With a sense of some relief – if this line of enquiry hasn't been closed, there may be hope for Catrin yet – I open the file and see the image.

Oh, God no.

I actually wonder, for a moment, whether I'm going to black out. I rub my eyes, close them for a second, then try again. It hasn't changed. Still a print I recognize immediately.

The afternoon I chased Catrin up the hill from town, turning around at the Grimwood house and heading back, the afternoon Peter Grimwood disappeared, I have no recollection of getting out of my car. And yet I must have done.

My usual walking boots – the ones that made the print I'm

looking at now, and there's no mistake, I'd know an ex-military boot print anywhere – weren't on my feet when I woke up, soaking wet, the night I had a blackout in camp. I'd changed them earlier that day. For my footprint to be in the mud outside the Grimwood house I would have had to get out of the car that afternoon. When I went back, around twelve hours later to drive Rob home, I was wearing different shoes.

Hearing a noise in the corridor I close the file and step away from the desk.

If I can't remember getting out of the car, what else have I forgotten?

Like flicking back through a video tape I run through the memories of my flashback. Noise, gunfire, screaming. Utter confusion. Terrified young eyes staring into mine. The Argentine boy I killed.

Except these are not brown any more, these eyes staring into mine. These are bright blue, wide with shock, a scream breaking free from small red lips. I walk to the outside wall and lay my forehead against its cool smoothness. Then I bang it, gently at first, but increasingly sharply, as though I'm trying to nudge some memory free.

Blue eyes. Fair hair. A terrified child.

I saw Peter that day. When I followed Catrin up the hill to the Grimwood house, I saw Peter. I feel a need to sit down and know I'm running out of time.

If I saw Peter, he wasn't in Catrin's car. If what I'm remembering now is real, she didn't take him. He wasn't in her car and he wasn't on her boat. She didn't kill him.

A hit-and-run. Another car, after Catrin's, coming along that road too fast. The driver with his mind elsewhere, not concentrating on where he was going. A small kid, escaped from the garden a second time, because if kids find something fun, they do it over and over again. A kid in the road. The daylight gone, taken away by some freaky solar event. A driver unable to stop.

A driver not in his right mind. Panicking when he sees the child is dead. Picking up the tiny body and hiding him away in his vehicle, perhaps wrapping him up in something, before anyone can see. Driving away. Telling no one. Wiping it from his mind, the way he has with so many other memories too dreadful to hold on to.

I'm at the window. I can see my Land Cruiser outside. There is a large lockable box in the back that a former owner used to store his weapons collection when he was on the move. I try to remember if I've looked inside it since the night Peter went missing. Someone is coming. I slip outside again.

There's a black fly on the back panel of the car. Nothing so unusual in that. It's summer, flies often land on hot cars. Is that was this is? Or . . .

I'm five yards away. I look back. The room I left is still empty. Four yards, three. I fish into my pocket and find my keys, before remembering that my car isn't locked. I never lock my car. Neither do I lock that box. I don't keep weapons in it any more. Whatever is in the box is there for anyone to see, has been these last forty-eight hours.

Two yards, one, I'm there. If Catrin didn't kill Peter Grimwood, then . . .

I press the button and open the car's rear door.

PART THREE

Rachel

I would cut off my own arm, rip my face to ribbons, if it were sufficient penance for what I did. I sometimes think there is nothing I would not do, no sacrifice too great, to get Catrin's forgiveness.

DAY ONE
Monday, 31 October

26

THE TIDE IS OUT, AS FAR AS IT WILL GO TODAY. THERE IS just a gleam on the sand to remind me that it was ever here at all and a flickering of light, a movement on the horizon, to suggest that it might come back again. The beach it left behind is wide and gently curving, surrounded by low cliffs. A necklace of driftwood lies inches out of reach of the returning waves, adorning sand that, like a young girl's skin, is smooth and white. Not far from me, a trio of oystercatchers tread rune-like footprints in a pattern that could be entirely random, but might hold the secret to the universe. Something catches their attention and their coral-red beaks turn in unison. They gaze in the exact same direction, as though they are three manifestations of a single soul.

I sit on a guano-stained rock about twenty metres higher than the beach, as I often do when the weather is decent, sometimes when it's not, and look out at a view that never changes, and yet never quite stays the same. Some days I watch surfers. When the surf is up, they appear like creatures from the deep, black and slick, only their faces exposed to the cold. Prone on boards, they paddle furiously, hovering in the spray, waiting for their moment. And then they take flight, soaring into the air, disappearing completely between frothing, turquoise waves, only to pop up again where you least expect them.

No surfers today, just a lone logger duck, leaving a trail behind it like the wake of a speedboat. Vrrrummmmmm. I'm making the sound under my breath, like a toddler playing with a toy car. The oystercatchers regard me, warily, as if I'm a simple soul, but one who might turn around and bite.

Around me and stretching further up the cliff are clumps of dull, grey grass. On a windy day, it will bend and sway, slap the rock like a thousand tiny whips. Today there is no wind and the grass is as still as the stones. I'm still too. I sit and stare at endless ocean until my vision blurs and it feels as though I'm on the very edge of the world.

A cluster of birds takes flight. They are cormorants, I think, their slender arrow-shaped bodies like splinters of glass as they shoot upwards from the beach. Directly ahead of me, the refuge the cormorants are heading for is the great prow of the wrecked ship, the *Sanningham*. It sits motionless, dripping seawater, crumbling with age. It was a supply ship, commissioned in the early years of the twentieth century, one of the first iron and steam vessels to make the long and dangerous run to South America. A few decades ago, it sprang a leak as it battled around Cape Horn and never made it home. When the tide is high only the cabins on deck can be seen above the crashing waves but as the water recedes the hull emerges, its rust stains like dried blood in the right light. I sit here and watch it rotting a little more with every fresh tide.

Years ago, when the boys were much smaller, when my life was very different, Catrin and I and the kids made our way out to the wreck at low tide and climbed up. Enough remained to catch a glimpse of the lives those sailors of old must have led: the narrow decks, treacherous in bad weather; the cramped hammocks, which must have been wet a lot of the time; the low-ceilinged cabins that, even decades after the ship was last used, seemed to stink of sulphur.

Catrin tried to teach the boys about the sea life that was colonizing the wreck, but I was way ahead of her. I'd sneaked out a couple of hours before and hidden fifty gold-wrapped chocolate coins in waterproof packaging. We had the best treasure hunt ever.

The boys loved it, of course, they've been begging me to go back ever since, but it's not somewhere I can let them go alone. At high tide, it's too dangerous, at any time it's quite difficult to get on

238

board. Sander has taken them once or twice. I simply can't bear to.

Instead I look. I sit and stare at the battered, rust-stained relic of better times and I think to myself: it's in better shape than I am.

There is movement at the far corner of the beach. I don't need to turn to see that it's Ralph Larken. Ralph always makes me think of Coleridge.

> *It is an ancient Mariner,*
> *And he stoppeth one of three.*

Except Ralph never stops me. I don't think the two of us have ever exchanged words.

Now that he's retired he wanders the length of the beach twice a day at low tide, looking for driftwood he can use as kindling, crabs left behind by the sea and even carrion: birds, penguins or fish that have been washed up whole. Rumour has it that he and the two women he lives with cook and eat what he finds, which isn't something I've ever wanted to dwell on too much.

Ralph is on the 'blacklist'. A list of known alcoholics to whom the pubs, restaurants and liquor stores are not supposed to sell alcohol. As a system, it works, but erratically. The determined drinkers will usually find a way. Something about his movements today suggests that he might have found a way in the last twelve hours. He's moving like a child's puppet, every step, every swing of the arm stilted and clumsy.

He scrabbles in the sand for a second or two, then stretches up again and seems to see me. We stare at each other, and I'm mouthing words quietly to myself.

> *By thy long grey beard and glittering eye,*
> *Now wherefore stopp'st thou me?*

'Rachel.'

My mother's voice, behind me on the cliff. I expected her later in the day. She's taking the boys out trick-or-treating. She's even made their costumes, including a stuffed pumpkin outfit for the little one. They will be the best-dressed little monsters in town and everyone who sees them will think: *Well, at least they have their grandma.*

The birds are making the most of the tide being out, strutting around, looking for stranded shellfish or over-confident worms. There must be a hundred or more, milling around on the sand and, for a moment, they make me think of worms on a corpse. Every now and again, something startles them. It can't be me, I haven't moved in the best part of an hour, and Roadkill is still too far away. But periodically they take flight, swooping upwards in a sudden storm of noise, feathers and shit. They shit every few seconds, these birds, as though the inside of their bodies is entirely fluid. You notice things like that if you watch for long enough.

'Rachel!' I can't ignore her twice. One time, I can claim the sound of the waves and the birds masked her voice. Twice would be pushing it and I can't fall out with my mum. I get up and turn around, to find she's walked further down the cliff path than she needed to. She'll be annoyed. It's a steep climb back up and if I'd turned around sooner, I'd have saved her a good part of it. She's breathing heavily, even though the downhill climb is easy. Not even steep enough to be hard on the knees. She's making a point. Again.

'We've been trying to get you on the phone for over an hour.' She breathes out a heavy sigh. It is the sigh of exasperation, the sigh of my teenage years. The one I seem to hear all the time these days. 'Where's Peter?'

She steps closer than she needs to, trying to smell alcohol on my breath. She won't. Today has been one of the better days.

There was a time when I felt a sense of dismay as I looked at my mum. I saw her plump body squeezed into clothes that were always a size too tight, the faded blonde of her thinning hair, the loosening around her jawline and I'd think: twenty years' time, that will be me. Now, I think twenty years might be over-optimistic, but find it rather hard to care.

'Peter's asleep,' I tell her. I give her a smile, although they increasingly seem to hurt my face.

She looks at her watch, registers that it's nearly four. 'What if he wakes up and you're down here?'

'He doesn't. He's a very good sleeper.'

'I'd better go and get him.' She sets off and I feel those invisible threads again, the ones that pull me away from the house, that make it so hard for me to go back. I follow her, reluctantly, trying to think of a polite way of asking her why she's here. 'To what do I owe this pleasure?' is the best I can come up with. I smile again, or try to, to take the sting from the words.

'Your father sent me. There's a child missing.' Her voice drops low, as though to thwart eavesdroppers. 'Another one.'

I have a sudden picture in my head of the oystercatchers turning to each other in pretend dismay. *A child missing? Another one? What are these people like?*

'What child? How?' I glance back. The second child to vanish, in recent times anyway, was last seen on the beach directly below us.

'One of the visitors. There's a big panic in town. People are going out searching.' My mother isn't particularly fit. She leads the way up and we go slowly. 'He and his family were fishing over near Estancia. The kids got bored and started playing hide-and-seek. The youngest still hasn't been found.'

'I take it they contacted the police.'

'People have been out looking for a couple of hours.' She stops, her sweater has caught on the gorse. I reach out to free it and she looks back, over my shoulder. 'Ralph's very interested in your boathouse.'

I follow her gaze to see that Ralph is directly below us on the beach, and has moved towards where the old boathouse is tucked against the cliff wall.

'He's welcome to anything he finds.' I give her sweater one last tug. 'There you go.'

We carry on up. Mum's already breathing heavily. She'll make me pay for this at some point. At the top, she pushes open the gate that separates the cliff from the garden. 'Are you sure this catch is safe enough?' she asks me, not for the first time. 'We wouldn't want Peter being able to open it.'

'So what's the plan? For the search, I mean?'

'I think he's gone in your boathouse, you know.' She's peering down at the beach again.

'That door hasn't been opened in years,' I tell her. 'And he isn't anywhere near it. Look, you can just about make him out, in front of the *Sanningham.*'

She sees I'm right and snorts. The dirty brown and grey of Ralph's clothes make him hardly visible against the prow of the old ship. He's getting close to it, his eyes intent on the sand. He must still be crabbing.

At that moment, a freak wave hits the ship. Spray flies high into the air and almost seems to hang there. For a second, maybe longer, I honestly feel as though time has paused. Please, God no. My days drag enough as it is.

'Where's the search meeting?'

'Near the farm. The spot where the family parked. They want you to take Bee. I'll take Peter and pick the boys up.'

Bee, or to give him his full name, Beelzebub, is my horse. An eight-year-old, seventeen-hand gelding from Chilean bloodstock. He's beautiful as the sunrise and has the nature of the devil he's named for. I'd have sold him years ago, but nobody else has ever been able to ride him.

In the old days here, before motorized transport became as sophisticated as it is, long before halfway decent roads were built, people got around by horse. My paternal grandfather, an Englishman, was the general practitioner on the islands. He learned to ride very quickly, visited all his patients on horseback, and the Duncans have owned horses ever since. Even today, huge tracts of land here are pretty much inaccessible by vehicle.

When a search is important enough, we do it on horseback.

We hear Peter complaining when we're halfway across the lawn. He's not distressed, just grumbling, but Mum shoots me a look. She waits for me to pick up my pace before pushing past. 'I'll do it,' she declares.

Makes no difference to me. I head round the back to hitch up the trailer. As soon as I appear, my horse starts kicking his stable door. I find tack and make sure the hay in the net is fresh. He's rubbing his neck against the side of the stall now. Horses can do a lot of damage to themselves that way, but he only ever does it when I'm around. He is a bloody great equine drama queen.

Beside him, a pale grey nose appears. Strawberry, the children's pony, is barely able to see over the door of her stall. I stroke her nose and slip her a mint, earning myself a pissed-off whinny from the horse next door.

'Come on, you grumpy old bugger. We've got work to do.' I flick the bolt on his door. He kicks it open himself and walks out into the yard, his coat gleaming in the sunshine. Officially, Bee would be described as a black horse, but that barely does him justice. I've counted over a dozen different shades in his coat, from deepest black to rich red brown.

'Any of those brats around?' He looks disdainfully for the kids he despises. 'I'm peckish.'

'Grandma's on the premises.' I drop my voice at this point. There are windows open in the house and you never know where she might be lurking. 'Plenty of meat on that ass.'

'Where the fuck are we going now?' I'm leading him to the trailer and he's not that keen. 'We've been out once.'

'Estancia. You like it there.'

'Fuck I do. Blue clay sticks to hooves for weeks.'

These conversations I have with my horse are imaginary, of course, I'm not completely mad. But so often these days, I find I'm spoiling for the fight I can never have in reality. Punching from both corners, sparring with myself in a make-believe skirmish, can sometimes be enough to calm me down. Sometimes.

'Get in there.' I slap him on the rump. He dilates his anus and lets fall three perfectly round, sweet-smelling balls of shit. One rolls on to my foot.

'Thanks,' I mutter.

'Welcome,' he grunts.

'Peter wanted to say goodbye.'

Mum has followed me into the yard. The child, still creased and grumpy from sleep, is balanced on one hip, clinging to her shoulder. He sees us and starts to cry.

'We don't bring him round here. He's scared of Bee.'

About a year ago he was on Sander's shoulders when my delightful horse decided to take a chunk out of him. Sander moved at the right moment, and all the nag managed was a tuft of hair. The child understandably took umbrage.

243

I walk over to say goodbye. He never leans towards me or holds up his arms to be lifted, although I see him do it all the time with Sander and even the boys. His big blue eyes, still damp from sleep, stare up at me with something like curiosity. 'Go with Grandma now,' I tell him. 'See Mike and Chris. I'll come get you later.'

'Ike and Kiss,' he repeats. 'Ike and Kiss.'

'Did you make that appointment?'

'I will, but I'm sure he's fine. Children develop in their own time. He's a bit lazier than the other two, that's all.' Recently, my mother has taken it into her head that my youngest son's speech isn't sufficiently developed for his age. 'Have you got everything you need?'

Lips pursed, Mum nods. 'Your father will meet you there.'

Oh joy, my father's involved too. I wait until Mum's car has disappeared down the road before getting what I need from the house.

'Have a nice time,' trills Strawberry as I climb into the car. Bee gives her the finger, which, in his case, is a desultory flick of both ears.

I'm about to set off when I see the corner of the plain white envelope sticking out of my bag. It was waiting for me this morning, in our box at the post office, sent from someone on the islands. I didn't recognize the handwriting. Neat, rather bold, a bit shaky around the extremities. Maybe someone who doesn't write that much, or who is trying to disguise their hand.

I pull out the single sheet of paper. Plain white, like the envelope. Handwritten, in the same blue biro pen. Four short words.

DON'T LEAVE HIM ALONE

27

I MAKE GOOD TIME OUT OF TOWN BUT HAVE TO SLOW AS I climb into the hills between Stanley and the great sea inlet of Port Salvador. As I drive across the stone run some small, grey birds that have been sheltering among the rocks fly up and, for a few seconds, I am surrounded by them. It's as though the rocks themselves have taken flight.

The stone runs are strange, almost unearthly rock formations. Barely known in other parts of the world, they are common here, snaking across the landscape like rivers. I like to think of them as ancient pathways, built for travellers as distinct from man as we are from the thousands of other creatures we share these islands with. There is a purpose to these stone runs, I'm convinced, a reason why ribbons of boulders should snake across the countryside.

There have been times when I've driven this way and sworn the stone run has come to life, started flowing again as scientists believe it once did. It happens when the light is playing a peculiar trick, when the clouds are low and both the wind and the sun are strong. Then, shadows are cast, millions of small absences of light that race across the ground, and the stones, which are anchored as firmly as any rock could possibly be, seem to slide, tumble, roll on down the hill. Blink hard and they stop. Glance back from the corner of your eye and they resume their crazy, imaginary flow.

A lot of visitors head out this way to see the stone run.

Estancia, too, is popular. The owners of the farm, George and Brenda Barrell, run tours in the summer months, most of them to see the king penguins at Volunteer Point. As I drive over the ridge and head down the other side, I can see most of the inlet ahead of me and so winding and fractured is the coastline around it that sometimes it is impossible to tell where land ends and sea begins. There are days when the sea seems to hold still and the land to be in constant, undulating motion. Not today though. The clear air is exaggerating the colours below me. The blue ocean, white beach, green, grey and yellow hillside. There are stagnant pools too, water that can't quite find its way back to the ocean, and these glow some of the most remarkable colours that nature can produce. Emerald greens, deep azure blues, even shades of violet.

On a dull day, my homeland looks barren and desolate, but when the sky is shining, these islands seem to have been spun from rainbows.

The search party has gathered at Estancia farm, using it for their base. As I get closer I can see several police cars, a couple of trailers, including my father's, and a few four-wheel-drive vehicles. One particular car seems to be the focus for the people milling around. I don't recognize it, so wonder if it's perhaps the hire car of the family concerned. It's a new Land Rover, silver, with black trim.

I park as far away from my father's trailer as possible and get out. Faces turn towards me and look away again. It's been like that for a while now. I'm something of a ghoul on the islands. No one looks at me and doesn't think: *woman who killed two kids.* I wonder if any of them are thinking, *Where's her own kid today? Has she left him alone? Again?*

DON'T LEAVE HIM ALONE

What does it mean anyway, 'Don't leave him alone'? Don't go into another room? Don't step into the garden if he's in the house? Don't exercise the horses unless he's in my sight?

I lean against the side of the car, thinking about it. We have no close neighbours, no one who can possibly know whether I am within touching distance of my youngest son or not. Friends have

246

long since stopped dropping in, especially when Sander is away. Ralph sees me on the beach, but I doubt Ralph can even write.

And yet someone has decided that the shame that fills my head from the second I wake up in the morning isn't enough. Apparently, when it comes to guilt, a woman can never have too much. I lean back into the car and find the note, tucking it firmly into the pocket of my jodhpurs.

Bee starts kicking to be free.

'Shut it for one minute,' I snap.

'Sorry?' The voice does not belong to my horse. I turn and see the policewoman, Skye McNair, hovering at the back of the trailer.

'Hello, Skye. How's it going?' I smile too brightly, inappropriately, given the circumstances, but she answers politely enough.

'Not well. He's been missing for two hours now.'

Closer to the farm, people are mounting up. Six riders that I can see; my father on his huge chestnut mare, trying to take charge.

'What do you want me to do?'

'Your father thinks the mounted searchers should work together. I think the plan is to spread out and make your way directly west. Those on foot will take the other side of the road. He really can't have gone far.'

Someone calls for her. She thanks me for coming and wanders away. In the trailer, the kicking resumes.

'OK, OK.' I lower the door, make a quick guess as to where the horse from Hades is most likely to aim his feet and slip past him.

'Someone's been watching you,' he tells me, as I toss the bridle over his head.

'Bite me.' I ease the bit in at arm's length in case he takes me literally.

'Been hanging round the house. Spying on you.'

'Shut it, will you?'

'Well, someone has to say it. You need to watch your back.'

I lower the saddle. 'Breathe out, Bozo. I'm not stupid.'

Like many horses, Bee puffs his chest out as I fasten the girth so that it's dangerously loose when I mount. On the one occasion I fell off, I swear I heard him laugh out loud.

247

'Bandits at six o'clock,' he tells me now.

From outside the trailer comes the sound of hooves. I take a deeper breath than usual and push my horse backwards into the world of judgement, negativity and point-scoring that is my relationship with my father.

'Afternoon.' I lower the stirrup, double-check the girth and mount. Bee staggers backwards as though I weigh fifteen stone not nine.

'Bad business,' my father tells me, nodding towards the mountains in the west. 'Fog coming in as well. We should have started before now. Afternoon nap, was it?'

I turn Bee and push him towards the other riders, all now mounted. There is no sign of fog that I can see. First thing in the morning, it's common around the water, not at this time of day.

'I thought your engine was missing when you drove down.' Dad is right by my side, stupidly close, given Bee's foul temper. 'When was it last serviced?'

'Sander takes care of that.'

'Along with everything else.'

I wonder how my father might react were I to tell him about the note I received this morning. Declare himself 100 per cent on the side of its author, I imagine.

'Be one of the buggers up at the barracks that's had the kid,' he mutters. 'Every couple of months we get a new lot in, we have no idea who they are or what their history is. I've told Bob Stopford he needs to check who was off duty earlier.'

'I'm sure no one's taken him. He'll just be lost.'

'Oh, excuse me for not seeking your opinion immediately.' My father raises his voice now, eager to drag in others to fight his corner, or witness my humiliation when I'm crushed by the weight of his argument. 'I imagine we can all go home, now Rachel thinks he'll be found in ten minutes.'

Why is he this way with me? Crikey, where would I start? For one thing, unlike 75 per cent of my peers, I didn't come back to the islands immediately after finishing university. God, how proud we are of that statistic: 75 per cent of our young people – our intelligent young people, mind you – come back to the islands at the first opportunity, so great a place is this cluster of rocks in the South Atlantic. By delaying my return, I joined the 25 per cent whose actions are inevitably seen as a personal and cultural rejection.

I told everyone from home who asked that the experience I was getting with an English newspaper would prove invaluable, make me a better reporter, eventually a better editor. That I was sacrificing my own inclinations for the good of the islands. It was a complete lie, of course; I didn't want to come home.

When people in the UK asked me why I stayed, I told them I liked London. I even wrote a piece about it for the paper. I loved the anonymity of the crowds, the sense that anything was possible and that no one from home would ever know; that I could be anyone I wanted, a different person every day, if I chose: demure and ladylike in the morning, all floating tea-dresses and violet-ink fountain-pens; a hard-smoking, hard-swearing Goth in the afternoons, with ripped black leather and white make-up; and in the evenings, I could put on sports clothes and run around the endless London parks. And nobody would say to me: Rachel Duncan, when did you take up running? Rachel, does your mother know you're dressed that way? Good Lord, Rachel, are you off to a fancy-dress party?

You have to come from a small island, in the middle of nowhere, I wrote, to truly value anonymity. That was all a lie too, of course. My real reason for staying away was quite different.

My father, though, took this stamp of independence as an assertion of superiority on my part. By not coming back immediately, I was saying as clearly as possible that I considered myself better than everyone I'd grown up around. In my father's behaviour towards me I see the contempt we reserve for those who try to outgrow us, who want to leave us behind.

Or maybe it's much simpler than that. Maybe he just can't stand to be around the woman I became three years ago.

And I had done an hellish thing.

A hellish thing that I will never be allowed to forget.

'Tally-ho!' I tell him now, heading off on to the moor. He kicks his mare, Primrose, and follows close behind.

The land we cross first is dry and windswept. Bare rocks poke out through thin soil and low-lying shrubs form dense, cushiony mats across the ground. They're soft enough to step on, but create a ground surface so pitted and uneven as to make travelling at any sort of speed impossible. Flowers poke through, though, as if to symbolize the resilience of Falkland spirit.

'Watch where you're going.' I've ridden too close to my father and Bee has aimed a bite at his mare's rear end.

'Sorry. Got my eyes peeled for a small child.' I steer further away, though. I have no desire to spend the rest of the afternoon chatting with my father.

There is a sudden shout over to my left. Something has been found. For a large, finely bred horse, Bee is pretty good on uneven ground and we soon catch up to the next rider, the island counsellor, Sapphire Pirrus.

After the accident, one condition of my avoiding prison time was that I would seek counselling. By the end of the third session, I was starting to think that prison would have been preferable. *How are you feeling today, Rachel? How does that make you feel, Rachel? What did you feel at that moment?* Good God above, how did she think I felt? My world had fallen apart. I could barely close my eyes without seeing the faces of those two dead boys, of hearing their screams as the car fell, and she thought talking about my feelings would help?

During my last session, I told her about the Coleridge poem, the one I'd never much liked, but had learned because I'd thought that Catrin, coming from a long line of mariners, would appreciate. As Sapphire's eyes glazed over, I told her the story of the long, perilous voyage south, about the albatross, something akin to a pet or surrogate child to the sailors, being shot dead by the titular Mariner.

The Mariner's remorse haunts him for the remainder of the story, and, either literally or metaphorically (I was never quite sure), he carries the dead bird, an outward symbol of his spiritual burden, around his neck.

I feel like Coleridge's Ancient Mariner, I told Sapphire. I did a stupid, thoughtless thing and now its consequences are impacting upon everyone around me. I feel as though I've cursed everyone I care about. I feel as though the people of these islands have hung the albatross around my neck, I told her. I feel as though everywhere I go, I carry the stench of a rotting creature with me, that everyone who looks at me sees the blood that still drips. Will always drip. What I didn't tell her was that it is only towards the end of the poem, when the Mariner finally learns to pray, that the albatross falls away.

It's going to take a lot more than a couple of minutes in church to cut the rotting carcass from around my neck.

Sapphire, on the grey gelding that matches her hair and clothes, and I on my mahogany-coated devil, make our way over to the small group to find a man holding up a piece of red fabric. We have already been told that Archie was wearing red.

'May I see it?' I press Bee forward. Sapphire keeps up with me and we approach together.

He gives it up reluctantly. Red check. A large print. A piece of brushed cotton about ten inches by eight, ripped from the bottom of a shirt, with the washing instructions still attached.

'No.' Sapphire shakes her head. 'I know this label. It's a clothing range sold in Stanley. Nothing to do with the little boy.'

People look at me for confirmation. We are the only two women and must naturally be experts on all matters of clothing.

'I recognize the label too. I think this belonged to someone who lives here. And the pattern looks quite faded. I'll keep it though, in case.'

I tuck the fabric into my saddlebag before Dad can get hold of it, because I can see his fingers itching. He suggests we re-form the line and we move on.

'We need to find him soon.' I glance round to see Sapphire is keeping up with me. 'Even if he's dead – and I pray to God he's not – but one way or another we need to find him. Nothing stirs up panic in a community like missing children.'

I think, but don't say, that few communities are fond of dead ones.

'It's our worst, most primeval fear.' I can hear her breathing. She's working hard to keep up with my bigger, fitter horse. 'The possibility that someone could be taking our children. Your father wrote an excellent piece about it about a year ago. Did you see it?'

Not only had I seen the piece in question – a consideration of how communities react to missing children by incorporating their tales into folklore – I'd written it. Dad had argued, probably correctly, that no one wanted to read a piece by me about mishaps to children and so he'd put it in the paper under his own byline. I think in the time since, he's actually convinced himself he wrote it in the first place.

'The little boy was playing,' I say. 'I'm sure he just got lost.'

'Let's hope you're right. But fear changes a community.'

'Watch Bee.' I pull ahead. 'He kicks. He's a nasty piece of work.'

'Look who's talking,' snorts my horse.

We see no sign of the child that afternoon, even though we stay out until the sun sinks below the mountains and the sky around us turns violet. As we near the farm, I edge closer to Tom Barrell, the farmer's youngest son, who is riding on my left. He is talking to Sapphire, who is on his other side.

'I'm not sure I've seen your dad around,' she is saying to him.

'He went out early this afternoon. He doesn't even know.'

'Do you think the little boy fell in the river?'

Tom's face creases, he has a young child himself. Of course, nobody wants to think that the child may have drowned, but given how close we are to water, it has to be a possibility. In spring, after the winter rains and snow, the rivers can be deep and fast.

'Starting to look that way,' he says. 'Tide will probably wash him up overnight or tomorrow.'

I close my eyes, take deep breaths. Ned and Kit didn't drown, their post-mortems made that perfectly clear, but so many times I've taken that sickening plunge with them. Every bad dream, every waking nightmare is the same. So, I know what it's like to feel water all around me, to see nothing but water, feel it hitting my face, forcing its way into my throat. I know what it's like to be lost, in a world of water, not knowing whether I will ever get out. Ned and Kit didn't suffer that, but I do, on a daily basis.

Water, water, everywhere.

No one should have to die in water, especially not a three-year-old child.

We're back. Bee sees his hay net and starts capering. He

skitters over towards it, nearly sending Constable Skye flying.

'Tom, I wanted to ask you something,' she calls up to him. Bee reaches the hay and starts eating before I've even jumped down.

'One of Archie's brothers says he saw another silver Land Rover parked down the road earlier.' Skye is jumping about like a nervous colt, scared of being stood on by one of the horses. 'Did any of you over at the farm notice anything?'

Tom thinks and shakes his head. 'We can't see that spot too well from the house, to be honest. But we do get a lot of people parking there in the summer. Sometimes a dozen cars a week. It's possible.'

'And this second Land Rover wasn't part of the group?' My father has crept up. He invariably has to be at the centre of things.

'Archie's family and friends came in two hire cars,' Skye explains. 'The Land Rover and a red Ford Mondeo. There was another group here when they arrived, in a blue Vauxhall estate, and those people are still here, helping with the search. So, three cars. Now we have the possibility of a fourth.'

Every second vehicle here is a grey or silver Land Rover, I think. The child could be confused.

'We really need to talk to your dad,' Skye tells Tom. 'He could have seen the unaccounted-for vehicle. He could even have seen the child. What time did he go, did you say?'

Leaving them to it, I lead Bee into the trailer, fasten his head collar and step back out to collect his tack. At the bottom of the ramp, I turn and almost bump into a man I know. Medium height, slim build, dark eyes that blink frequently and heavily. Sallow skin. His once dark hair is now sprinkled with silver.

Ben Quinn. Whose sons died at my hands. While we've been out searching, an ambulance has arrived and I guess he came with the medical team.

'Oh. Hello.' He seems as surprised as I am. He can't have recognized my trailer.

There is a moment when neither of us knows what to do. So we simply stare at each other. I must be the last person he wants to be anywhere near, and yet the rules of civilized society demand that, at the very least, he offer a token social pleasantry.

'You OK?' he asks, blinking hard, as though trying to break

253

whatever spell is keeping him within reach of the woman he has probably fantasized about choking to death.

'Good. You?'

What next? Ask him about his family? His seven-month-old baby? I don't get a chance to do anything so stupid, thank God, because he turns away first, half stumbling over a clod of earth. Forgetting the tack, I head back into the trailer. I go in as far as I can and lean, trembling, against my horse's solid front quarter.

Bee shifts, uncomfortably. 'What is it now?'

'Shush, give me a minute.' I let my head fall. Bee's coat is warm and damp with sweat. I can feel his heart beating.

'You are pathetic, you know that?' He tosses his head.

'Yeah, I know.'

Dust makes me want to sneeze, but still I don't move. I stay cuddling my horse, telling myself I need a minute, just a minute, and all the time knowing that a thousand minutes, a million, would never be enough.

Being in the same school year, Catrin and I went to England together, although not to the same university. She was studying marine biology at Plymouth, I'd chosen English and drama at Bristol.

I don't think I'll ever forget the excitement of that first trip. There were five of us heading to academia on the RAF TriStar, including Ben, in his third year at medical school. The older ones slept but Catrin and I stayed awake all night, watching the light fade and reappear unnaturally quickly as we crossed time zones.

We told each other this was simply a new phase in our friendship. We planned to buy travel mats and sleeping bags so that we could sleep on each other's floor at weekends. Catrin's new friends (she'd be selective and particular, she had high standards when it came to the people she allowed into her life) would be my new friends too, and mine (I was planning to spread my net as widely as possible, dip my toe into every river, lake and puddle – *because how else will I know who I really like, Catrin?*) would be hers. In the last months before we left, I seem to remember talking endlessly about the nature of true friendship, of the synergy of two souls growing closer as each individual part gets stronger. Catrin checked railway timetables and worked out how much of our annual grants needed to be set aside for train fares.

'I'd love to see Scotland,' I said, as the plane took off again from its refuelling stop at Ascension Island. I'd been reading Sir Walter Scott and having Rob Roy fantasies about tumble-down castles, tartan-clad warriors and heather-strewn mountains.

'The drama society at Bristol usually takes a couple of shows to the Edinburgh Festival,' I tried again, when she didn't respond.

'Isn't the festival in summer?'

As first years we were expected to fly home for the long summer vacation.

She twisted round in her seat. 'Ben, when's the Edinburgh Festival?'

He was sitting three rows back, with Josh Savidge, who was in his final year studying law at Bath. Ben invariably looked as though he'd just woken up in those days. Maybe it was his heavily lidded eyes, or his habit of blinking rather quickly and forcefully. Maybe he didn't sleep enough.

'August.' He flicked hair from his eyes. The silver that was to claim it hadn't yet staked its hold. It was still black as a Spaniard's. 'Why? You thinking of coming up?'

'Rachel is.'

'Come for Hogmanay. It's mental. We usually have floor space.'

We did go for Hogmanay, the Scottish New Year. Our sleeper train arrived at six thirty on a Tuesday morning and Ben was at the station to meet us. There then followed five days in a city that seemed to be carved from black ice. We were dazzled by Edinburgh, as imposing and as permanent as the mountains around it. Coming from settlements where, if you want your house to stand the test of time, you give it a stronger tin roof, we were in awe of the castle and its surrounding mansions, towers and churches, of the wide colonnades and sweeping steps, the cobbled roads and subterranean bars, of skies that were so like home, above a city that could not have been more different to anything we'd known in the past.

The New Year cold sucked the air from our lungs and tore the skin from our fingertips, but the amber liquor we drank burned all the way to our toes. For five days, we barely stopped to rest. I don't think we spent an hour sober. We didn't both sleep on the floor, though, not after the first night. That was the trip when Ben and Catrin got together.

Leaving my snorting, stamping horse I creep to the rear of the trailer and look out. Ben is over by the ambulance, talking to the paramedic who drove it here.

The people we love fall into two distinct camps, it seems to me. First, those whom we are obliged to care for, connected to us through ties of blood and, occasionally, other people's marriages. Then there are those few souls who suit us so perfectly that we cannot help but love them. Those whose very presence seems to lift our spirits, soothe our ruffled feathers, tilt the disturbed world so that its axis is true again.

In all my life, there have been only two people I've loved in that way. Two people whom I simply couldn't help but love. My best friend and soulmate, Catrin, of course.

And the man she married.

28

THE FIVE DAYS IN EDINBURGH BECAME FIVE NIGHTS OF physical and emotional torture. Alone in my sleeping bag on a greasy living-room carpet, I dreamed of Ben's hands on me, of the warmth when our skin touched, of the soft tracing of his fingers, just as Catrin was experiencing those things for real only a few yards away. I told myself it wouldn't last, that one day he'd be free again and next time he'd choose more wisely, but it did last. It lasted all the way through the three years of university, and by the final term she was wearing his diamond.

When she went home to work for the Conservation and plan her wedding, I simply couldn't follow. I didn't go back until the big event, over a year later, when I cried the whole day. Luckily, everyone assumed it was sentiment. I've always cried easily. After that, I decided I might as well stay. It wasn't as though things could get any worse.

Besides, there was a new young man on the islands, a Dutchman called Sander who'd come over to work in the Secretariat. He obviously had a thing for girls with damp blue eyes because he barely left my side the day of the wedding. I've wondered, occasionally, if he knew that those were real tears and that, beneath the pale gold satin, my heart was shredded. If he did, he's never once let on.

Thinking of Sander has calmed me somewhat. It usually does. I don't love him – I'm not sure I ever did – but I'm a better, stronger person when he's around.

I gather up the rest of the tack, listen to a half-formed plan to meet in the morning – if we have to – and then we all head back towards Stanley. Desperate not to see Ben again, I'm the last to leave apart from the police cars and the family's vehicles.

A few yards before the road crosses the stone run I spot an old green Range Rover coming in the other direction. It pulls over to let me pass. I raise my hand in thanks and George Barrell, back from his errand, raises his in return.

By this time, I seem to be alone on the road and realize it's getting quite close to Peter's bedtime.

Something has been digging into my bum and I remember I still have the anonymous note in my pocket. A note that I know I should report to someone, if only to Sander. And yet, I cannot tell anyone about it without admitting that, for large chunks of the day, I do leave my youngest son alone. He goes for a nap, and I head for my rock above the beach, or take one of the pills my GP prescribes for when I'm having a rough time sleeping. Often, he wakes before I do, or before I get back from the beach, but he can't climb out of his cot. He's perfectly safe.

I'm nearing the point where the road out of Stanley forks, the left arm heading towards Darwin, Goose Green and the airport, and the right (the one I'm driving back along now) towards Estancia. Another vehicle is heading for me from the west, travelling faster than I am, as though determined to reach the fork first. I brake, let the pale-coloured Land Rover get ahead, but not before I catch the final three registration letters, SNR, which makes me think of the stone run.

Halloween is in full swing as I drive through Stanley. I pass groups of tiny witches, miniature devils and half-pint skeletons, all carefully supervised by attending parents. Older, bigger children are out too, their masks altogether darker, more threatening. A zombie lurches across the road in front of my car, forcing me to stall.

Before I can restart the engine, I see that some of the adults are getting into the spirit as well. Mel, the chef from the Globe, struts down the street in the costume of a pantomime dame. He sees me and stops, one hand on his purple-silk-clad hip, the other pushing a Carmen Miranda hat more firmly on to his head. 'How do I look, darling?'

Mel is one of the few people on the islands who is genuinely nice to me. So I look him up and down and try to smile. 'There is nothing like a dame,' I tell him.

He pretends to rearrange his crotch. 'And I'm nothing like a dame.' He winks before tottering off along the street.

I find the boys at home, up and playing with their grandmother, even though it's long past the youngest's bedtime. She's found some old cardboard boxes and built a series of tunnels and caves in the living room. There is no sign of any of them as I walk quietly in through the back door, but I can see boxes shaking and hear the scuffling sounds of small people scurrying along inside.

'Mwa, ha, ha, ha!' Grandma sounds even more like a goblin than usual. She emerges from one end of the cardboard city and looks abashed when she sees me in the doorway. Crawling out, she gets awkwardly to her feet.

'Is your father with you?' She brushes the cardboard dust off her clothes.

'I think he went straight to the newsroom. They're planning to stay on air for longer tonight.' All scuffling has stopped. Chris appears to grin at me, then Michael. Finally the little one stands up. He ignores me. 'Ganny chase us!'

All three boys are in their pyjamas. I can smell shampoo and biscuits.

'Any luck?' my mother mouths at me. I shake my head.

'Did you find him?' Chris misses nothing. Michael comes over and wraps his arms around my waist. He has always been a very cuddly child. Peter sees my arms around his older brother and, predictably, gets jealous. He runs over, holding up both hands to be lifted. He's looking at Michael, not me, but I pick him up.

'How about some hot chocolate?' Grandma suggests.

In the kitchen, dishes are washed and away in cupboards. The table is clear of clutter. The worktops shine. I try to see it as it was meant, as a kindness, but the very sparkle on the taps seems to be telling me I'm a failure.

'What will happen to him?' Chris asks, as we sit down.

'I'm sure he'll be fine,' I say. 'He'll be cold and a bit frightened, but there's no real harm can come to him. The weather forecast is good tonight. Do you want to take Peter, so I can help Grandma?' I hand the small boy over to the bigger one.

'Will he die?' asks Michael.

'Of course not. How could he die? Pecked to death by a penguin?'

Quick as a flash, Michael becomes a penguin, arms stiff by his sides, hands sticking out at right angles, mouth pursed like a beak. He starts pecking away at his little brother, who naturally decides it's the best game ever.

'Sam Welsh's mum says he'll die of exposition,' says Chris.

'Exposure, and that's very unlikely. Lots of people sleep outside in the summer.'

'More,' demands Peter.

'In tents. In sleeping bags.' Chris still looks troubled.

'I'm not saying he won't be uncomfortable, just that a night out of doors won't do any permanent damage.' I can tell no one is fooled by my determination to look on the bright side.

'We blew out the pumpkin candles,' says Michael. 'So that if he comes near here he won't be frightened.'

'I said they should.' My mum won't let an eight-year-old take the praise that is her due. 'I expect his parents were there,' she says, in a low voice, as though Chris and even Michael aren't hanging on to every word. 'You never know what you have till you lose it.' Mum puts two mugs and a covered plastic cup down on the table. 'Goodness, what that poor mother must be going through. Oh, did you want some, Rachel?'

'I'm fine,' I say, although I've eaten nothing since lunch.

Mum helps me tuck the boys into their respective beds and then I walk her out to her car.

'Do the police think there's any connection?' she asks me as she opens the door, and I press into the hedge to avoid the wind. 'With the other two?'

'No one's said anything.' Except my father, I think. He's determined to see a conspiracy.

'All three vanished from near water.' She lowers her ample frame into the driver's seat and looks up at me. 'Maybe we have to be thinking about people with boats.'

Half the people who live here have boats and she knows it. 'I'm sure we'll find him tomorrow. Goodnight, Mum.' I bend to peck her on the cheek and pretend not to notice when she half flinches away from me. 'Thanks for all your help.'

She snorts and drives away before I have the chance to step clear. She doesn't drive over my foot but it's a close-run thing.

An hour or so later, a startled cry rouses me. I wait for a few minutes; there is always a night light in the little one's room and he's pretty good at settling himself. Not tonight, though. He starts crying in earnest and I know he'll wake the others.

A flicker of light outside the house catches my attention as I'm making my way down the corridor. I step closer to the window, knowing it's unlikely I'll be seen from outside.

There is a vehicle in the road. One I know immediately, even if I didn't recognize the pale-faced, dark-haired woman in the driver's seat. Once again, Catrin is parked outside my house at night, looking up at my youngest son's bedroom.

I lock the door as I leave the house, which I almost never do, but the missing child, not to mention my anonymous correspondent, is bothering me. The wind that has been absent for much of the day has picked up now, forcing the buildings to creak and groan in protest.

Unusually, also, I left a note on the kitchen table for Chris. I've never known him wake and come down in the night, but this doesn't feel like a normal night.

Gone to check on the horses, I'd written. *Back soon.*

'Oh, you are kidding me,' moans my horse.

'Come on, you lazy bastard. Earn your keep for a change.'

I have him saddled in a matter of moments and then I lead him out of the yard along a strip of grass that effectively muffles sound.

Catrin's house is several miles away by road, but across country I can get there in a little over half an hour. We've been playing this game for a while now. She drives past my house at night, sometimes stopping for minutes at a time. I ride over to hers. I seem to know when she's out there and I can't help thinking she knows when I'm close too. Yet we do nothing. One night, maybe tonight, one of us will do something to break this deadlock.

And maybe, if we do, maybe I can start to find myself again. To pull myself, *with penance done*, from the depths in which I've been floundering.

For over twenty years, most of our lives, Catrin was the other half of me. Even when I was sick with jealousy that she had Ben, I still needed her in my life. Now, years after we last spoke, I am lost without her. I would cut off my own arm, rip my face to ribbons, if it were sufficient penance for what I did. I sometimes think there is nothing I would not do, no sacrifice too great, to get Catrin's forgiveness.

To wash away the albatross's blood.

The islands are transformed by the setting of the sun. As the colours fade to monochrome, as the fine contours of the landscape melt into shadow, so the sounds and scents and textures of the land wake up. People who live in the populated parts of the world talk about the quiet, the stillness, of night. Here, when the sparse population goes to its rest, the opposite happens. Here, night-time means an endless cacophony of noise. The nesting birds that Bee and I ride past chuckle and gossip, in a constant, squabbling carpet of sound. Overhead, avian teenagers carouse in high-pitched revelry, drunk on flight and freedom. Hawks sing, penguins on the nearby shore bray at the howling of the wind, while the clifftop albatross colony might be discussing politics, so varied and intelligent seem their conversations. Beneath it all is the endless grumble and roar of the ocean.

I leave the track, heading out across open countryside, knowing from the sweetness around me that I am travelling through gorse. When we reach the peat, the smell will become one of dank, rotting vegetation. The wind has gained in strength, irritating Bee, but we soon arrive at the point where I can turn him, and now the wind is behind us, urging us on.

Halfway, I almost turn and go home. I have left all three of my boys alone. If someone has been watching me, maybe they saw me leave the house.

'Maybe they're there now, sneaking around, looking for a way in.'

Trust my horse to make a helpful contribution to any internal debate. And it's a ridiculous idea. No harm can come to sleeping children here. I tell him so.

'Archie West's parents left him alone.'

'Archie is lost. He wandered away. That's as sinister as it gets.'

'You keep telling yourself that, love.'

'We go home when I say so. Now shut it.'

There is light in Catrin's bedroom. I see it when I'm still over half a mile away. It's not so unusual, though, for Catrin to be awake late. She takes her boat out at night, anchoring in some isolated bay. Maybe she, too, has trouble sleeping.

The last stretch takes me along the road, although I keep to the verge to muffle the sound of Bee's hooves. I can see the upper storey of the house, the tips of the skeletons, but the gorse hedge that grows around the garden screens most of it from view. I get down and in a sheltered spot behind a rocky outcrop I tie up Bee.

There is a weak point in the hedge. It's uncomfortable, pushing through thorns, but I've done it before. Head down, I squeeze myself in tight and I'm soon through. The light I saw from a distance is still shining. As I step closer to the house, I think I'm half willing her to look out and see me, or for Queenie to sense my presence and start barking.

A short distance away, Bee snickers and a second later, I hear a soft, low, human sound. A grunt of effort, a fraction more than a sigh. Someone is coming. I slip back into the hedge and wait.

A tall man strides to the gate and steps over it. He stands on the edge of the garden looking around.

'Hello?'

I recognize the accent immediately, if not the voice it belongs to. This is a Scotsman. Coupled with the man's height and breadth, it can only be Callum Murray.

Who seems to see me, to be looking directly at me as he crosses the garden to the point where I'm hiding. I shrink back further, but know I can't get away without making a sound. I'm saved by the fact that he doesn't know this garden as well as I do and doesn't see the stack of harpoons. His foot catches one. Thrown off balance, it falls and dislodges the others; they clatter to the grass.

I take advantage of his distraction to get further into the hedge, but as I'm about to turn and go, the back door of the house opens.

'Bit late for trick-or-treat.' Catrin is in the doorway, barely visible against the darkened room. Callum mutters something about thinking he'd seen her in the garden. As he steps closer their voices are masked by the wind, and I can no longer hear what they are saying. The voice in my head, though, is loud and clear. Catrin and Callum are together again.

Three years ago, I'd known there was something Catrin wasn't telling me. I'd known for months. She'd changed. Her time was suddenly much more limited, for one thing. And she'd lost that openness, that willingness to share everything that was going on in her life. I knew she was holding something back. I toyed with the idea that she and Ben might be having problems, but deep down I knew it wasn't that. There was no sense of unhappiness coming from her. Then, one day, I rode Bee up here without telling her I was coming. I tied him up, in the exact spot he's tied now, approached the door and heard her voice from round the back of the house. I made my way round and stopped at the corner.

At the rear of Catrin's house, the side that faces the sea, is a suntrap. When the wind is light, and the sky clear, it forms a small patch of bright warmth. It was late spring, and this was a hot day by Falkland standards.

Catrin was lying naked on a cluster of scatter cushions with a man, also naked, whom I knew instantly wasn't Ben. The broad shoulders reaching over her were fair and overly muscled, his legs so much longer than those of her husband. The tension in her body, the way her toes curled and pointed, her fingers clutching his shoulders, told me they were about to make love. Then he raised his head and I recognized the sandy hair.

I fled the scene, wondering how I'd keep a secret so immense, so important. It was beyond belief – for me anyway – that a woman whom Ben came home to every night could even think of looking elsewhere. At the same time it made perfect sense, and Catrin's barely concealed interest in the Scotsman who'd fought in the conflict became entirely understandable.

What I felt that day, when I got over the shock, was nothing less than joy. Catrin had met someone else. I knew her well enough to be sure she wouldn't be having an affair with a man she didn't care for. Catrin had fallen in love with another man. Ben could be free again. Free to be with me. It would be complicated, of course, and I would feel bad about taking the boys from their father, but we could work something out. Suddenly, my life was full of possibilities. For the first time in years, there was hope of happiness, not just consolation. Something more than solace.

I'm feeling something of that now, as I lead Bee away. Catrin is seeing Callum again. If he's back in her life, is it a sign that she's recovering? If she can find happiness again, maybe she can find a way to let me back in too.

DAY TWO
Tuesday, 1 November

29

THE SEARCH FOR ARCHIE CONTINUES THE NEXT DAY. ALL morning, the horsemen of the apocalypse, as my father insists on calling us, patrol the beaches, looking for the sand-smeared remains, the tiny shoe poking out from behind rocks. Others, including Catrin and Callum, fine-tooth-comb the hills. As noon approaches, optimism is becoming an effort. If the child did nothing more than wander off, he would have been found by now. If he died on the moor, he would have been found.

There remain two possibilities. The first, that he fell into the river and was swept downstream and out to sea. In which case, if the tide hasn't brought him up already, it is unlikely to do so. We may never find him.

The other possibility, over which opinion is sharply divided, is that someone may have taken him. No islander, other than my father, will admit openly that this is a possibility but the visitors are thinking it. The military are thinking it. Everywhere I look I see an undercurrent of concern building in strength. People are openly dissatisfied. They are starting to take sides.

I have to leave the search at midday. Mum, who had Peter all morning, has a hospital appointment, and it's one of my days for picking the boys up from school. I collect my youngest and, not being able to face even an hour at home alone with him, I head into Stanley.

There are more people in town than we would ever normally see. A lot of them are service personnel, in town to help with the search. Others are coming off the *Princess Royal*. Nothing new in that, of course, but visitors typically come ashore for a few hours at a time, to watch wildlife, travel to the less accessible beaches. They don't hang around in Stanley. This lot, though, seem drawn to trouble the way flies are to rotting meat.

It's not as though any of them can know Archie's family, because the Wests came here independently, not on the cruise ship. These people with their big hair, their bright man-made fabrics and their gleaming white trainers are here for the drama. They are here to inhale the stench of our trouble.

I collect a bundle of post, tucking it into my bag without looking properly. In the store, I see Roadkill Ralph buying roll-up paper and tobacco. He nods to me and seems about to say something, but the woman at the counter speaks to him and he turns away.

When I've got everything I need, I still have an hour before school finishes, so I head to Bob-Cat's Diner for coffee. The swing door is heavy, difficult to manoeuvre with a buggy, so I'm not really concentrating on who's inside.

'Bang, bang, bang!' A child's voice. My child.

Something shatters on the stone-tiled floor as the door slams shut. Behind the counter, Bob-Cat curses. Everyone else in the room has fallen silent.

Callum, standing between the counter and the door, is staring down in horror at my son, at the gun in his hand. The remains of a coffee mug are scattered across the floor. My child bursts into ugly loud sobs.

'For God's sake, mate, it's a kid's pop-gun, what's with you?' Bob-Cat is seriously pissed off about the broken mug and spilled coffee.

Callum is still staring and there is a light in his eyes that I don't like, certainly don't recognize. I pull the buggy back as Bob-Cat leans across the counter and tugs at Callum's shoulder. It does the trick. He shakes his head, as though to clear it, then looks down at the mess on the floor.

'Shit, I'm sorry.' He bends down, starts to gather up the broken pieces, then stops. 'Rachel, I think the coffee caught him. I think he's burned.'

Suddenly, everyone in the diner is an expert on first aid, determined to make a massive fuss of the child, who stops wailing once he realizes he's the centre of attention. There is a pink mark on his left shin and coffee stains on his sock, but we strip it off, wrap cold, wet cloth around his leg, and in a minute or two there isn't a mark to be seen.

While the rest of us are seeing to Peter, Callum clears up the mess and offers to pay for the mug. Bob-Cat takes him at his word and charges him enough to buy a set of bone china.

'It was my fault,' I say, when some semblance of peace is restored. 'I didn't realize he had that with him. It's his brother's. It must have been tucked away at the bottom of the buggy.'

'No harm done.' Callum has also insisted on paying for my coffee and my son's milkshake. I'd intended to head for an empty table at the back of the room but that seems rude now. Besides, Callum and Catrin? I take a stool beside him at the counter. The child complains, predictably enough, so I unfasten his reins and lift him on to my lap. He tries to climb off, on to the counter, but is distracted by a biscuit.

'No luck this afternoon?' I ask.

Callum lowers his voice. 'Stopford's a fool. He won't accept any possibility other than the kid wandering off. So he's keeping the search in one area only. No one's looking anywhere else.'

I think about this for a second. About the sheer size of the islands. 'Yeah, but fair play, where would he start?'

'There's been no real attempt to find this other Land Rover the kid's brother saw.'

Behind us, the door opens and a smell of frying food, seaweed and diesel fumes blows in, as though we are at the end of a wind tunnel leading directly to the harbour. When I turn, I see Roadkill Ralph, his nicotine-stained fingers clutching a half-smoked roll-up.

'Them boys o' yourn been playing on the wreck?'

It takes me a second to get over my surprise that Ralph has actually spoken. 'I don't think so. They know they're not allowed to go out there by themselves.'

He nods and sucks on the thin, straggling cigarette, before turning and leaving the diner.

'Must get him and the girls round for dinner some time.' Callum's face is completely deadpan and in that moment I see exactly what Catrin saw in him. Sees in him? I am amazed to find myself laughing. A second later, he joins in.

I stay too long in the diner, too long chatting to Callum about nothing, when all I really want to say is, how is Catrin? Will she talk to me, do you think? And by the way, I know I never thanked you for what you did that day. I know you went into the water looking for me, for my sons, that you risked your life to save ours, but that was the day when her sons died, when I became the monster that nobody can quite bring themselves to look in the eye, and we can't talk about that, can we? Not ever?

He leaves first. I follow more slowly and push the buggy up the hill to my car. I must be more distracted than usual because I actually get in the wrong one. It's easy enough, no one locks their vehicles here and we have a lot of light-coloured Land Rovers. I open the rear door and think that someone has stolen the child's seat. Then I see the cardboard box of bacon labels, register that my car has never been this filthy, this covered in sand, and realize I've opened Bob-Cat's by mistake. Embarrassed, I climb out and look around, but no one seems to have spotted me, so I take hold of the buggy and slink a few yards further up the hill to my own car.

When I get home with the boys, I look at the post for the first time. There is another white, hand-addressed envelope. Local postmark.

Even though I can hear them playing, I nevertheless have to go into the room and do a head count. Big boy, middle boy, little boy, all present and correct, engrossed in building a Death Star from Lego. I want to throw the envelope away but can't bring myself to.

I open it. Same as before. Almost.

DON'T LEAVE HIM ALONE. LAST WARNING.

*

I don't sleep much. Every hour, it seems, I get up, check the locks, pull the curtains a little closer and peer in at the boys. Each time I do, I work out the time where Sander is. I surprise myself by how much I want him home. I surprise myself by how afraid I am.

On my third bedroom round I see the fires. A dozen or more, stretching up the hillside, dancing in the wind. Beacons for little Archie West. All over the island, people are camping out, keeping vigil, so the child won't be entirely alone. It is well meant, I know, but I wish they hadn't, because the picture up on the hillside seems the living embodiment of verses I can't get out of my head.

About, about, in reel and rout
The death-fires danced at night

Each small flame looks to me like a funeral pyre.

DAY THREE
Wednesday, 2 November

30

Two nights now, Archie West has been missing, and everywhere I go there are reminders of what Sapphire said to me that first day of the search. Fear changes a community. It's certainly changing this one. As I drive the boys to school, I pass four cars whose drivers don't wave at me. It's what we do here, when we pass someone on the road, we raise our hand in greeting. Visitors find it funny, think we must constantly be lifting our hands from the wheel, but when there are so few of us, it's a courtesy we wouldn't think of letting go. Today, even though I know the cars, I don't get the familiar sign of recognition. And then I realize I'm not doing it either. We are all preoccupied. We are all thinking about the dead child. Not missing child, any more, although that's what we still say when we mention him aloud. In our heads he's become the dead child.

Another dead child. What is wrong with us? Why can't we keep our children safe?

Two men are arguing outside the post office as I drive past. I don't know them, nor the crowd that watch them at a distance. Someone lurches into the road and I brake sharply. The man, plump and middle-aged, sees the boys in the car and leers closer for a better look. He spots the youngest in the back and his eyes widen. I press my foot down. On the drive home, I decide, I'll lock the car doors.

I hold Chris and Michael close when I say goodbye at the school gates and, around me, see other parents doing the same thing. There are more mothers here than usual. Normally, even primary school children walk to school by themselves. Their mothers wave them off at the door, happy for them to journey a couple of short, quiet streets. Not today. Mr Savidge seems to be counting them in, reassuring himself that each one of his charges is safe so far.

'I can't take my eyes off them,' says one mother. Not to me. They rarely talk to me, but they are close enough for me to catch snippets of their conversation.

We all wait, until the last child is safely inside and the doors slam shut. I wonder how many of us will come back at break-time, just to be sure they're still safe.

I push the buggy to the shops, as I often do. My life has become one long exercise in killing time. There are too many soldiers on the streets. They are here to make us feel safe, but today they seem to be a reminder of how we've failed. How we continue to fail.

'A bunch of bloody whales! They're all heading over to some back-of-beyond island to save a bunch of bloody whales. What's wrong with these people?'

'Especially after last night, you'd think missing kids would take priority.'

I slow down. I'm back at the group of visitors I saw arguing earlier. I think one of them is Archie West's father. The others I'm not sure about.

'Phone the papers. Get the number for the *Daily Mirror*.'

'It's bloody disgraceful, your little lad's still out there.'

Discreetly, I change direction and head to the offices of the *Penguin News*. With no particular desire to see my father, if there are calls from British newspapers in the offing, he needs a heads-up.

As I enter the hallway I hear his voice coming over the airways, which means the red light will be on above the studio door and he won't be receptive to interruptions. I can leave a message though. My grandmother pounces on Peter and releases him from the buggy.

'It's getting ugly out there,' I say to Cathy, an old friend of ours who works with Dad and who brings the boys home from school a couple of days a week.

278

She knows I'm not talking about the weather. 'Tell me about it. Phones have been going off the hook. Like we know anything.'

As if on cue, one of the desk phones starts ringing. Cathy leans across, activates the answering machine and holds up a finger for silence. The music fades and I realize my father is interviewing Chief Superintendent Stopford.

We all listen, my son being so quiet I feel sure Grandma Mabel is slipping him Polo mints. She never misses a chance to sneak them to my children or my horses. Apart from me, she is the only human Bee will tolerate.

'Now, obviously we care about the local wildlife, Bob, but can you assure us that the search for little Archie still takes priority?' My father's voice always sounds deeper, more cultured, when he is on the radio.

'Absolutely, Robert. Very much so.' Stopford clears his throat. 'We're widening the area that we're searching. The military are up at Estancia at the moment, as are as many volunteers as can spare the time.'

'Except for those who've gone out to Speedwell to help the Conservation rescue the beached whales?'

'Robert, it's not my place to tell people here what to do with their time. They decide that for themselves. What I can tell you is that we have a lot of people out looking for Archie today and, God willing, we'll find him.'

'Have you searched the *Princess Royal*?'

Stopford half answers, loses his thread, and starts again. He emphasizes that they have enough personnel to search the area where Archie went missing.

'Have you had any success tracking down the sighted silver Land Rover?'

More bluster, about following a number of leads, but there being no certainty there was another silver Land Rover at Estancia in the first place and the important point, for everyone to take away, is that the search for little Archie is continuing and will do until, well, for as long as it needs to.

'What about a house-to-house search? What are there, seven hundred properties in Stanley? With all the military personnel you keep talking about, it can't take more than a day, surely?'

'Well, you know, Robert, we can't go searching people's houses without warrants, and everyone's been more than cooperative. I'd go as far as to say every resident of Stanley has searched their own property in the last twenty-four hours, just to be on the safe side. I think we have to concentrate police resources on where they are most needed.'

'Will you be requesting police assistance from London?'

'If need be, of course, but there is nothing to suggest, at this moment in time, that the situation is anything other than . . . What I mean to say is, we are putting all our available resources into the search for little Archie and, I have no doubt, we'll find him soon.'

There is a pause in the studio. A second or two of dead air. Mabel and Cathy share a look. 'Wait for it,' says Mabel.

'There's a rumour flying around this morning that the body of a young child was found at Port Pleasant last night, Chief Superintendent. Can you tell us anything about that?'

What? I spin to face Cathy. She shushes me again.

On air, Stopford makes a low-pitched choking sound. 'Information will be released in the fullness of time, Robert. You know it would be wrong of me to speculate.'

A body? At Port Pleasant? The boys and I listened to the radio over breakfast. Nothing was said about a body.

'Do you think it was Archie?' Dad is asking now.

'At this moment in time, we have no reason to believe . . . That is, we are almost certain that it isn't Archie, and we've informed his family accordingly.'

A child's body? No wonder people in town were jumpy. But if not Archie, then—

'Jimmy,' Cathy mouths at me. 'Jimmy Brown.'

'How soon do you expect to have a positive identification?'

'I really can't speculate.' I can practically see Stopford getting out of his chair, inching towards the door.

'Do you believe the two cases are connected?'

'There is no— absolutely no reason, at this stage, to connect, well, to believe the two cases are connected. It would be irresponsible to speculate. And very unfair on the families.'

280

'Three young boys in the past two years. All disappeared near water – and you're still asking people to believe they're not connected?'

'Robert, this is unhelpful and upsetting for the families concerned. We're going to have to leave it there.'

Music begins to play, and we hear the sliding back of chairs, then the studio door opening. Chief Superintendent Stopford doesn't acknowledge us as he strides through and out the front door. My father stands in the doorway, watching him go, as the sound of 'Sweat' by Inner Circle blares out across the islands. 'Gonna make you sweat,' warns the lead singer.

Some days, even I have to love my dad.

Home again, I give Peter something to eat and then take him down to the beach with me, something I never usually do. He'll get grumpy fast, he really should sleep after lunch, but I feel the need to be out of the house and for some reason – which is almost certainly the notes – I don't want to leave him by himself.

As I left the house I heard, via Dad on the radio, that the initial examination of the body, that police have still to confirm is that of Jimmy Brown, is taking place at the hospital this afternoon.

I wonder again whether I should tell someone about the notes, but with everything else the police have going on, my anonymous, judgemental pen-pal is hardly going to be a priority. It's not as though Archie's family received notes before he disappeared.

Or maybe they did and it's been kept quiet. So, what do I do? Report them and risk wasting police time, not to mention drawing attention to my poor parenting, or . . . I will report them, I decide. Definitely. Soon.

The novelty of being on the beach makes my youngest child forget that he's tired. He takes a few, fast steps towards a flock of birds and they take to the air around him. He spins on the sand, entranced by his power to have such an impact upon so many other lives.

It's a dangerous power, I think, watching his fair head bounce, his feet scuff the sand, his eyes widen in wonder. I should know.

When Chris was born, in those first few days after becoming a mother, I found the sudden responsibility close to terrifying. So much of our time, in those early days, we were entirely alone. Just me, a tiny creature completely at my mercy, and my head filled with sickeningly violent fantasies.

They came from nowhere. I'd be making tea and think how easy it would be to tip the contents of the kettle over his cot. I'd take him out into the garden for air, walk to the edge of the cliff, and wonder, were I to loosen my hold on him right now, how long it would take him to reach the bottom. Would he cry? Would I be sorry? In the few short moments before he hit the rocks who – he or I – would scream the loudest?

I struggled to feed him and switched to formula quite quickly. I could put anything in these bottles, I'd think, as I made them up every morning. Drain cleaner? Neat Scotch? Who was there to stop me?

I had no idea what had gone wrong with the wiring in my head, why these unspeakable thoughts kept bursting their way in. It wasn't as though I didn't love my baby. Sometimes it felt as though the love I had was so intense there wasn't enough space in my head to keep it all in. I could hardly bear to be in a different room. I'd wake at night, find my hand resting softly on his tummy as he lay in the crib beside me, and wonder how I'd spent so many years of my life without him. And still the dark, twisted thoughts kept coming.

I became afraid of myself, afraid of what I might do, and there was no one to whom I could turn for help. How could I confess that I was fantasizing about killing my baby? Other mothers would open their eyes wide in fright and make an excuse to get out of the house. My GP would section me. Sander would apply for custody. My best friend had a new baby herself, she was hardly in a position to deal with my paranoia.

In the end I did tell Catrin. I broke down completely one afternoon and told her everything. Inscrutable, unflappable as ever, she thought about it for a while.

'I think it's your subconscious processing a fairly cataclysmic life change,' she said, eventually. 'On some level, you're aware that you could do those things so, on that level, you're acting out, exploring the boundaries. I wouldn't worry. I think they'll go in time, once you get used to the whole motherhood business.'

'What if they don't? What if I actually do one of these things?'

She looked at me like I was dim. 'Rach, I've seen you catch wasps in your hands because you can't bear to swat them. They're fantasies.'

In time I came to think that she was right. The fantasies became less frequent, eventually stopped altogether, and when Michael was born they didn't repeat themselves.

It's still a dangerous power, though, control over another human life. There came a day when I had an impact on other lives and, years later, the consequences of that one mistake are eating me away like a cancer.

A police boat appears around the headland and I watch it draw closer. It's heading for the wreck. They are all going to be searched over the next couple of days. The old ship on which people I loved played pirates is going to be crawled over by police officers.

A sudden gust hits us hard, almost knocking my child over. He's wandered some way down the beach and for a second looks round in panic, imagining himself lost.

Sometimes it feels as though everyone around me is lost. A dozen miles away, people are still looking for a lost little boy. Fifty miles away, other people are trying to get over a hundred lost whales back to where they belong. I sit on the cold sand, watch a skinny two-year-old chase shags and guillemots across the beach, and wonder who's going to find me, and how I'll ever get home.

Chris wakes me in the night. The phone is in his hand. It must have been ringing for a while but didn't penetrate my drug-assisted sleep.

'Mummy.'

He's on the bed with me, pulling at my shoulder. Panic hits and I pull myself up.

'It's Granddad. They've found him. They've found the little boy.'

I grab the phone and try to concentrate. It isn't actually that late, not long after midnight, but the drugs have a powerful hold. Yet I take in enough. Archie West has been found. Alive and reasonably OK.

Chris is leaning close, trying to catch what Dad is saying, a smile of relief on his young face. I can hear the excitement that Dad is trying so hard to conceal, the chattering of my mother in the background. I have a sense of everyone around me taking deep breaths, allowing the tension to leave. It's over.

Dad is still talking. Little Archie was found by Catrin and Callum, of all people, on their way home from Speedwell. Dad can barely contain his joy at the story that has landed at his feet like a pot of ambrosia tossed down from Olympus. They slaughtered nearly two hundred whales after an unprecedented beaching and, on their way home, spotted a cold and hungry little boy by the roadside.

When Dad stops to take a breath, and I've grasped the opportunity to wish him goodnight, Chris is snuggled up in my bed, almost asleep again.

I get in on Sander's side. It feels cool beneath me.

The nightmare is over, has ended better than anyone could have hoped. The small child from far away is found. There are signs that Callum and Catrin are together again. Suddenly, so much seems possible. I settle down, glad of the feeling of Sander's cool clean sheets beneath me, of the sound of Chris's breathing at my side. It's over. Whatever happened to Archie, it's—

Then I remember what day it is. The third of November. The day I killed my best friend's children.

Sleep feels impossible now, so I pull the covers up over Chris's shoulders as I get out of bed. In Michael's room, there is an unusually large lump beneath the quilt with two fair heads peeking out. The little one can't get out of the cot by himself, so I can only surmise that he woke, Michael heard him and carried him into his own bed.

On my way back to my own room, I lean in to close Peter's door and even though I know exactly where my youngest is, the sight of the empty cot startles me.

They should be the most precious of all, our youngest children. Youngest, sweetest, most loved, the last children of our bodies. Archie is a youngest child. Holding him in her arms again, his mother must feel as though the thin, fragile shell of her heart can't

284

possibly hold the swell of emotion inside it. She will stay awake all night, holding his tiny, cold body within her own, hardly able to believe she's been given this second chance.

Is it possible, that there's a second chance for me?

'Mummy.' In my room, a sleepy young voice is calling me back to bed. I don't go. I stand here, thinking, staring down at the empty cot.

DAY FOUR
Thursday, 3 November

31

'SHE'S NOT RIGHT. SHE HASN'T BEEN RIGHT SINCE—'
One of the gossiping mums at the school gate spots me. I see an elbow shoot out, the speaker interrupted.

'Well, so what? I'm not saying anything we don't all know.' Her voice has lowered, but fractionally. I long ago ceased to be someone whose feelings are taken into account.

We are waiting for the school to open. It's one of those days when the sky is still clear, but the clouds are gathering and we know there's going to be rough weather later on. They're banking up, out to sea, the line getting thicker and darker as each new mass joins the ranks and the shadow beneath is spreading across the ocean. Right now the sunshine-streaked coloured roofs of Stanley are gleaming. Another couple of hours and they'll be cowering like washing left out in the rain.

Three years ago today it was unusually calm, unseasonably warm. The kids had been on the beach and as I drove Ned and Kit home I remember thinking I'd have to vacuum the car. I never did, of course. The sand, pebbles and other beach debris went into the sea with the boys.

The weather was perfect, the day Ned and Kit died.

Storms come quickly here, but we learn to read the signs. The massing army out to the west of us will grow in strength throughout the morning. Then, to anyone watching, a moment of stillness will fall, when those unfamiliar with the place might think the worst is over, but then a newcomer arrives, a long low shadow of a cloud, moving faster, sinking down. It's the advance guard, coming on hard and fearless, spurring on the rest, and then the full force of nature rains down.

> *And now the storm-blast came, and he*
> *Was tyrannous and strong*

Ignoring the gossiping women, I pretend to watch Michael being chased around the playground by his brother. The older child jogs ahead then waits for the younger to almost catch up, before sprinting away again. The little one will tire of this soon, but for now it's entertaining him.

'I don't know how she could. One after another, like an execution.'

'That is her job, though, isn't it?'

'Could you do it? I couldn't. Over two hundred of them. Tiny ones and pregnant mums and everything.'

It's Catrin they are talking about. Not me.

'She found the little boy though.'

'She found both boys. One of them dead. That tells you something.'

'I wouldn't want to get on her bad side, I know that.'

That's it. I turn and step closer to the group. 'How many lambs does your Allan slaughter every spring, Alison?' I stare at the woman with permed blonde hair and red cheeks. She and her husband own a sheep farm on one of the smaller islands. 'How does he do it, exactly?'

She stares back. 'That's different and you know it.'

Alison and I were at school together, although she was a year or so older than me. I seem to remember her wit being faster than her intellect, which makes her tricky to argue with.

'Mass slaughter driven by necessity,' I say. 'Lambs are killed because we need the food. The whales were put down to prevent them suffering. Arguably, what Catrin did was far more compassionate than what you and your husband do.'

She sneers, takes a little step forward. My chest tightens. She leans towards me, puts her face directly in front of mine. 'Well, excuse me. I was forgetting you're our expert on killing innocent creatures.'

And there is nothing I can say to that. No possible way I can react. Most of the women around us – we have attracted a sizeable crowd by this time – look uncomfortable, but I can see a few faces enjoying the drama.

No way can I win this. What I did has taken away for ever my right to have an opinion on anything, to argue any case. I cannot, ever, challenge anyone again, because they have a weapon that can destroy me utterly. I killed two kids. And for that I will pay, over and over again, every hour of every day.

'They're going in.' The group breaks apart, some of the mothers run to say goodbye to their children. The rest cluster around Alison like a pack of dogs waiting for me to show just enough weakness. I feel tears pricking. No, I cannot cry. Not now, not in front of them.

'Mum! Peter's trying to come inside.'

Chris's voice. He is over by the railing, holding up his brother. Michael has already disappeared. I go to meet him and bend to take the child. He doesn't want to come with me, of course he doesn't, who would? He leans back towards his big brother, squirming and kicking. Great, a full-blown tantrum.

Boys of nearly three in a rage are incredibly strong. It is as much as I can do to pin him in the buggy while I fasten the restraints, and it is mortifying that I have to do it under the judgemental stares of Alison and her mates. One of his flying fists catches me in the eye, causing a second of extreme pain, and I shout at him without thinking.

'Stop it, you little shit!'

Conscious that all of them are still watching me, that even Chris, at the railings, has seen my humiliation, is sharing it, I cannot do anything but turn the buggy and walk away.

We spend most of the morning crying. I surround my son with toys, put a video he likes on the TV and stay in the room with him. He's picking up on my mood though, is difficult and fractious, sometimes clinging to me, other times taking himself into a corner to hide.

My heart aches with pity for him. When Sander and the boys are out, which is most of the time, this tiny little thing has no one but me to rely on. I can see him longing for something his small, unformed brain can't visualize or articulate. He has no idea what it is that he needs, only that something essential to his life is missing. He cries and he screams and each sign of his misery yells at me to sort myself out, to be a mother, to take care of him the way I did, still do, with my older two and I just can't.

I can't.

Eventually, I turn on the radio to find something, anything, to take my mind off myself and my own life. I've missed the big press conference but the later news bulletin brings me up to date.

The remains found on the *Endeavour* have been formally identified and the family of seven-year-old Jimmy Brown will be able to bury him soon, to grieve properly. The police have no reason to believe his death was anything other than accidental.

The news reader, not Dad, goes on to say that the police now believe that Archie was abducted after all, and that they are working on the theory that whoever took him lost his nerve and abandoned him. The hunt is on for an abductor, and the *Princess Royal* will not be allowed to leave in the immediate future.

At three o'clock, when I still have the better part of an hour before the boys get home, I strap Peter into the car and drive to Catrin's house. I know she'll be at work. Not once, in three years, has she been on the spot where her sons died at the exact moment the car went over the edge. It is a grim vigil I keep alone.

I get out of the car, having first checked that my small charge is safely strapped in and the handbrake firmly on. I didn't do either three years ago. Then I walk up towards the house. Three years ago, I did this with my face glowing and my heart hammering, knowing Ben was at home and that I was an hour earlier than Catrin had told him I'd be. Three years ago, I was walking into the unknown.

I turn back at the door, I never go any further than this, and for a second, my car seems to be sliding forward, just as it did then. It isn't, of course, it's a trick of the light, but it has me racing back to it all the same.

*

The sound of a car turning in the road outside drags me from the doze I'd fallen into. I hear Cathy calling goodbye, the sound of Michael and Christopher running up the path. I sit up, shake my head, rub sleep from my eyes.

As I stand there is a rush of blood to my head and I wobble on my feet. Beneath the window I can hear Chris and Michael talking quietly to each other. In the next room, Peter calls out to them.

I head for the bathroom, use the toilet and wash my hands and face.

'Mum!' Chris usually comes straight into my room when he gets home. Other boys get back from school to find their mums in the kitchen, making dinner. Mine wake me from drug-induced sleep.

'I'm in here.' I try to sound normal. 'Give me a sec.'

'OK.'

He runs back downstairs again. I hear voices outside. I look at myself in the mirror and don't recognize the woman staring back.

Then I realize the room is darker than it should be and remember the eclipse. Chris and Michael. I don't want them climbing down the cliff path in semi darkness.

Another car, coming up the hill. At this time of day it can only be Cathy. She must have forgotten something.

Not the red saloon I'm expecting. This is a silver Land Rover with a black roof. Catrin's car. I've never seen her drive past the house in the daylight before. She's going fast. Much too fast on this narrow, poorly repaired road. She brakes hard and a second later I can smell the burned rubber.

She's getting out. She's actually out of the car. Her dark hair is flying up around her head. There is something in her face that frightens me. So many times, I've wanted her to initiate contact.

Not today. I can't face her today.

She vanishes from sight, ducking down low behind the hedge. Then she stands again.

She has my child in her arms.

I watch, open-mouthed, as she turns back towards the vehicle. The woman who hates me, who wishes me dead, the woman who revealed herself yesterday as a cold-blooded killer, has her hands on my child.

DAY FIVE
Friday, 4 November (late evening)

32

ONLY WHEN THE HOUSE IS QUIET DO I BREAK THROUGH the stupor that's engulfed me for most of the day. The police, the well-wishers and the merely inquisitive have gone home, my mother is snoring in the spare room and my two remaining sons are collapsed in miserable exhaustion, curled up together in one bed. Only now do I get up and leave my bedroom, make my way through the darkened house.

I can't actually remember much of the day; were it not for the night sky outside, I'd be unsure whether it had happened at all. And yet the hours have ticked past and something must have filled them.

I step carefully down the stairs, not sure who I'm frightened of disturbing, and as I do so I look in each dark corner, just in case. Just in case there's something small and insignificant that I've forgotten. Such as what I actually did with my youngest child. *Oh yes, here he is! How could I forget I tucked him into the small boot cupboard at the bottom of the stairs? Sorry, everyone, panic over, he's been here all along.*

I gasp for breath, and not nearly enough seems to make it inside me. I tell myself to think back through the day, to remember everything, to give my mind some anchor to hold on to. Breathe in, breathe out.

We heard the news of Catrin's arrest early this morning. Of course, as soon as the police arrived yesterday, I told them about her stopping outside the house, about her picking up the child. What

297

could they do but make her their prime suspect? They learned quickly that she'd left harbour in her boat and naturally they launched a full-scale search, but Catrin knows the Falkland waters very well and in the time it took to get a helicopter in the air, darkness had fallen.

They didn't find her until first light, by which time there was no sign of anyone on the boat but the dog and Catrin herself. No one has said to me that Catrin had Peter for over twelve hours, that she could have done anything with him, abandoned him anywhere, but I know that's what they are all thinking.

Yesterday was the third anniversary of the accident, when I left two children unattended, in a car dangerously close to a cliff edge, never dreaming for a moment that my doing so would result in both plunging to their deaths in icy water. The anniversary cannot have escaped people's notice. How many will be wondering if Catrin chose that day, deliberately, to do the same thing to my son?

We've had courtesy phone calls from the police throughout the day, mainly, I suspect, because Dad would drive them daft if they didn't keep us informed. So we know that Catrin has been interviewed at length, but has admitted nothing beyond seeing the child in the road, picking him up and returning him to the garden. There were hairs on her sweater and a child's fingerprints on her bag, but alone they'll prove nothing beyond the fact of her picking him up, and that she freely admits.

At the bottom of the stairs the hallway is cold, the tiled floor uncomfortable beneath my bare feet. Sander has been calling continually. I think he's going out of his mind so far away, unable to do anything. As if he'd feel any different, any less powerless, were he here.

The police are convinced that Catrin is lying, mainly because they found a toy on her boat, a little stuffed rabbit that I identified immediately. It's an old one of Michael's that his younger brother adopted and that we have been unable to find anywhere in the house. The police see it as proof that she had him on the boat, that she took him out to sea. Divers have been in Port Pleasant for much of the day, looking for anything Catrin may have thrown overboard.

At least, that's the official line. We all know they're looking for my son's body.

The kitchen still smells of the spaghetti bolognese that Grandma cooked for the boys. We all watched her put out three plates, including the little Peter Rabbit one that Peter always uses, and nobody had the heart to say anything. When she realized what she'd done, she fled the room. We could hear her sobbing in the hall. It was Chris who got up and put his brother's little plate away in the cupboard, who served spaghetti to himself and Michael.

The two anonymous notes I received are being kept confidential for now. Stopford himself says it's usual in these cases, to keep something back from the general public, although we do know that Catrin herself has denied sending them. A close examination has found no fingerprints other than mine and those of the woman who manages the post office. She, of course, sells lots of the stuff. A sample of Catrin's handwriting will be sent away for comparison but until it comes back with a positive result, the notes don't constitute evidence of any useful kind.

With nothing else to do, I go back to my bed. Fireworks have started to go off around Stanley. Each one sounds like gunfire.

I'm first up next morning. I dress quickly and go outside, across the garden, to the cliff path. As I draw near to the edge, the sky starts to colour, picking up reflections of a sun that I know is coming up fast. Normally, there are few sights more heartening, more lifting to the spirits than a sunrise, the glorious announcement to the world that night is over. Nothing uplifting about this one. There are no soft pinks, no pastel shades of orange in the colour palette building around me. The clouds, as thick and heavy, and banked as high as they have been the last twenty-four hours, are becoming a mass of dark shadows and the harsh Falun-red that we used to see dug out of copper mines. This is *the hot and copper sky* of Coleridge's poem. Then the sea colours too, and its rise and swell starts to look like congealing blood. The deep, dark reds around me intensify, even the grass, the gorse, the rocks are gleaming crimson. The world has turned red.

If ever a red sky in the morning felt like a portent of something sinister, this one does. This feels like the dawn to mark the death of a child.

I get back to the house to find the police waiting for me. Catrin has confessed.

DAY SIX
Saturday, 5 November (five hours later)

33

I DON'T GO HOME WHEN CALLUM AND I FINISH READING Catrin's diary. I cannot. In any case, I don't need to. The boys are with my mother and, for all that she drives me nuts, she is a great grandma. Chris will feed, muck out and ride Strawberry. Dad will guard them all with his life, if he has to, I know that much about him. In a few hours, Sander will be home and he is the best father any child could ask for. They don't need me. They think they do, but they don't.

I need never go home again.

Once the initial shock, the misery, is over, they will be so much better off. Like an otherwise healthy body after a gangrenous limb has been removed. So I don't go home. I ride instead to the nearest cliff tall enough for what I have in mind.

God, the wind. It's howling, screaming into my face. It feels strong enough and angry enough to lift the whole of East Falkland up out of the sea. It will help, I think, take responsibility away from me. I can lean into it, hover beyond hope of changing my mind and allow the wind to choose the moment when it lets me go.

I slow Bee when we get within twenty yards of the edge. The wind is bothering him, I don't want to scare him by taking him any closer.

She isn't human in my eyes now.

How well she puts it. I'm not human in anyone's eyes. What is it

303

she called me? *An event, a living disaster, a void.* I am the storm that wiped out two young lives, the foul wind that blighted so many more.

The man I loved, my best friend, the man who loved her, all of them twisted by grief into something even they barely recognize. And then there are my sons, husband, parents, all tainted by their association with me. One of them has already paid the reckoning that should have been mine. One of us, the smallest, most vulnerable, has been sacrificed. That has to be enough.

I slide off Bee's back, remove the saddle and bridle and lay them on the ground. They'll be found, soon enough, like clues in a treasure hunt.

'What in the name of God do you think you're doing now?'

I hadn't really expected my horse to take this quietly so am hardly surprised. I lean against his ribs, feel his coat damp from where the saddle lay and stretch my hand up to cradle the underside of his jaw. 'Shush now, be good. Go home.'

She's the reason the world has lost all balance. While she's around, the universe is tilted and those of us on the underside are on the brink of falling straight down into hell.

People I love are on that underside. One of them has already fallen. No more. Or maybe, just one. Just me.

I step away from the warmth of my horse, push his head in the right direction and shove at his hind-quarters. Then I turn and face the cliff.

'I've seen you do some stupid things, but this . . .' Bee hasn't gone. His head hits me square between the shoulder blades.

'Go home, you daft horse. I love you. Don't bite anyone.' I push him again, hitting him hard on the flank, and he trots off. I can't watch him any more. I turn and can't see anything very much, what with the wind on the brink of ripping my eyes out. Blinded, feeling my way, I take one step, then another.

Why couldn't it have been Rachel standing there on the dock, falling apart? Rachel suffering as that poor bitch is doing. Why not Rachel dying inside, right now, instead of curling up on her son's bed, rocking his warm body back to sleep? Why isn't she staring at that bed, cold and empty, wondering where on God's earth he is?

I am. I'm doing all of those things. Enough now. I walk faster. I won't stop and think about it. I will keep walking. In fact, better if I run. Run straight, and leap.

I can't run. I don't quite have the nerve for that. But I'm at the edge. One last look. The beach below is covered in big, solid rocks, densely packed with sharp edges. They will shatter my skull, if I'm lucky, because that will be the fastest death, but even if my head survives, the multiple ruptures will pierce my vital organs, the bleeding will be extensive, will kill me in minutes. Maybe I'll really luck out and my neck will break.

I spread out my arms and lean, the wind takes me, holds me on the brink of oblivion – and my frigging horse takes a chunk out of my shoulder.

He staggers back, planting his hooves firmly on the soft ground, taking me with him.

'Let go.' I try to pull away. I would have done it, I know I would, I'd felt my balance give way, my weight tilt.

He can't talk to me. His teeth are clamped together around the loose fabric of my shirt. Besides, the effort of dragging me back is taking most of his energy. Unable to pull away, I sink to the ground. He lets go and takes a swipe at my head with his mouth.

'Get up, get that saddle back on me and let's get home.'

'Bee, I can't. I just can't.'

'Lady, twenty-four hours from now, I'll push you off myself. But there's something you have to do first.'

I turn to look at the soft, black muzzle, those chocolate-brown eyes, and against every inclination I know that he's right. I'll come back here soon, if I can. But there's something I have to do first.

34

I T IS BONFIRE NIGHT. BEING BRITISH – WELL, SORT OF – WE celebrate it. Of course it's not so easy here because November is late spring and the evenings are long. Bonfires don't have the same impact in the twilight, we have to wait till much later before setting off the fireworks, but we make the effort all the same.

As soon as Bee and I get home, I ask Mum if she can stay with the boys, but she's anxious to leave. She and Dad are committed to the ongoing search for my son, and I can hardly argue with that. She does, though, agree to take them to the bonfire in the evening. I have a few more hours to get through.

I'd like to say I spend the day putting everything in order – seeing to the horses, tidying the house, cooking dinner for Sander and the boys – but the truth is that everything has already been done for me. So I fill the hours by watching my sons, sitting close to them whenever I can. I try not to think about whether the decision I made on the clifftop is the right one. I watch the hands of the clock creeping round.

At six o'clock it's time. I leave instructions for Sander, where I've put things, how to feed the horses. I don't tell him what I'm planning to do, or why. The first he'll know soon enough, the other he'll never understand.

'We don't want to go to the bonfire.' Chris starts grumbling before he's fastened his seat belt. 'We want to stay here.'

It's an effort not to yell at him, *Just get in the bloody car!* 'We always go,' I tell him. 'It will take your mind off things for a while.'

'What if Peter comes back and we're not here?'

'Daddy will be home soon. And I'll try and pop back, once I've done what I need to.'

'You're not coming with us?' Michael wants to know.

'Peter doesn't want you.' Chris is struggling not to cry. He always gets a bit mean when he's upset and trying not to show it. 'He knows you don't love him. He wants us.'

I take a deep breath. Chris was always the smart one.

'I love you,' I tell him. 'I love you and Michael more than anything else in the world. Please do this for me.'

'But not Peter.'

'Of course I love Peter.' I take hold of him and press him close to me so that he can't look me in the eye. He'll be taller than me soon. One day, I'll hug him and he'll be the bigger party. And then I realize that may never happen now and it feels as though an Antarctic wind has blown straight through the car. I let him go and he pulls sulkily away.

I say goodbye to them in their grandparents' driveway. I want to hold them both again, to say something that might be meaningful in time. Except, I know that if I start I'll never get away.

It's a short drive to the police station and stray fireworks are already going off around me. I pass houses with their coloured tin roofs, see Guys slumped against fences, families setting out for the bonfire, and I feel as though I'm seeing it all for the very last time.

'Hello, Rachel.'

I've known the desk sergeant since I was little. Now, I watch his face fall. 'I'm not sure we have any news, I'm afraid, but I can call DS Savidge down for a word?'

The station has an empty feel about it – everyone must be out supervising the fireworks, or simply enjoying them. I feel the need to be close to the sergeant all the same, to speak quietly.

'Is Catrin still here? I know she was released last night, allowed to go home. Has that happened again?'

Frowning, he shakes his head. 'She's still here. But, Rach – let me call Josh down.'

307

I wait in the reception area, watching the lines of the sergeant's face twitch as he has a muttered telephone conversation.

'He's on his way.' The telephone receiver clicks back into place. 'Can I get you something? Tea?'

I shake my head. I don't want him to do anything now that he might be sorry for later. And that includes showing me acts of kindness.

Josh Savidge looks tense when he appears after a minute or two. He thinks I'm here to demand answers, to blame him for my son's continuing disappearance. He'll soon be wishing I were.

'Rachel, I'm sorry. There's nothing new.' He looks round, as though for inspiration. 'Look, come and have a cup of tea. The interview room's free, isn't it, Neil? No, actually, let's go into the staff room.'

Everyone is determined to be kind to me. 'You might want to make it a bit more formal. I've come to make a statement.'

He blinks at me. 'OK, right.' He blinks some more. 'Remembered something, have you? OK, then. Well, if you'd like to follow me.'

The walls on either side of the corridor seem to be closing in.

'Next on your right.'

We enter a standard box of a room, with a barred window high in one wall and a table that is too big for the four chairs arranged around it. A pile of four more chairs is stacked in one corner. There is recording equipment. Through the window, I see a rocket fly into the sky. It explodes into lilac stars and I can't help remembering that Peter hated fireworks, that he cried and cried last year when we took him to see them. 'Bit too horrid, Daddy,' he whimpered into his father's shoulder.

'It seems quiet here. The station, I mean.'

'Most people are out at the fireworks. There's a lot of people from the *Princess Royal* in town still and things are a bit – we only have a skeleton staff here.' Josh is looking guilty, as though expecting me to blame him for not having all hands on deck when my son is still missing. Except, why should they? They believe Catrin has killed him and the urgency to find his body doesn't merit running up a massive overtime bill.

Skye McNair joins us seconds later, banging her shin on the table as she sits down. There is what looks like a ketchup stain on her collar and her bun is crooked.

Savidge has a notebook open in front of him. After a few seconds of fumbling around, Skye pulls one out too. They both find a moment of stillness, wait for me to start.

'You said there was something you'd remembered, Rachel,' Savidge prompts.

I take a second to steady myself, then look him directly in the eyes.

'I killed my son, Detective Sergeant. I killed Peter Grimwood.'

35

SILENCE IN THE ROOM. SOMEWHERE THERE IS A CLOCK, maybe on the wall behind me, I can hear it ticking. Then the rumble from someone's stomach. I look steadily back at Savidge, can see Skye from the corner of my eye. They think they're hearing things. I give them time. In fact I start to count in my head. One, two ... when I reach four, Savidge leans across the table towards me.

'Could you repeat that, Rachel?'

'Sarge—'

'Hang on a minute, Skye. Rachel?'

'Sarge, we need to caution her.' Skye turns too quickly and her chair almost tips. 'We should switch the recorder on.'

He sees the sense of this and gets up.

Skye looks at me with wide frightened eyes, then round at the senior officer, who is fumbling with the recording equipment. 'Rachel Grimwood, you are here voluntarily to make a statement,' she begins. 'You are not under arrest at present, but may be in the near future. You do not have to say anything. But it may harm your defence if you do not mention when questioned something that you later rely on in court. Anything you do say may be given in evidence.'

Savidge takes his seat at her side and looks at me as though I've changed right in front of him. As, I guess, I have.

'Sarge, was that OK? What I just said?' Skye is glancing nervously at the man next to her.

'It was fine. Well done, love.' He can't take his eyes off me.

'Rachel.' Skye again. 'Do you understand your rights as you've just been, I mean, had them read to you?'

Their utter bewilderment has a calming effect. It feels as though I am in charge, not they. 'I do, thank you.'

Savidge speaks the formalities into the tape. We give our names, and then he asks me once again to repeat my confession.

'I killed my son,' I say. 'It wasn't Catrin Quinn. It was me. I'm sorry I've been wasting your time.'

They're struggling to take it in. I wait for them to ask me when, where, to give a full account of how, exactly, I committed the most unspeakable act that either of them can think of.

'Why?' Skye asks instead. I don't mind. This one is easy to answer.

'I didn't love him,' I say.

They continue staring.

'I never did love him,' I repeat. 'I couldn't.'

'You love your other two sons?' Skye asks me.

'More than anything.'

'Then why not Peter?' Her voice is pitched low, gentle, as though she is speaking to an invalid.

It's a good question, but one I'll struggle to answer properly. This is something I have never before articulated. I've spoken to no one about my relationship with my youngest son. Not to anyone, husband, parents, even my horse, have I admitted my feelings for him to be anything less than they should be. I've never even allowed myself to think it, but the truth is, it has always been completely impossible for me to feel anything akin to love for him.

'Three years ago, before you came back from college in England, Skye, I killed two children. I know you know about it. Josh certainly does.'

'I know there was an accident.' In the dimly lit room, Skye's hair seems to be an extra source of light. 'A terrible accident. That's not quite the same thing.'

'Try telling that to my best friend.'

'Go on, Mrs Grimwood,' Josh tells me. 'In your own time.'

'After the accident, I never felt I deserved my own sons to be alive, let alone that another one should be born. I used to think it would have been fairer if one of my boys had gone over that cliff and one of Catrin's. That would have been dreadful but fair, don't you think?'

I wait for the answer I know I'm never going to get. As if fairness has anything to do with the random cruelty that is accidental death.

'One of my sons should have died. Then Catrin would still have had one child. Her life wouldn't have fallen apart, she wouldn't have become ill, wouldn't have lost the baby she was carrying.'

They are looking at me as though I am slightly mad. Only slightly? I have more work to do.

'If that had happened, we'd both have two children now and the grief would have been terrible, but we'd have coped with it, together. We did everything together. That's how it should have been.'

'You're saying you wish one of your sons had died?'

'No, of course not. Just that it would have been fair. If you have to choose between terrible grief and terrible guilt, I think grief is easier, in the end. Don't you?'

Skye starts to speak, but it's suddenly very important to me that I get something in first. 'Not that I could ever decide which I'd have given up. I love them both so much, my big, serious clever boy and my little cuddly one. I love my two sons more than anything.'

'But not your youngest one?' She has asked me that already, just doesn't seem able to absorb the truth of what I'm telling her. I gave birth to a child. I didn't love him.

'I couldn't. I was never cruel to him. I didn't mistreat him. I fed him and kept him clean. But I couldn't play with him, or sing to him, or cuddle him the way I did with the other two. And the bond wasn't there. The postnatal chemicals didn't flood my brain the way they're supposed to, telling me that I'd give my life for this tiny soul. All the normal mother–baby stuff simply didn't work with him.'

And the guilt that was already eating me up had a fresh banquet to feed on.

From outside comes the sound of shouting, running footsteps. A can is kicked along the street. It's time for the bonfire to be lit, for

312

the barbecues to start serving food, but not everyone, it seems, is at the school field.

'Were you diagnosed as having postnatal depression? That can be pretty serious.' Skye seems to have taken over the interview.

'I had every type of depression ever listed, and quite a few new ones as well.' In a strange way, saying all this aloud for the first time is something of a relief. I certainly never said any of it to Sapphire Pirrus during the enforced counselling sessions. 'I barely remember the first year of his life, if I'm honest. Then suddenly, I had this screaming, demanding toddler to deal with. It was as though he'd appeared from nowhere. As though a little changeling had come to live with us.'

'Changeling?' Josh has woken up. 'What's a changeling?'

Skye turns to him for a second. 'Fairy child. British folklore, Sarge. The fairies stole away human infants and left fairy children in their place. Only they were mean and bad-tempered and ugly. Is that how you thought about Peter, Mrs Grimwood?'

I have a sudden image of the child, gazing at me through the bars of his cot, plump from sleep. 'No, of course he wasn't any of those things. He was a pretty little boy. Just not my pretty little boy.'

Josh clears his throat. 'So what happened on Thursday afternoon? The afternoon of the third of November.'

I give myself time. This will be harder.

'I was in my room.' I'm seeing it as I speak. Waking to find the late-afternoon sunshine had fled, to be replaced with an eerie, ominous darkness. I can hear the sound of the ocean through the open window, catch the bitter salt smell that wafts in from time to time.

'The boys came home.' I hear the car that drops them off, Cathy shouting goodbye, their footsteps on the stairs. I hear the baby yelling for their attention, but they always come to me first.

'They came into my room.' I was in the bathroom by this time, trying to shake off the dopiness. 'I told them I had a headache.' I didn't, I just couldn't face those noisy few hours before bedtime. There are times when I feel as though my children are throwing tiny stones at me, because one demand comes after another. *Mum, can I have a packet of crisps? Mum, can I have a biscuit? Mum, Peter's got a dirty nappy. Mum, my finger hurts.* It's relentless, dealing with three boys, even when they're not quarrelling, which is a good 50 per cent of the time. Sander knows I struggle with tea and bedtime. He usually comes home early.

Something hits the outside wall. Savidge jumps up and goes to the window. 'Kids,' he mutters when he comes back. 'Go on, Mrs Grimwood, the boys were home from school, you had a headache.'

'Chris and Michael went into Peter's room.' I hear his squeals of delight when he sees them, the low grunt Chris makes when he picks his brother up. 'I think Chris changed him.'

More shouts from outside. Both pairs of eyes opposite flick to the window and back. Skye nods at me to go on.

'Then they all went outside. I could hear them, running about, shouting to each other.

'They were so good with him, my two. So fond, so caring of their little brother. Then the sounds of giggling and shouting fell quiet. I couldn't hear them any more. I remembered my mother's warnings about the loose garden gate. I remembered the eclipse, that Chris and Michael would probably head down to the beach to watch it.

'I got up. I heard a car outside and went to the window. I saw Catrin's car, then Catrin herself getting out and bending down in the road.'

'You told us all this when we spoke to you before.' Skye frowns and starts flicking back through her notes.

'When she stood up again, she was carrying the child,' I ignore Skye's interruption. 'He must have got out on to the road somehow. I told you all this. What I didn't tell you is that I then saw her lean over the gate, put him down and get back into her car and drive away.'

A sigh seems to escape both police officers at once. They look at each other, and back at me.

'So what she told us was true?'

'Of course it was.' I feel an odd, twisted pleasure in defending my former friend. 'Catrin doesn't know how to lie.'

A pause. They look at each other and again sigh in unison. I have a sense that Catrin's exoneration pleases both of them.

'Carry on, Mrs Grimwood,' says Savidge.

The terse instruction takes me by surprise but, of course, in the story I've been telling, my youngest son is still alive. I have to get to the end.

'I could see him near the gate. I waited for his brothers to come and collect him but they must have gone further down the garden towards the beach. I couldn't hear them. Then he made for the hedge again and started to climb through. He'd found some weak point and was getting out. Obviously I had to go down there.'

'So you did?'

'It took me a few minutes. I wasn't quite dressed. But when I got down, sure enough he was on the road again.'

'And was Mrs Quinn anywhere to be seen?'

'No. There was no sign of her car. I thought I could hear an engine, someone else coming up the hill, but I didn't hang around. I picked the baby up and carried him back into the garden.'

'Go on.'

'As soon as we got back through the gate he went mental.'

'Mental as in . . .'

'Completely berserk. A proper tantrum. Screaming, kicking, crying. Hitting me with his fists. I'm not sure how much experience either of you have of tantruming two-year-olds but they can be very strong.'

'We'll take your word for it,' says Josh. Skye has fallen quiet and I'd be willing to bet she'd rather not listen to what's coming next. God knows I'd rather not say it.

'He wanted to be out on the road, or to be with his brothers. What he didn't want was me spoiling his fun.'

I stop. There is water on the table although I have no recollection of either officer providing it. I pick up the glass. Warm, like the room. Pale in colour, like a fine Scotch whisky. It tastes bitter, as though it was poured days ago. The officers are waiting for me. I look at him, then her and see the condemnation that I know will be in every pair of eyes that looks into mine from now on.

'Go on,' says Josh.

'I put him down, he went straight for the gap in the hedge again. I physically blocked it, he started kicking and punching me. Two-year-olds can be monsters, they really can.'

'And what did you do, to this monster in front of you?'

315

Skye looks reproachfully at her colleague. She doesn't want him condemning me, not until they've heard my full confession.

'I don't remember much of what happened next.' I try. 'I'm sorry, it's actually very difficult to talk about.'

We all jump as a stone hits the window. Josh picks up the phone, has a brief muttered conversation with the desk sergeant about sorting out the bloody hooligans outside, then looks at me again.

'What did you do to him?' he asks.

I look at the man I've known since childhood and I can see sympathy seeping from him. With every second that passes, his judgement is hardening. Of the two of them, Skye is holding up better. She leans towards me and pats my hand. 'I'm afraid we do have to know exactly what happened, Rachel. Take your time. You're doing really well.'

She sits back again and rubs her fingers where they touched mine.

'I took hold of him by the shoulders and gave him a shake to stop him crying. He was hysterical. He needed a shock.' I can't look at either of them as I say this, so I stare at the tabletop.

'The shaking seemed to make him worse. I don't really remember much. I must have shaken him again. I honestly don't know. I just remember looking down and seeing him limp in my arms.'

Out of the corner of my eye, I think I see Skye drop her head into her hands. She recovers quickly. When I look up again, her face is pale but composed.

'I let him fall to the ground. He wasn't breathing.'

'Did you try mouth-to-mouth? Did you give him CPR?'

I stare back into cold blue eyes. 'There wasn't a lot of point, Josh. His neck was broken.'

'How could you be so sure?' Skye is practically whispering at me. I'm tempted to tell her to speak up for the benefit of the tape, but common sense prevails and I don't.

'Have you ever seen a broken neck, Skye? Trust me, they're pretty much unmistakable. Besides, it only takes a few seconds for a corpse to start turning blue.' The confession is getting easier. I practically have to remind myself that I'm talking about my own son.

'Did you consider calling for help? Letting the authorities know?'

'Not really. I was more worried about getting him out of the way before the boys could see him.'

I hear myself. My youngest son. My baby has turned into a nuisance. An inconvenient piece of rubbish I had to get rid of. I've crossed the line.

'The boys weren't anywhere near at this point?'

'Good God, no. As if they'd let me harm their brother.'

'So what did you do?'

'Panicked a bit, I think. I thought about throwing him over the cliff, pretending he'd got out through the gate and stumbled in the bad light. But I wasn't sure whether the post-mortem examination would find the broken neck and realize it couldn't have been sustained in a fall. Besides, I could hear the boys coming back. I could hardly have pitched their little brother over their heads, could I?'

Now, it is the two officers who need to take their time. Savidge leans back, holds up a finger, in a half-hearted attempt to slow me down. I give him a few seconds, but it is Skye who speaks first. 'The boys were coming back. You had only a few minutes to dispose of the body. So what did you do?'

'I put him in the boot of my car.'

'Your car?'

I shrug. 'It was handy.'

Savidge looks as though I've slapped him. 'Not possible. We searched that car. We searched the whole premises.'

'Actually, Josh, your officers did a very perfunctory search. Even I could tell their hearts weren't in it. Everyone assumed he'd either been taken by Catrin or by the same person who abducted Archie West. They assumed he was heading for a sex fiend's lair somewhere in camp or on a boat out to sea. No one expected him to be close to home. And no one looked in the boot of my car.'

There is some small level of satisfaction in being able to point out that they screwed up too.

Savidge is on the point of getting up. Skye puts a hand on his arm. 'We can check, Sarge,' she tells him. 'Let's see this through.

'So what did you do with him then, Mrs Grimwood?' I am not Rachel to her either, any more, I notice. There is no sympathy, real or fake, in her eyes. 'Or am I to assume he's still in the boot of your car?'

'No. I disposed of him.'

'Where?'

They're not going to like this next bit. They wait, give me a moment. Only a moment.

'Mrs Grimwood?'

Still I say nothing.

'Mrs Grimwood, what did you do with your son's body?'

'I won't tell you,' I say. 'I'll tell Catrin.'

36

I HAVE A SENSE OF AIR BEING SUCKED OUT OF THE ROOM, OF tension prickling between the three of us. I see a battle imminent and know it's one I have to win.

'That isn't going to happen.' Josh Savidge looks like I've slapped him.

'Why not? What do you think I'm going to do to her? I know she didn't hurt my son, I know that better than anyone. And if she was going to do me harm, she could have done so any time the last three years. I want to talk to her. If you let me see her, I'll tell you where you can find my son's body.'

'We'll find him, whether you tell us where he is or not,' says Josh. 'He has to be somewhere on or near your property. There simply wasn't time for you to do anything else with him and I know you've hardly been alone since he vanished. This time we'll do a proper search. We'll find him. We may have been distracted by what happened to Archie West last time, but—'

There is a knock on the door. Josh runs his hands across his face, but I think he half welcomes the interruption. He suspends the interview, gets up and opens the door. The voice on the other side is one I don't recognize.

'Get on the phone to the boss,' I hear Josh say. 'We need some uniforms down here.'

More mumbling.

319

'I don't care what they've got kicking off up there, tell him I've got two women in custody, exactly five officers and a gang outside intent on causing trouble.'

The door closes. The tape is switched on again, and Josh crosses to the window to look out before he sits back down.

'Sarge.' Skye has been flicking back through her notebook, a crease line between her eyebrows. 'The thing that's been puzzling us is which, if any, of the four cases of missing children are connected. People have been arguing that Catrin must have taken Fred and Jimmy because they both looked so much like her sons and because she found Jimmy's body. On the other hand, Archie was fair, completely different to the other two, and wasn't harmed.'

Blue eyes fix on me. 'So, did you take Archie West as well, Rachel? Did you kill Fred and Jimmy?'

I'm glad she asked. 'Of course not. I have no idea what happened to Jimmy and Fred but my guess is their deaths were both accidents, exactly what Chief Superintendent Stopford has been arguing for years.'

'They did look a lot like Catrin's children, though,' says Skye.

'A quarter of the kids on the islands are of South American descent,' I say. 'I don't think it means anything.'

Savidge starts to interrupt. I don't let him. 'I can, though, tell you exactly what happened to Archie West. I realized a couple of days ago.'

Another puzzled glance between them. They speak almost in unison. 'Go on.'

I fold one hand over the other on the tabletop, trying to look relaxed, like the monster they now believe me to be. 'I'll tell you if you let me speak to Catrin.'

Savidge taps both hands down flat. A ring on his left hand clatters, making the gesture more aggressive than I think he meant. 'Why is it so important for you to speak to Mrs Quinn?'

'I want to tell her I'm sorry. I want to look her in the eye and tell her I'm truly sorry for destroying her life. For killing those boys, who I loved almost as much as she did, by the way.'

Savidge doesn't buy it. 'You've had three years to do that.'

'No, because for three years she hasn't been anywhere near me and I've been afraid to go to her. She didn't want to hear my apologies or my excuses. She didn't want to set eyes on me.'

'It's quite likely she may still not,' says Skye.

'But she will, if she knows it will lead to my son being found.'

Silence while they think about it. They clearly want nothing more than to huddle in a corner, whisper through a plan. But if they leave the room now, momentum will be lost.

'Oy, Quinn! What's it like to kill a kid?'

'Murdering bitch! What have you done with Fred?'

'Tell us where they are, Quinn!'

The voices sound as though they are directly outside. Skye can't stay focused on me any more, her eyes are constantly flicking to the window.

'Those bozos outside are here for Catrin,' I say. 'Where is she? Is she safe?'

'She's fine.' Josh's voice is louder than it needs to be. 'Tell us what you know about Archie West's disappearance.'

'Can they get inside?' Skye looks at Josh in alarm.

He shakes his head. 'Neil's locked all the doors until we have more guys back here. Won't take long.' His smile looks forced.

'Ask her if she'll talk to me,' I try again. 'Just ask.'

'I think it better if you talk to her once we've sorted this out.'

Josh's assumption that I'm stupid annoys me. 'What bargaining power will I have then? Why should you or she agree once there's nothing more I can tell you? Besides, when this is over, I'll be sent to England, to prison or some psychiatric hospital. I'll never see her again. This is my only chance.'

Behind me the clock ticks. I count four, five, six beats. Outside there is a constant rumble of noise. Beer cans thrown, complaints and shouts. Stones flung at walls. What I don't hear are police sirens. I wonder what can possibly be going on up at the bonfire to prevent officers being sent down here and remember that Chris and Michael are up there. This needs to be brought to a close, now.

'How about you tell us what happened to Archie, as a gesture of good faith, and then we let you see Catrin?' says Skye.

Josh stands up. 'Interview suspended at twenty zero four hours. Word outside, Constable McNair.' He gestures towards the door and Skye gets up too, pushing the chair over in the process. It is she, though, not the man in charge, who remembers to switch the tape off.

'I agree to that,' I say, as they reach the door. 'Come back, switch the tape on and I'll tell you what happened to Archie. Then you can check it out and when you find I'm telling the truth, you can let me see Catrin. This whole nasty business could be over with before the bonfire burns low and you two could be well on your way to your next promotion.'

'We don't care about that,' says Skye quickly. Without even thinking about it, I believe her. 'We just want – wanted – to find your son alive and well.'

Josh says nothing, merely switches the tape back on. They look at me like a pair of dogs, hungry, but wary. I throw them the bone they need.

'Archie's disappearance from Estancia farm was entirely accidental.' In spite of the tape running, Skye is scribbling notes, and I give her time to catch up. 'He and his brothers and friends were playing hide-and-seek,' I say, once her pencil stills. 'How much have we heard about how Archie loved hide-and-seek? It was his favourite game. That's why the parents weren't too worried at first. They thought he'd found an extra good hiding place.'

In spite of everything, I'm actually quite proud of myself for working this out.

'So where did he hide?' Skye's pencil is tapping away on her pad.

'In his parents' hired Land Rover. Or, what he thought was his parents' Land Rover. There was actually another car there that day, of identical make and colour. It was only parked for a few minutes, while a visitor popped into Estancia farm, and the rear door left open. Then the owner returned, closed the door, with no idea there was a small child tucked away inside, and drove off.'

'Archie's brother talked about another silver Land Rover,' Skye reminds Savidge.

'Which no one else had seen,' I say. 'So because no one could corroborate, and because he was only a kid, you discounted his evidence.'

Savidge doesn't like this. I can confess to murdering an infant, but no way is he going to admit to making a mistake. 'We asked the Barrells. No one visited the farm that afternoon. They knew nothing about a silver Land Rover.'

'Did you ask George Barrell?'

As Savidge blinks, trying to remember, Skye shakes her head. 'He wasn't there that afternoon but we talked to him the next day. Nobody came to the farm.'

'He's lying to you. For a good reason, but he's lying all the same.'

Another pause, while they think about what to ask me next. Savidge goes first. 'OK, so Archie is in this mysterious Land Rover, being driven God knows where. Why doesn't he say something?'

'At first he assumes it's the family driving the car and he's still hiding. When he realizes it's not, that he's actually in a car with a perfect stranger, he keeps quiet because he's scared. Quite possibly frightened out of his wits. How often do we tell our kids not to get in cars with strangers? Well, not so much here, but in Britain people are paranoid about stranger danger. Archie was a British child.'

'And this Land Rover is headed for the food shed where we found him?' Skye looks puzzled.

'Yep. For an assignation. The driver has been meeting someone there for some time. The two of them fixed it up to suit their purpose. They thought it would be the last place anyone would think of, and it probably would have been, had they not picked up a little stowaway.'

'They were having an affair.' Skye looks like she's discovered alchemy. 'Two islanders, married to other people. That shed wasn't a paedophile's lair, it was a love-nest.'

'Who?' Savidge demands.

'George Barrell, for one,' I say. 'That's why he lied about the silver Land Rover. His girlfriend came for a quick visit, they arranged to meet at the shed, she drove away, unseen by anyone but Archie's brother. A few minutes later, George followed her. He passed me coming back, early evening.'

'Who's the woman?' Skye asks. 'Who was George meeting?'

'Roberta Catton.' In different circumstances, I think I might have rather enjoyed my Miss Marple moment. 'Bob-Cat from the diner.

I saw her car as well that afternoon, silver Land Rover, exactly like the one the Wests hired. The registration letters are SNR. It's quite a bit older than the Wests' car, but I'm not sure a three-year-old would appreciate that. She was coming back from the direction of Darwin when I pulled on to the main road. At least, I didn't recognize her at the time, but I saw her car registration and then I saw it the next day outside her diner.'

Skye's face is creased with concentration. 'They must have seen the kid when they got to the shed.'

I shake my head. As far as I can see, Barrell and Catton are only guilty of adultery and I'm not going to beat them up about that. 'Not necessarily. Archie would have been terrified, remember. I think he got out of the Land Rover and hid. He talked about a man and a woman, when you spoke to him later, didn't he? He hid while the two of them were in the shed, doing what they had to do, then I imagine they left quite quickly, driving away and leaving him stranded. He did the only thing possible. He sheltered inside, lived off the bits and pieces of food they kept there, and finally, when he couldn't stand the loneliness any longer, made for the road. Luckily for all concerned, Callum and Catrin were driving by at the time.'

'Oh my God, poor kid,' Skye mutters.

Savidge dry-washes his face. His hands come away looking slightly oily. 'OK, it's plausible. But that's all it is. A theory.'

'And one we may never be able to prove.' Skye, I can see, is still dwelling on the fear of a young boy, abandoned in the middle of nowhere. I wonder if she has too soft a heart to make a really good police officer.

'Talk to George and Bob-Cat. Promise them discretion and I'm sure they'll admit they were in the shed that afternoon, and that Bob-Cat was parked by Estancia earlier. It's probably occurred to them already that she was the means of getting little Archie to that shed.'

'They'd have said something, surely?' Skye isn't convinced.

'Why would they risk the affair becoming public knowledge? Archie had been found, no harm done. I imagine they thought least said, soonest mended. Oh, and there is this—' I reach into the pocket of my jeans, pull out the polythene bag. I put it on the table directly between Skye and me. She reaches out; Savidge puts a hand on hers.

'We need an evidence bag for that,' he says. 'What is it, Mrs Grimwood?'

'Sand. I scraped it from the back of Bob-Cat's car on Thursday. I'll bet it's the exact sand that can only be found on Estancia beach. And I'll bet it got into the car on the soles of Archie West's shoes.'

'Interview suspended at twenty fifteen hours.' Savidge gets up, finds another clear plastic bag, and puts mine inside it. 'I'll send you in a cup of tea, Mrs Grimwood.'

Skye follows him out, and I'm alone.

It will take time, a couple of hours or more, to track down Bob-Cat and George. Even if they cooperate, nothing will happen in a hurry. They can look in Bob-Cat's car, she won't have cleaned it, but even supposing they find more sand, they can't prove it came from Estancia without sending it away for analysis. It all depends on the two lovebirds coming clean. I can't expect to see Catrin for some time.

A flickering of blue light on the wall opposite the window tells me at least one police car has arrived. I hear it driving slowly around the building.

My father will turn up soon, demanding to know what's happening, why I'm being kept so long. He'll probably be told that I've confessed. He'll demand to see me. I presume I'll be allowed to refuse, so of course that's what I'll do.

Never having to look my father in the eyes again, never again see myself falling short of whatever standard he's chosen to hold me up against this time, could be the silver lining I'm looking for.

All is quiet outside. The police car is gone. So, presumably, is the unruly Catrin-hating crowd they were sent to quell. Soon that crowd will turn their bile from Catrin to me.

Trying not to listen to the clock's ticking, I sit and think about my sons, my darling boys, and what it will be like not to watch them growing up. To see them only across a desk, something like this one, a handful of times a year. To look into eyes that are different each visit, trying to find some remnant of love, and see only condemnation and shame.

A wave of pain hits me so hard I have to stand up, to move around, to lean against cold hard walls. It is silent outside. And yet somehow, the lack of sound feels more ominous than the shouting and running we heard previously.

The clock ticks out the remaining seconds of the life I'm still clinging to, and I think about Sander, who deserved so much better than me. He is a good man, my husband. Wise, hard-working, loyal. Fiercely protective of his family and so very, very fond of me. I wish I'd tried that bit harder. There is so much to love in that big, ugly Dutchman of mine, why didn't I see it when I had the chance?

The ticking of the clock gets louder. I walk laps of the room, stare up at the sky, at what could be the last firework display I ever see. And I think about prison. I will be a child-killer, something no one tolerates. I think about the beatings, the abuse that I'll suffer, and think that perhaps, in some way, I'll welcome it.

I think about the people who were outside earlier, baying for Catrin's blood. It will be mine they want soon. I have a sense of them coming back. I can't hear them, but I feel some lurking presence very close.

I cannot think about Catrin. Every time I try, it is as though there is a barrier keeping the thoughts out. Catrin and I will meet tonight but it's not a meeting I can prepare for. When she and I do at last come together, I'm going to have to wing it.

And so, finally, I think about my youngest son. He should have been the most precious of all, the beloved last child, the one I kept a baby long after the age I let his brothers gain their independence. He should have been my favourite, my pet. Instead he was the intruder, the changeling, a constant reminder of the most dreadful act I could possibly have committed. He was the living embodiment of my guilt.

I think about his skin, turning the ivory colour of cheap wax. I think about him being so cold, so alone, out there in the dark. I see his body rotting and his soul crying out for me, for the love I denied him when he was alive.

I can't see the clock any more. I can't see the walls of the room. I can see nothing but the shining drops of water falling from my eyes on to the table.

When the door opens again, I'm calmer. My head is resting on the tabletop, sore from where I think I might have been banging it, damp with tears or sweat. Not blood, I hope, that will just result in more delay. It's the desk sergeant. He's brought me tea.

'Your husband's here.' As he puts the mug down, keeping his distance, I meet his eyes. He knows. His body doesn't move but I can see his mind recoiling from the monstrosity in front of him.

Get used to it. This is how the world will react from now on. He's said something. Focus. Sander. He managed to get a flight.

'He's here? In the station?'

A single, short nod of the head. Unnecessary words are not for the likes of me.

'Is he asking to see me?'

'He is.'

'Do I have to?'

He shrugs. Were it in his power, I think he would force me to come face to face with my husband. And be there to watch while I'm doing so. 'Up to you.'

'I don't want to see him. Tell him the boys are at their grandparents.'

'I'll tell him two of your boys are.'

The door closes and the lock is turned. I drink tea. I wait.

The next time I hear the door, I'm standing by the window, my hands clutching the bars. A breeze is making its way in through an ill-fitting pane of glass, bringing with it the smell of peat-smoke and burning salt that always fills the air on Bonfire Night. We have few trees here, and wood is always at a premium, so we burn driftwood, and keep the fire going with peat. I've been watching the fireworks fly towards the stars they aspire to be, and thinking that, in a parallel world, I could have been at home, huddled in a chair by the window, my youngest son on my lap. At a distance, the fireworks wouldn't have frightened him. At a distance, in my arms, he'd have fallen in love with the strange, transient beauty of fire flying through the sky.

'Your husband was here, Rachel.' Skye's voice.

'I know.' The firework display is building to a climax. The explosions have increased in intensity. The revelry will go on, of course, long into the night, but the celebrations will be private ones. On clear nights here, you can climb to high ground and watch firework parties taking place all over the Falklands.

'*And to and fro, and in and out,*
The wan stars danced between.'

'Sorry?'

'Samuel Coleridge.' I'm still looking at the sky. '*The Rime of the Ancient Mariner.* The fireworks made me think of it. What were you saying about my husband?'

'He's gone to look for Christopher and Michael. He'll take them home.'

I send a silent message of thanks to my husband for making it home tonight, for ensuring the boys aren't alone.

Skye and Savidge are standing either side of the door. A uniformed constable is in the doorway. The three of them look like an execution squad.

'We've spoken to George Barrell and Roberta Catton.' Savidge speaks first. 'Both admit to the affair, to being at the food shed on the afternoon in question. They're going to come in separately tomorrow to give official statements. Both deny any knowledge of the boy being with them, of course, although—'

'You'll never prove it, so don't try,' I interrupt.

Savidge looks as though he wants to slap me and I make a note not to provoke him any more. We need to get on with it.

'Come on.' He gestures to the door.

'Where are we going?' I don't move. 'I want to see Catrin.'

'And much to my amazement, she's agreed. We're all in the boardroom. Come on, we've wasted enough time.'

I couldn't agree more. So I follow as quickly as I can. We turn at the bottom of the corridor and another constable is holding open the door of the boardroom. Catrin will be waiting inside. I picture her looking out of the window, her long hair streaming down her back, turning to face me at the last moment.

She isn't, of course, Catrin never does anything for effect and wouldn't dream of playing to the gallery. She is still the most unassuming person I've ever met. She is sitting quietly at the table and doesn't look up as I come in.

I'm steered into the seat directly opposite hers. She's wearing clothes that are far too big. Cotton trousers pulled tight at the waist. A shirt that drowns her slim form. Her hair has been tied back with an elastic band. Her arms are folded on the table in front of her and she's looking down at them. She is the picture of stillness, except that the fingers of her right hand are shaking. Her face looks thin, drawn. The lines I remember are more pronounced than they were three years ago. They are lines of grief, now, not merely creases caused by wind and sun.

Around the room people are taking their seats. Skye on my right, Savidge to my left. The other two flank Catrin. We are two opposing armies, except there is only one enemy here and that is me. The recording equipment is switched on and we all give our names for the record. When it is Catrin's turn her voice breaks, as though she hasn't used it in a while. She coughs and tries again.

'Right.' Savidge tries to take control. 'Mrs Grimwood, you asked to speak to Mrs Quinn and she's agreed. Mrs Quinn, I have to inform you that if, at any time, you wish this interview to end, you only have to say. You are under no obligation to speak to Mrs Grimwood. Can I remind you both that you are still under caution?'

There is scuffling outside and what sounds like a football being kicked against the wall. One of the uniformed constables stands up and speaks softly into a wall phone. I can't take my eyes off Catrin's face. She can't take hers off the sleeve of her shirt.

'OK, Mrs Grimwood, you've got what you asked for. Now, please can you tell us what you did with Peter's body?'

She looks up then. Calm grey eyes. They stare into mine and I know they won't look away until we leave this room. 'I want to hear Rachel tell me what she told you.' Her voice is the same. A little shaky perhaps, but basically the same.

'We've been through that.' Savidge is speaking softly, as though Catrin's calm is rubbing off on him. 'We filled you in with everything she said. We don't need to go through it again.'

'I need to hear it in her own words.' Catrin is speaking to him, looking at me. 'I want her to tell me how she killed her son.'

I expected this. I'm ready for it. I tell her, exactly as I told Josh and Skye earlier, about my seeing her car stop outside my house, my watching her pick up Peter and lift him back into the garden.

Her brow lifts; she doesn't take her eyes off mine.

I tell her I saw her drive away down the hill, effectively clearing her of any involvement in my son's disappearance. Still she doesn't speak. I give her back her liberty, absolve her of all blame, open up the possibility of a future with the man she loves. I take my life in both hands and give it to her and she offers me nothing in return. Except her undivided attention.

I leave nothing out. I repeat, almost word for word, the confession I made to Skye and Josh. The two constables, who haven't heard any of this before, are shocked – I can tell from sharp intakes of breath, from furtive glances at each other – but Catrin is unmoved.

'I put him in the boot of my car.' I can't bring myself to say his body. 'I knew there'd be a huge fuss. People looking for him. So I hid him, to deal with him later.'

Grey eyes blink and moisten. Blink again. Their focus doesn't shift.

'And that's all,' I finish. 'That's how, and why, I killed my son.'

Everyone is waiting for Catrin. For a moment, she does nothing. And then, her hands lift and clap together, once, twice, three times. A slow handclap, cutting through the otherwise silent room. No one else moves. It is as though she holds a spell over us. I can't break eye contact. We're playing that game we loved as kids, the one where we tried to outstare each other. The first one to look away was the loser. She always beat me. She won't this time.

Outside fireworks explode. Someone has set them off right next to the building. On the wall behind Catrin I can see reflections of red, blue and lilac sparks. A ribbon of silver stars. The pops and bangs continue for the better part of a minute then silence falls again. And with it, the spell is broken.

'OK.' Savidge is determined now. 'That's it then. We've done what you asked, Mrs Grimwood, we've done what you asked, Mrs Quinn. Now I want to know where the child is.'

I'm waiting for Catrin to speak. She's waiting for me.

'Mrs Grimwood. Rachel.' Savidge knows he's taken a risk, allowing Catrin and me to talk, he's panicking it hasn't paid off. 'For your family's sake, for everyone's sake, including your own, tell us where we can find Peter.'

'She can't.' Catrin seems to have spoken without moving her lips, or maybe I'm so fixated on her eyes that I can see nothing else. 'She doesn't know. She's lying to you.'

'What?' Skye whimpers at my side. The men are looking at each other. Catrin and I are still locked in our weird staring competition, and I am praying as I've never prayed in my life before. I see her lips soften, twist.

'She always was a manipulative cow.'

All four officers stiffen in their seats, either nudge their chairs back or think about doing so. They look from Catrin to me, as though expecting one of us to leap at the other any second now.

Oh, please God, please God, please God.

Catrin sits more upright, before taking her eyes from me and fixing them on Savidge.

I'm not sure I can breathe again. Not until . . .

'Rachel didn't kill Peter.' Her tone is disparaging, verging on incredulous. 'Shame on you for even entertaining the thought, Josh Savidge. You've known her since she was five, what were you thinking of?'

'She confessed.' Skye looks a little afraid of Catrin. 'We have it on record.'

People are running around outside again. We ignore them.

'She confessed because she thinks I killed him.' Catrin is looking at me once more. 'She thinks she owes me. She destroyed my life, so she's giving me hers in return. She's going to let me get away with killing her son, and she's going to serve the prison time that is rightfully mine, because that's the only way she thinks she can make it up to me.'

331

'I don't—' Savidge sounds as though he's going to burst into tears. I can't look at him. I can't take my eyes off the woman who holds the rest of my life in her hands.

That woman sits back, she might be completely at ease. 'She may have seen me pick Peter up from the road but she couldn't possibly have seen me putting him in the garden. You can't see the garden gate from her bedroom window.' She looks round in exasperation. 'For God's sake, I've been in that room dozens of times. I know what you can and can't see from the window. She saw me pick her son up, she panicked and came racing downstairs to protect him, but by the time she reached the garden I was gone. And so was he.'

'Rachel, is this true?'

My hands are clutching the tabletop. If I let go, I'll fall.

Catrin hasn't finished. 'Except, my former best friend is a bit more cunning even than that. She's gambling on me not letting her go through with it. That I'll relent at the last minute and make my own confession, tell you what I did with Peter and where he is. She's willing to risk going to prison, just to get her son's body back. That's how much she loves this little boy she's just told you she killed.' She shakes her head, and something in her cold, stern face softens. 'You poor, poor, stupid cow.'

I don't mean to wail, I simply can't help it. It comes from nowhere and suddenly both Skye and Josh are holding me, trying to stop me from banging my head on the hard surface of the table. Finally, after what feels like for ever, but is probably only a couple of minutes, I'm being held in my chair. Skye's arms are around me, but it feels more like a big hug than a restraint. Josh is crouched at my side, panting heavily.

'I'm telling you, I'll bloody well charge the pair of you if I don't get some answers.' He doesn't mean it, I can tell. He's as confused and unhappy and bewildered as the rest of us are. Except, perhaps . . .

Catrin waits for me to calm down, to stop sobbing, to look her in the eyes again.

'Please,' I say, knowing that I will beg, get down on my hands and knees if I have to. I will do anything to see my little boy one last time. I feel my face collapsing and know I'm about to start crying again.

332

'Rach.' She's leaning across the table. The two minders copy her, ready to pull her back. 'Listen to me.'

I think her voice is the only thing tethering me to sanity.

'I've spent three years thinking about how I'm going to hurt you. Three years with nothing in my head but misery and stupid plans for revenge. I even wrote some of them down, which is why I'm here in the first place. And everyone is quite right that Thursday had a special significance. Thursday was the day I was going to bring everything to an end.'

I can't do this. I thought I was strong enough. I'm not.

'Rach, listen to me, look at me. I was going to call you on Thursday, round about three o'clock, before the boys got home from school. I was going to say that we needed to talk, that things had gone on long enough, and I was going to suggest we go out on my boat, so that we could be alone, so that no one would know what we were doing or try to interrupt us. I knew you'd agree.'

'Yes.' I would have done. I'd have agreed instantly.

Catrin's eyes remain on mine but her lips are curling upwards in the faintest hint of a smile. 'I was going to drive us out of harbour and then, when we were out of sight of anyone on land, I was going to shoot you with a tranquillizer gun.'

No one was expecting that. I can tell from the starts, the puzzled frowns, the nervous eye movements.

'It was risky.' Catrin ignores the police officers. It might be only the two of us in the room as far as she is concerned. 'I roughly knew your weight, of course, and could calculate the amount of anaesthetic I'd need for a marine mammal of similar size. But different species react to drugs differently. There was a chance I'd end up killing you.'

'You weren't going to kill me?'

Her grey eyes are cold as steel. 'Of course I was. Just not quickly.'

Again, the mood in the room shifts. Savidge clears his throat, but doesn't seem to know how to begin. It is Skye who speaks next, from her position on the floor beside me. 'So what was the plan? When – if – Rachel woke up?'

'We were going south.'

The officers are exchanging looks around us. 'What's south?' asks one of the constables.

'Nothing,' I say, because in those four words she's told me exactly what the plan was. 'We were going to die together, weren't we? After days, maybe a week or so, the seas would get too big for that small boat and we'd be lost.'

Catrin inclines her head. 'I was planning on a few days at least. Enough time for you to dwell on what was going to happen. On what you were leaving behind. A few days of agony didn't really feel enough, but it was the best I could come up with.'

'Until you saw Peter in the road?' says Savidge. 'When suddenly you had a much better plan. You decided to take the child, rather than the mother.'

'Yes.'

This is it. It's coming. I reach out for Skye but she's moved. I can't look for her. I can't take my eyes off Catrin.

She gives a heavy sigh, as though her confession, like mine, is proving exhausting. 'When I saw Peter in the lane that day, I stopped the car, got out and picked him up. Just as you saw.'

I want her to stop. I've changed my mind. I can't bear to hear this.

'It was the second time in two days that I'd held a young child. Archie, when I found him, was too shocked and cold to do anything but cling to me, but Peter was quite different. He wrapped his arms round my neck and pushed his face against my shoulder, the way Kit used to at that age.'

Her eyes stay on mine but their focus drifts. She's slipped away, is reliving the moment she held Peter in her arms. I think I can see the gleam of a tear.

'And . . .' prompts Savidge.

She comes back to us, blinks, gives a half shrug. 'And everything changed.'

Savidge opens his mouth, she doesn't give him chance.

'I knew I could never kill Peter.' She's speaking directly to me again. 'I didn't even want to kill you any more. So I carried him to the gate and put him back in the garden. I turned the car and I drove back down the hill. The last time I saw your son, Rachel, he was alive and well.'

And again, we stare at each other for what feels like a very long time.

Until Savidge interrupts. 'So if you didn't take Peter, Catrin, why did you race down to your boat? Why did you disappear for hours?'

Her eyes drift briefly from mine. 'Because I needed to think. I'd spent months planning that my life would effectively end on Thursday. I needed to come to terms with the knowledge that it wasn't. That I wasn't going to die and I wasn't going to kill Rachel.'

'Why didn't you tell us any of this before?'

She tosses her head in exasperation. 'It would hardly have helped my case, would it? And it was completely irrelevant, because as far as I was concerned, the last time I saw Peter, he was absolutely fine.'

She seems to lose interest in Savidge and turns to me again. 'I know what happened that day,' she says. 'You know, the day Ned and Kit died?'

I can only stare back. She knows? She knows what I did that day?

'I know how you felt about Ben.' She shakes her head sadly. 'No one cries for five hours at a friend's wedding. And I know you knew about Callum.' She shrugs. 'I guess the temptation was too much to resist.'

She reaches out towards me but the table is too wide. 'It's OK,' she says, and there is a ghost of a smile on her face. A smile of pity, but I'll take what I can get. 'You know what? If it hadn't been for the accident, you'd probably have done me a favour. Really, it's OK.'

I hadn't known it was possible for misery to hurt this much. And yet, somewhere, out in the universe, a cog slips back into its rightful place. The wheels start turning again, and their movement is smooth.

> *He'll shrieve my soul, he'll wash away*
> *The Albatross's blood.*

'I'm so sorry,' I say.

Her small, slim body relaxes as her hatred of me slips out of it. She knows that I've seen it. 'I know,' she says.

'If there was anything, anything at all that I could do . . .'

She gives a brief, almost amused, look around the room. 'Clearly.'

The sound of wood scraping along the floor. 'Enough.' Savidge is on his feet. 'I'm getting the boss in. I'm separating you two. One way or another, we're going to get to the truth.'

I open my mouth. Catrin beats me to it.

'Don't be such a twat, Josh. Get Stopford by all means, get the entire bloody constabulary back, but splitting us up will achieve nothing. We've told you everything we know. Rachel did not kill Peter. She couldn't kill to save her own life.'

'And Catrin doesn't know how to lie.' I'm talking to Josh, but looking at my best friend.

She's looking right back. 'Unlike you. You're a bloody master at it.'

'Could never fool you, could I?'

The tiniest of smiles and then she's talking to Savidge again. 'Josh, come on. While you're focusing all your efforts on us, no one is looking for Peter. You haven't been looking for him since you made up your mind I took him.'

She hasn't convinced him, I can see from the look on his face. He's had two suspects today, he's not going to let us both go without a fight.

A knock on the door. It opens. The desk sergeant. 'Josh, I need a word.'

'Give me a minute, Neil.'

'No, has to be now. I'm serious, Josh.'

'For God's sake, what is it?'

The desk sergeant looks around and seems to decide. 'I've got Callum Murray in the interview room. He's claiming he killed Peter Grimwood.'

37

I'M BACK IN THE INTERVIEW ROOM, ALONE. CATRIN HAS BEEN returned to her cell. Callum's arrival – not to mention his confession – has floored all of us, but Josh Savidge has wit enough to realize that he needs to talk to him alone.

Already, ten minutes have passed and they won't even have finished booking him in yet. There is no time for this. My baby is out there. Peter. I've started whispering his name to myself like a mantra. Peter, Peter, Peter.

I can't sit down. I pace the room, pound my fists on the walls, but not so loud as to attract attention, because I mustn't waste any more time. I peer out into the corridor and see nothing. I walk to the window and look up at the sky.

I don't believe it. Not the man on whose shoulder I wept only this morning. I have always liked Callum. He is big, friendly, larger than life in every respect and yes, there might be shades of him that are darker, no one can have been through what he did in the war and come out of it unscathed, but he keeps his dark places hidden away and private. I have never thought him dangerous.

My dad thinks the world of him, and he's never wrong about people. He certainly had me pegged years ago.

Callum could not have harmed my child. And yet I no longer believe it was Catrin. I've looked into her eyes. It wasn't Catrin.

Was it me? Did I kill him and wipe the memory from my mind?

Is that even possible? Much more of this and I'll start to believe anything. I think back, watching Catrin walk towards her car with Peter in her arms, losing sight of her (she was spot on about that), running from the room, out of the house, across the garden.

Outside, a large engine roars into life and I can't help but step away from the wall. The revving sounds continue, increasing in volume. Then a burst of forward momentum. I back up, almost to the door, and the truck stops. Its headlights are shining in through the window. Then, equally quickly, the engine squeals, tyres scrape across the road and it speeds away.

Inside the building I hear footsteps running. Another siren sounds but it's heading up the hill to the bonfire.

I want to bang on the door, demand to know what's going on, but there simply aren't enough people in the building to deal with hysterics on my part. I may be losing my mind, but I have to do it quietly.

There's something going on up at the bonfire, otherwise more police would be here. I'm praying Sander had the good sense to take the boys home; that wherever my three men are, they're safe.

An alarm sounds, drowning out external noise. From inside the building I hear more running footsteps.

An escape? Callum changed his mind and ran for it?

The alarm continues, painfully shrill. Then someone is at the door. I step back and Skye rushes inside. She is wearing her high-visibility jacket.

'Get your coat.' Without waiting for me to move, she grabs it from the back of the chair I've been sitting on.

'What's going on?' I speak without thinking because from the corridor comes the faint but unmistakable aroma of smoke. Skye has brought it into the room too, clinging to her like cheap perfume.

'Someone sent a firework through a window. The main office is on fire.' She's holding out handcuffs. 'I have to cuff you, I'm afraid. Sergeant's orders.'

The smoke is thicker in the corridor and from somewhere close by I can hear crackling as Skye, now cuffed to me, drags me towards reception.

'Breathe as little as you can till we're outside.' She succumbs to a fit of coughing.

My eyes begin to sting. There are footsteps at our rear but I don't look back. We run through the security doors into the reception area. Neil, the desk sergeant, a handkerchief to his face, is holding open the front door.

Smoke is racing ahead of us, thickening in the cooler air. Skye pulls me outside, beyond its reach, beyond the wave of warmth that has been increasing with every second. The cool clear air feels like a huge relief.

A window shatters as Catrin, handcuffed to the uniformed constable, follows us out. She rubs her eyes with her free hand and looks around. Her eyes settle, not on me, but on Callum. He is already in the car park, similarly restrained, standing with his minder by the police minibus. He keeps his eyes on his feet, his shoulders lifting visibly with every breath he takes.

Josh Savidge is last to leave the building. 'Fire brigade?' he asks.

Neil throws up his hands. 'On its way. But guess where everyone is?'

Josh strides towards us. 'Everyone in the bus.' He feels in his pockets. 'Come on. We don't know who threw that firework and I'm not having you three out in the open.'

'Where're you going?' Neil asks.

Josh doesn't know. It's obvious from the look on his face. 'I'll be on the radio,' he tells Neil. 'Get hold of the boss for me.'

We are dragged and coaxed on to the bus. Josh has the engine on before the rest of us are even sitting and we pull out of the car park.

'Town hall,' Skye suggests.

'Bad idea,' the constable with Callum pipes up. 'It'll be swarming with people tonight. You really want to throw three confessed child-killers into the mix?'

'Holy shit.' Josh leans on the steering wheel. We are right in the middle of the road.

'Cathedral?' suggests the constable cuffed to Catrin.

'It's locked at night,' she says. 'Josh, go to the Conservation. We keep a key hidden in the porch. No one will look for us there and you can hide the bus round the back.'

Josh sees some sense in this, or maybe he's grasping at straws by this time. He releases the brake and we head towards the offices on Ross Road where Catrin works.

At the Conservation, we all file out. No one is around. Or, if they are, we can't see them. Smoke from various bonfires has filled the atmosphere. It is as though fog has covered the whole of the Falklands and the endless fireworks sound like artillery fire.

Catrin finds the key and we all go inside. Once the doors are closed and locked, Catrin and I are uncuffed and she leads us to a conference room. It is eerily similar to the one we left behind at the police station. She pulls down the blinds and we are cut off from the world.

Callum isn't released from his restraints. The four officers are taking no chances with a fourteen-stone former soldier. They lead him to the head of the conference table and he sits, separate from the rest of us.

'What now?' He still can't look anyone in the eye, least of all me. 'What happens next?'

What happens next is that we argue. Josh insists we wait for Stopford, for others to join us. Procedure has to be followed, he says, and we three suspects need to be interviewed separately.

Catrin pitches in, arguing that it will take too long for Stopford to get here, for him to be brought up to speed. 'And he's not exactly quick off the mark,' she reminds them. 'Splitting us up is stupid,' she says. 'Every time one of us says something, you'll have to double-check it with the others. We'll be here all night. And while we're faffing around, Peter is out there.'

It becomes a mantra for Catrin. Every time she presses urgency upon us, she reminds us that Peter is out there, waiting for us to find him. I'm sure if I weren't here, someone would point out that Peter is dead, and that a few hours will hardly make much difference. But I am and they don't.

'We'll never secure a conviction if we mess up the interview,' Skye warns Josh.

'He's confessed,' one of the constables says. 'The conviction is a done deal.'

'Yeah, well I've had three bloody confessions in one evening,' snaps Josh. 'Forgive me if I can't take them seriously any more.'

For nearly ten minutes Catrin argues, with me joining in occasionally. Josh wants backup, but his attempts to get information out of Neil back at the station come to nothing. The desk sergeant's priority, understandably, is to stop the building burning down. Callum appears almost to have gone into a trance. Eventually, with misgivings that are practically etched on his eyeballs, Josh agrees. He wants the truth as much as anyone.

Catrin finds a tape recorder. It's checked and switched on, we all give our names for the record, Callum last of all.

He is redder in the face than normal. He has the sort of fair skin through which every emotion he's feeling shines. He is breathing heavily, but otherwise seems calm enough. Until you look at his hands, clenched tightly behind his back. Those hands cannot stop moving.

Josh has taken a chair at the foot of the table, opposite Callum. Ten minutes to eleven. It is completely dark outside.

'Tell us what happened on the afternoon of November the third,' Josh begins. 'The afternoon Peter Grimwood went missing.'

Callum swallows. 'I was worried about Catrin.' He doesn't look at her, although she's barely taken her eyes off him since we entered the room. 'I knew she'd seen her photograph in the *Daily Mirror*. I knew she'd be upset. I wanted to find her, make sure she was OK.'

He glances right, meets her eyes for a second. She seems on the point of speaking, then shakes her head.

'I followed her in my car.' His eyes flick in my direction. 'Up towards your place, Rachel. I didn't think she should be on her own.'

'What time was this?' asks Josh.

'A few minutes before four, I think. I know it was starting to go dark.' He looks at Catrin as though for confirmation. She seems bewildered. Catrin, who kept an icy calm all the time I was confessing to killing my own child, has gone to pieces now that Callum has started speaking.

'OK, carry on, please.'

'I shouldn't have been driving. I could feel an attack coming on.'

'An attack?'

'A blackout. No, that's not quite right, I'm not epileptic or anything, but I have episodes.'

Around the room, faces are puzzled.

'I suffer from post-traumatic stress disorder. I have flashbacks to what happened in the conflict. They can last for several hours, and afterwards I remember practically nothing about where I was or what I did.'

Around the table light is dawning. We've all heard of PTSD.

'Can anyone corroborate these flashbacks?'

'Dr Pirrus. I've been seeing her for a couple of years now. And Catrin. I nearly strangled her a few nights ago.'

At the mention of flashbacks, Catrin's head dropped into her hands. She peers at him now, over the top of her fingers. 'You didn't hurt me. Not really. I hurt you much more.'

His eyes soften. 'You don't take shit from anyone. But imagine if I got hold of a kid . . .'

Alarmed glances flicker my way. I concentrate on breathing in, breathing out, knowing that if I show signs of being too upset, they'll remove me from the room. I look at a spot on the wall, behind Catrin's head. I try not to look at Callum, try not to think of those strong hands on my child.

'OK, so you were driving along the Airport Road after Catrin, and you could feel an attack coming on?'

'That's right. But before I got to the Grimwood house, before I could even see it, Catrin's Land Rover came charging back down the road again. I'm not sure she saw me, although she practically drove through the ditch to get past me. She sped off, leaving me facing the wrong way.'

'I saw you,' Catrin says.

'I was half tempted to go home, leave you to it.' He's talking directly to her now. 'Then I realized you were probably heading for the boat, and that didn't feel like a good idea. So I carried on up the road, meaning to turn round and follow you to the harbour.'

'A few minutes before four,' Josh says. 'Catrin has just put the little boy back in the garden, Rachel has seen her from the window and is running down the stairs. Carry on, please.'

'I'm driving too fast at this stage. I'm worried about Catrin, and I'm slipping.'

'Slipping?' Skye this time.

342

'Losing my grip. Feeling the flashback taking over.'

'Almost four o'clock. You must have reached the house by now?'

Almost four o'clock. Callum is at the house and I'm – where? Pulling on shoes? No, I was barefoot when I ran outside that day.

'I reached the house.' Callum is continuing with his story. 'Driving far too fast. Not concentrating. Peter had got into the road again. I hit him, head on. He flew up, hit the bonnet, the windscreen and then disappeared under the wheels.'

Catrin's white face looks from Callum, to me, and back again. I don't react. I can't. I'm thinking, *that was quick then*. He wouldn't have been afraid. He didn't suffer. He probably didn't even feel much pain. I can keep telling myself that, can't I? There are worse ways, surely, for a little boy to die.

Callum is still talking. 'I stopped the car, of course. I got out, but the boy was dead. I could tell straight away. If he hadn't been, I'd have done something, called someone, I know I would. But I've seen enough corpses to know when someone is beyond help.'

Killed outright. If he's going to be dead, that's the best way, isn't it? I realize that Skye is holding my hand. I squeeze hers, to let her know I'm grateful.

'What did you do with him?' asks Josh.

Callum isn't looking at anyone as he goes on with his story. 'Picked him up, wrapped him in a blanket from my car and put him in the gun case in the back. Then I turned round and drove back down the hill. I think I went to the harbour, still looking for Catrin, but I'm not sure about that bit.'

Exactly what I claimed I'd done. In my stupid, fabricated story, I said I put him in the boot of my car. I'm paying for that now.

'You're not sure about that bit?' Skye has let my hand go. 'You remember the accident clearly, but you don't remember what you did immediately afterwards?'

'Not exactly.' He takes a deep breath, ready to try again.

'You said a few seconds ago that you remember very little about what you do when you have a flashback,' Skye says. 'Just images of the conflict, you said. And yet you remember hitting Peter and putting his body in your boot?'

'You're going to have to hear me out, guys.'

Josh clears his throat. 'Carry on, Callum. Let him go with it, Skye.'

'I disposed of his body later that day,' Callum says. 'I'm not sure about the exact time, it all gets a bit hazy, but I know I drove up to the cliffs above Port Pleasant.'

Catrin's head lifts, like a dog with a scent.

'I left the road, drove as close to the edge as I could, then took Peter out of the car. I threw him over the cliff.'

Skye's hand grabs mine again. It makes no difference, I'm telling myself. He was past being afraid by then. Past being hurt.

'Sarge, I think I should take Rachel outside.'

'I'm fine,' I say, although I'm squeezing her hand so tightly I doubt she is. 'Thank you, Skye, but I'm fine. Carry on please.'

'Did you see him reach the bottom?' asks Josh, after a worried glance at me.

Callum shakes his head. 'I didn't look. I think the tide was in. I would have assumed the water would take him away.'

I wonder if I've blacked out. I can see nothing. After a moment, I realize I've closed my eyes.

'Why didn't you say anything before?' asks Josh. 'Why come in now?'

'Because I remembered none of it. I had no idea until I saw the footprint on your system at the station.'

'Hang on, hang on. Footprint?'

They are just voices now, swirling around in the darkness.

'I went to the police station earlier today. There were a couple of officers in the back room but they had to attend to something and I was left alone. I looked on your computer, Skye, and found the footprint you'd lifted from outside Rachel's house. I recognized it immediately as mine. But I'd only been wearing those boots the afternoon Peter disappeared, so that meant I had to have got out of the car, even though I couldn't remember doing it.'

I have a sense of heads nodding, following the argument.

'When I saw that print, I knew I must have killed Peter that day, and blanked it from my mind. I went straight outside to my car, fully expecting to find him in the lock-up box. He wasn't, of course, and neither was the blanket.'

No, he was lying on the beach, broken by rocks. Oh God, what if he wasn't dead? What if he was clinging to life down there, crying for – not me, he wouldn't cry for me.

'Rachel, are you OK?'

Skye's question brings me back to myself a little. I open my eyes and nod. The four officers are all looking at me. Catrin's eyes are on Callum. His are staring somewhere into the middle distance.

'I do think you should be waiting outside,' Josh tries.

I shake my head at him. I'm going nowhere.

Something has occurred to Skye. 'Callum, I understand why you're worried, but there's nothing in any of that to suggest you killed him.'

'I agree.' Josh isn't looking any happier than Skye. 'If I understand correctly, you don't actually remember any of this, you just surmised it after you saw the footprint on our system and your missing blanket.'

Callum's eyes are fixed on the tabletop now. I cannot share the relief of the officers around me. Neither can Catrin, I see. We both know there's more to come.

'I went to the beach this afternoon,' he says. 'The one where the child's body would have landed.'

We wait.

'I found him.'

I can't help the sob slipping out. Across the table, Catrin's face has creased in misery. I think I see her reach out towards me, but then her hand pulls back sharply.

'You found him? He's on the beach? He's there still?' Josh demands.

Callum lets his head fall forward and back up again. My baby is still on that beach. I try not to see it. Try to make my mind go blank. Those skinny little limbs, that pale, perfect skin.

Josh is giving instructions to the two constables. 'We need to get down there. Quick as you can. Call as soon as you find him.'

'Wait.' Catrin's face is as white as the walls.

Josh isn't having it. 'No, I'm not waiting any longer. Off you go, both of you. Let me know as soon as you find anything.'

'Be careful,' Catrin calls after them. 'That cliff is steep enough in the daylight. Take good torches and watch your step.'

The second the door slams behind them she turns to Callum. 'What did you see, on the beach? Tell me exactly what you saw.'

What is she doing? Skye reaches out to take my hand again. Josh clears his throat. 'I don't think so. We need to get Rachel back to her family. Catrin, are you OK to stay here until we can get all this stuff processed?'

Catrin is looking at me now. 'Trust me,' she says. 'Rach, trust me.'

I nod. It feels like the least I can do, and she faces Callum again. 'What did you see on the beach?'

Callum looks at me, as if for permission.

'Go on,' I tell him.

'I found the blanket pretty quickly,' he says. 'It was caught by a rock, just out of reach of the tide. I couldn't see anything else at first, but as I got closer – I'm sorry, Rachel – I saw his body.'

I want to be brave. I want to trust Catrin, but the thought of my baby lying at the bottom of a cliff . . .

'No!' Catrin slaps her hand down on the table. 'Tell us what you saw. Not what you think you saw. What did you see?'

'For God's sake, Catrin!'

In response, she gets up, strides to him before either officer can stop her, and leans across the table. 'Did you see clothes? Peter was wearing blue shorts and a yellow-and-white-striped T-shirt when I picked him up. Did you see those?'

Somehow he holds it together and shakes his head. 'The clothes weren't there. I think they must have been ripped off. Catrin, he's been on a beach in spring for two days. You know what will have happened to him.'

My baby's body, at the mercy of every creature flying or crawling or swimming around these islands. I feel a cry building at the base of my throat. There'll be no holding back, once it reaches the point where I let it go.

'Did you see shoes?' Catrin is relentless. 'I'm pretty certain I remember buckled sandals. They wouldn't have come off his feet easily.'

He seems to be thinking about it. Did he see brown leather sandals on tiny plump feet?

'What about hair? Peter is blond. His hair looked quite long to me. He looked like he needed a haircut. Did you see hair?'

'I saw enough! I wasn't about to carry out a frigging autopsy!'

I've pulled away from Skye, wrapped my arms around myself. I'm starting to rock, forwards and backwards, the time-old physical response to grief. Is this her punishment, then? To put me through this?

She's kneeling down by Callum's side, has reached up to take his face between her hands. I think he's trying to pull away. She won't let him.

'Tell me what you saw. Rachel can deal with it. She's tougher than she looks.'

I doubt that. I'm hanging on by a thread here.

'Ribs, a skull, a spine. What looked like fingers. That's all I could bear to look at. I saw those and I came away.'

'Skeletonized, or still with flesh attached?'

He's almost sobbing now. She's tormenting him, as well as me. 'Mainly skeletonized. Some flesh, but there were birds feeding on it as I approached. There was very little left.'

Catrin gives a heavy sigh, then stretches up, bends over and drops a kiss on his forehead. I can't believe what I'm seeing. I knew she hated me but . . .

'You saw a seal, you idiot,' she says.

'What?' say Josh and Skye simultaneously.

She straightens up. 'South American fur seal, at a guess. The young adults are a very similar size to small human children.' She looks round, towards the door. 'I can show you. Let me fire up the computer and I'll show you a seal skeleton.'

Josh and Skye are staring at each other. Callum can't take his eyes off Catrin. I simply can't allow myself to think. Without waiting for permission, Catrin leaves the room. Josh motions for Skye to follow her. I go too. Behind us Callum and Josh bring up the rear.

Everything seems to be happening in slow motion now. For me, anyway. I focus on the back of Catrin's head. She's switched on a desktop computer and entered log-in details and password.

'You did drive up to Port Pleasant that day.' She raises her voice so that Callum will hear her. 'Early evening, around six thirty p.m. I heard your engine first, then I saw you.'

We form a semicircle around Catrin. All eyes are on the screen, but Josh and Skye make sure to keep between Callum and me.

'Around six thirty on third November, you can confirm that Mr Murray drove up to the cliff above Port Pleasant?' Josh says.

'About that time, yes.' She's distracted, searching through databases. She enters something into the search engine but types too quickly for me to read it. 'He stayed for around thirty minutes. Most of the time he was in his vehicle, but he got out and walked to the clifftop at one point.' She turns to Callum. 'You had me worried for a second. You came very close to the edge.'

'Was he carrying anything?' Josh demands. 'Did he have anything with him?'

She's flicking from one image to the next. 'Not a thing. He was wearing a faded denim jacket and jeans. Blue and brown scarf around his neck. Not what he'd been wearing earlier in the day. I remember wondering why he'd changed.'

'Did I see you?' Callum asks her.

She shakes her head. 'I was below, watching you through the hatch. I didn't take my eyes off you, though, all the time you were there. I was just about to come on deck and wave when you turned round, got into your car and drove away.'

'I did it later then.'

'You did come back later.' She nods sharply in agreement. 'Much later. The next morning. I watched you park, get out and walk to the edge again. This time you had that blanket wrapped around your shoulders. I don't blame you. It was a very cold dawn. You watched me get arrested and taken on to the other boat.'

He's nodding. 'I remember that. The flashback was over by then. Had been for several hours. I'd been up all night.'

'You did look a bit rough. Before the police boat arrived, I was watching you through the binoculars.'

'Did anyone else see him?' Josh asks. 'Any of the arresting officers?'

'Possibly, but I think their attention was mainly on me. I tell you what I did see, though, just before they made me go below deck on the police boat.'

'What?'

'I saw you turn round and walk back towards your car. And I saw the blanket blow away from you, up into the air, and then down towards the bottom of the cliff.'

He's shaking his head, not daring to believe what she's telling him.

'You didn't even notice, did you? All you were thinking about was me. There you go.'

She enlarges the image on the screen. We are all staring at the skeleton of a South American fur seal. About a hundred centimetres long, unmistakably a seal.

'Catrin, I really don't—' Josh begins.

'It wouldn't be whole and complete, like this one.' She raises her voice to make her point, keep our attention. 'It will have been mauled by scavengers. Callum, on the beach today, you saw the blanket and that confirmed your worst fears. Then you saw a ribcage, very similar to that of a human child. You saw parts of the spine, again virtually indistinguishable, maybe part of the skull. Even the bones of the flippers could look like those of a human hand to someone not quite in his right mind. But now you know you didn't throw the blanket, there's no reason to think you threw the child.'

Faces around me look far from convinced. I want to be convinced, but . . .

Catrin has turned away from the computer now, is looking directly at Callum. 'All the time you were on that clifftop, I was watching. You didn't throw Peter off. You didn't kill Peter.'

'So who the hell did?'

They both look at me. I shake my head. I didn't kill him. I don't know who did. Three of us looking at each other now. It is as though the two police officers have ceased to exist. Callum speaks first.

'He disappeared in what – fifteen minutes? Both Catrin and I were outside your house then. Three cars on that road in that time? Not possible.'

'I didn't see him,' I say. 'When I ran outside, he wasn't there.'

'Exactly, it must have been me. I'm sorry, Cat, but I'm the only one with time unaccounted for. I'm the only one of us with an established psychiatric condition. I'm the only one with a history of violence against other people.'

She shakes her head. 'No.'

'There wasn't anyone else there.'

'Except his two brothers,' says Skye in a small voice.

38

I'D THOUGHT I WAS NUMB. HOW WRONG I'D BEEN. I CAN SEE my own shock mirrored on the face of my friend. 'No,' she says again.

Callum isn't going to hand over guilt easily. 'Don't be ridiculous, Skye.'

'Five people were on or near the property when Peter vanished.' Skye is quiet but insistent.

'When you came down to the garden, Rachel, were your two older boys there?' asks Josh.

I pretend to think about it. 'No,' I say, after a few seconds. 'They were down on the beach somewhere. They'd talked about going down there to watch the eclipse. They came back up when they heard me calling. They helped me search for Peter.'

'Did you stay together?'

We didn't. The second I knew Peter was missing, I went into panic mode, stopped thinking straight. 'They went back down to the beach, I think,' I say. 'I searched the house and the stables. We were separated for about twenty minutes. Then I called the police.'

Silence. I can't deal with what I'm seeing on the faces in front of me. 'They love their brother. They take better care of him than I do. They wouldn't hurt him.'

'I'm sure they wouldn't, Rachel.' Skye takes my hand again. 'But there could have been an accident. Maybe they felt responsible. Couldn't bring themselves to tell you.'

The garden gate. The one Mum has nagged and nagged me about. The cliff path could have been in shadow. 'I have to get home. I have to talk to them.'

'Are they there? I thought they were with their grandparents.'

'Sander is back. He'll have taken them home.' I look at Josh. 'I have to talk to them.'

'We can't go charging over there now. We haven't enough officers.'

Callum shrugs his shoulders to indicate he's still handcuffed. 'I shouldn't be much of a threat.'

I watch Josh decide that, having bent or broken so many rules tonight, he might as well toss the book out of the window. We run outside and pile back into the minibus. Skye drives, Josh sits in the back, keeping an eye on the rest of us. He needn't worry. All we are focusing on is the road ahead, all we are interested in is getting to the house faster.

Skye heads out of Stanley, swinging her way around people in the road. It's not far off midnight.

Every time I think it can't possibly get any worse, it does. If my son has to be dead, I would a million times rather he'd been killed by Catrin for revenge, or Callum in a trauma-induced flashback, than by his own brothers.

I remember Ralph asking me if my boys had been hanging round the old wreck. He must have seen something, footprints leading to it, one of them climbing on board. Is that where they put him? How will I ever convince them it wasn't their fault? That it was mine. My job to take care of him. My failure, not theirs.

We reach the house and I'm first out of the bus. I hear Josh call at me to slow down but I'm through the gate, running across the garden and in through the front door before the rest of them have left the vehicle.

I'm expecting the boys to be in bed, but I can hear the TV playing softly in the living room. Sander looks up at me from the sofa, his blue eyes paler than usual, dimmed by grief. On either side of him, their heads resting on his lap, are the boys. Both have blankets covering them. Both are asleep.

Skye has caught up with me. She puts one hand on my shoulder. 'Steady, Rachel,' she whispers.

'I need to talk to them.' I look from Chris to Michael, both still so young, so beautiful, when they're asleep. 'Wake them up.' I'm whispering too, talking about waking them up in a voice low enough to keep them asleep.

Sander's hands stretch out to shield each child, protect them from me. I see in his face that he believes me to be the killer of his youngest son. 'What are you doing?' he says. 'Get out of here.'

'Mr Grimwood, we need to talk to Christopher and Michael.' Skye steps in front of me. Behind us, Josh, Catrin and Callum have arrived.

Something, either the noise or the colder air, has roused Chris. He rubs his eyes and opens them. 'Mummy.'

He springs up, as only the young can after being asleep, and as I run forward his arms wrap around my neck. Over his shoulder I address Sander. 'Did you tell them?'

Chris stiffens. 'Tell us what? Mummy, tell us what?'

I hold his head in my hands. I don't think I've ever loved a face more than I love his. 'Chris, I need you to tell me the truth now. Daddy and I love you and Michael more than anything else in the world and whatever happens we will always love you and always take care of you, but you have to tell us the truth.'

I see it in his face. The start of his features, the dark light in his eyes. He doesn't need to ask what I'm talking about.

Oh, God no.

'Rachel, what is going on?'

I can't go on. I don't want to hear it. Chris's mouth is trembling. His eyes are starting to gleam. 'I'm sorry, Mummy.' He starts to sob. I pull him close. I've lost one son, I will not lose another.

'It's OK, my angel. Whatever happened it's OK. I love you.'

He's sobbing hard now, against my shoulder. Every time he takes a breath, I hear the word sorry and I think one more might just break my heart.

'Rachel.' Sander, still on the sofa to avoid disturbing Michael, is pleading with me now.

'There was an accident,' I say, because it's all become so clear to me now. 'That day Peter disappeared. It was my fault completely, I wasn't watching him. He tried to follow the boys down to the beach and fell. They saw what had happened, saw that he was dead and thought it was their fault. But it wasn't, my darling, it really wasn't.' I'm rocking Christopher. I think he's trying to pull away from me but I'm not ready to let him go just yet.

'They panicked and they hid his body somewhere. Probably on the old wreck. They thought I'd be angry. They thought I'd blame them, but I never would have done, my angel. You must never think it was your fault.'

Behind me, I hear Skye sniff.

'You must tell us now though, my love. You have to tell us where he is.'

'Peter's not dead, Mummy. He's in the boathouse.'

I stop moving. Everyone does. Without our noticing, Michael has woken and pushed himself upright next to his father. His eyes dart from me to the group in the doorway. 'Hi, Auntie Catrin.'

'What?'

I'm really not sure who said that. It wasn't me. I can't speak. I can only stare.

Michael blinks sleep from his eyes and they drop to the floor, the way they always do when he knows he's in trouble. 'We hid him in the boathouse when everyone was watching the eclipse. We gave him your sleeping pills so he wouldn't cry. Chris said if you thought he was gone you'd start to love him like you love us. He said you'd be like the other little boys' mummies, all sad and everything. It was Chris's idea.'

Chris has stopped moving. His head feels as though it's glued to my shoulder. I don't think he's breathing.

'Chris wrote the notes too. I saw him. He posted them in town.'

I'm vaguely aware of Sander getting to his feet.

'I think Peter wants to come out now,' says Michael. 'We ran out of pills. He's been crying a lot today.'

I am not moving. I cannot. So the world moves for me. The house dissolves into mist and I'm outside, feeling the rush of the wind, the salt spray in my face. Sounds hit me in the darkness from all sides. Fireworks exploding. The shouting of people I love. The screaming of gulls. The deafening thunder of the wind and, from the nearby town, the sound of the cathedral clock striking midnight.

'Rachel, let us go. Come back.'

'Rachel, slow down. You can't run down there in the dark.'

'Someone get these friggin' cuffs off me!'

'Mummy, I'm sorry.'

'Mummy!'

I see the beach, gleaming pale in the glow of a thousand fireworks. It's far below me; then not so far, the beach is rising up to meet me. Explosions like gunfire echo around the rocks. I fall and the beach catches me. I have no breath, no strength in my limbs, no thoughts in my head, but the old stonework of the boathouse is in front of me now. The boathouse that nobody has been inside for a decade or more.

'Rachel!' Sander's voice from the clifftop. 'They say the skylight is loose. That's how they got in.'

I'm looking round, for the route the boys must have taken to get on to the roof. I see rocks, loose stonework in the walls, and just as I throw myself against it, Callum is beside me. He kicks out and the door flies inwards. The smell of wet straw and soiled nappies hits us. Callum heads in first, I pull myself in front of him.

Peter, tear-stained, dirty, dopey with sleep and drugs, is sitting on an old horse blanket. He is surrounded by straw and clutching his stuffed rabbit. A look of bewildered desperation takes over his face and he lifts his arms towards me. As I drop to my knees, I hear rushing feet and then a strangled cry that tells me my best friend is back by my side. My son's arms reach up, clasp tight around my neck, and with his chubby fingers, he loosens the rusty, slime-ridden chain that hangs there.

The albatross falls from me, and sinks, deep down, into the sea.

Friday, 3 November 1995
(Twelve months later)

39

DAD'S VOICE IS COMING OUT OF THE RADIO AS I ARRIVE AT Catrin's old house above Whalebone Bay.

. . . that was John Wilcock, of the Falkland Conservation, updating us on the oil-spill clean-up currently taking place around Carcass Island, and this is a reminder to everyone out and about on boats around the islands, any sign of pollution on the water, get in touch with the Conservation straight away. At this time of year it can have a devastating impact on our wildlife.

I park, in the safest place there is, nowhere near a slope of any description, pull the handbrake on tight and turn to check that Peter is sleeping peacefully in the back seat. I can't help but smile. He's grown so much this last year. And when he's awake, he just will not stop talking. A real mummy's boy, as well, follows me everywhere.

You're listening to Rob Duncan and this is the afternoon show on Falklands Radio. I'll be signing off in a few minutes, but first some news I've been saving all day. Good news at that, all the way from St Andrews on the east coast of Scotland, about some great friends of ours who, sadly, left these shores not quite a year ago.

Right, better do this properly. Where's that bit of paper? Thanks, Mabel. Ahem.

Catrin and Callum Murray are delighted to announce the safe arrival of their first child, a daughter. Skye Elise was born at ten fifteen this morning, GMT, weighing seven pounds and two ounces. She has light red hair and both her eyes, it says here, are exactly the same colour. As for what that colour is, well, stay listening. I also understand that mother and baby are doing very well.

I get out of the car and walk to the clifftop. On the horizon, a boat is heading this way. A boat that, even at a distance, looks familiar.

It's an unusually warm, still day and there are families on the beach below. A group of children some distance away are playing football. One boy, about six years old, has wandered away from the rest. He seems intent upon the sand. Behind me, I can still hear Dad.

Anyone wanting to send a card or a message of congratulations to the new family will be interested to know that my daughter, Rachel, who I'm sure won't mind my telling you has already been asked to be godmother, is coordinating a parcel to be flown out next Wednesday. So get in touch with Rachel if you want to save yourself some postage.

The boat is getting closer, has cut its speed, is aiming for the small jetty down on the beach. I can barely make out a solitary figure at the helm.

Catrin and I can never be real friends again. I accepted that shortly after the night we found Peter in the boathouse. It is impossible to be friends with someone who has taken so much from you. So, I was almost relieved when Callum persuaded her to move to Scotland. At a distance, we can keep up the pretence, and by asking me to be godmother she is signalling to the world that I am forgiven. It's enough. It has to be.

In the meantime, I maintain my annual pilgrimage to the place where I killed her sons.

It is exactly four years ago today that I came here, an hour earlier than arranged, in the vain and rather pathetic hope of spending some time with Ben, when Catrin was safely out of the way. I had a feeling she was going to leave him soon and I was determined that I'd be the one to pick up the pieces. Ben. It was all I could think about. A life with Ben.

Above me, in the car, Dad is signing off.

I'm going to leave you now with a song from 1982, when Callum first came to these islands. For his new daughter, Skye, this is Elton John, singing 'Blue Eyes'.

I would never have told Ben about Catrin and Callum's affair, she was quite wrong about that. If you ask me what happened, Ben realized when her third child was stillborn. A son with hair the exact shade of strawberry blond as his biological father's. I did come here to betray her four years ago, I won't deny that, but not quite in the way she imagined. I came to begin my own affair with her husband.

I'm breathing fast, the way I always do when I come here, but above the sound of my own breath, I hear the engines of the boat down in the bay fall silent. It's Catrin's boat, no wonder it looked familiar, but it isn't Catrin at the helm, she's thousands of miles away in a maternity ward. That's Ben down there, tying up on the jetty.

That dream is over, of course. It was over before I killed his sons, because he turned me down that day. He knew, before I'd spoken a dozen words, why I was there. Kindly, because Ben was always a kind man, but firmly, he told me it was impossible. That even if I hadn't been his wife's best friend, he simply didn't think of me that way. And he never would.

'Where are the kids?' he said, as I turned from him, choking back sobs, about to flee the house. 'Rachel, where have you left the boys?'

He followed me out. Saw what was happening almost before I did. He ran towards the car but it was too late. I don't think I'll ever forget the sight of his fingers clutching at the car bumper, of Kit's terrified face as he looked into his father's eyes one last time.

To my dying day, I will hear Ben's scream as the car disappeared.

And yet, Ben proved the strongest of all of us. While Catrin, Callum and I were floundering, lost in our grief, he found a way to cope. When Catrin cut herself adrift from the world, seeking only the ghosts of those she'd lost, Ben sought out life, found love and began the world anew. When Catrin was eaten up with hatred, hatching endless but ultimately fruitless plans for revenge, Ben found the courage to forgive.

The pain tearing through him must have been as savage as that which stabbed at Catrin, Callum and me but Ben, the healer, found a way to heal himself.

I watch him now, stepping from boat to jetty, walking slowly towards shore in that loose, easy way he has. He pushes his sunglasses up on to his forehead and looks all around. I step back but I don't think he can see me all the way up here. There is gorse in front of me, for one thing, and the sun behind. He squats down now, and I see that the young boy is at the jetty too. They start talking. Ben seems to be showing the boy something in his hand, something he pulled from his pocket, and I see now that the child is skinny, dark-skinned and dark-eyed, like Ned and Kit – the two boys I killed.

Ben gestures back towards the boat. The kid's eyes follow his.

Skinny, dark-skinned and dark-eyed, like Fred and Jimmy, the two boys whom everyone has learned to believe died tragic and accidental deaths. Whom, for a short time, people believed Catrin had killed because, in her grief-crazed state, they reminded her, unbearably, of her dead sons.

A sudden cry of panic from my car. Peter has woken, alone and disorientated, and I'm glad of the excuse to run back, to bend into the car and kiss him quiet again. It's time to go. His brothers will be home soon and I always try to greet them at the garden gate these days.

As I wipe Peter's tears and promise him chocolate brownies when we get home, I hear a boat engine firing up again.

I don't want to look back at the beach but I can't help it. I just can't. The boat with Ben at the helm is moving slowly, the engines running quietly, but already some distance from the jetty. It picks up speed as it leaves the shallow waters behind and turns away from Stanley, heading out towards The Narrows and open sea. There is no sign of the child.

I get into my car, start the engine, and reverse back. I head home, knowing that I will never come here again. I don't look at the sea, or the sky. Above all I don't look at the beach. I do not look at the patch of sand, roughly two hundred yards from the jetty, where a picnicking family will be starting to wonder where their youngest son is.

Author's Note

Little Black Lies is a work of fiction, inspired in part by the Falklands conflict of 1982. In the story, I make reference to a few events that actually happened, but my characters are from my own imagination. Any similarity to any real person connected with the Falkland Islands, whether alive or dead, is entirely coincidental.

There really was a solar eclipse on 3 November 1994, but I have delayed its impact upon the Falkland Islands by a couple of hours.

Bibliography

I enjoyed the following books, and found them useful:

A Little Piece Of England by Andrew Gurr (John Blake, 2001)

Storming the Falklands by Tony Banks (Little Brown, 2012)

Forgotten Voices of the Falklands by Hugh McManners (Ebury Press, 2007)

A Falkland Islands Story (A Doctor on Horseback) by Tom Hopwood (Lulu Press, 2007)

Atmosphere, Landscapes of the Falkland Islands by Ian and Georgina Strange (Design in Nature, 2005)

Birds and Mammals of the Falkland Islands by Robin W. and Anne Woods (Wild Guides Ltd, 2006)

Falkland Adventure by Andrew Coe (Bluebell Publishing, 2000)

Old Whaling Days by William Barron (Irving Lewis Press, 2007)

Acknowledgements

Books are rarely the work of the author alone and mine certainly are not. My thanks to the following:

Adrian Summons, whose idea it was to set a book in the Falkland Islands.

Trish Preston Whyte, who served as an RAF officer in the Falklands for some time, and Andy Williams, who lived there for many years.

The Transworld team, who continue to give me support, encouragement and friendship. I cannot imagine working with a nicer group of people. Special thanks to Sarah Adams, Alison Barrow, Larry Finlay, Frankie Gray, Claire Ward, Suzanne Riley, Kate Samano and Bill Scott Kerr.

Elizabeth Lacks, Andrew Martin and Kelley Ragland of St Martin's Press, my publishers in the US.

Belinda Bauer, who let me steal her title.

The Buckman family (Rosie, Jessica and Peter), my lovely agents, at home and overseas.

And finally, Anne Marie Doulton, who deserves a special mention in dispatches this year. (She knows why.)